FALLING FOR HAMLET

FALLING FOR HAMLET

A NOVEL BY MICHELLE RAY

poppy

LITTLE, BROWN AND COMPANY
NEW YORK   BOSTON

Poppy

Hachette Book Group
237 Park Avenue, New York, NY 10017
For more of your favorite books, visit our website at www.pickapoppy.com

Poppy is an imprint of Little, Brown and Company.
The Poppy name and logo are trademarks of Hachette Book Group, Inc.

The publisher is not responsible for websites (or their content) that are not
owned by the publisher.

First Edition: July 2011

Library of Congress Cataloging-in-Publication Data

Ray, Michelle, 1972–
    Falling for Hamlet / Michelle Ray.—1st ed.
    p. cm.
    "Poppy."
    ISBN 978-0-316-10162-2
    [1. Revenge—Fiction. 2. Murder—Fiction. 3. Princes—Fiction. 4. Denmark—
Fiction.]   I. Shakespeare, William, 1564–1616. Hamlet.   II. Title.
    PZ7.R210157Fal 2011
    [Fic]—dc22

                                                                        2010034259

                                10 9 8 7 6 5 4 3 2 1

                                        RRD-C

                        Printed in the United States of America

"FRAILTY, THY NAME IS WOMAN."
—WILLIAM SHAKESPEARE

"WILLY, THY NAME IS SEXISM."
—OPHELIA

PROLOGUE

"Thank you, ladies and gentlemen. Oh, thank you!" Zara shouts as she feigns surprise at the audience's outpouring of affection and its standing ovation. She gestures for the audience members to sit down, though she smiles broadly when they continue to stand. "Please. Please," she gestures, and since they have all been watching her for years, they know that she means business even when she's giving a casual instruction. They settle into their seats as Zara flops precisely onto her overstuffed cream couch, smoothing her dark hair.

She leans forward and begins: "Today we have a guest who will amaze you." She pauses to punctuate the drama and yells, "Ophelia is in the house!" Her tone sends the audience members to their feet again. They know how lucky they are to be in the audience on this day, and this is their moment to show it. The camera cuts to mostly middle-aged women in seasonal sweaters gasping, clapping, smiling. One even dabs a tear of excitement, or is it sadness? Who can tell, and who really cares? It's a tear that some cameraman was lucky enough to capture, a cameraman who is planning, as he films, what he will buy with the bonus the segment producer will give him for catching an actual tear wipe.

The audience calms down after a last twitter and exchange of

1

amazed glances. "Our nation has been so deeply saddened by the tragedies surrounding the royals of Denmark. Today, we will speak to Ophelia herself and find out how this young woman was caught up in the secrecy, the revenge, and the madness... madness that we all thought had consumed her.

"You are a lucky audience, indeed, to be here this afternoon. Ophelia has agreed to make one appearance, one exclusive appearance, to tell her story. So, ladies and gentlemen, here she is. Ophelia, come on out here, girl."

Ophelia walks out onto the stage tucking her bobbed blond hair behind her ears. Her black turtleneck and jeans fit her perfectly, and she has the air of someone who looks great no matter how much time she does or doesn't spend getting ready. She's slim but curvy, and healthy-looking, except for circles under her wide green eyes. When she sees the crowd, she pauses to take a deep breath and raises her hand in a little wave. The crowd jumps to its feet again, and Ophelia winces. Zara reaches out an encouraging hand and guides her toward the couch. Ophelia looks at someone offstage and then looks back at the audience, clearly trying to smile. Zara, after prolonging the moment just a second longer, invites Ophelia, and therefore everyone present, to sit down.

"Welcome, Ophelia," Zara begins, patting Ophelia's hand.

Ophelia nods and says quietly, "Thank you for having me."

"So, you're not dead?"

"That... is true." Ophelia smiles.

"Ladies and gentlemen, you will recall that on this show just a few weeks ago, we joined our kingdom in mourning what we thought was our guest's shocking death. In fact, we will replay the video my incredibly talented staff compiled to commemorate her life, a life entwined with that of the royal family owing to her relationship with our beloved prince, Hamlet." A montage begins: Ophelia as a newborn, Ophelia on the junior high swim team, Ophelia and

2

Hamlet at the prom. As it plays, the music is quieted so Zara can continue. "Ophelia, we were all so amazed and relieved when you were found alive. What happened? Take us back."

Shifting in her seat, Ophelia replies, "I really wouldn't even know where to begin."

[transcript #81872; Denmark Department of Investigations; interview room B; interrogators: Agent Francisco and Special Agent Barnardo]

Francisco: Ophelia, you are here because you're being investigated for treason.

Ophelia: Is this a joke? Am I on one of those shows where they scare you and then film it? Okay, you got me.

Barnardo: Sit down. This is no joke.

Francisco: You vanish. Things go to hell. You return. Interesting timing.

Ophelia: I vanished because things had *already* gone to hell.

Barnardo: We think you conspired against the royal family.

Ophelia: That's ridiculous. I'm innocent. You have to let me go.

Francisco: We don't have to do anything. We're the Denmark Department of Investigations. You're ours until we are done with you. And we want to know what happened.

You wanna know the truth? Here it is. Not the truth I tell Zara or the truth I tell the DDI or anyone else. I'll tell you, but no questions. I've had enough questions.

1

Zara leans in, looking like a schoolgirl sharing a secret. Her eyes bright and wide, she asks, "You spent a great deal of time with the royal family. What were they like?"

"Oh, you know...royal. Fairly proper. Serious. And, uh..." Ophelia looks off camera and adds, "But nice, I guess."

Hamlet's father had the kind of laugh that made wineglasses vibrate and clink if the staff set them too close together, and Hamlet's mother, Gertrude, loved to hear it so much that she went to great lengths to provoke it. At this moment, she was telling a story and proceeded to launch herself out of her chair to act out the punch line. The king cheered her with a "bravo," and we all clapped. She took a little bow before kissing the king and nodding to his brother, Claudius, who was smiling but not laughing. He never seemed to laugh.

As many times as I had been in the family's private dining room, I would always be slightly surprised to see Gertrude relaxing in track pants and without her characteristic French knot. Gertrude's gaze met Claudius's, and her face suddenly grew pinched. She quickly looked back at her husband as she fluffed her blond hair and sank back into her giant pink-and-gold dining chair.

Claudius glowed. "You tell a wonderful story."

"Indeed, indeed," the king agreed, his eyes fixed on Gertrude. The king missed Claudius winking at Gertrude, who blushed but pretended to take no notice.

I acted as if I hadn't seen it, either. From the time I could speak, my father had told me this was my role: silent observer and keeper of secrets. He said it was the only way to survive living so close to the royals.

Claudius was creepy and seemed to dislike everyone but Gertrude. He was so different from the king, who was funny and youthful despite the wrinkles and graying hair. When Hamlet's dad had time, he tried to see movies that Hamlet liked or listen to some of the bands we talked about. I'm sure he hated a lot of it, but he tried, you know?

The adults turned to one another to converse about some associate who told the most dreadful stories, which left Horatio, Hamlet, and me to chat. The three of us had been friends for as long as we had been alive. Horatio's parents and my father had been advisers to the king, and we had grown up in the castle.

Ever since we were in elementary school, Horatio and I had been invited to dinners with the royal family. As an only child, Hamlet grew bored at the table, and it annoyed his parents endlessly that he couldn't sit still and be quiet while they ate. Once we were in high school, our invitations were limited to Sunday dinners. Since the king often missed dinner with his wife and son during the week, his staff knew that Sunday was to go untouched whenever possible. In a matter of weeks,

Hamlet and Horatio would leave for their second year of college, making these last Sundays more precious for us all.

"You've got to come visit this semester," Horatio said to me.

"I'll try, but you know my father."

"And your brother." Hamlet rolled his eyes. "Laertes is going back to grad school soon, I hope."

I nodded. "Tomorrow, actually."

Hamlet replied with a sigh of relief.

"He's not that bad," I said.

Hamlet picked up his knife and pretended to stab an invisible figure, so I added, "He's not. Hamlet, you know I love my brother. Please don't do that."

Hamlet leaned over to kiss me, but I pushed him away. He grabbed my wrists and kissed me anyway. "Jerk," I grumbled.

"Are you two dating again?" asked Gertrude from across the table, her voice dripping with disapproval.

Hamlet and I looked at each other. We had been together all summer, and it seemed odd that she hadn't noticed. She had been so distracted during the past few months, and I fleetingly wondered again if it had something to do with Claudius.

"Are we?" I asked, somewhat amused.

"Are we?" he answered back.

"For now," I answered, looking at Hamlet rather than Gertrude.

"What kind of nonsense is that?" bellowed the king, which made everyone except Claudius roar with laughter.

"It means, sir, that your son likes to be unencumbered when he is at school," I answered when we had all quieted down.

"To being unencumbered," Horatio toasted, and I threw my napkin at him.

Horatio and I would play our part in the light repartee, but both of us knew how many hours he had spent comforting me after the tabloid exposé that had led to my breakup with Hamlet in the spring.

Gertrude knitted her brow and looked at me squarely. "And where does that leave you?"

"Unencumbered as well, I suppose."

"And have you been seeing anyone else?" she asked, tapping her sculpted fingernails on the table, her eyes narrowed.

I shifted in my seat. She was not only the mother of the only guy I had ever loved but also someone with the power to kick me out of the castle, which made the question all the more awkward. "Well…" I stalled, grabbing my glass of water and sneaking a sip before she could ask another question.

She sat very still, which I knew was the only reply I was likely to get. Gertrude had never liked my dating Hamlet, and she hated that I had hurt her son's feelings more. When I broke up with him the last time, it took her weeks to even look at me, and Hamlet had to convince her to let me sit at her table again.

"There have been other…" I swallowed hard and didn't look at Hamlet. He cleared his throat as he ripped a dinner roll and dropped half of it onto his bread plate, clattering the butter knife. Still feeling his eyes on me, I told her, "I've been asked out…."

"But you have never brought anyone here," she said.

I couldn't figure out if she was being serious or not.

The king interrupted. "Gertrude, can you imagine how that date might go? Between the guards and you, I'm not sure which would be more intimidating." The king laughed, and she joined him but eyed me suspiciously as Hamlet snickered into his wineglass, which was nearly empty.

The king turned his attention to Hamlet and said, "You are just lucky, my boy, that your flirtations have not angered your subjects. Luck can only last so long." He jutted out his sharp chin and glared ever so slightly at Hamlet.

I looked down, a familiar hurt washing over me. I tried to push away memories of last April's multipage spread of Hamlet and a girl sunbathing at an exclusive resort, images some of the girls at school were only too happy to have on hand for weeks afterward. Hamlet had said the pictures were taken out of context, but I still wasn't sure how out of context a girl draping herself across him could be. Months later, my desire to punch him for whatever the context was had only slightly diminished.

Hamlet leaned back in his chair. "I've never cheated, and you all know it. How can I help it if the public wants to believe that I have?"

His father squinted at him. "You should know as well as anyone that perception is all. If your subjects believe you've cheated, you're a cheat. They won't trust a liar as their leader."

Hamlet reached for the wine bottle, and his mother slapped away his hand.

"Enough talk of cheating," she declared, her brow furrowed and her cheeks ablaze. "Why don't we retire to the sitting room?"

We all stood and wandered toward the cozy, overstuffed couches in the next room. Hamlet put an arm around me and kissed the top of my head. I shoved him away, pretending I was kidding but taking the moment to pull myself back together. More than anything, I was kicking myself for giving credence to the whole thing. Lots of people had reasons to sell inaccurate, inflammatory stories to the press. It had happened to us before. Hamlet said it wasn't true, and I knew I had to stop letting such things bother me if we were going to have a future together. And as for being grilled by his parents, if one planned on spending time with the royal family, one couldn't be overly sensitive.

Hamlet pulled me onto the couch next to him and put his arm around my shoulder. I leaned into the curve of his body, and Horatio plopped down next to me.

"There are other chairs," the king said, smiling.

"We can't stand being apart. You know that," answered Hamlet.

Gertrude sighed.

Hamlet's father said, "Horatio, your mother tells me you've chosen a major."

"Yeah. Political science."

"Bah, politics." The king waved his hand as if clearing the air of something foul. "All of that power, deceit, and corruption."

"You've done well with politics," Claudius said, his eyes narrowing at his brother.

The king shifted in his seat. "As have you. But we were born into our roles. If you had been able to make the choice, wouldn't you have done something other than work for me?"

Claudius leaned forward, scratching at his beard, which was short enough to be considered overgrown stubble. "I would have been king."

Hamlet's father raised his eyebrows. "You know, being in charge is no picnic." When Claudius merely sniffed, Hamlet's father sighed and added, "Don't be bitter. It was an accident of birth. I'm older, so I'm king. What can we do?"

Claudius ran his fingers through his thick dark hair as he glared at his brother. Then he rose and poured himself a drink.

"Dad, what would you have chosen to be?"

The king looked right at his son and said, "A florist."

Hamlet began to laugh, and his father joined him with a sound so loud that a security guard poked his head through the door. The king waved the man away.

When he'd settled down, he asked, "Ophelia, is your passion still art?"

"No, it's Hamlet," whispered Horatio, and I poked him in the ribs.

I nodded at the king.

"I have that painting of yours hanging in my study."

I took a moment to think. "The one of the unicorns and the rainbow?" I asked, amazed he still had that thing. I'd presented it, with great solemnity, when I was in the second grade, and he had received it with a bow. "I should make you a new one."

"I look forward to it."

The clock chimed ten, so the king excused himself to go back to his office, as he did each evening. Gertrude rose and pecked him on the cheek without comment, which was peculiar. For as long as I could remember, the king's long hours had driven her nuts. How many times had I heard her say that her husband worked too hard, that he neglected her, and that another few hours wouldn't change the kingdom one way or another? The tension had been worst right before Hamlet went to college. But then, to my surprise, a few months after he left, she stopped bringing it up as often, at least publicly. I wondered why.

The king's departure was, as always, the cue for the "young people" to leave. Gertrude and Claudius would stay up talking and, even if it had not been exceptionally boring to be with the two of them, we were not welcome. What she found so fascinating about the king's reptilian brother, I couldn't understand.

We got in the mirrored elevator that would stop first at my floor and then continue down to Horatio's family's apartment. "I really meant it," Horatio said. "You've got to visit Wittenberg this semester. It's always so much more fun when you're around."

"You really should," said Hamlet.

"We'll see," I said, walking out on my floor. "You coming?" I asked Hamlet, reaching out my hand.

"Is your brother there?" he asked, poking his head out, pretending to be scared.

"She's right," said Horatio. "You are a jerk." He pushed Hamlet out with his foot and yelled, "Good night, sweet prince!"— a mockery of how I sometimes said good-bye to Hamlet. We both turned around and shushed him, laughing.

The king's Cabinet was expected to live within the castle, as were other high-ranking officials and their most vital assistants. The two-hundred-year-old marble, gilt, and stone portion of the castle was reserved for state dinners, meetings among diplomats, and the like. That part acted as a grand facade to a twenty-story black glass building that loomed over it. The modern section housed the royal residences and included a rooftop pool and gardens, ten floors of meeting rooms and offices, and nine floors of apartments. Upper-level staff, like my father, had apartments on the north side of the building, which looked out at Elsinore's spectacular skyline, as well as its sparkling river and harbor.

Staff apartments were on the floors directly below the royal residences. Ours had no grand lobby into which the elevator opened. By some strange design, there was not even an entryway. The elevators just opened into our sitting rooms. Everyone in the castle knew this to be the situation, so people were careful about which buttons they pushed. In addition, one needed a code to go anywhere above the tenth floor.

Even so, with an ever-rotating staff that was often overworked or preoccupied, the chances of an error were great, so one never got the feeling of complete privacy. When we were younger, Hamlet, Horatio, and I found it funny to push all the buttons and see whom we could find in nightgowns or mid-argument. It took a few groundings to teach us that it wasn't worth it. Every so often I was tempted to do it again but never did.

With the elevator doors closed and Horatio's laughter fading away, Hamlet and I stood silently, checking whether it was safe to proceed. City lights streamed in through the high windows, giving the large sitting room and open kitchen an eerie blue glow. We listened a minute at the entry to my father's hall, which branched off to the right of the elevator. We could hear my father's snore through his closed door, and I tried not to laugh. His bedroom and study were at the opposite end of the apartment from Laertes's and my hall, so I led Hamlet the other way. We paused again, and since we heard nothing, I kept going. Hamlet shoved his hands into the pockets of his jeans and sauntered behind me. Laertes's door was open, but the light was off, so we continued into my room.

"Finally," he said when we climbed onto my bed.

I kissed his shoulder, then his neck, then his cheek.

But he pulled back and asked, "So, who have you been seeing?"

"What?"

"You told my mom you've been dating other people."

"Leave your mother out of this room, please," I said, trying to kiss him again, but he stopped me.

"No, seriously. Who?"

"It was nothing," I said, trying to sound casual, which is precisely what it had been, anyhow. He kept glowering at me. I added, "No one you would know."

It wasn't true. Hamlet knew Sebastian from the lacrosse team in high school. He knew that Sebastian was in my circle of friends and that Sebastian and I were always in the art studio together. But Hamlet didn't need to know that Sebastian took me to hear a band called the Poor Yoricks and asked me out several times afterward. I wanted to torture Hamlet after all he'd put me through, but he didn't need details.

"That's—"

"Hey, we agreed: Don't ask about last semester. This is what you wanted, so—"

"Well, I hate it."

"Oh, you hate it? Then I am tremendously sorry," I said with exaggerated sympathy. "Last spring, I totally should have been thinking about *your* feelings in case we got back together."

He bit back a smile but then furrowed his brow and looked genuinely troubled, so I added, "Hamlet, it was nothing. If you want me to trust you, then you have to trust me. It's not easy for me, knowing that once you're back at school, you'll have those girls in little skirts fawning all over you. I'm not supposed to give that any thought?"

He sat back on his haunches. "I don't like any of them like I like you. I've broken things off in the past because I *have* been tempted...because I never wanted to cheat or lie. But honestly, Ophelia, there's no one else for me."

My stomach jumped a little, but I didn't want to get too

14

excited. I was trying to keep my emotions more in check this year. I had to protect myself.

"I think..." he started, "I want to stay together."

Again I felt fluttery, but I could not allow myself to trust the sincerity of the sentiment. "Hamlet, you always do this. You decide one thing and then change your mind. It's hard to know what to believe."

"Believe that I love you."

"I do."

"Let's try then. Let's commit to being together."

"If you say so," I said, picturing Horatio's "I told you so" face if Hamlet broke my heart again. But then Hamlet kissed me, and my fears evaporated. I sighed with happiness, thinking that this time things between us would work.

Francisco: So you were tight with the royal family.

Ophelia: We spent a lot of time together.

Barnardo: How much of that time did you spend plotting against them?

Ophelia: None. Why would I—

Francisco: Okay. Different question. You were alone with Hamlet constantly, yet your father, from what we understand, was very protective of you.

Ophelia: My dad was too busy and too tired to notice what I did a lot of the time.

Barnardo: So you took advantage of his schedule and his position?

Ophelia: *(pause)* No more than any other teenager.

Francisco: So that's a yes?

2

"Did the queen take you out for 'girl time'?" Zara asks as a picture of Ophelia and Gertrude in front of Elsinore's most notoriously expensive shop is projected.

"Sometimes."

"What did you two talk about?"

Ophelia blinks a few times and then her mouth curls into something resembling a smile. "I'll never tell."

Zara leans in. "I guess a girl has to keep her secrets. But, just between us, did you talk about Prince Hamlet?"

Ophelia winces almost undetectably but then flips her hair. "What do you think?" she asks as she reaches for a glass of water. Her hands shake slightly, and she spills a few drops on the armrest of the couch.

Zara seems not to notice and winks at the audience.

"Gertrude may dress you up and welcome you at her table, but she's not your mother and you're not her child."

I turned away from my reflection, letting my new dress slip to the floor.

Laertes continued. "You can never have what they have.

You can never be rich, like they are. This whole thing with Hamlet can only end in disappointment."

I picked up the dress, threw it across the plaid couch as if it didn't cost a month of my father's salary, and stomped toward our kitchen. "Laertes, I'm aware of all that. Do you think I'm an idiot?"

"Sometimes I think you are," he said while following me.

"Nice." I scowled. "It's a dress."

He slid onto a bar stool at the kitchen island. "It's not just a dress. Every time that woman gives you something, there is a reason behind it."

"That is not true."

"If you broke up with Hamlet—*you*, and I mean you crushed him—do you really think she'd invite you the next morning for tea and shopping?"

I shook my head, knowing he was right.

"Be careful, that's all I'm saying."

I handed him a soda before slumping on the kitchen island and asking, "Where were you last night?"

"Movie. I heard Hamlet leave around two."

I had to concentrate to swallow my tea.

"What if Father saw him?" he asked.

"He didn't."

Laertes shook his head. "You shouldn't trust Hamlet. This thing you two have, it's like…like a violet."

"A violet?" I asked.

"Yes, a violet," he overenunciated. "Sure it's beautiful and perfect, but it can't last. This is a diversion, nothing more."

"Nothing?" I asked, my blood starting to heat.

"No. And even if it was, let's say he loves you now…do you really believe he has a choice in who he marries?"

"Marries? Laertes, no one is thinking of marriage."

"You've been together on and off for, what, two years?"

I nodded as I counted.

"In another few, you'll be at an age where people *do* think about marriage."

The thought was too foreign to me.

He continued, "Let's say you do stay together. You know Hamlet can't make any major decisions alone. And he certainly can't choose the daughter of an employee as his queen."

"But—"

"I know you'll say he loves you, but if something goes wrong, what'll happen to your reputation? Worry about that, Ophelia."

"My reputation? Jesus, Laertes, exactly what century do you think we live in?"

"Have you seen the tabloids? You think there is no such thing as public shame these days? You're so naive."

"Shut up," I said, walking toward the dress I had cast aside.

"Very eloquent," he retorted.

I spun around, annoyed as much by his implying that I was stupid as by his calling me naive. "You are such a hypocrite. Are you saying you've never treaded on the primrose path of dalliance?"

"On the what?"

I was enjoying one-upping my brilliant brother. "I asked if you're telling me you've never screwed around."

"You and those poetry classes." He sighed. "Of course I have."

I lifted my hands in a grand "touché."

He added, "But never with someone famous."

I dropped my arms and threw myself onto the couch. I hated that he was always right.

He sat next to me and said, "I worry about you. That's all. Mom's gone, and Dad's, well, Dad. You have no one to say these things to you. I'm telling you, Ophelia, this thing with Hamlet can only end in disaster."

"I know it's been rocky, Laertes, but I actually love him. I don't know how to be without him."

He sighed and said, "Then we have a problem," and sympathetically stroked my hair.

Before I could knock his hand away and tell him to cut the crap, the elevator *ding*ed, and out stepped our father.

Laertes whispered, "We should talk more about this later."

I shoved a pillow over my face and groaned. I didn't need another father. My first father was frustrating enough. And why couldn't Laertes just let me be happy about Hamlet?

My father said, "Ah, Laertes, come with me into my office, my boy. Before you go back to school, I would like to have a word with you." Laertes stood heavily, bracing himself for one of my father's wisdom-filled lectures, and winked at me. My father, down the hall already, was still talking and did not notice. I stayed hidden until the door to the study was closed. Then I ran back to my room to text Hamlet about going out that night.

Francisco: Our records show that Gertrude took you shopping. Quite a bit, actually.

Barnardo: Seems odd.

Ophelia: Gertrude was odd. And manipulative.

Francisco: So she took you shopping to manipulate you?

Ophelia: Yeah.

Barnardo: She punished you with expensive dresses. Scary.

Ophelia: No, she took me with her to get information about my life and about her son.

Francisco: And you went along with it?

Ophelia: It was part of the game.

Barnardo: And it was fun to have expensive things.

Ophelia: Yeah.

Francisco: And a mother for a few hours.

Ophelia: That's not how it was.

Barnardo: Oh come on. Every girl needs a mother.

Ophelia: Not one like Gertrude.

3

"So what was it like jetting all over the world with the royal family?" Two dome-haired women exchange wistful glances. Ophelia catches them, as does Zara. "Sounds like a fairy tale," she says, beaming.

"Well, we didn't actually go that many places."

"Come now, Ophelia." Photos are projected of the two families in Africa, China, and Paris. "What are all of these?"

"Official business," Ophelia answers, her mouth drawn into a line, though she fights to turn it into a smile. "My father had to go, and sometimes he brought me and my brother along."

Not to be hindered, Zara presses, "So did you and Hamlet ever get away? Just the two of you?"

"Once."

"When you and Hamlet went to Florence? Last summer, right?" Ophelia nods. "Was that trip as romantic as it looks in this picture?" Zara winks and the audience oohs as a striking photo is shown of the couple on a flight of marble steps. They look tan and happy with their arms around each other, each wearing sunglasses and sandals, casually fabulous.

Ophelia smiles, relaxing a little. "Yeah. That was a great trip. That picture was taken our last day."

"Was it a good day?"

"Perfect, start to finish."

"So, Dad, what do you think?" I literally held my breath as I squeezed Hamlet's hand. It had been a few weeks since my argument with Laertes, and things had been going so well with Hamlet. We had never been so at peace, never had so much fun. My father had seemed to notice and had been less wary of our being together. So when I asked if Hamlet and I could go on a vacation alone, I was fairly confident he would agree.

He nodded gravely. "Yes, that sounds fine."

I clapped excitedly. "Thanks, Dad."

"A few things first, though," my father said, scooting forward. I felt Hamlet shift in his seat, but I elbowed him subtly and kept smiling. "It goes without saying that you will have separate rooms. And you need security with you at all times, even if they're in plainclothes. You can never be too careful."

"Polonius, we know," Hamlet said with a sigh.

"Do you?" my father asked him, squinting and leaning farther toward us. "Has Marcellus told you about the latest rash of threatening mail your father has been getting?" Hamlet grew very still. "I thought not," he said, leaning back again for emphasis. "And please, please remember that when you are abroad, you are representatives of your kingdom. Ambassadors, as it were. Thus, let me be clear"—and he leveled his gaze at Hamlet—"that you should behave accordingly." Hamlet was fighting a smirk. "Plus you will be in charge of my daughter. See that neither of you embarrasses yourself, your parents, or Denmark." His last words built to a crescendo, and I swear if

22

he had pulled out a flag, I would not have been altogether surprised.

Once we were in the hall, Hamlet muttered sarcastically, "Well, that was fun."

"Hey, at least he's letting us go."

Hamlet rolled his eyes and said, "I can't wait till you're out of high school and we're free to do what we want."

"You're followed everywhere. We'll never be that free."

"Being followed doesn't bother me. Neither do the tabloids. You're the one who has to stop caring what everyone thinks."

I was going to argue, but instead I started to laugh as a thought occurred to me. "We could scandalize everyone and run through Florence naked."

Hamlet's mouth twisted. "If you would agree, I would agree."

Thing is, I knew he would. How he could be immune to public scrutiny amazed me.

"Maybe next time. Let's go pack," I suggested.

The trip was incredible. It was the first time Hamlet and I had slept in the same bed for a whole night, and to be honest, it was almost too shocking to enjoy. I couldn't believe that my dad had allowed it. I mean, he kind of didn't when he asked us to get separate rooms—which we got, though Hamlet's body-guard, Marcellus, not I, slept in the second room. Did my dad really expect us to be in one of the most romantic places in the world and then, like, not stay together? Maybe he did, but if so, that was a little naive. I was worried that he would find out, but Hamlet rightly asked, who was gonna tell? The hotel staff was paid for discretion, and Marcellus never divulged secrets.

The first night, Hamlet slept and I stared at him, unable to believe my luck, foolishly listening for the sound of my dad or brother coming down the hall. Old habits die hard. By the second night, even though it was still pretty unbelievable, I could at least relax and appreciate a boyfriend who wanted to sleep with his arms around me and who told me he loved me before we both drifted off. If it was possible, I fell in love with Hamlet even more that night and each day of the trip.

As for the sights, I was overwhelmed at seeing Michelangelo's chisel marks still in *The Captives* and Raphael's subtle brushstrokes. The Ghiberti doors were glorious, and Brunelleschi's cathedral dome transcendent. Vespas coughed shrilly and constantly, a sound I will forever associate with intense joy. Everything was perfection.

Our room overlooked the Arno and the Ponte Vecchio, a bridge of unmatched romance and allure. Three times a day I insisted on walking across, taking note of how the vendors and the pace of life changed. When not sightseeing, I sat with my colored pencils and pad, staring out the hotel window, so enraptured by how the sun painted the city anew that I kept forgetting to sketch it. But I remember how each morning pink light kissed the bridge awake. Midday, its yellow and burnt-umber stucco beckoned. At dusk, the river looked like liquid sapphire, and the buildings, though plunged into darkness, seemed to glow from within as if fighting off the coming night.

On our last full day, I sat drinking espresso on the balcony of our room, watching and listening to the city already in motion. Hamlet was completely hungover from a party we'd attended the night before and was lying on a lounge chair with his eyes closed. We had planned on going to the Museo Firenze, but he looked so wrecked that I decided to leave him alone. As I slipped on my sandals, he asked where I was going.

"I really want to make the museum before we leave. I'll just go myself," I said cheerfully.

He slapped his face a few times and hoisted himself up. "Don't be silly. Of course I'm coming. Seeing the new sculpture gallery is what you wanted most from this trip, right?"

I nodded, touched that he knew without my telling him.

He took my hand, put on his sunglasses, and led me outside.

A skeevy-looking photographer with too-tight pants followed us from the hotel to the museum and trailed us to the entrance. Marcellus started to go after him, but Hamlet told his bodyguard to let him handle it.

Hamlet let go of me and calmly approached the photographer. He said, "Listen, we really want to enjoy this alone. Take our picture now if you want, but don't follow us in, okay?" To my surprise, the guy agreed, snapped a few posed pictures and a few of us walking inside for good measure, then sat down outside, leaving us in peace.

Inside, the cool stone structure was dark and moody. Arm in arm we walked through the halls with their vaulted ceilings, cluttered with paintings that were centuries old. The velvet overstuffed benches looked inviting, but I felt I did not even have a moment to sit. There was simply too much to see, and I wanted to get to the new sculpture gallery before it grew too late or Hamlet grew too bored. He kept checking his watch as it was. Marcellus touched his earpiece and turned to Hamlet, nodding. I was afraid they were deciding to leave, so I quickly suggested we skip the illuminated manuscripts and go right to the new wing.

As we exited the elevator and approached the exhibit, I was surprised to see the glass doors closed and museum guards standing in front of them. My stomach sank with disappointment and I slowed my gait, trying not to seem too upset.

Hamlet looked at me proudly. "They closed it for us for the rest of the afternoon. I knew you'd want it quiet up here."

I was speechless and pulled my arm tighter around his. He did this for me. Me! Hamlet had done sweet things in the past—sent flowers, written notes and poems—but this was the most romantic thing he'd ever done. And the fact that it wasn't jewelry but a unique experience he knew I would treasure made my legs go to jelly. It's a memory that I still hold dear, even though it's hard for me to think of Hamlet now.

The guards nodded at Marcellus and opened the doors. The gallery itself was a work of art: tall glass walls with ethereal curtains fluttering all around. The dreamlike quality of the room made the white marble statues seem to breathe and sway. I let go of Hamlet's hand and roamed around one of Aphrodite, marveling at her milky perfection.

Hamlet followed behind, and I noticed he was looking at me rather than the art. I stopped and cocked my head. "What?"

"Happy?" he asked, beaming.

I walked up to him and whispered, "Thank you for this."

He shrugged modestly and said, "I know you love great art." Then he squinted and asked, only half joking, "Do you just love me for my money and power?"

I put my hands on his shoulders and said, "I love you because you think of doing things like this and you try to make me happy." I kissed him and continued, "Hey, you're just some guy who happens to live in my building, right?"

He laughed appreciatively and added, "But having this all to ourselves is pretty nice."

"Yeah," I said, nodding, "pretty nice."

There was a sudden *click-clack*, and when I turned I saw Gertrude rushing toward us, silk scarf flapping, giant sunglasses perched on top of her head. "Darlings!" she shouted, opening her arms wide.

"Mother?" Hamlet asked, befuddled.

"You're kidding," I muttered.

"I knew it was your last day and I thought, 'Well, it's been ages since I've been to Florence,' and I simply *had* to see what the fuss was all about with this gallery." She turned around once and said in faux astonishment, "Fabulous." Then she took Hamlet by one arm and me by the other and said, "I simply must take you both to lunch now. I heard about a divine little place for pasta."

"Pasta? Imagine," he said slowly. "That's…um, it's really late for lunch."

"Dinner then. Shall we?" she asked, and drew us toward the entrance.

I stopped walking, and my pulling against her nearly made her trip. "Gertrude, we're not ready to leave."

She sniffed, her face impassive but for the fire in her eyes. "Excuse me?"

"What she's saying is—" began Hamlet.

"I was pretty clear, Hamlet." My head was light from defying her. It wasn't my habit, but I was sick of her trying to come between me and Hamlet, which she had been doing since she realized we were back together. "We're not ready to go."

"*You* might not be, but what about my son? He hates art." She turned to him and, in her sweetest voice, said, "Keep me company, Hamlet. You know I despise eating alone."

He worked his arm out of her grip. "Ophelia wants to stay. We'll catch you back home. Tomorrow."

Her lips curled around her teeth as she said, "Fine," and clacked out stiffly.

My hands were shaking from the confrontation, and Hamlet squeezed them. Kissing my cheek softly, he whispered, "She'll get over it. Let's go find a Donatella."

"Donatell-*o*," I corrected.

He winked at me, and I realized he was teasing. For a guy who professed to not care about art, he knew quite a lot about it.

Barnardo: Gertrude showed up and ruined your little getaway.

Ophelia: Yes, she did.

Barnardo: Is that when you tried to come up with a way to get rid of her?

Ophelia: I didn't try to– She was intrusive my entire life.

Francisco: So you must have hated her.

Ophelia: No. It was just how it was. To be with Hamlet was to be with Gertrude.

Francisco: How romantic.

Ophelia: Not like that. Jesus.

4

"How did you feel being left behind when Hamlet went to college?"

"Honestly, I hated it."

Zara laughs. "I can imagine the rumors of other girls didn't make it any easier."

"No, it certainly didn't." Ophelia's eyes flick to the screen behind her, and she relaxes when no photo appears.

Zara asks, "You and Hamlet began dating when you were almost sixteen, right?"

"Yes."

"That's a long time." Two young girls in the audience nod at each other, as does Ophelia. "What attracted you to him?"

"He was funny and fun and smart."

"Sexy, too, our viewers would agree."

Ophelia lowers her head but doesn't say anything.

Zara adds, "As would the folks at Courtier Magazine, who named him Sexiest Bachelor of the Year."

The audience sighs as Zara holds up the cover.

Zara crosses her legs and leans back. "You and Hamlet broke up a few times."

Ophelia nods.

"Yet you kept getting back together. Why?"

"We made each other happy...most of the time."

Zara raises her eyebrows and asks, "And the rest of the time?"

"It was complicated." Ophelia turns quickly and looks over her shoulder. "You're not going to get Dr. Dave out here to analyze the relationship, are you?"

Zara laughs. "No, but that's a great idea. Would you come back?"

"Uh...we'll see."

After Hamlet finished packing for his sophomore year at Wittenberg College, we sat in the conservatory looking at pictures from our vacation on his camera. I was just recalling my irritation at Gertrude's intrusion when Hamlet made the mistake of trying to get me excited about my last year of high school.

"It's gonna fly by. Senior year's awesome."

To me, senior year had become like a vacation you're looking forward to, but when you finally get there, you find out the hotel's pool is closed and the sights looked better in the brochures. The thing is, I had done most of the great stuff when Hamlet was graduating and, more than anything, I just felt ready to move on.

"Even if it's fun and whatever, you know my dad says I can only go to Denmark State after I graduate."

"So you'll go there. They've got classes, books, parties."

"It's a commuter college. Nothing like Wittenberg. Your school is gorgeous. Everyone's relaxed, hanging out on the quad. And you can practically smell the money."

"And you can't here?" he asked, his arm sweeping toward the elaborate fountain at the far end of the courtyard. He knew

I loved it in that room. The exotic flowers' perfume filled the air, and enormous leaves drooped low across the paths, making it one of the only private public spaces in the castle.

I shook my head, completely annoyed beyond what was called for. The thought of another year in the castle with Gertrude watching my every move, another year without Hamlet, another year of surveillance cameras and bodyguards, was getting under my skin. "This isn't mine."

"And Wittenberg's not mine."

"You know what I mean," I said, getting up angrily to go. All I could think was that everything I could see was actually his mother's. I imagined she would have been hovering at that moment if not for a ladies' luncheon that she was obliged to attend.

"Phee, come on," he called after me. I kept walking, so he gave chase. "I know it's not the same. It's a joke."

I spun around, whacking at a large leaf that dared to hang near my head. "It's not funny to me. Denmark State sucks."

"So don't go there."

"The only place I want to go is Wittenberg, and my father won't let me."

"Wittenberg's a great school. What's Polonius's problem?"

"Duh…you're there, you idiot. My father wants to keep us apart. It's what he's always wanted."

"And with good cause," he said, stepping forward and slipping his hand under my shirt.

"Jesus, Hamlet," I said, pushing it away. "Not here." I looked at the glass conservatory door, hoping no security guard was passing by.

"You're so paranoid," he whispered in my ear.

A chill ran through my body as he kissed my neck. "Not

without reason." He smiled that deadly smile and I whispered, "Let's at least go downstairs," and grabbed him by his T-shirt.

As we walked out into the hallway, he asked, "Why do you listen to Polonius? If you want to come to Wittenberg, come to Wittenberg."

"You know that's impossible. My father would cut me off."

"So what?"

"How would I pay for Wittenberg without money?" I asked, punching the elevator button so hard, I broke a nail.

"I'll pay."

I scoffed. "I can't let you do that."

"Why not?"

"Whose boyfriend pays for her to go to college?"

"Who else is dating a prince?" he asked.

My mouth twisted into a smile rather against my will. "Good point, but no. It'd be too weird."

Hamlet shrugged. "Suit yourself."

The elevator doors opened on Claudius and the king. Though they were silent when the doors opened, it was clear they had been arguing, as they were both slightly red-faced and the king's hands were clenched awkwardly. "Father!" Hamlet exclaimed, taking his hand off my back.

"Are you two coming in?" Claudius asked.

"No, we'll wait," said Hamlet, looking from one man to the other.

"Don't be absurd," the king said, so we hastened in. "What floor?"

"Mine," I said.

Looking over the top of his glasses, the king asked, "Hamlet, will you be up this evening? I want to spend some time with you before you go." The doors opened, and he smiled warmly at Hamlet.

Hamlet smiled back. "Yeah, sure, Pop."

We walked out together, and the door slipped shut behind us. "That was weird," I said, heading to my room.

"What?"

"Your uncle and your dad."

"They've been really uptight lately. I asked about it, but my mother just said 'business.' She's been weird, too, but whatever. I'm gone tomorrow, so…" Hamlet flopped onto my bed. "Speaking of classes, what are you taking?"

"Oh, um, swimming, art history, English with Ms. Wallace—"

"She's a nut."

"Yeah, but she loves poetry, so that'll be cool. Uh, still-life painting, and Math for Poets."

"Math for Poets?"

"Code for idiots. Or an easy A." I sat on my floor, grabbed a squishy pillow, and started mushing it around.

"No science?"

"You know it's not required for seniors."

"Sounds challenging."

"Screw it. I figure going to that lame college means I'm not meant to do much with my life, so I won't bother trying."

"Taking those classes, you won't need to."

I'm going to interrupt and be honest here: The thing with Denmark State was my fault. I remember the fateful day early in the summer when my father had stood waiting for me with a large envelope in his hands.

"This arrived today," he had said. "It's a letter of invitation to start Wittenberg a year from now."

"Oh my God!" I had shrieked, grabbing the letter—

handwritten by the dean and signed by the provost—and reading the delicious words about how thrilled they were to offer me a place in their future freshman class.

My father had pulled the papers down, so I could see his angry eyes. "You aren't applying there. Why are you getting letters from them?"

"Actually, I did. Talk to them, I mean. I've been recruited."

"For what?"

"I don't know. I guess they know I'm a straight-A student in all advanced courses."

"And Hamlet's girlfriend. It'll look good for them in the papers."

"That's not the only reason, Dad."

He had grabbed the letter and envelope out of my hands and thrown them on the counter. "Well, you're not going."

I had crossed the room and started drying the spilled orange juice that was seeping into the middle of the page. "I have to, Dad," I said, preparing myself to unleash the secret I'd kept for months. "I don't plan on applying anywhere else."

"Why would you do such a foolish thing?"

"It's not foolish. It's an incredible—"

"You can go anywhere but Wittenberg."

I stood for a second, trying to process what he was saying, and then my anger began to pop. "You never care about what I want."

"Not when what you want is shortsighted and irresponsible. I'm not letting you go to school with him."

"This isn't about Hamlet."

My father had scowled at the half truth. "Then you'll go to State," he had said, before tucking his reading glasses in his pocket and disappearing into his study.

I felt like I had no choice. Part of me knew I could apply to other schools, but I hadn't researched any others and was so pissed about the whole thing that I didn't plan to. And, more important, I figured if I stayed in Elsinore, I could at least see Hamlet whenever he came home.

But now, ready to begin my senior year with a loser schedule that my father didn't even know about—one that would take me out of the running for any competitive colleges if I changed my mind about going—I was freaked out but too stubborn to do anything about it. And having Hamlet disapprove didn't make it easier.

I punched the mushy pillow hard. "I don't see the point of even going to college. I don't know what I want to major in or what I want to be someday."

"What do you think you *might* want to be?"

"I don't know." I rolled up a magazine and started tapping at my head with it. He took the magazine away and rubbed my shoulders. I relaxed under his touch. Quietly, I admitted, "I just want to be with you."

"You must want more than that. That's pathetic."

I pulled away. "Thanks. I thought you'd think it was a compliment."

"It kind of is but, Jesus, I'm not that great. Why not pursue art or—"

"Whatever." I grabbed back the magazine and started flipping through it.

"Phee," he said. "Ophelia, come on."

I didn't look up but offered, "Why don't you go hang out with your mommy? Or maybe both of us are simply too pathetic to be graced with your presence these days."

"I can't believe this is how you want to spend your last day with me."

He grabbed his camera and walked down my hall to the elevator. I took a deep breath and chased after him. He didn't turn around even when I was right behind him.

In my most conciliatory tone, I asked, "Hey, let's just go out, okay? Get you back in time to hang with your dad?"

He paused a moment, then stretched his hand out behind him. I took it and he pulled me around in front of him.

"Can my mom come?" he joked.

I swatted at him, and the elevator arrived. This time, it was empty.

The next morning, he was set to leave. I was getting ready for our official public good-bye when Hamlet surprised me by coming to my apartment. My father was still home when Hamlet walked in. They shook hands, and my father wished him well. I was just about to be relieved that they hadn't irritated each other when my dad looked at his watch and said, "You two are expected downstairs in five minutes. People count the faults of those who keep them waiting."

Hamlet rolled his eyes as my father took his coffee into his study and shut the door.

"I wanted a minute alone with you," Hamlet said, taking a few strands of my hair and pushing them behind my shoulder.

As much as I wanted nothing more than to hang out with him on the couch all day, the choice wasn't mine to make. "We should go."

"I know, but I just wanted to say...God, there's so much. This summer was..."

"What?" I asked.

He opened his mouth, but then closed it again. I waited for him to finish, hoping it was going to be sweet and romantic and as perfect as he'd been for weeks, so I was disappointed when he smirked and asked, "So, do I look ready for my public?"

No one could pull off effortlessly devastating like him. Damp blond hair tucked behind his ears, slightly wrinkled linen shirt, board shorts just below his tan knees. I sighed despite myself even as he did a mock catwalk. He stuck his sunglasses on his head, took my hand, and led me to the elevator.

"Well…I don't know." I wrinkled my nose. "Too bad you didn't get the looks in your family." He laughed. "You know I love this," I said as I ran my palm down the length of his linen-covered chest, "but that can't be the outfit your mom had the stylists pick for you."

"I decided to take off the suit."

"You should have come down earlier. I would have taken it off for you."

He smiled and said, "You're wicked."

"Only because you made me that way."

He put his arms around me. "What am I gonna do without you?"

"Not a whole lot, I hope," I said, squeezing his cheeks between my hands.

When we got downstairs, my father's secretary, Reynaldo, was waiting with his arms crossed and his lips pursed. As he hurried to Hamlet's side, Reynaldo slicked back the few remaining wisps of hair on his shining head and said, "Stormy Somerville is waiting with her cameraman at the top of the steps. She's going to ask a question or two, then you kiss chastely."

Hamlet snickered. "Does that mean no tongue?"

I elbowed his ribs.

Reynaldo cleared his throat and wiped his head again. "Then Ophelia waves briefly and comes back inside. Is that clear?" We both nodded.

I smiled wryly and stood on my toes to whisper in Hamlet's ear. "If you stick your tongue down my throat, I'll kill you." I pinched his butt and put on my public smile.

Laughing, he threw one arm around my shoulder and the other hand in the air. The crowd roared as we walked outside. Dozens of flashes went off. Spread across the steps were mostly teen girls with their mothers. Many held handmade signs with slogans like "Don't go, Prince Charming" and "Elsinore's a snore without you." A few held *Courtier Magazine*'s Sexiest Bachelor of the Year issue with Hamlet's photo emblazoned on the front. As often as I had posed for these photo ops, there was still a part of me that found them amusing and thrilling.

Stormy Somerville walked over, hot pink microphone in hand. I tried not to gawk at the fact that her skirt was so tight, you could tell she was wearing a thong. "Ophelia," she said, leaning close to me, "your guy is going away. Any parting words?"

"Hamlet—" I began. I was supposed to say, "Study hard and make Denmark proud." But I just couldn't bring myself to do it. Hamlet's eyes were blank as he waited for my scripted farewell, and a spark of rebelliousness flared in me. "Listen," I said, and he cocked his head as he snapped out of his stupor. "Don't do anything I wouldn't do, sweet prince."

I heard Stormy and Reynaldo gasp, and Hamlet's eyes now danced with glee. That was for us, so now I'd give the adults what they wanted. "And study hard. And make Denmark proooud."

"Aw," said Stormy as she turned to the crowd. I noticed tiny beads of sweat had popped up on her forehead, and I wondered if my actions could actually get her in trouble. A girl in the front screamed uncontrollably and then slumped into her mother's arms. I forced myself not to laugh.

Suddenly Hamlet grabbed my arm and dragged me a few steps away from Stormy, who looked impatiently at Reynaldo.

"I'm so glad you did that," Hamlet said quietly. "I should have said this upstairs, but this was the best summer of my life, and all we did was hang out. I wish you were coming with me. It's a whole week before your classes start."

"But you know I can't." Stormy was glaring at us, so I said, "We'd better go back."

"This is so lame," he muttered.

I shrugged, hoping he meant the staged good-bye and not my decision to go back to Stormy. "It's part of your job."

He nodded slightly then whispered, "I love you, Ophelia."

I got the chills. "I love you, too, Hamlet." I wished he'd been able to say that and more when we were alone. We kissed simply, he returned to the scheduled interview, and I went inside.

I hurried upstairs and flipped on the TV, knowing that his departure would be televised, replayed, and dissected on the morning talk shows. Hamlet posed for some pictures with the scream queens, and then he actually kissed a baby.

My friend Lauren called and asked if I was watching. I said yes as Hamlet wished a happy birthday to an elderly woman in a purple housedress who was turning one hundred.

"He's quite the charmer," narrated Stormy.

"No kidding," Lauren said into the phone. "So," she asked, "now that he's gone, you wanna hang out? Sebastian, Keren, and all those guys are grabbing coffee. Sebastian really wants you to come."

I hesitated but knew I should. The first days after Hamlet left were always the hardest for me, so I tried to keep busy. "Yeah. See you in ten."

I grabbed my bag, and while I waited for the elevator I texted Hamlet.

Barnardo: You sent this message to Hamlet: "u bin gn 2 long. im w/ sml new. sry."

Ophelia: When did I...? Oh. I sent that about five minutes after he left. Check the records. *(pause)* It was a joke.

Francisco: Did Hamlet find it funny?

Ophelia: Do you have his reply? *(shuffling of papers)* See? He wrote back "me 2." And for the record, I laughed.

Barnardo: Interesting relationship.

Ophelia: You had to be there.

5

Zara tilts her head. "So Hamlet left for college not knowing that his life would change forever."

Ophelia looks at her lap. "None of us did."

My friends and I met for iced coffee but decided it was too hot to be anywhere but the river. We piled into Justine's car, and because there were so many of us, I ended up squished between Lauren and Sebastian. Lauren grabbed the sunglasses off my head and put them on.

"Gertrude buy you these?" she asked.

I tried to take them back, completely annoyed by the memory of the shopping trip during which Gertrude had chosen these glasses for me. She had spent the outing asking why Hamlet was refusing to declare a major, and she wouldn't take "indecision" as enough of an answer.

"What's it to you who buys me what?" I asked Lauren, brimming with irritation.

"Why do you go out with her?" Lauren checked her

reflection in the window before Sebastian grabbed the glasses off her face and handed them back to me.

"You are a true gentleman, sir," I said to Sebastian. "Thank you for coming to my rescue."

Lauren leaned into me. "Careful not to compliment him too much. He might take it the wrong way with Hamlet out of town."

Sebastian whacked the back of her head, and she smoothed down her short dark hair.

"Be nice to Sebastian," I said, putting my hand on his thigh. "He's sensitive."

Sebastian shifted in his seat and pushed my hand away. Guilt overwhelmed me when I saw him blush.

"Uh," I said, leaning toward the front seat to break the tension, "we going to our usual spot?"

Everyone agreed, and soon we were by the river setting up towels and kicking off our shoes.

"Dan and Greg coming?" I asked.

Keren shook her head. "They have to work. Dan wants to have a barbecue tomorrow, though. You in?"

I nodded as I stripped down to my bathing suit, pretending I didn't notice Sebastian staring. We all walked to the water's edge, and Lauren suggested a race. She and I plunged in and stroked hard against the current. She won, and when we emerged on the other bank, we found we'd been carried downstream a fair way. I wasn't surprised by either fact, since she was a stronger swimmer, and the current, though slower than in the spring, was still powerful. We swam back across and then walked together along the shore.

"You joining the swim team again this year?" she asked.

"I don't know. I'm definitely doing lacrosse in the spring."

"I love how they call it a spring sport but practices start in January."

I shrugged. "Nothing logical about sports or school."

"I'll miss you if you don't swim."

"You'll miss giving me a hard time."

"True," she said. "Who will I mock if not you?"

"I'm sure you'll find someone. You shouldn't let that talent go to waste."

When we reached the others and sat back down, Justine asked, "So how was Florence? Your pictures were gorgeous."

"Oh my God, it was fantastic."

Sebastian pulled out his sketchbook and rolled onto his side so we couldn't see his face.

I hesitated, but Lauren waved for me to continue. "Well, uh, you should go there someday. The galleries are amazing and the buildings are—"

"I meant Hamlet. How was it being there with *him*?" Justine asked, leaning back to get more sun on her face.

My eyes flicked again to Sebastian's back. "Good."

"That's it?" asked Justine, sitting up on her elbows. "You're with the girls. Dish."

"Not all girls," I reminded her, "and I don't want my business to end up in your blog."

"I would never—" she began, but then lay back down and laughed. "It was one mistake, Ophelia. I didn't know I wasn't supposed to tell about—"

"Anyone hungry?" asked Sebastian, reaching for the food bag.

"No. And no details. That memory's all mine." I put on my sunglasses and lay on my towel thinking about Hamlet and Florence and how much I wished we were there at that moment.

*   *   *

After school started, it was ridiculously boring around the castle. Horatio, Hamlet, Laertes, and I all e-mailed and called, but it wasn't the same. Gertrude invited me every so often to have lunch or shop or sit through a fitting, but I was certainly not welcome at her table on Sunday nights without the boys. And with my dad working all the time, I was alone night after night.

School was unchallenging, and every time I sat staring out the window or dressing reluctantly for swim practice, I thought about what Hamlet had said and knew the boredom was my own doing. I considered changing my schedule to take something enriching, but it sounded like a lot of trouble. Besides, being in shape and having time to paint were more appealing than learning about politics, a subject that seemed to be all too much a part of my life as it was.

Late one afternoon, I went to the conservatory to get some reading done. I liked working in there because it made me feel close to Hamlet, and few people in the castle had the time or the inclination to go in there, especially midweek. I stepped out of the elevator and hesitated when I saw Hamlet's uncle, Claudius, outside the glass entryway. He was shoving a bottle into his coat pocket as he walked. He stopped short and I thought he spotted me, but he was looking over his shoulder at the cameras pointed at the door to the conservatory. He furrowed his brow and hurried down the hall in the other direction, so I proceeded.

Inside, the thick, moist air was fragrant with blooming sweet peas and I considered picking some for my room. I looked up at the surveillance camera that Claudius had been checking out and thought better of it, having previously been caught and reprimanded for filching flowers. Only after I had tucked myself into the coziest corner by the fountain did I realize that I had brought the wrong book, and so I unenthusiastically headed back to my apartment.

Just as I grabbed the correct book from my nightstand, I heard sirens. I looked out the window and saw an ambulance and a fleet of police and security cars screaming to a stop in front of our building. Racing onto the balcony, I leaned over as far as I could. Royal guards fanned out and blocked the street in either direction while police set up barricades. I started breathing really fast, and everything looked all wobbly. Ever since my mom died, sirens had triggered panic attacks. And when I saw a stretcher being rushed into the lobby, I had to hold the railing really hard because I was terrified they were coming for my father. With hundreds of people working in the castle, it was pretty unlikely, but I was so scared of losing him, too, that I had to make sure it wasn't him.

Moments later, a stretcher raced past. I couldn't make out who it was under the oxygen mask and buckled sheet, but once Gertrude shrieked out after it, I froze. I knew it was the king. I shouldn't have been relieved, but for a second I was, because it meant my dad was okay. And then I realized it was a man I loved almost as much as my dad. My chin began to tremble, and I clutched the railing, watching with horror as the stretcher was pushed into the ambulance.

They moved so fast that Gertrude didn't even have time to hoist herself into the back of the ambulance. One of the royal guards grabbed her by the arm and, at a near run, guided her into a black town car with tinted windows. The cavalcade sped off toward the hospital.

"Papa Don't Preach" blared from my phone. I usually found the ringtone funny, but not just then. My father, usually a man of many words, simply instructed, "Stay in our apartment. Do not leave until you hear from me again. And do not call Hamlet." He hung up before I had time to argue or question.

I pressed my lips together and told myself to breathe. The king would be okay. He had to be. He was young and healthy. But what could have—

A new set of engines rumbled outside, and heavy sliding doors opened and closed. I was all too familiar with the sounds of various news vans pulling up in front of the castle for special events and scandals alike. I flipped on the TV and moved back to the balcony feeling as if I were walking through molasses. I leaned over the railing and then decided to sit. Then I jumped back up and ran inside. There was nothing new on TV, so I went back out and leaned over the balcony again, and then dropped onto a patio chair. I started shivering and chewed on my nails while I wondered if Hamlet knew what was happening, wondering if his father was going to be all right, wondering what we would all do if he wasn't. I wanted to be with Hamlet. To reassure him. To have him reassure me.

I was about to defy my father and call Hamlet when the soap opera that had been on was interrupted by a Special Bulletin logo and thumping music. I raced back inside as a camera zoomed in to a chiseled blond who began to speak, her voice shaky. Something about her expression made my breath short and kept me from focusing on her words. Unexpectedly, she broke down and cried, so the camera cut to an equally chiseled man. His face crinkled as he said, "This just in. Our king…is dead."

I breathed out slowly and sank onto the couch without

realizing it. Tears filled my eyes, but my arms could not move to wipe them as they slid down my cheeks. It couldn't be. The man who had made me laugh at my fifth birthday party by pretending he'd stolen my nose could not be dead. The man who had told me not to worry when I was starting a new middle school could not be dead. The man who had put his arm around my shoulder and led me gently to my mother's graveside could not be dead. It could not be that man. It could not be Hamlet's father they were talking about. No. Not Hamlet's father. Hamlet.

Oh God, I thought. I stood back up quickly, focusing my thoughts with all my strength. I grabbed for my phone and typed: "find hamlet." My thumb hovered over the Send button momentarily before I punched it.

I gripped my phone hard and stared at it, waiting for a reply. Helicopters were circling the castle by that point and, from the sound of it, they were over the hospital as well.

"Answer, damn it," I muttered. I tapped my feet to try to keep my legs from shaking. I opened and shut my phone as if that would make something happen.

My phone *bing*ed and I jumped. A text message:

Keren: What's going on?

Another *bing*.

Justine: King dead?

And another.

Lauren: OMG

47

And another.

Sebastian: U ok?

I couldn't deal with my friends' questions, so I hit Ignore over and over and paced.

My phone rang and when I saw Horatio's name I flipped it open so fast, I almost dropped it. "You got my message?"

"Yeah. How did this happen?" Horatio was shouting. He sounded like he was running.

"I don't know. Are you with Hamlet?"

"No, the royal guards grabbed him out of class. He's on the helicopter already."

"Is he okay?"

"I don't know. I can't believe this."

"Me eith—" I fought away tears so I could ask, "Where are you?"

"Running to one of the cars. Officer VanDerwater said I could ride along if I hurried. Ophelia, try to meet him at the hospital."

"I don't know if they'll let me in."

"Oh please," he said skeptically.

"I'll try. Let me know if you hear anything."

"Same. Later." He hung up.

I ran for my room and grabbed my bag and keys. Stopping to turn off the television, I noticed that the streets were blocked all around the hospital and the castle. No point in getting my car or even a driver.

I pushed the elevator button. The first time it stopped, it was packed with very angry-looking faces. "No room!" some-one shouted before pushing the Door Close button. The next time, it was equally crowded, but at the front stood Marcellus, who was Hamlet's bodyguard everywhere but Wittenberg, as he was too old to blend in at college. He reached around the people in front of him and pulled me in. Everyone jostled impatiently to make space.

After being shoved into its midst by the crowd behind me, I stood in the lobby slightly disoriented by the sheer volume of people. The common area was full of workers who made the castle run but who suddenly had nowhere else to be. Some were crying; some were talking on cell phones; some were staring blankly at the flat-screen TVs.

"Come with me," offered Marcellus. "We'll have to run, but I can get you into the hospital."

"Thanks," I squeaked out through my clenched throat, checking to be sure I still had my phone in my pocket. I wanted to text Hamlet, but I resisted the urge to do so.

Marcellus's uniform caused everyone lingering in the castle lobby to move out of his way, and we were out in the air sooner than I could have hoped. I was in shape, but he ran five miles a day and it showed. As he sprinted down the street, I struggled to keep pace with him.

"Have you heard anything?" I asked, trying not to sound too winded, afraid he'd slow down or, worse, leave me behind.

"Maybe a heart attack. Maybe a stroke. Sudden was all we heard."

He grabbed my arm and tugged me in the opposite direction of the cameras, down three blocks, and around to the back entrance of the hospital. A guard waved us inside and we ran for the elevator.

The hospital had an eerie stillness about it. Everyone was standing around various televisions watching the latest emergency report. Nothing had changed since this had all begun, and yet the people acted as if staring would alter the outcome or make something happen. Running had kept my mind free, but once we stopped, thoughts of the king tugged at me. Images of his kind face rushed through my head, and his laugh seemed to echo in the silence. I pressed my fingers to my eyes to keep the tears in.

Marcellus and I got into the elevator, which was antiseptic and cold. The only sound was our panting as we tried to catch our breath. I felt sweat trickling down the small of my back, so I dried it with my shirt. A gentle *ping* announced our arrival at the tenth floor, the one reserved for the king and his family, whatever the cause.

As we emerged, a door opened midway down the hall, and I spotted corn-silk hair bobbing between the black trench coats. "Hamlet!" I called, but he couldn't hear. The group was headed away from me, and I knew I had to do something since, once he found Gertrude, it would be ages before he and I could speak. I needed to know he was okay.

"Marcellus, where are they— Can you—?"

Marcellus lifted his wrist and spoke into a tiny microphone hidden under the cuff of his shirt.

The flock of guards halted and I heard, "Phee?"

"She's here," called out Marcellus, and I put my hand up.

Hamlet rushed around his detail and flew at me. I was relieved to finally talk to him, to touch him.

His cheeks were as cold as his hands. He started to break down but wiped his face hard, looking at the doctors and nurses who had stopped to stare. "Come on," he said, grabbing my hand and yanking me into the circle of guards who had followed. "Privacy, damn it. We need a place that's empty!" His voice was shrill. Two guards fanned out and began opening doors. When one signaled, Hamlet dragged me along with him.

I was suddenly fearful that when we were alone, I would have nothing to say. What words would make him feel better? None. I knew from experience that talk meant nothing at a time like this. But I could hold him. And I could listen.

He nodded almost imperceptibly at the guard, who nodded back and shut the door behind us. Hamlet's angular face was pinched and red, his eyes unfocused. "Hamlet," I said softly, and put my arms around him. My chest ached with sympathy and my own loss. I couldn't help but mix this moment in with the day my mother died, and thinking of how much he had helped me that day, I determined to push aside my own feelings so I could help him.

He sank into my embrace and wept openly. I could hardly hold him as his body shook and heaved.

"My father, my father," he rasped over and over. My shirt was soaked with his tears, but I held him still, stroking his smooth hair and kissing it every so often. He broke from my arms and put his hands on his knees, gasping like when he was cooling down from a run. When he finally stood up and tucked his hair behind his ears, every bit of his face was wrinkled and distorted. "I have to go back out there. Damn it." He walked to the sink, splashed water on his face, and pulled the paper towels with a sharp *tch-tch*. He dried his face, furiously crumpled the paper towels, and let the flap on the trash can close loudly. Every sound was exaggerated. I just wanted to be somewhere quiet and familiar.

"Come on," he said, and he opened the door.

Guards surrounded us as soon as we stepped into the hall, and we all began walking toward a set of double doors.

Knowing there might be a dead body on the other side forced acid into my throat. I squeezed Hamlet's hand. He misinterpreted it as checking in because he whispered, "I'm okay."

We all came to an abrupt halt. Too short to see around the guards in identical black trench coats, I could only hear Claudius's voice. "Leave Ophelia out here," he commanded.

"But Uncle Clau—" began Hamlet. His request was cut off when Marcellus stepped between us, and the rest of the huddle moved forward through the double doors. Hamlet's fingers slipped from mine and I stood on my toes, hoping to catch at least a glimpse of him. I couldn't.

"Marcellus, this is ridiculous. He wants me with him," I argued.

"But Claudius doesn't."

"Why does he get—"

"Go home, Ophelia. Don't make this harder than it has to be."

I left to find Horatio and tried not to think about hating Claudius, feeling bad for Hamlet, or how much I was going to miss the king.

Francisco: *(clears throat)* Why did you text Horatio "find hamlet"? Was it so he could kill him, too?

Ophelia: Of course not. They were best friends.

Barnardo: We think it was a code. We think Horatio was in cahoots with you.

Ophelia: *Cahoots?* Who even uses that word?

Francisco: Answer the question. Did you and Horatio plan to murder the king and then get to Hamlet?

Ophelia: That's ridiculous. It was a text to—

Barnardo: You two exchanged a lot of messages.

Ophelia: Yeah, we're friends.

Francisco: Maybe we should bring him in.

Ophelia: No, please. He had nothing to do with this.

Barnardo: Unlike you?

Ophelia: No. I didn't either. God!

6

"What a shocking day for us all," Zara says solemnly. A mother in the audience puts her arm around her young daughter. "That day you sent a message to Horatio but not Hamlet. Why is that?"

"My father told me not to communicate with Hamlet."

"Did you always listen to your father?"

Ophelia looks down and blinks rapidly. "No. But I should have."

Zara pats Ophelia's leg.

Ophelia twists the bottom of her sweater between her fingers. "Each decision that day seemed really important, but I didn't know what to do, how to make things right."

Zara nods hard in agreement. "We were scheduled to tape a show that day on dog makeovers. It just didn't seem right to carry on, but the puppies were ready, the stylists were all set with their specially designed outfits, and the runway had been built to scale. Hard to know what to do on a day like that. I think that day we were all feeling it."

Ophelia blinks a few times, her lips pressed together. Then she says, "So you know then."

"You look dashing, Dad," I said, pulling at my father's tie.

"I'm not supposed to look dashing. I'm supposed to look mournful. A man who does not know his place is a man who loses it."

I cocked my head and answered, "Then you are a man who, despite himself, looks great, but in the most respectful, unpresumptuous way."

He pinched my cheek. "Ready?" he asked, putting out his arm.

"Yeah. I told Hamlet I'd meet him upstairs."

He clucked quietly.

"What?" I asked impatiently.

"He should be with his family."

"Dad, he's been trapped with his family for the past few days. He told me he can't stand it anymore and just wants to be with me."

He raised an eyebrow.

"I can't not show up. He's waiting."

"Double negative."

"Dad!" His grammar lessons always irritated me.

"Sweetheart, you put too much effort into that boy at the expense of what's good for you. As the saying goes, 'To thine own self be true.'"

I rolled my eyes. "Dad, when I'm with him, I *am* being true to mine own—my own—whatever. True to myself. He's important to me, as is keeping my word. I'll see you in a while."

He shook his head and walked to his room.

As I rode up, my phone *bing*ed.

Sebastian: Going 2 the funeral?

Me: Course

Sebastian: If u need anything, im here 4 u

Me: K

I hadn't seen my friends in a few days, but they kept checking in, which was sweet. I couldn't really tell any of them what was happening—not the real stuff. Not how I hadn't been able to sleep in a few days because I kept having nightmares about hospitals and funerals. Not how Gertrude had tried to keep Hamlet from everyone, including me, for days. Not how he had cried on the phone and how last night he had snuck down to talk after a sedative had pulled his mother into a deep sleep. I would never be able to share these things with them, and I felt a wall being built between my former life and my current one. A wall I didn't realize would be so hard to break through.

When I left the elevator, the chambers were surprisingly quiet. One of the guards nodded at me and opened the door to Hamlet's hall. I heard Gertrude talking as soon as he did. She was shouting about how she could not possibly go out and be seen in her current state. The pause must have been someone answering, but she did not give whoever it was much time before she continued shouting, "Your father. Your poor father!" I stopped, deciding whether to go on, and turned to face the guard, who gave an encouraging nod. I had made a promise, so I continued to Hamlet's room. The door was open, so I waited in the doorway until someone looked up.

Hamlet saw me first and waved me forward, but I didn't enter. I knew better than to walk in with Gertrude's back to me. She saw him gesturing again and turned, ready for me to be an intrusive servant she had to dismiss. Full of rage, her eyes met mine. To say her fury dissipated would be an overstatement, but she pulled out of her full mistress-of-the-house posture and settled on annoyed. "What is it, Ophelia?"

"Uh, Hamlet asked me to come up."

"Of course he did," she said, then stood and straightened her skirt. "One time, Hamlet, one time it would nice if I was enough." She turned back to me, her eyes narrow. "Your father will be waiting for you, though. We must all leave in a few minutes."

"I want her to ride with us," Hamlet explained.

Gertrude's eyes flew open and her lips curled into a snarl. "Absolutely not. The plan has been set. The event scripted. It will be you, me, and Claudius."

"But Mother, I need her."

She drew her lips into a thin line. "*I* need *you*. Alone."

"But Uncle Clau—"

"Nothing more. I need you to do as you're told. Don't think I've forgotten the leaving-for-college debacle. Stormy was very disappointed by that, as was I. I will see you, and only you, in one minute. Ophelia." She nodded as she left, wiping her smeared mascara.

He made to argue, but I put up my hand as I walked to him. "Forget it," I said, trying not to be angry myself, knowing it would only make it worse for both of us. I laced my fingers through his and said, "I'll be in the car behind yours. I'll be sitting behind you at the service."

"I prefer being behind you."

I wrinkled my nose. "Even today with the sex jokes? That's really…"

He blushed slightly. "Sorry. I'm just…I'm trying not to think about any of this. It's too—" His forehead crinkled and he looked away.

Like Hamlet, I was also trying not to think about what was happening. I focused on him because the rest was too hard. Too strange. Too familiar. I kissed him and he walked me to the door.

When I got to the car, my father was standing next to my brother, who had returned from Paris for the funeral. Laertes was shaking his head. I pretended not to notice and climbed across the backseat to sit by the far window. Laertes slid in next to me, and my father sat across from us so he could continue glaring at me.

I refused to look at him but stared at all the people who were laying flowers and candles and pictures of the king out in the street. For the past three days, people had streamed to the castle and added more. There were layers and layers, and I wondered who would clean it all up in the end and if the stuff would be thrown away or saved. Probably thrown away.

I saw a large man who looked like he spent his days lifting very heavy things weeping openly, letting thick tears drip down his face and onto his nylon jacket. It was a face I wanted to sketch, but I wouldn't. Instead, I would try to forget it, because I couldn't watch his grief without thinking about the man we had all just lost. A lump formed in my throat, but I didn't want to cry in front of anyone that day. I had promised myself that I wouldn't. And I couldn't be there for Hamlet if I was wrapped up in my own feelings. I pulled my sunglasses over my eyes and stared at my lap.

Moments later, I heard the crowd let out a cheer and I looked to see what it was. Gertrude and Claudius were leaving the lobby. He was supporting her, and she lifted a hand weakly to acknowledge her subjects. Hamlet trailed behind, hands in his pockets, head down. For once he did not play to the crowd. Reporters and average citizens alike took pictures as the family got into the lead car. His tie flapped over his shoulder, blown by the wind just before he dove into the backseat. I knew Hamlet would have preferred to have a hood to hide himself further, but it was not to be. The caravan moved as soon as their door was closed.

"Unbelievable. They can't even mourn in peace," said Laertes, scowling.

"This is the life they expect. Part of the job," my father answered. "Everything about their lives is prescribed," he said, staring at me. I sighed and looked back out the window at the people lining the streets. Another wave of sadness passed through me, so I returned to staring at my lap.

Hamlet's father was a man I'd always loved. He was so important and so busy, but he tried to make life seem as normal as possible for all of us. He always made time for Hamlet and made me feel like family. He came to a couple of Hamlet's lacrosse games and even attended my school art show the time my father couldn't make it.

Sitting in the limo on the way to his funeral, I remembered a ride I'd taken with the king right after Hamlet broke up with me for the first time. Hamlet hadn't even bothered to come home from Wittenberg but called to do it. Bastard. Somehow someone found out, which meant I was left in Elsinore to deal with the press myself. Not exactly myself. The guards and PR people camped out at the front of the lobby, blocking the reporters' entrance and answering questions when they could. But still, it was intimidating. And I was pissed.

Marcellus escorted me to the underground garage and told me I should travel with an extra guard until the whole thing quieted down. While I waited, a stretch limo pulled up and the king exited the elevator.

"Ride with me," he said, though it was a question rather than a command.

I looked at Marcellus, who nodded, and I slid onto the leather seat.

As we passed the crowd of cameras, he shook his head. "I wish I could outlaw all of that nonsense, but reporters are like my wife — they listen only when they want to." He smiled broadly and patted my hand.

His kindness actually made it worse, and I had to look out the window so he wouldn't see my tears.

"You don't have to talk about it, but what happened?"

When I had composed myself, I turned to him. "Your son," I began, attempting to keep some accusation out of the word *son*, "decided that he didn't think it made sense for us to stay together now that he's away. Said it wasn't me and asked if we could be friends. He couldn't have come up with anything more original?" My voice quaked with fury.

"Ah," was all he said for a while. Then, in the voice he used to soothe his subjects, he continued, "You are right in saying that those phrases are too often used. But as his father, I must confess I think he might mean both."

I clenched my teeth but listened to him despite my intense desire to open the door of the moving car and let the reporters have me.

"It can't be *you* because he loves you. He always seems a little…lost or sadder when you're not around. Being a young man, especially one in his position and with his looks, there are many…temptations."

My stomach turned as I imagined the temptations and what they were doing with him at that moment.

"And as for being friends, well, I'm sure he's sincere about that, too."

"Right." My bitterness threatened to swallow me whole. When Hamlet and I began dating, we said it wouldn't ruin our friendship. Ah, the lies we tell ourselves. "Because it's always been Hamlet and Ophelia. Ophelia and Hamlet."

"Not always. When you were three, he asked to have you removed from the castle because you kept stealing his toys." His glass-rattling laugh exploded from his throat, and I couldn't help but smile a little. "Hamlet even wrote a proclamation. Misspelled half the damn thing, but it was very impassioned."

We pulled into the driveway of my school, and my smile faded. The driver had called ahead, so their security guards were waiting out front to escort me past the reporters.

I smoothed my plaid uniform skirt, worrying more about having to face my classmates and their stares than the cameras. No one ever thought I might need protection *in*side the classroom.

The king sighed. "This will pass, and if my son has half the brain I think he has, he will come back to you. And then *you* can decide if you still want him when he does."

I wiped my face and asked, "How do I look?" My lashes were still wet, and I knew my eyes were red and puffy.

The king's lips twisted just like Hamlet's did whenever he was about to tell a lie. "Well…do you have any makeup?"

"I'm not allowed to wear it at school."

"Then you're gorgeous." He handed me my backpack. "Deep breath and good luck."

At the cemetery, the scale of the event overwhelmed me. Enormous flower arrangements flanked the walkway and encircled the graveside. Flags flew; soldiers stood at attention in their dress whites; a brass band played melancholy versions of patriotic tunes. Leaders and dignitaries from other lands had come to pay their respects and waited as our group passed. After the ceremony, most would try to speak to Gertrude, and probably to Hamlet and Claudius, too, but until the king was laid to rest, they would keep a deferential distance. As we walked, Hamlet turned a couple of times to look back at me, and I smiled as small as I could.

I noticed my father looking through the crowd on our right, and I knew it was for my mother's grave. It had been a long time since we had visited. Involuntarily, we all looked in its direction as we turned the last bend in the path to take our seats. Laertes put an arm around my shoulder. After we walked a few paces, I whispered, "Maybe we should come back tomorrow."

"Not a chance. This place creeps me out," Laertes whispered back.

"Mom would like it," I suggested.

He grimaced and walked a few steps ahead of me to catch up with our father. I craned my neck one more time, then walked to my seat next to my father.

We were, as expected, directly behind the royal family. I touched Hamlet lightly on the back before sitting and folding my hands demurely in my lap. I thought of the reporters taking this in and knew that, were the occasion not so solemn, they might take a swipe at us, asking why we weren't sitting together or maybe even why we were back together at all.

My mind drifted again to our first reconciliation. Everyone advised against it—my friends, my brother, my father, and, of course, Gertrude. But when he came back from Wittenberg for Christmas vacation, our families had to travel together to Switzerland. On the plane he told me he couldn't stand being without me, that there were no other girls he liked as much, and my anger dissolved almost instantly. Our being together wasn't just convenience. It was an inexplicable attraction that had grabbed hold of us when I was fifteen and hadn't let go of us since. Oh, how I wish it hadn't been that way, but it was.

The minister began the service, and everyone sang a hymn, the sound enveloping us as it rose and echoed eerily at the end.

My father stood to deliver the first speech. "Our king," he began, overenunciating as he did only at press conferences and when lecturing me, "was not only a great leader but a man whose moral character was beyond reproach. He taught his subjects through his actions. He was never false to any man. He was never one to speak without thinking. He was careful never to begin a fight, but if pulled into one, his opposition quickly realized he was a force to be reckoned with. He was not flashy or gaudy. He was neither a borrower nor a lender.…"

I slid down slightly in my chair and hoped my father would not speak for so long that he would embarrass himself. A few years back he had delivered a speech at Gertrude's birthday party that was so long, the candles on her cake had nearly melted away. Finally, the king had tapped my father on the shoulder and raised his glass to toast his own wife. Gertrude had sighed and blown out the few candles that were still ablaze.

"…And so we bid him a solemn farewell." My father tucked his speech into his pocket.

Too many others spoke, but I couldn't focus on their words. Most of the speeches were about the position, not the man. Even the portrait on display looked little like the king I knew from sitting around the dinner table, the one who liked card tricks and to play racquetball in his rare free moments. All I wanted was to sit with Hamlet on the green hill above us and remember the man we'd loved.

After an extraordinarily long time, the ceremony came to a close. The final song, sung by the kingdom's most treasured soprano, was one of the king's favorites. As the coffin was lowered, I got goose bumps and could think only of my mother and the king lying under deep piles of dirt for all eternity. Unable to consider it for another second, I distracted myself by checking on Hamlet. He had dropped his head, apparently unable to watch anymore, and I wished I were sitting at his side so I could comfort him.

As soon as the minister nodded the end, Hamlet stood and turned around. His face was flushed, and I could see he was fighting back tears. A folding chair separated us, so he put one knee on it to get closer to me and I quickly embraced him. He buried his face in my shoulder and whispered, "This sucks," before he lost it and wept into my neck. When his shoulders had stopped shaking, he lifted his head and wiped his face, which was streaked with red and white. He pushed his hair back and I reached up and touched his cheek. Hamlet looked so pitiful and alone, despite the hundreds who surrounded the grave.

"This will be over soon," I whispered. He pushed his hair back again and looked around. When he saw the grave behind him, he shuddered. "What can I do?" I asked.

"Ride back with me," he said, his eyes scanning the crowd.

"I can't. My dad—"

"I need you, Phee," he pleaded.

I turned to ask my father, but he was talking to a visiting dignitary. "Ask your mother," I said quietly.

"It's not her decision."

"Hamlet, she doesn't like surprises. You have to tell her."

Gertrude was shaking hands with a duke when Hamlet tapped her on the shoulder. "I'm going with Ophelia to the car. She's riding with us."

Gertrude's face grew stony and, barely opening her lips, she replied, "I said it before. There is a plan in place. No." Turning back to the duke, she continued her conversation.

"Then I'm going with her."

"No."

Frustrated by my inability to help Hamlet hurt less, and too full of emotion to control myself better, I stepped forward. "Let him do what he wants for once," I said quietly. "This day is hard enough."

She glared at me but said nothing. I took him by the hand and he pulled me toward the cars. Gertrude did not shout after us, but I knew she must have been furious.

The crowd was pulsing around us, milling and sharing greetings, gloomy faces fixed in place. They looked properly attired for mourning, but I got the feeling that much of their grief was just for show. Hamlet did not acknowledge them, keeping his eyes down as he walked.

"Hamlet. Ophelia," called out a familiar voice. Horatio was chasing us. We stopped and waited for him to catch up. Soldiers were keeping the photographers out of the graveyard, but all around the perimeter their cameras poked through the gates. As we walked down the hill to the long line of black cars, the cameras turned to follow us. Hamlet put his head down as we approached, then got into the second car in line. I followed him in with Horatio right behind me.

As he closed the door, Horatio said, "I can't stay long. My

folks are waiting for me." After a moment's silence, he asked, "So, Hamlet, they figure out what happened to your father?"

Hamlet loosened his tie. "No. Doctors are thinking it was a heart attack, but he was healthy at last month's exam, so it doesn't make any sense."

"I'm surprised they buried him without an answer," Horatio said.

Hamlet rubbed his eyes. "My mom insisted. Said the nation needed closure."

Horatio and I both looked at Hamlet, who had dropped his head into his hands. I ran my fingers through the back of his hair and kissed his shoulder. Horatio looked at my face, then at Hamlet, then back to me.

We sat silently until Hamlet said, "I can feel you watching me. Just talk, you two. Please."

"Uh…okay. Horatio, how long are you staying in town?" I asked, feeling a little stupid about engaging in small talk.

"A couple days. Class has been suspended until Monday."

"Hamlet, are you going back with him?" I asked.

He shrugged and reached for a crystal carafe of Scotch.

"Hamlet," admonished Horatio.

"What? Of all days, this is a day for drinking." He held up the bottle and both of us refused. All I needed was for my father to smell alcohol on my breath.

Horatio grimaced. "Not too much, though, man. Okay? You have to stand and face people in a few." Hamlet took one more swig, then put the stopper back in with a flourish.

The car door opened. My brother, seeing us all inside, stopped short. Hesitantly, he said, "Oh. Hey."

"Hey, Laertes. I was just getting out," Horatio answered, winking at me.

Laertes paused, expecting Hamlet to follow. When he didn't, Laertes got in the seat across from me. "Dad'll be here in a minute," he hinted.

"It's just a car ride," I said.

"You know it's not," he replied. I kicked off my heels and thought about how stupid it was that where Hamlet rode was such a big deal. Hamlet took my hand in his and squeezed. Laertes watched us levelly and asked me, "So, did you see that bouquet of *violets* out there? Pretty delicate for this weather, don't you think?"

I realized Laertes was referring to our last conversation before he had left for school. If my love for Hamlet was like a violet, then my father was likely to yank off its petals when we got home. I had broken from my scripted existence. It was one thing to do what Hamlet and I wanted within castle walls, but another thing entirely to mess with orchestrated events. I rubbed my forehead and wished I were somewhere else. Or some*one* else.

The car ride was nothing if not uncomfortable. Once my father assessed the situation, he decided to stay silent and deal with me later. Just before we left, Gertrude's driver knocked on our window, wanting to be sure Hamlet was, indeed, in our car. She didn't try to get him to come out. The damage was done.

Anyone who wanted it had fodder for speculation in opinion columns, tabloids, and talk shows, but it would take a few days before they used it. Once the appropriate amount of grief had been displayed and seemingly enough restraint had been exercised, reporters would have photographic evidence of Hamlet choosing not to be with his mother. "What could it all mean?" they would ask.

When we arrived at the castle, my father made sure Hamlet

exited first and was at his mother's side before he would even consider letting me out.

"It wasn't my idea," I offered.

"Do not come to the reception," he instructed, jabbing his finger at me before he hopped out of the car and raced inside.

Barnardo: This picture shows you looking at your mother's grave.

Ophelia: Yeah. Very perceptive, Detective.

Barnardo: Don't use that tone with me, little girl.

Francisco: Did you blame the king for your mother's death?

Ophelia: I didn't blame— The assassin was trying to kill him, not my mother.

Barnardo: And that's why you wanted the king dead.

Ophelia: I didn't want him dead!

Barnardo: Payback. We get it. Get revenge on the king while at the same time you make Hamlet feel what you felt.

Ophelia: My mother's death has nothing to do with this.

Francisco: But something does. What is it? It's late. We all want to be done with this. Just tell us why you wanted to hurt the royal family.

Ophelia: So I could end up in here with the two of you. Oh good, my evil plan worked.

Francisco: We're getting nowhere with her.

7

"So Hamlet rode back from the funeral with you rather than his mother. How did the queen feel about that?" asks Zara.

"Gertrude was fine with it. She always had Hamlet's best interests at heart. I mean, she basically lived to make him happy."

"He disappeared during the reception. Any idea where he went?"

"Nope."

Zara squints at her and sniffs. "All right, then how did Prince Hamlet feel about being king?"

"He knew it would be a challenge, but it was a job he was born to do," Ophelia tells the audience.

Later that night, Horatio and I snuck up to the rooftop garden with a bottle of wine and waited for Hamlet. We walked to the edge of the roof and looked down at the crowd below. Average citizens were still dropping off flowers and lighting candles. Official cars were still coming and going with dignitaries paying their respects. Horatio had had less than a minute to speak with Hamlet, but it was enough to tell him where to find us. The night was crisp, since the temperature had dropped significantly. I had brought a sweater, but I should have put on something warmer. I crossed my arms and tucked my hands in my armpits. Horatio offered his jacket, but I refused.

"Wonder what it would be like to just live a regular life like all of those people?" I pondered, watching the cars and pedestrians pass by.

"Our life's pretty regular," he mused. I gaped at him, so he added, "Okay, mine more than yours, maybe."

"Mine should be normal. I mean, I just live here. I'm not one of them."

"You had to fall for Hamlet. Your downfall, you might say."

"Thanks," I said. "How are your classes so far?"

"So far so good. You?"

"Fine. Whatever." I sighed.

"You think your dad's gonna let you go to Wittenberg?"

"No."

Horatio put an arm around my shoulder. "Woulda been fun to hang out."

I wanted to scream, but I just stood there, enduring having my life decided for me. "Yeah. Woulda been."

As we stood in silence, I recalled how our trio had changed from three friends to a couple with a sidekick. It was the winter of my sophomore year, and our families had gone to the French Alps for a long weekend of meetings and skiing. Hamlet, after promising to hang out with us on the last night, instead hooked up with an ambassador's daughter, leaving Horatio and me to our own devices. Sore from a day on the slopes and too tired to bother getting dressed up for a fancy dinner or a wild party, we decided to kick around at the lodge—a spectacular, two-centuries-old wooden structure with a great room full of books and mounted animal heads.

Horatio and I sat in front of the roaring fire chatting about one of our favorite subjects: Hamlet's playboy status. The conversation morphed into a half-kidding discussion of how much easier it would be if Horatio and I were a couple. We decided that we would have to kiss and see what we thought of it. We both admitted to not having feelings for each other but thought the benefits of the experiment would be twofold: (1) we could each say we had kissed someone on vacation, and (2) once we were lip-locked, attraction might spring up—a convenient outcome, we agreed, given how often Hamlet left us alone together anyway.

And so we sat knee to knee on the burgundy velvet love seat, trying not to crack up. "You first," I said, which was stupid because a kiss kinda takes two to accomplish. It made him laugh, so that when he leaned forward our teeth knocked, sending both of us backward in hysterics.

"Okay, okay, be serious," he said after a minute, and took me by the shoulders. "We can do this." He leaned in. I felt the warm dampness of his lips and then he pulled away. We looked at each other and considered the kiss—a reaction that proved there wouldn't be another. All I could think was that it had been no more exciting than kissing my brother. Which, let me be clear, meant not at all.

"I, uh…" he began, and I could tell he was afraid to hurt my feelings. "I didn't, um…"

"Me neither," I interrupted, and the tension left his face. "You're a good kisser, though, Horatio."

He settled sideways into the oversize sofa cushions. "Yeah?"

"Where do you learn moves like that?"

He narrowed his eyes. "Martha Kensington."

The Elsinore Academy junior was the worst combination: ugly, bossy, and mean, but she was part of the popular crowd. "Gross," I said. "Do *not* tell me my lips just touched lips that have touched Martha's."

He smiled. "She critiqued me the whole time, but it did make me a better kisser."

"*Ew*," I said, and then pretended to be the hair-flipping, sour-faced Martha, telling him where to better place his hands, when to move his tongue, and how to tilt his head just so. This sent us into an uncontrollable fit of giggles that Hamlet walked in on.

"What's so funny?" he asked, pulling off his sweater before sitting in front of the fireplace.

Horatio opened his mouth to explain, and I shook my head.

"What?" Hamlet asked, getting a little offended.

I locked eyes with Horatio, then said, "Fine," and turned to Hamlet. "We were doing an experiment."

"What kind?" Hamlet asked.

I squinted at him. "We kissed," I said lightly.

"Reeeally." He looked from one of us to the other. "And?"

"And," Horatio jumped in, "turns out we're both good kissers, but we have no future together."

"I'm a good kisser?" I asked, and Horatio nodded.

"Cool," said Hamlet, "my turn." He got on his knees and leaned toward me.

I lifted my eyebrows and put up a hand. "You can experiment on Horatio but not me."

"Why not?" he asked, puffing himself up.

I climbed over the side of the love seat and headed for the door. "Because it's late and I don't want to kiss you. Good night, boys."

Horatio called out his good-bye, but Hamlet gave chase up the dimly lit, dark wood lodge steps. "Why don't you want to kiss me?" he asked.

"It'd be weird," I said, taking the stairs two at a time. The suite my parents and I were sharing was the first floor up from the great room, so I was on the landing quickly.

"And it wasn't weird with Horatio?" he asked, still following me.

"It was," I said, stopping at my room, nearly catching my long hair on the antlers hanging from the door.

"So?"

"So nothing. I don't want to." The truth was I *did*, and that was what had me worried. I'd always been more than a little curious, and every once in a while, when I thought of Hamlet, it wasn't just as friends. I had pangs of jealousy when he skulked off with some girl, and occasionally I looked a little too long when he locked lips with one of them. But with him front and center, and the possibility of his kissing me being real, I knew I should decline.

"Horatio got to," Hamlet argued. "That seems a bit unfair." He was acting like a spoiled little boy, which made me want to kiss him far less. Which is why I did it.

"Okay?" I asked, flinging my arms wide after planting a fast, annoyed kiss on him.

He stood really still, and because the torch-shaped hall light was directly behind his head, it made it hard for me to see his expression. Then he inched forward and I could see there was no mirth on his face, only intense desire. His palms cupped my face and when his soft lips brushed against mine, I wanted to both run away and stay there forever. This was bad because it felt so good. Better than good. It felt right.

I yanked my head back and said nervously, "Okay, then, so we did it. Now…good night."

I fumbled with my key and then opened my door. When I stepped inside, he was still standing in the same position. "Huh," he said, bemused. "Good night." He walked away, running his fingers through his hair as he pounded down the steps, presumably to rejoin Horatio.

That night I could hardly sleep. I spent the first half of the night thinking about how beautiful Hamlet looked as he had come closer, and how amazing he smelled, and how confident yet gentle his touch was. I spent the second half of the night thinking about how stupid I'd been to allow it.

The next morning, I didn't talk much to my parents at breakfast. And when we all got on the royal jet, I put my backpack on the seat next to mine and pulled out my homework. When Hamlet and Horatio tried to sit with me, I shook them off, claiming that I had tons to do, and tried to ignore the kick in my stomach when Hamlet leaned in to say they'd be mere feet away if I changed my mind.

When we were waiting for our bags to be unloaded, Hamlet sidled up next to me. "You're acting weird," he said. "We okay? I mean, last night—"

I waved my book right in front of his face. "I'm fine. Mrs. Bernstein is tough, though, and there was a quiz while we were gone. I need to do well on the makeup. That's all that's wrong." In my attempt to sound normal, I knew my voice had gotten higher and less convincing.

He shrugged, fighting back a smile, or so I thought. "Movie tonight?"

I shook my head. "Studying," I said, looking down at my book, hoping he couldn't see the pages shake. How had I never noticed how darn good he smelled? Seriously. Like pine trees and musk and rosemary. Had he changed deodorant? Was he suddenly wearing cologne? He was going to have to move away or I was going to fling my book aside and smooch him right there on the tarmac in front of all our parents.

He left, and I was quite relieved to have escaped such embarrassment.

The next day, Horatio drove Hamlet and me to school, much to my concern. We rode together every day, and saying no would have been an even bigger clue that I'd totally lost it. But in the car, I couldn't talk or join in the conversation. I sat in the back telling myself to stop thinking of Hamlet. Obviously, it didn't work.

Wordlessly, I got out and waved over my shoulder to them, slipping into a circle of my friends, resisting the urge to watch him walk to his locker. Lauren asked how France was, and I answered in as few words as I could, and then Sebastian brought up a party they'd all attended in my absence. I breathed for the first time in over twenty-four hours.

First period was history, and Ms. Stone was delivering a heartfelt lecture on the importance of due process when Hamlet opened the classroom door and said I was needed in the office. As often happened when Hamlet spoke to the female teachers, her eyes glazed over in acquiescence. I never knew if it was his good looks or his celebrity that got them, or a combination of both. Leaving my stuff behind and wondering why I could be needed, I hurried out of the room and into the hall. Hamlet closed the door for me and followed.

When we were on the stairs, I stopped. "I know where the office is, Hamlet."

"They didn't actually call for you."

I hesitated and started to get mad. "I have to go back to class," I said. I had never gotten in trouble and didn't want to start.

He caught me by the arm and said, "Ophelia, we should talk."

I didn't walk away, but I didn't speak.

"I..." he began. "I never thought much about you in that way. You're adorable and have a great body and—" He stopped when I crossed my arms around my middle. "This is coming out wrong. You're younger and we've always just been friends, you know?"

I did. And though I knew he would be right to say things shouldn't change, I braced myself because it was gonna suck having him tell me anyway.

"But," he said. A magical word. "I...Oh, hell." He stepped forward and pulled me close. My legs went weak as his tongue slipped into my mouth and he wove his fingers into my hair.

I stepped back. "This is such a bad idea," I said, barely able to stand. "We *are* friends, and this could be a disaster." He seemed as dazed as I felt, so I had the chance to continue. "When was the last time you dated someone for more than a month?"

The question snapped him to alertness. "Well—" he began, looking like he had evidence to the contrary, and then started to laugh when he realized he didn't. "Ophelia, most girls are interested in dating a 'prince' and are not especially interested in me, which gets old fast, or they're classmates who might see the difference, but once I spend more than a few minutes alone with them, I realize they're really dull."

I smiled. He had complained about this problem before.

"But you..." he said. "I know you don't want me because of what I am—"

76

"I don't?" I asked, batting my eyelashes.

His smile matched mine. "And I know you're not dull." We stood in silence. "I'm going away in less than a year, and who knows what will happen then? But after I kissed you the other night, it was weird because, well, I suddenly couldn't think of spending the rest of my time home without you. And not the way things were before, but like this." He stepped close again and planted a kiss on me that was so intense that neither of us noticed Mr. Johnson, the assistant principal, walk up behind us.

He cleared his throat. "Hamlet, this is not—" I leaped back in shock, and he said, "Oh. Ophelia. I didn't realize—" Unexpectedly, he looked embarrassed. Then he went back to stern professionalism. "Why are you both not in class?"

Red-faced, I looked down and mumbled that I was just going. Hamlet ambled a few paces behind me and when I reached for the door to Ms. Stone's room, he said quietly, "We're not making a mistake. Don't you see we were meant for each other? How can this bring us anything but happiness?"

I knew it was naive. I just didn't realize how complicated it would become.

Almost two years later, when I was waiting for Hamlet to leave the reception of his father's funeral, the memory was oddly comforting and sweetly distracting. I shivered, and Horatio threw an arm around me, making me glad that kiss between us had been so mutually unappealing, because Horatio was the best friend I ever had.

Hamlet came banging through the stairwell door, ripping at his tie. "Get this thing off of me," he called out, then ran toward us and threw the tie over the edge.

"Hamlet!" I cried out.

"Someone can sell it on eBay." He shook hands with Horatio, and we all moved to the patio furniture by the roses.

"How bad was it?" I asked as we settled on a pair of lounge chairs. Lying next to him, I felt warmer already.

"Hell. All those people talking to me like I could help their futures. And most of them didn't know my father at all. Just met him during handshaking photo ops." Horatio and I nodded. I shivered, and Hamlet put his arms tighter around me. "Actually," he said to me, "your dad was the coolest." "Coolest" and my dad were never before and never since mentioned in the same sentence, as much as I loved him, so this took me by surprise.

"He told me things about my dad I didn't even know and gave me a letter my father wrote to me when I was first born." Hamlet touched his suit pocket reverently, and I heard the paper crinkle. "It's about my father's hopes and dreams for me. About how he never expected to l—" His voice broke and he breathed deeply. "Never expected to love anyone as much as he loved me, and h…how it had only been a few days since I'd been born, and how he couldn't im…imagine how he could grow to love me more as I got older, but that he knew he would. Pretty amazing stuff." He looked away, and I held his hand tighter, willing myself not to think about the box of my mother's journals that I had hidden under my bed, journals that said the same kinds of things about me.

Horatio got a text and, after he shoved his phone back into his pocket, Hamlet asked, "Kim?"

Horatio nodded and told me she was a girl he met at school. Hamlet said he liked her but didn't sound too enthusiastic.

"What's your problem with her?" Horatio asked. "Kim's pretty."

"True," Hamlet agreed.

"And she's an amazing writer."

"Also true."

"She's fun."

Hamlet remained silent.

"Life isn't always about acting like an idiot," Horatio said, his voice rising.

"Maybe not, but I know fun, and fun she is not."

"Screw you. I like her." Horatio turned onto his back and looked at the starless sky.

"Cut it out, Hamlet," I said. For a cute guy, Horatio had been alone for a long time, and I thought it was nice he had someone. "Tell me about her, Horatio."

He told me how smart she was, that they spent their time together reading and studying. I hoped they did more than that, though I didn't say so.

I said he should bring her to the castle, to which he replied, "She doesn't know I live here."

I was shocked.

"It's easier. I want her to like me for me."

"Yeah, but that's a hell of a secret," I said.

"I'm good with secrets. Who knows if she is?" He shrugged. "This is separate from school."

"I wish it was for me," Hamlet interjected.

We nodded sympathetically.

"Funny thing is, I don't even want to be king."

"You don't?" asked Horatio, as if it were the first time Hamlet had mentioned it. Maybe it was. I couldn't remember it ever coming up. We'd thought his father would live for a lot longer, and Hamlet was rarely serious enough to bother talking about something so important.

"So don't," I countered.

"Oh, that's rich. Your father tells you not to call me, and you don't. But you want me to stand up to everyone? Say no to this position?"

I stayed quiet, knowing he was right.

"Hamlet, you have to do it," Horatio said. "It's expected. Your family's been in power for generations. You're next in line."

"I know, but there's no way. I'm not ready to lead anyone."

"That is true," Horatio agreed with a smile.

"Shut up," said Hamlet, starting to laugh.

Horatio continued, "You can't even decide what dining hall you want to eat in each day. How are you going to decide on matters of state?" Hamlet took off his shoe and threw it at Horatio, who caught it and threw it back.

As Hamlet put his shoe back on, he said, "You know I'll be a figurehead as much as anything. Parliament makes all the real decisions. Even so, I'm not sure I want to…"

I asked, "Without thinking, what would you do if you could do anything with your life?"

A satisfied smile crept onto his lips. "I'd play my guitar."

We all laughed.

Horatio teased, "You'd starve. You really suck at it."

"I do not. Ophelia?" he asked, trying to get me to agree with him.

"Well…" I hesitated, trying to imagine Hamlet on a street corner with an open guitar case at his feet, hoping for spare change.

"Okay, you two, enough kicking a guy while he's down. Have a drink." We passed the wine around.

"Hamlet, what about someone else doing the job until you're older? At least until you finish college," I suggested.

He shook his head. "I don't know how that would work. Maybe."

Horatio looked perplexed. "Didn't anyone mention a plan to you? They must have rules or contingencies for these sorts of things."

Hamlet turned to me and said, "Your father started talking about it yesterday, but my mother stopped him. Said it wasn't necessary to bother me with it in my grief."

Horatio pressed on. "But you have to deal with it soon, right? I mean, the public wants to know—"

"The public?" said Hamlet. "Whose side are you on?"

Horatio took his iPod out of his jacket and focused on untangling the wires, knowing better than to keep arguing.

"Talk to my dad tomorrow," I suggested.

"Can't wait." Hamlet sulked and drank more wine.

The next morning we were all in Hamlet's room. Horatio was texting Kim, Hamlet was strumming his guitar, and when I wasn't sketching Hamlet, I was staring at him. I admit it was pathetic, but I fell to pieces watching him play the guitar, no matter how good or bad the sound. Classic girl crap, I know. The hair falling over the face, the furrowed brow as he tried to get the chord right, the guitar resting on his knee just so. Sigh and sigh. I dug it. What can I say?

Anyhow, we were all doing our thing when Gertrude stumbled in, and she did not look pleased to find Hamlet with company. She was still in her shiny sea-foam bathrobe; her hair was matted and she had not taken off her mascara from the night before. My guess is someone had given her something to help her sleep, because it was eleven, and by that point in the day she had usually done her Pilates, showered, dressed, and answered selected pieces of fan mail. She clutched her bathrobe around her and asked if Hamlet would follow her out. Horatio and I exchanged glances, and he went back to Kim.

I was cold, so I walked to Hamlet's dresser and took out a long-sleeved shirt. Before I pulled it over my head, I stopped a second to smell the collar. I knew it was clean because, at the castle at least, his stuff was taken care of. But I loved the combination of his scent and the detergent the laundry staff used.

Horatio caught me. "That's just sad," he said.

I covered my face. "I know. I don't get to have these creepy moments when you guys are gone. Having you back is a bonus."

He lifted his eyebrows in mock disapproval. "The king's death is a bonus? Nice."

"You know that's not what I mean," I said, throwing the shirt at him.

Hamlet walked in to find us having fun, and his dark mood sobered us immediately. He looked like someone had touched his jutting cheekbones with pink finger paint. He crossed the room quickly and sat on the floor facing away from us.

"What's wrong?" Horatio asked.

Hamlet wouldn't answer but picked up his guitar and closed his eyes. I saw him wipe away a tear, so I sat on the bed behind him and kissed the top of his head. He strummed with his eyes closed and tried to calm himself.

"She wants me to go back to school tomorrow," he said finally.

"You're kidding," I sputtered. "Tomorrow's pretty fast." I wasn't sure if I was disagreeing with Gertrude because she was wrong to push him or if I just expected him around for a while more.

"Did she say why?" asked Horatio.

He stopped playing and said angrily, "She said that while she would prefer I stayed by her side, I should get on with my life. We would sort out all the being-king stuff later. God, it's been one day since the funeral! Get on with my life?" He shook his head and banged on the strings, making a discordant howl, then sat quietly staring out the window.

Horatio tucked his phone into his back pocket and asked, "You think you'll come back with me?"

Hamlet shrugged. "Maybe."

"It might help you keep your mind off of things," I suggested, not really wanting to encourage it but remembering how busy I kept myself after my mother's death. Busy to distraction. Busy to exhaustion.

He went back to strumming, but mid-song he threw his guitar across the room, cracking the neck. "No. Forget it. I'm not going. I can't be in class right now. Who cares about macroeconomics or protozoa? My dad is dead. What am I gonna do, party, for God's sake?"

Horatio went to pick up the broken guitar and I slid off the bed to sit next to Hamlet. "She'll understand," I said.

"Who cares?" Hamlet grumbled.

I rushed home from school each day for the next week, declining invitations to hang out with my friends, skipping swim practice and time in the art studio to be with him. I tried to keep Hamlet from grieving. More than a minute or two of silence or stillness, and he would retreat into a depression, and it would take hours to pull him out of it.

My friends, my coach, and my art teacher were pissed, which seemed unfair because I'd lost someone, too (though not an actual parent, so I guess everyone else saw it differently), and if I'd been taking any tough classes, my grades would have slipped. It did occur to me that it was probably a good thing that I wouldn't be going to Wittenberg with him. My father, I begrudgingly admitted, might have been right about that after all.

Given my efforts to help Hamlet, I was slightly disappointed when we were swinging on the hammock on my balcony and he announced, "Being around the castle is too depressing. I've decided to go back to school."

"I thought…" I began. "I thought we were doing all right."

He ran his fingers along my thigh. "It's not you. It's my mother and my uncle. One of them is always hassling me about going back to school or wanting to discuss my future. I'm sick of it. And when my mom isn't crying, she shuts herself behind closed doors. Most of the time, she acts like she doesn't want me around."

Well, that's a change, I thought. I couldn't remember a single time when she hadn't begged him to join her for a meal, tried to separate him from me, or otherwise sought him out. It didn't make sense.

I asked, "Then who's she turning to for comfort?"

"Claudius. She says he understands her…that he feels the same pain. But I don't know what she's talking about. His brother died, and I've never seen him cry or even look more than a little sad. And that's only when someone else mentions what a loss it's been. My uncle and I have never been close, but I've never wanted to be around anyone less."

"Leaving's probably best then," I conceded, then snuggled tighter against his body, trying to soak in the last moments I thought we'd have together for a while.

Barnardo: Did you try to talk Hamlet out of being king?

Ophelia: Why would you even ask that?

Barnardo: Just wondering.

Francisco: You get into his head...make him doubt that it's the right thing to do.

Barnardo: Hamlet hesitates, so Claudius takes over, driving Hamlet over the edge.

Ophelia: That's not why Hamlet was pissed.

Francisco: Come on, all that power in the wrong hands.

Ophelia: Hamlet didn't care about power.

Barnardo: What did he care about?

Ophelia: *(pause)* Me.

Barnardo: And look where that got him.

Ophelia: Does the DDI give lessons on cruelty or does it just come naturally to you?

8

"So, one minute we're all mourning the death of the king, the next we're hearing about a relationship between Gertrude and Claudius. When did you become aware of it?"

Ophelia smiles elusively. "Around the same time as everyone else."

Watching two people kiss is about the most annoying thing ever, unless it's in a movie. Somehow if it's on-screen you can put yourself in the place of those beautiful people, and you can imagine the leading man running his fingers through your own hair, stroking your own face. You are suddenly gorgeous and the object of his desire, not sitting alone in sweatpants with racing stripes that you hope make your legs look thinner. But when a real couple is actually in front of you kissing, all you can think is, *I'm right here! Take your big ol' tongue out of her mouth.*

Happening upon two people kissing who don't want you to see them kissing is not only gross but really, really awkward. Such was the case when I walked into Gertrude's sitting room and found her lip-locked with Claudius. I'm not sure who was less happy about it. She had asked me to come see her, so the fact was, she was expecting me. Why she wasn't more careful if she didn't want to get caught, I just don't understand. Of course, I haven't always been as careful in my life as I should be, so maybe it was a mistake. Does it even matter? I froze in my tracks and then left the room as fast as I could, all the while considering Hamlet's reaction to this stunning turn of events. I couldn't decide if he'd be more devastated or furious when he found out. I knew *I* was more disgusted than anything.

Unfortunately, running away wouldn't do for Gertrude, who chased after me shouting my name.

"I'll just…come back later!" I called behind me.

"Ophelia, stop!" she commanded, so I did. Her smile fixed, she suggested, "Let's go shopping."

"Uh, I'm swamped with work, so…"

"I'll write you a note or something."

"I'm already really behind—" I began.

She interrupted my refusal. "Come now. In the weeks since Hamlet went back to school, I don't think we've spent any time together."

Let me just say that was all her doing, and I doubt she missed the time with me any more than I missed hanging out with her.

"Ophelia, sweetheart, we'll buy you something fabulous. Ooh, we can even catch high tea at the Crown."

I forced a smile of my own and replied, "Sounds lovely. Let me just get my jacket."

"No need to say that this is just between us," she said, winking at me. I shook my head as she closed the door behind me.

On the way home, Gertrude admired the suede blazer she had purchased for me, the one piece of clothing I actually liked all afternoon. The kiss went unmentioned. Though she thought she had bought my silence, more than anything I was too stunned to take action. I liked the blazer, yeah, but I didn't stay quiet over designer clothes. I just wasn't sure what to do. Was I supposed to alert the press? Tell my dad? Call Hamlet? Probably. Maybe I should have gone to Wittenberg and told him in person. But it was so surreal. So gross. So personal. As tempted as I was to tell him immediately, there was a part of me that thought Gertrude ought to do it herself. And if she and Claudius had ended things quickly and quietly, we wouldn't even be having this conversation. Part of me thought—maybe hoped—they would, and that would have spared the three of us—okay, me—having to tell anyone anything. And I never would have stayed quiet if I'd realized how serious things were with Claudius and Gertrude or how quickly they would progress. So I admit it: I took the blazer and I stayed silent. I'm not sure if telling Hamlet right away would have changed anything, but I wouldn't feel quite so bad about what came next if I had.

And she didn't write me any blessed note, which didn't matter anyway, because I would never have handed it to my teachers if she had. I just stayed up later than I wanted and did terrible work, which I had been doing a lot even without her help.

Less than a week later, I was up in Hamlet's room grabbing a CD he said I could take to download when Gertrude came walking in.

"Oh," she exclaimed, "I thought you were one of the maids."

"I was just leaving," I said, holding up the case.

She gestured broadly to the door, and that's when I spotted the sparkle of an enormous diamond. On her finger.

"What's that?" I asked, pointing at her hand, my eyes wide.

She looked down and quickly covered her left hand with her right, then said, "Please follow me." She clip-clopped down the hall to her receiving room. The walk must have given her time to think of what to say. I know it gave me time to think of a lot of questions.

She sat behind her desk and pointed at the chair I was to sit in. "Well, dear, things have developed, and I am truly glad that you found out, well, even before Hamlet." I knew this could not be good. "Perhaps you can advise me on the best way to tell him that…Claudius and I are engaged."

My mouth actually dropped open. I searched my mind for the date to be sure I wasn't crazy for being so surprised. Nope, not crazy. One month. It had been one month since her husband had died of unknown—one might even say mysterious—causes. "Are you kidding?" I asked.

"No," she said, clutching her hands together, hiding her new ring again. "It only happened this morning, you see." She blushed and let out a little half laugh. "I'm simply afraid that, well, Hamlet is not going to take this well."

"I imagine he won't," I answered, still in shock.

Gertrude stayed cool and patted her perfect French knot. As she did so, I had the chance to study the ring, and it was, to say the least, lavish. Twice as large as her original (which had been no small diamond) and sparkling dazzlingly. She said in a clipped voice, "The thing is, I'm very, very happy about this, and I am hoping that you can convince Hamlet that it is a good thing."

I blew out a burst of air and smiled, though not for the reason she probably thought. I was laughing at what an impossible request it was, and how improbable it was that he was going to be anything but livid. "I'll try."

When I got back to my apartment, I decided to text Horatio first but didn't want to make it too specific. Hamlet, I thought, should be the first to know.

Me: Strnge thngs r afoot @ the circle K
Horatio: ?
Me: Go hm. H wl need u.

My phone rang in my hand and I hoped it wasn't Horatio because then I'd be sorely tempted to explain. It wasn't. It was Lauren.

"You coming over tonight?" she asked. "Everyone's watching *Denmark Divas* at my place. The theme is classic rap. Totally ridiculous idea for a bunch of pop singers, right? I can't wait to see how vicious the judges get."

"I can't. Listen, I gotta go—"

"He's not even in town," she said with unadulterated irritation. "I get we're invisible when he's around, but—"

"You can berate me later, Lauren, but something just came up."

"Whatever," Lauren grumbled.

I sat on my bed, fleetingly considering how much I neglected my friends and how I was once again becoming the lamest kind of girl—the kind whose boyfriend came before all else. And then I thought about what to do…about Hamlet. I would have kicked myself if I weren't so preoccupied with the Gertrude situation.

I didn't want to be the one to tell Hamlet, but I certainly didn't want him to hear it from anyone else, especially his mother. I decided to call rather than send a message. He did not, as you can imagine, take it all that well.

"Hamlet," I began. My legs were shaking. "Hamlet. Okay. Can you sit down? I need to tell you something that…I don't think you're gonna like."

"You're not pregnant, are you?"

"What?" I asked, completely distracted. It might have been a funny miscommunication except that I was so dreading telling him the real news. "No. It's about your mom."

"Is she okay?" he asked, his voice tight.

"Yeah. I think *she* might think she's more than okay. She's, um…she's engaged…to your uncle."

He was silent for a moment. "Is this a joke?"

"No," I assured him.

"What the hell?" he screamed. He didn't say anything else. He just started throwing things, including his phone, which is when we lost contact.

After wrecking the room, Horatio was able to get Hamlet to agree to go for a walk down by the river, which would be more private and where he would have fewer objects to throw. That's where Horatio called me from, and eventually Hamlet got on the phone.

"Hamlet?" I asked.

Without taking a breath, he continued with what he had been saying to Horatio. "Are you kidding me? Not even a month. The shoes she walked in behind my father's casket aren't even worn in. Did she want to save money by using the leftover food from the funeral? Maybe the flowers are still alive, so she figured she could save on centerpieces, too. Goddamn it! My uncle? Were they sleeping together while my father was still alive?" He paused as if waiting for an answer, but I had none. "I can't even…*argh*! It's too disgusting to even consider."

I didn't say a word, though I agreed with everything he said.

"Any animal would have mourned longer. Marrying my uncle? He's no more like my father than I am like…like Superman. What could she see in him?"

I sat down to continue listening to him rant.

"My father treated her so well! I swear he would punish the wind for blowing too hard on her face. She hung on his every glance, every word. Was it all just an act? I don't understand. She can't love my uncle like she loved my father. That's not possible, right, Ophelia?"

"Hamlet, I—"

"How soon after my father's death did she hop into bed with my uncle? Or was it before? I can't—I can't—"

I heard Horatio say, "Give me the phone, Hamlet." Hamlet's voice faded, though I could still hear him shouting, and Horatio said to me, "I'll call you back."

I waited for about fifteen minutes before grabbing my keys. I decided to call my dad from the road. Better to ask forgiveness than permission. I'd driven for over an hour before Horatio called.

"Christ, Ophelia, I don't know what to do. He just keeps shouting. His security detail blocked the area for now. They want to bring him back to the castle, but I think that's the worst idea."

"I agree. Don't let them do that. Tell Hamlet I'll be there soon."

I found them at the river. Hamlet and Horatio were sitting side by side, and Horatio had his arm around Hamlet's shoulder. When I approached, they both looked up. Hamlet's eyes were bloodshot, and dirt streaks ran down his cheeks.

Hamlet shook his head slowly. "How could she do this to my dad? My dad. God, I miss him." He groaned and clutched his stomach.

I knelt down, a lump forming in my throat. "Me too." I looked at Horatio, who stood and walked a few feet away.

"Why did you tell me about the—engagement? Why not my mother?"

"She thought you'd take it better if you heard it from me."

He laughed, tucking stray strands of hair behind his ears. "She was afraid of what I would say."

I nodded. "Probably. Listen, let's go back to your room and talk, okay? Those guys must need a break," I said, pointing to the two guards waving students away.

He agreed. Horatio joined us on our quiet walk back to their house. My shoulders were finally starting to relax when Hamlet asked me, "When did you know about all this?"

"This morning."

"You never saw Claudius and my mom—" He interrupted himself and shuddered.

An icy wave of panic swept through me. My hesitation caused Hamlet to stop walking. Horatio's mouth popped open and he shook his head subtly. I had to choose between telling the truth and keeping the hard-won calm. But I had never lied to Hamlet, and I didn't want to start, especially when his mother could so easily expose my complicity.

"Last week I saw them kiss," I said.

Horatio grimaced, and Hamlet's face went slack. I reached for Hamlet's arm, but he pulled out of my grip. A passing student held her camera phone to capture this tense moment, but a guard grabbed the phone out of her hands.

"You know the rules," he barked as he smashed it under his boot.

I was watching the shards fly across the sidewalk when Hamlet walked away from me. "Hamlet, wait!" I shouted as he bolted into his fraternity house. I started to follow him, and

Horatio followed me. I waved Horatio away. I didn't want to be protected and I didn't deserve to be.

I ran inside and upstairs. Hamlet's room was locked. I pounded on the door, and to my surprise, he yanked it open and pulled me inside. After closing and locking the door behind us, he leaned heavily against it.

"You saw them kiss and you didn't tell me?" he asked.

It occurred to me that he had never suspected anything was between them. He had never noticed anything odd. Not at the family dinners. Not in Claudius and Gertrude's late-night chats. Not in the way Claudius looked at Hamlet's mother when she was passing in the hall, like a snake taking its time before it ate a mouse. To go back that far right then would only add to Hamlet's pain. I decided to take the fall and clarify later. So you know, I didn't do it for Gertrude. I did it for him.

"She asked me not to," I said as I perched on the edge of his bed.

He kicked the door with his heel. "Why, Ophelia? Why can't you just do what you know is right?"

I sat up tall, trying not to show how much that question hurt me. "Because my having access to you depends on my pleasing *your* mom and *my* dad."

He shook his head and looked at me, his eyes narrow. "How do you figure? You honestly think I would let them keep you away from me? Not possible." He came and sat next to me, his voice urgent. "No matter where they would send you, I'd find you and we'd be together."

I started to cry from guilt and relief that he still felt that way even after I had kept such a big secret from him. Through my tears I said, "Maybe so, but you have freedoms I don't have."

He wiped my face gently. "True. But I have a lot of limitations, too. Look at what just happened. I can't even freak out without it being a major security concern. You've just got to stop worrying about them."

"Papa Don't Preach" blared, and Hamlet jerked my phone out of my hands. "Polonius," he barked, "this isn't a good time." He snapped the phone shut. "Boundaries. See? Not hard."

"Give it back," I commanded, my palm thrust forward.

"Not if you're going to call your dad."

"I'm not. I want to call your mom so she and I can plan a slumber party," I said sarcastically. Then I leveled my gaze at him. "Give me the phone. Now."

He slapped it in my palm, but I shoved it in my pocket, deciding to deal with my dad later.

To be mean, but also because it needed to be discussed, I said, "I guess Claudius marrying your mom means you're not going to be king for a while."

"That's not true. My mom said she would reign for now, but then after I graduated...Son of a—!" He leaped up and kicked the door.

There was a knock. "Everything okay in there?" a guard called out. Hamlet answered quickly, knowing that if he didn't, they'd break down the door to be sure all was well.

Hamlet paced around muttering. "That jerk stole everything! I can't believe my mother would promise me...unless she wanted Claudius to be king all along. Wait. No. She's not like that. And she never lies."

"Everyone lies, Hamlet."

"Do you?"

I paused. "Not to you."

He stood still, breathing hard. Then of all things, he asked, "Are you disappointed?"

"About?"

"Not being queen. If we, you know, stay together."

"I don't think about that," I said, twisting my hair between my fingertips.

He raised his eyebrows.

"Okay, I think about the glamorous part sometimes. The parties. Owning all that art. But seriously, you could walk away from Elsinore tomorrow with nothing—no title, no money—and I'd be happy as long as we were together."

He curled his lips from a smile to a frown and then in between. "Really?"

I nodded.

He sat on the bed, leaning back on the headboard. "And what would you do if we had nothing? Or if we weren't together? What else do you want in your life?" he asked.

I shrugged and laid my head on his chest.

"Still undecided?"

"Pretty much," I admitted. It sounded so ridiculous that I came up with something on the spot. "Although…I've been thinking lately about being a museum curator."

"Cool."

The idea did sound cool. Being surrounded by art all day. Picking pieces for a collection. Deciding where to place them. "Yeah. I was thinking even of handling the collection at the palace."

He cocked his head. "Don't you want to get away?"

I shrugged. I really never let my mind wander far. I couldn't separate visions of my future from a future that involved Hamlet. And I couldn't imagine leaving my dad. My brother had chosen to go far away from our home, my father, and the empty hole left behind by our mother's absence. But, as crazy as my dad made me, I couldn't picture leaving him alone. Even if I moved out, which I would someday, I wanted to be close enough to check in on him. It was important to me, but I didn't want Hamlet to comment, so I removed myself from his embrace.

I stood and crossed to the window. Horatio was sitting on the curb talking to the second security guard. The sun was hanging low on the horizon, and I knew I had to head home. I reluctantly said, "Sooo, back to the wedding."

Hamlet snapped his tongue.

"Your mother wants you to come up—"

"I'm not going. I would rather eat glass than be a part of that."

"Isn't that a little overdramatic?"

"No, Ophelia, it's not. Why don't you try being a little *more* dramatic? Or critical of the things you see happening around you?"

I put my hands on my hips and said, "I am critical. I'm just smart enough to keep it to myself."

Hamlet chuckled.

My irritation drained away. "So what should I tell your mother?" I asked.

"Tell her to go to hell."

I whistled and smiled. "Yeah. I'll get right on it." And with that, I hugged him good-bye.

Horatio ran up to me as I came out the front door. "So?" he asked.

"He's all yours. I wouldn't bring up Mommie Dearest if I were you."

He laughed and blew me a kiss as I was escorted to my car.

*   *   *

I didn't hear from either of them until late that night. I tried to paint, but it was impossible for me to focus and I was really relieved when Horatio finally called to tell me that Hamlet had passed out in his own room. Horatio had taken him to a bar, where they drank excessively. As they stumbled home, Hamlet swore it would be the last time he had a drink. Incredibly, he stuck to his word and stayed sober through all but one night of the sordid events that were yet to come. Maybe if he had been drunk through the rest, it could have all been excused or dismissed. But how Hamlet changed was all his own doing, his own sober, crushed, depressed doing.

Barnardo: "Strange things are afoot at the Circle K." What does that text mean?

Ophelia: It's from an old eighties movie the boys and I loved. Jesus, for being "intelligence," you seem not to know much.

Barnardo: Watch it.

Francisco: We think it was a code.

Ophelia: Yeah, it was code for: "You're not going to believe that the queen was (whispers too low to be heard)."

Barnardo: Hey, hey. Have a little respect. You kiss your mother with that mouth?

Francisco: 'Course she doesn't. She doesn't have a mother, and all because of the royal family.

Ophelia: I have to go to the bathroom.

9

Zara's excitement returns. "It happened pretty fast. Don't you agree?"
She fans herself, asking the audience as much as Ophelia. The audience members look at one another, a mix of laughter and disapproval.

Ophelia is enjoying this moment. "Indeed it did."

"What did you think of the whole...affair?" Zara winks.

Almost sincerely, Ophelia replies, "I'm not sure it's my place or anyone else's to judge."

Zara turns to look at some photos of Gertrude in an elegant gown with Ophelia at her side. Both women are smiling and waving. "Despite our opinions of its speed, it must be said that the wedding was beautiful."

"That it was," Ophelia replies, eyeing the series of pictures that follow: the church, in front of the castle, inside the reception.

Zara flips her hair and furrows her brow. "Hamlet did not, as had been announced, act as Claudius's best man."

Ophelia squints and says, "Uh, nooo, he did not."

"And yet you were a bridesmaid."

"Well, Gertrude was like a mother to me. How could I refuse?"

Whenever I spoke with Horatio, I updated him on the latest development. They seemed to be coming so quickly that I found myself speaking to him a couple times a day. I should have known the castle phones were tapped. I sort of did. I mean, my father had always warned me to watch what I said on the apartment phone or in the public spaces of the castle, but it had never mattered in the past. I always figured that I had nothing to hide, which I usually didn't.

Horatio asked, "Why is she making you a bridesmaid?"

"I've been thinking this over, and there are three possibilities. One, to keep me close. Two, because she thinks the pictures will look nicer with Hamlet and me in them together. Or three, she thinks he's more likely to show if I'm part of the whole thing."

"Probably all three."

"That's what I think."

That afternoon when I went to meet with Gertrude and the dressmaker, she was perturbed. "Ophelia, would you like to know why I asked you to be my bridesmaid?"

I was taken aback, totally unsure if she had already been told what I said or if she was just in a snit because of my hesitant reaction when she asked the day before and felt she needed to explain. In either case, I vowed to myself that I would use my cell phone and watch what I e-mailed, too, from that point on. As far as I knew, my cell phone was still safe.

"I asked you because I thought you would be honored. I thought we had a good relationship. Sort of like a mother-daughter thing." I felt a chill. She was nothing like my mother, and I did not need adopting.

I had found out about my mother's death after going to the movies with Hamlet. We were in the middle of a very silly comedy, and despite the constant pratfalls and bodily fluids that kept spewing, I spent much of the movie thinking about what my mom said before we both went out for the night. I had asked what she thought of my dating Hamlet. It had only been in the last few months that we had gone from friends to boyfriend/girlfriend, and she had been very quiet on the subject.

"He's a smart boy with quite a future ahead of him. But being with him won't be easy," she warned as she put on her lipstick.

"I know," I said, hopping onto the marble counter next to her bathroom sink.

She looked at my reflection. "I don't think you do. Sweetheart, think about what we go through with your father. Even that sort of a public position is hard enough. We are never alone. We rarely do precisely what we want."

I picked up one of her discarded necklaces and jangled it. "But I really like Hamlet."

She smiled a little sadly but added, "Then be with him. Your father is against it, but I say you cannot stop love."

I hesitated, blushing. "I don't know that I love—"

"I know. Maybe that will come. Maybe not. But let me assure you that you will sacrifice a lot to be with him. If it's worth it, make the sacrifice. If it stops being worth it, let go. You're young. Go have fun." She smiled. She studied herself once more in the mirror, then turned and added, "And make sure he drives carefully. And don't get pregnant!"

"Mom!" I gasped.

"Kidding. Sort of," she said as she chucked my chin and kissed me. She looked like she had more to say, but my father hated when she was late, so she grabbed her shawl and beaded bag, then left for the opening of a gallery.

I'd been trying to put my mind back on the movie when

the theater lights flicked on suddenly and guards came swarming at us. They surrounded our seats, and two grabbed each of us by the arm and pulled us out of the theater. Hamlet was shoved into one car and I was thrown into another. I could see guards pushing Hamlet's head below the seat as they sped off.

"Assassination attempt on the king," the guard driving me explained. "We'll meet up at the castle."

We pulled into the garage under the castle, where the king, Gertrude, and Hamlet, whose car had arrived ahead of mine, were waiting.

Gertrude stepped forward and said, "Your mother...There was a shooting." She stopped and looked at Hamlet's father, who nodded his encouragement. Wringing her hands, Gertrude continued, "She's...she died."

The power of the last word knocked me to my knees, and everyone rushed forward. The king put his hand on my shoulder, as did Hamlet. I looked around frantically, hoping to find a direction in which to run. But I couldn't think clearly and the garage was dim and cement walls surrounded us. I sobbed uncontrollably, grabbing and squeezing Hamlet so hard, my arms hurt. I was sure if I let go, I would faint or die myself. My cries echoed off the walls and made me weep all the more for hearing my own anguish.

My parents had been riding in the limo that an assassin believed the king would be riding in. Misinformation from someone inside the castle. The informant didn't know that my mom would be on time for once, and that she and my father, not the king and queen, would be the first to leave for the event. If my mother had stayed to chat with me for just a few minutes longer, all of our lives might have been different. But she hadn't.

We never found out much about the assassin. As far as we

ever knew, he worked alone and was a former soldier who had become convinced that the only way to save the kingdom was for Claudius to be king. "Long live King Claudius!" were his final words before his execution. Maybe that was why I always dreaded Claudius. Or maybe it was because he was a jerk who hated kids.

"Gertrude," I said wearily, "I'm happy to be your bridesmaid, okay? What color is the dress?" And with that, the dressmaker brought out an assortment of fabrics, most the color of babies' bedrooms.

I spent the morning of the wedding in Gertrude's private rooms as a team dressed and made up both of us, all while Gertrude stressed. "Hamlet's not here yet?" she asked, tapping her fingertips together.

A servant standing at the door answered, "No, ma'am, not yet."

She turned to me, messing up the work her hairdresser had just begun. "Ophelia, is he coming?"

I answered, "I have no idea."

"He didn't say anything?"

I put down my coffee and thought of how to tell her again not to expect him. I didn't want to say what he had actually said, that he would rather be thrust onto a thousand spikes than watch his mother betray his father's memory with this display of incest. "When we first discussed it…he implied that he wouldn't be here."

"Oh. Lately?"

"He won't talk to me, so I don't know." Once he found out that I intended to be in her wedding party, he had hung up on me and wouldn't pick up when I called back. I had texted and e-mailed but got no reply. I'd considered driving to talk to him, but Gertrude had kept me too busy with wedding plans. And my keys had disappeared. I suspected my father, but I couldn't be sure. During my frequent calls to Horatio, he had reassured me that Hamlet would calm down eventually. It had been three very long days.

"Heavens," she said, checking that her pearl necklace was in place for, like, the hundredth time. Her face was lined with worry and showed more vulnerability than I could remember seeing. I didn't like the idea of this wedding, but it had to suck to have your son be so pissed that he wouldn't even show up or talk to you, and to know that much of the kingdom was judging the whole thing. I kind of felt sorry for her.

News stations from around the world covered the wedding. Funerals brought out reporters for the macabre spectacle, vultures hoping to catch a breakdown or at least a tear. On the other hand, weddings brought out the cheerful, envious public, thousands who were seemingly unconcerned about the scandal and were just hoping to see something pretty and to dream of what it would be like to ride to a wedding in a carriage.

A horse-drawn carriage might seem romantic, but it's really slow, which did not suit my mood. I guess the slow pace is the point if you're a queen who wants to be noticed in all of her matrimonial glory. At least Gertrude had the good taste not to wear a big white gown. I had honestly thought she would skip the whole thing, get it done privately, but neither she nor Claudius would hear of it.

"The public likes its shows. And after the sadness that has befallen us lately, it would seem we owe it to them," he declared.

I was also amazed at how quickly such a large event could

be put on. Every party planner and caterer had been mobilized, and the results were fairly spectacular, though I found the scale of this dubious second wedding vulgar nevertheless.

The carriage door opened, and a footman with gold fringe jangling from his shoulder pads and cuffs held his hand out for me. I stepped carefully down the petite stairs, holding the full silk skirt with my free hand to keep from tripping. The crowd squealed in anticipation, and a thousand flashbulbs went off. I hadn't had a choice in the style of shoes, nor had I had a chance to break them in, so my peach-colored heels pinched with each step. I hoped my grimace appeared to be more of a smile.

I stepped forward, and Stormy Somerville, wearing a tight pink suit, thrust a microphone in front of my face. "Isn't this thrilling?" she gushed.

Hoping Hamlet wasn't watching, I gave the answer I'd been ordered to give. "What a wonderful day for us all." I moved forward and winced as the skin of one heel peeled away.

Gertrude stepped down next, holding the train of her de-mure cream gown. She raised her head and one hand in a prac-ticed gesture of welcome to her subjects. I had seen it so many times, as had the crowd, but they shouted as if it were the first time. I'm fairly certain I rolled my eyes.

We trudged up the steps and, upon reaching the top, I gaped at the aisle that ran the length of the cathedral. We had practiced walking it the night before, but it suddenly looked much, much longer.

To distract myself, I fantasized about the wedding I might have with Hamlet. I tried to picture walking down this very aisle in a flowing white gown, my father holding my arm. Hamlet would be waiting for me, his blond hair sparkling in the glow from the stained-glass windows. Horatio would be standing next to him, smiling broadly, and maybe Lauren, if she didn't get sick of my disappearing acts, would be a bridesmaid. I would never make her wear peach. Or pinchy shoes. But the crowd would be there and that bummed me out. If only we could do it quietly, do it somewhere else.

I don't want a public life. The thought came suddenly and filled me with horror. My legs went weak and I wasn't sure I could make it to the end of the aisle. *I don't want this. I just want Hamlet.* I tried to breathe while keeping my face neutral. The skin on my other heel ripped.

Horatio smiled at me as I passed. I couldn't return the smile, and his faded.

I walked up the few steps of the altar and turned to the crowd. I started to calculate. There must have been fifty rows of pews with about ten people per pew, but that was just one side, so...

My mind was so preoccupied that I missed the opening words of the minister, the Dearly Beloved part. I caught up at "Marriage is not to be entered into unadvisedly or lightly—but reverently, discreetly, advisedly, and solemnly." I could give Claudius the solemn part, and he and Gertrude could apparently be discreet (which wasn't the same as "using discretion"). As for the "advisedly" part? Not so much. This wedding seemed ill-advised at best.

The drone continued, and my attention waxed and waned. I perked up for "If any person can show just cause why they may not be joined together—let them speak now or forever hold their peace." In movies someone always steps forward right around this part. In real life, they never do. Even when they should. It would have been awesome if Hamlet had come bursting into the sanctuary just then, or if some random earl had stood and pointed out how wrong it all was. I knew I didn't have the courage to do it, but I momentarily hoped someone, anyone would. Sadly, no. The wedding carried on.

By the time Claudius and Gertrude were told to kiss, I was nearly crying from the pain in my feet and from my keen desire to be anywhere else. I decided not to think about the whole marrying Hamlet thing. We had a long way to go before that happened. And maybe I would change my mind about crowds and public scrutiny.

We recessed, and I winked at Horatio on the way out. I knew he wouldn't be reassured until I actually spoke to him, but it would help. I decided to keep the actual reason for my distress to myself. It sounded bizarre, and I didn't want to admit how far my imagination regarding my future had run.

Gertrude and Claudius took their damned time getting into their carriage, which meant we all had to stand on the steps of the church smiling and pretending it was all so fantastic. I stood next to my father and stared at the crowd like it was a growling dog, telling myself I wasn't afraid of it.

We were driven to the formal, original part of the castle, where the reception was being held. A servant brought me bandages and sneakers, which I put on immediately after I was excused from the receiving line. Guests filled the room, and once a critical mass was reached, I was able to fade away.

Horatio and I stood on the side of the ballroom waiting for Hamlet, who Horatio assured me planned to show up at some point. We watched Claudius and Gertrude greet hundreds of people as hors d'oeuvres were passed.

Marcellus came up behind us. His gun holster peeked out from beneath his tuxedo jacket as he gestured with his long arms, and his badge glinted in the lights from the dance floor. "Lord Hamlet is here," he announced.

"Thanks, Marcellus," Horatio said.

Horatio and I went running out of the ballroom and found Hamlet coming up the spiral staircase.

"Hamlet!" we shouted.

He kept trudging up but did not answer.

Horatio met him at the end of the landing, and they shook hands. Then Hamlet walked past me without any acknowledgment.

"Hamlet?" I called after him, my stomach sinking. I knew he'd be pissed, but there was a part of me hoping that once he saw me, he'd be happy enough to let it go. Wishful thinking.

He heaved his book bag and it skidded across the lobby, then he reached for the door.

"Don't go in there angry," I begged.

He spun around and yelled, "But I am angry. I'm angry at my mother. I'm angry at those people for pretending this is all perfectly normal. Most of all, I'm angry at you."

"Hamlet, what else could I have done?"

When Gertrude had asked, I hadn't felt like I'd had a choice. I really hadn't. And yet seeing Hamlet's fury completely melted away all my rationalizations. His anger was justified, and I was an idiot.

"You could have said no. How could you walk down the aisle with her, stand next to her as she married my *uncle?*" He rushed back toward me and grabbed my shoulders, almost shaking me as he added, "You say you're on my side, but your actions just told the world that what my mother is doing is right!"

Horatio came between us and moved Hamlet away. Hamlet shook him off and went toward the windows overlooking the city. "How could you?" he asked as he slammed his hands on the oversize pane.

I was on the verge of tears, but I forced out, "Right and wrong don't matter in my position. I had to put on this stupid dress and walk her down the stupid aisle because she asked me to. You can get away with saying no to her, with not even showing up!" I caught my breath and went toward the railing, then leaned over it, wondering how far a fall it would be. Three grand flights of red-carpeted stairs swirling downward. It would work if one were inclined to do such a thing. I shook my head at Hamlet, sick of dramatic scenes like this, sickened by my own bad decision and by the knowledge that, if pressed, I would probably do it again. Gertrude was the queen of drama as well as Denmark, and I suddenly couldn't wait until I was able to leave the castle and not be drawn into these moments so often.

Still pressed against the railing, I called out, "Your mom's mad, but she'll forgive you. She always does. She wanted you here, and you hurt her by not showing. Fine. You made your statement. Go in to her party or don't. Horatio and I have to go back in because we're expected to. You…I can't imagine the next time she'll ask anything of you."

I started walking toward the ballroom when I heard Hamlet say, "She asked me to wear one of those dresses, too, but I was afraid it would make me look fat."

I turned back, and Hamlet was smirking. All three of us began to laugh and came together in the middle of the lobby once again.

"I'm sorry I grabbed you," he said, stroking my arm.

"Don't do it again." On the outside, I shrugged off his

apology. Inside I was still a little shaken and hoped he really did feel bad.

We walked in as Claudius and Gertrude began their first dance. I knew the song from the first notes. It was one of my parents' favorite songs, and my father used to sing it to my mother with some regularity. *"What a difference a day makes,"* crooned the lead singer, the white flower pinned behind her ear shimmering in the spotlight. *"Twenty-four little hours."* Claudius dipped Gertrude to applause from the guests. Hamlet made a gagging motion, which cracked me up. "Would that have been twenty-four hours after her husband's funeral?" Hamlet asked in a stage whisper. "That's a picture, isn't it?" he asked those around him.

Horatio, smiling slightly, put his hand over Hamlet's mouth while some very serious woman in front of us shushed him. When she realized who had spoken, she turned back around red-faced. Her helmet of hair did not move, though her hands shook slightly.

The song played on, and the newlyweds danced, pretending not to hear the murmur from our direction. The next time the singer reached the chorus, *"Twenty-four little hours,"* Hamlet interrupted with, "Is there much difference between twenty-four hours and two months, when it comes to remarriage?"

He was loud enough that Gertrude faltered in her steps and Claudius made a move toward us, but Gertrude composed herself and pulled him back.

The dancing, I'm sure, was meant to continue, but when the song ended, Claudius took the stage. The singer grabbed her silver train in her hands and moved swiftly toward the drummer, making way for Claudius to use the microphone stand.

"My guests," Claudius began, holding up a champagne glass.

Cameramen crowded in front of the festooned stage.

"For Hamlet, my brother's death is still a fresh memory…"

I turned and saw Hamlet wince at his own name.

"…and I am aware that the kingdom is still in mourning. Because of this, I attempted to act with discretion, to push aside my feelings. Yet I couldn't fight nature. It was in my heart to love this wonderful woman, and my heart won the fight. And so my sister-in-law has become my queen."

"Bloody hell," Hamlet muttered.

Claudius carried on with his formal, overly practiced speech. "It is with tempered happiness that Gertrude and I stand before you today. We have reluctantly felt joy in the midst of our mourning, and to this happy event, our wedding, we bring sadness. While we know not all have embraced our joy," he said, narrowing his eyes slightly and scanning the crowd as if to root out the traitors, "we thank those of you that have come here today to celebrate with us. Cheers." He raised his glass a little higher, and the crowd applauded.

"I'd say I need a drink, but I made a promise…." Hamlet grumbled.

Horatio messed up his hair.

Gertrude stood at the microphone wringing her hands and said, "Would everyone," and she looked directly at her son as she said this, "please join us on the dance floor?"

I suggested to Hamlet that he acquiesce, but he refused. As he walked to the cheese platters, he yanked the hood of his black sweatshirt, which he had defiantly worn to flout the black-tie requirement of the affair, onto his head. We all huddled in the corner for a while, chatting.

Just before dinner, my father came and found me and invited me to dance. I did not know the song, but I was content to be with my dad as the band began the jaunty tune. The singer's voice was playful as she sang, *"Maybe I can't live to love you as long as I want to / But I can love you as long as I live."* I knew it was meant to be sweet, but its lyrics made me feel melancholy.

"I miss Mom," I whispered in his ear. "I wish she could dance with you right now."

He squeezed my hand and pulled me closer, so I wouldn't see his eyes fill, I was sure. I stepped on his foot and we laughed.

"She was a better dancer," he teased. We kept listening to the accidentally sad song and I wished the band had chosen to play something else. When it was over, he bowed and kissed my hand, then released me to be with my friends. I lingered a minute to watch him transform from doting father and lonely widower to statesman with a mere lift of the shoulders and a purpose to his step.

When I turned around, Marcellus was whispering to Hamlet. Marcellus held up his hand to me as I approached, and I stopped short. They whispered a few moments more, then Hamlet came toward me, his eyes dancing with excitement.

"Sorry to do this, Phee, but I gotta run."

"Where are you—"

"You wouldn't believe me if I told you." He took my hands in his and kissed them. His hands were shaking, which didn't match the thrill I saw on his face. "I'll come down later. You think your dad'll be asleep by one?"

"Probably, but your mom—"

"Screw her," he grumbled as he turned to go.

"No thanks," I joked.

He stopped and swatted my butt. "Watch it," he said, and

his laughter calmed me. He walked out the side exit of the ball-room with Marcellus.

My phone vibrated in my purse.

> Lauren: U lookd pretty
> Me: I lookd like cotton candy
> Lauren: Hamlt there yet?
> Me: Yep. intrstn

That night, I waited up for hours listening to music. When Hamlet walked in, he sat on the bed, pulled off his sweatshirt, then kissed me. It was a more passionate kiss than he'd given me in weeks. Looking back, maybe it wasn't even passion. A better word might be desperation.

Taking my hands in his, in a voice so quiet it was nearly a whisper, he asked, "If I did something bad, would you still love me?"

I started to pull my hands away, but he gripped them harder. My breath caught as my mind raced through the possible mis-deeds he might have committed.

"I haven't done anything yet," he assured me. "But if I did."

I exhaled slowly and studied his face, which was lined with worry. "What are you planning to do?" I asked.

He shook his head. "I don't— It's not— Could you just answer my question?" He tucked his lips in and blinked rap-idly. He twisted his mouth one way, then the other as if that effort would prevent more emotion from leaking out.

"Hamlet, I think it depends—"

"Yes or no?" he demanded, squeezing my hands so hard, I nearly yelped.

I couldn't think of what to say. No matter what I said, I was screwed—it was an impossible request. Placating him seemed to be the only option. If he was relaxed, I figured, he might explain himself. "Sure, Hamlet," I said. "I guess...."

He nodded with chilling finality and walked out again.

I thought of telling my father, but he tended to overreact under the best of circumstances. I thought of telling Gertrude, but that would have been the greatest betrayal of all. I picked up the phone to call Horatio, but it was the middle of the night, so I changed my mind. I decided to wait and watch. More and more, I was feeling trapped. I was both in the middle of things and left out of them, and it was a place I was quickly growing to hate. But what could I do? Listen, don't pretend you have an answer. You weren't there.

Francisco: What'd you think of the hasty remarriage?

Ophelia: Not my business.

Barnardo: Bull. You were against it. We have the phone records.

Ophelia: Fine. So what if I was? Did it change anything?

Barnardo: Yeah, it helped you get Hamlet to want revenge.

10

Zara leans in to Ophelia. "We hear Hamlet started acting very strange after the wedding."

"People like to talk." When Zara lifts her eyebrows, Ophelia concedes, "Well, he was under a lot of pressure. Especially from Claudius."

"Was he crazy?"

"That's a loaded term." Ophelia recrosses her legs. "Um...I will say he wasn't quite himself."

In the days following the wedding, Hamlet said he didn't want to be anywhere near his mother or Claudius, but he also insisted that he didn't want to go back to school. He refused to go outside into the world, because he didn't want to be followed or questioned or photographed. And as discreet as people within the castle were supposed to be, they were more curious and watchful, too. So during the day, he hung out in my apartment even when I was in class, creating a kind of half-life for himself.

When I was with him, I spent most of the time worrying

about how troubled he looked and how little he would speak and what "bad thing" he was planning on doing. I asked a couple of times, but he wouldn't answer. I tried to go back to my routine, staying in the art studio after school and going to swim practice. But when I wasn't with him, I worried even more and was totally distracted, so my coach kept yelling at me, and my art teacher, Ms. Hill, just stared with silent concern, which isn't exactly good for the creative process. I couldn't miss practice, since the end of the season was fast approaching, so I dealt with the shouting, but I decided to skip studio time and paint at home. But every time I got there and picked up the brush, all I could do was stare at Hamlet sprawled across my bed and think, *What are you going to do? What are you going to do?* Needless to say, I accomplished little.

My father did not notice Hamlet's constant presence, or else he would have insisted on a change or at least offered his thoughts on the matter. Things had been so busy following the wedding, what with the shift of power and the flurry of requests for interviews and appearances by the royal couple, that he had not noticed what was happening.

Gertrude finally asked my father to ask Hamlet to leave our home. My father, taken by surprise, stormed into our apartment and began lecturing Hamlet, who was watching an infomercial about tall ladders. (I had wandered away out of boredom, as we neither needed a tall ladder nor did I understand how an entire hour could be filled by discussing a ladder.) As soon as I heard my father, I ran back in from the balcony where I had been sketching, only to hear Hamlet say, "Got it, Polonius. No need to go on." He stood, zipped up his black hoodie (his uniform at that point), and reached out a hand to me.

I followed, and my father cleared his throat. "Dad, I'll come back later. I'll cook you a special Sunday dinner."

"I believe Gertrude wanted to speak to Hamlet alone," he advised.

Hamlet interrupted, "Then *Gertrude* can say so herself!"

"Hamlet!" I admonished.

He softened his tone and said, "If she wants me so much, she'll have to deal with Ophelia being there. I really can't be left alone with my mother right now. I don't trust myself."

My father looked apprehensive but nodded in agreement.

We found the newlyweds in the office of their social secretary. Gertrude fluttered over and kissed Hamlet in greeting. His arm tightened across my back, but he said nothing.

Claudius called out, "Son, how are you this bright afternoon?"

"Son?" Hamlet spat. "I don't think we're ready for that." Hamlet turned to leave, pulling me behind him, but Claudius's words stopped him.

"Fine. Then, Hamlet, how are you this bright afternoon?"

"Too much sun, if you ask me," he answered sharply.

Claudius *tsk*ed and asked, "Why is a dark cloud still hanging over you?"

I wished I hadn't followed Hamlet upstairs, but I squeezed his hand to try to bring him back from his deepening anger.

"Darling," Gertrude said, stroking Hamlet's cheek, "why are you still in this wretched sweatshirt? It is neither stylish nor becoming on you, and the color…it will seem to our subjects that you are still in mourning."

He ducked away from her touch. "Seem? *Seem?* I'm not wearing black to make it *seem* like anything, Mother. If all of these things *seem* like grief, it's because I *feel* grief. I—am—in—mourning. Aren't we all?" He raised his eyebrows and glared at her.

Gertrude's face became its typical mask, and her eyes flicked to me. She paused for a moment, then decided to speak in my unwelcome presence. Through thinly drawn lips, she counseled, "Be kinder to your uncle, dearest. You know you could spend the rest of your life looking for someone who will measure up to the *image* you have of your father, but you will find no one to match it."

Hamlet's face was pinking, but he listened to the rest.

"You know this is common. All living things must die. Ashes to ashes and all that," she said.

"Yes, it is *common*," he fumed.

I had the feeling that he didn't mean only the death of his father, but that he referred to her, as well. She seemed to sense his insult and walked away irritated, though she had enough presence of mind to glance at Claudius, who stepped forward. It was clear that they had planned this verbal attack.

"It is sweet and commendable, Hamlet, to mourn for your father. But you know that *your* father lost a father, and *that* father lost his. Each of them mourned for a suitable amount of time. But to carry on like this…it is a sign of, well, stubbornness. And, frankly, it's unmanly."

I sucked in my breath, and Hamlet muttered, "Son of a bitch."

Claudius heard what he said but simply narrowed his eyes and said in forced sincerity, "I love you, Hamlet, and I hope you can think of me as a father."

Hamlet yanked me out of the room at this point. I don't

know what possessed Claudius to keep speaking, but he yelled, "We hope you will stay with us and not go back to college!"

Hamlet's gait caught, but then he continued on.

Gertrude chased after us and begged, "Please do this for us...for me. Stay with us. Do not go back to Wittenberg."

He would not look up but mumbled, "I'll think about it."

She couldn't feel his sweating palms or see the pinched pain on his face, but I could, and his agony made me snap. I turned on her. "Gertrude," I said, but paused to keep myself from telling her how much I hated her and wished her husband—her first husband—were there to scold her. "Don't you see you're messing with his head? First you told him to go, now you want him to stay."

"I love my son."

"So do I, which is why I think you should leave him alone. Can't you see he's upset?"

"We are all upset," she said slowly, carefully.

With condescension that would have killed my father, I asked, "Are you?"

If she were a cobra, this would have been the moment when those weird flaps would have popped out of the sides of her head and her fangs would have spewed poison. She opened her mouth, but before she could say anything, the elevator arrived and Hamlet snatched me away from her.

As soon as the doors separated us from them, he said, "You're crazy to talk to her like that."

I shrugged and gritted my teeth. "Aren't you always telling me to stand up to her?"

"Yeah, but wow. Hell of a way to start."

"It's not the first time," I said with a sigh, and leaned my head against the metal elevator wall, wondering what the exchange with his mother would cost me. "I used to hold back, but since your dad...it's been harder for me to keep quiet. Especially when she treats you like a pet or a little boy."

His face darkened and he kicked the wall, making the elevator shake. "God, why? Why did my father have to die? Why did she marry Claudius? Why so soon?" In what had recently become a common gesture, he ran his fingers roughly through his hair, making it stand up in every direction. "Everything just seems so...wrong. I have no use for them...or for anything."

"Not even me, sweet prince?" I asked, not at all hurt, but looking for a way to distract him. His eyes met mine, and it seemed to pull him out of his head. I pressed, hoping for a smile if not a laugh, "What, no sex joke? No, 'But I have a lot of *uses* for you, wink, wink'?"

He stared at me for a moment and added coolly, "I never say 'wink wink.'"

"Maybe not, but you're not even going to make a snide remark? You're slipping."

He gave an exaggerated wink and said suggestively, "I could use a little slipping."

I clasped my hands in a mock prayer of thanks. "And he's back."

I didn't feel much like kidding around, to tell the truth, but I knew Hamlet needed it. I found everything Claudius and Gertrude had said to him distasteful and disturbing. What was their rush? They had obviously moved on, but most of us hadn't, and certainly not Hamlet. It had been merely two months since the king had died, and they wanted life to return to normal. For Hamlet, there would never be a "normal" again, and the fact that Gertrude, especially, didn't see it was shocking. I hoped he would go back to school, and fast. In truth, I was not sure how many more of those conversations he could take, nor could I imagine the consequences if his mother and uncle (for I would never call him Hamlet's father, or even step-father) did not let up. With dread I wondered if the "bad thing" Hamlet had spoken of might involve them.

When we got back to my apartment, my father came out of his office. "Why are you back? Didn't your mother want you home?"

Hamlet kept walking, so I explained, "They had a fight. Can he just stay a little while, Dad?"

My father chewed his lip and watched Hamlet's slumped figure pass down the hallway to my room. Reluctantly, he nodded and said he'd be working from home for a while and that Hamlet had to leave before dinner.

When I got to my room, Hamlet was sitting at the foot of my bed with my sketch pad in his hands. He didn't even look up, so I sat at my desk and started doing homework. After I finished analyzing a poem, I tossed the textbook aside and slid onto the floor next to him.

He was scrawling "To Be" and "Not to Be" over and over.

"What's that?" I asked.

"That is the question."

I studied the scribbled page and tried to figure out what he meant.

He leaned his head back and closed his eyes, his voice distant. "Is it better to suffer through life, to deal with all the crap thrown at you, or to fight against your problems by *ending* your life? To die is to sleep. That's all. And by sleeping, we escape everything that tortures us. That's the dream, then, isn't it? The perfection of nothingness."

A chill ran through me. It sounded like he was talking about suicide. Was he just thinking aloud, or was he formulating a plan? If I came at it headlong, I thought he might freeze up, so I tried to follow his logic and keep him talking. I suggested, "When you sleep, it's not nothingness. You dream."

He opened his eyes and looked at me. "There's the catch, huh? When you die, who knows what dreams might come? What's in the afterlife—if there is one? That's the scary part. That's what keeps us living out our long, painful lives. Who would put up with the heartache and the injustice of life when one could just get a knife and end it...except for the fear of what comes next? Fear of something worse makes us too scared to do anything."

My own fear bubbled over. "To do what, Hamlet? What are you thinking of doing?"

"Nothing."

"It's not nothing." When he didn't answer, I started to get up. "I'm going to get my dad."

"Don't," he begged, grabbing my arm and pulling me down again. When I stiffened under his grip, he let go and leaned back. "I was just talking, Phee," he said, pushing a smile into the corners of his lips. But his eyes were dead. He took the page, ripped it out of my sketch pad, crumpled it, and tossed it aside.

It rolled under my bed, but I didn't get it. Instead I took his face in my hands and pleaded with him, "Please, Hamlet, tell me what you're thinking of doing. I can't lose you, too. I can't."

He rose, and my hands fell pointlessly into my lap. "You won't, Phee. Everything's gonna be fine. You'll see." Then he zipped up his sweatshirt and walked out.

Francisco: So Hamlet considered suicide.

Ophelia: I don't know.

Barnardo: You were his girlfriend. How can you not know?

Francisco: Ophelia? He asked a question. *(pause)* He never spoke about it?

Ophelia: Well...yeah, he talked about it, but not in a real way.

Barnardo: Not in a real way? What does that mean?

Ophelia: Hamlet talked about a lot of things. He said he was going to climb Mount Everest one day. Maybe you should haul in some Sherpas and find out if they knew about that plan.

Francisco: Don't be smart.

Barnardo: No risk of that with her.

11

"So if Hamlet wasn't crazy, was it an act?"

Ophelia purses her lips. "No one is that good an actor."

Zara raises her eyebrows. "Are you admitting to all of us that he was crazy?"

Ophelia looks up at the stage lights and sighs. "I don't know what to tell you. Truly. He was troubled."

Zara leans forward and touches Ophelia's knee. "Both your personal life and school life were unraveling because of the attention you paid to Hamlet. Was it worth the sacrifice?"

Ophelia pulls at her sweater. "I did what I thought was right at the time."

The next week, Horatio came home for Christmas. He canceled his trip to meet Kim's parents, saying that I sounded tired, and after the weird messages he was getting from Hamlet, he thought he ought to return. Horatio and Hamlet spent most of their time together and, though I never told either of them, it was a relief to be alone. Knowing Horatio was taking care of Hamlet, I let go a little and was able to sleep and paint, and painting helped me to stop thinking. I didn't check e-mail or call anyone. I ignored my texts. I painted until my hands were as colorful as a garden and I'd filled paper after paper with images that had nothing to do with Hamlet or the king or the castle.

Finally I showered and changed, and when I went into the sitting room, I found a message from my dad that the boys wanted to go out for a movie and it was fine with him if I went. I headed up to Hamlet's room, where I found him completely engrossed in something he was reading on the Internet and Horatio looking annoyed.

We waited for over an hour for Hamlet to log off, and I knew if we didn't leave the castle soon, we would never make the movie. Of course we could have mentioned any film to the social secretary and it would have been played for us in-house, but there was something so much better about being in an actual theater with regular people, especially for a comedy. As long as the guards were in plainclothes and Hamlet kept his sunglasses on or his hood up and his head down, no one bothered us, at least most of the time. We got the occasional tween girls screaming or hugging him without permission, but more often than not he went undetected, or people just whispered as he passed. It made their months that they could go around telling everyone they'd been in the same place as the prince, and it made us feel better for having done something together that was normal. And if Hamlet couldn't stop fixating on his computer, we were going to lose out on our last chance for normal that night, and we all needed a laugh.

Horatio and I had been trying to entertain ourselves as best we could, but Horatio was getting impatient and my worries were starting to creep back. He signaled to me that it was my turn to try, so I walked up behind Hamlet, put my arms around him, and kissed him on the head. He didn't look up, just patted my hands.

I started massaging his shoulders and said, "You shouldn't be reading those message boards. They'll drive you nuts."

Horatio jumped in with, "Some of the things people say are so ignorant."

"You don't believe this junk?" I asked, hoping that leaning in front of the screen might work.

Hamlet just leaned the other way and kept reading.

I continued, "Conspiracy theorists, crackpots. Come on, Hamlet, let's just go."

Ignoring us, he frowned and read. "Listen to this: Someone claiming to be a servant here says he saw Claudius putting poison in my father's ear."

"His ear?" Horatio laughed. "How the hell would Claudius get poison in an ear?"

"My dad was probably asleep. He loved to nap in the conservatory. Said the flowers soothed him."

"Fine," said Horatio, "but why not just poison his drink or something?"

Hamlet scrolled down and said, "Because my uncle's a sneaky piece of crap, and I bet it'd be harder to notice."

"Wouldn't poison have showed up in an autopsy?" Horatio asked.

"My mother rushed that whole thing, remember?" Hamlet rubbed at his temples.

Horatio shook his head and walked over to the computer. "If what that person says is true, why has no one else mentioned it? Publicly, that is? It would have to have been an incredibly elaborate cover-up. I mean, not a peep anywhere else? These things never stay quiet. Not for long, anyway."

"Exactly," I added. "And I didn't see anyone there besides Claudius."

"Wait, what?" asked Hamlet, finally turning to face me.

"In the conservatory that morning. When I got there, Claudius was leaving." I felt a little shocked as the words left my mouth. It was the first time I had mentioned it to anyone. The first time I had actually thought about it since that day. It sounded suddenly important, and yet it had been nothing more than a fleeting vision of Claudius with…a bottle in his hand.

"You saw Claudius?" Horatio asked. His large brown eyes widened, and my stomach flipped.

"Yes," I said, trying to act very casual, "but he wasn't acting suspiciously. If he had just murdered his brother, don't you think he would have been running or something?"

"No," Hamlet replied quickly.

"Hamlet, like I said, I was there. No one else was. Not a guard. Not a servant. Just me and the flowers."

"And my dad."

"I didn't even know he was there. He must have been tucked in that back corner."

"The only place with no cameras…" Hamlet's voice trailed off.

"I was certainly caught on video. If anyone was suspicious, don't you think I would have been questioned?"

Frowning, Hamlet said, "Not if Claudius didn't want it investigated."

I looked at Horatio, who merely shrugged.

I wanted to reassure myself that it couldn't have been anything, that I hadn't missed something so important as a man escaping the scene of a murder. It looked like a bottle of water, the fancy blue kind we got at special events around the castle, just smaller. I wasn't sure if I should insist that we all talk to security or if I should run from Hamlet, who was sure to be more than a little miffed if it turned out I had witnessed the whole damned thing and done nothing about it.

We waited in silence as Hamlet continued clicking the mouse manically. Ten minutes passed. Then another ten.

"Come on, Hamlet," I finally said, not the least bit serious, "Horatio and I will take you to a strip club."

After a second, he turned his head, and a smile crept into one corner of his mouth. "You performing?"

I pulled my long hair on top of my head and pouted my lips. "I'm not on the schedule tonight," I joked. "But I've got a stack of singles for ya. I'm sure we could get your security detail to look the other way just this once. Or maybe they'd welcome the distraction."

He half laughed, said, "If your dad joins us, I'm in," and turned back to the screen.

I shuddered and then shrugged at Horatio.

"How about that movie?" asked Horatio. Hamlet didn't even look up, so I fell backward on the bed with a surrendering sigh.

Horatio turned to me and said, "We could go."

I shook my head.

Horatio picked up the remote and started flipping through the channels. After a few minutes he muttered, "So much for coming back and cheering him up." He turned off the TV and said, "Ophelia, I'm leaving tomorrow, so there's not much else I can…"

I tried to give a reassuring smile. He had done his best.

"Hamlet," I said, "you said you were thinking of going back to school. Are you going with Horatio tomorrow?"

Leaning closer to the screen, he mumbled, "I don't think so."

"Why not?" I asked, somewhat surprised. He had been clear after their last conversation that he wanted to get as far away from his mother and Claudius as possible, and that if his going would upset them, then all the better.

"I have business here."

Dread crept into my chest and I asked, "What business?"

"My business," he said, still looking at the screen, his frown deepening.

I turned to Horatio and asked, "Has he talked to you about this?" Horatio shook his head weakly, which made me not believe him. "This is crazy, Hamlet. Whatever plan you have, you should drop it."

My frustration and confusion were growing. There were clues everywhere, but I couldn't put them together—not in any way that made sense. It was like being thrown into a maze blindfolded. A maze with an invisible monster that I knew I had to stop.

"Hamlet," I said, "as much as I'd love to be with you more, you can't stay here. What are you going to do, skulk around the castle indefinitely, watching your mother and Claudius do… whatever it is they do? Yuck." I was grasping for anything at this point.

He was finally looking at me, which was something, but he didn't reply.

I knelt at his feet. "Hamlet, I know what I promised, but I don't want you getting into trouble."

"I can't go, all right?"

"This is madness!" I stood, grabbed my coat, and walked out. I clutched my hands together, praying that he wouldn't do something that would ruin both of our lives.

Hamlet woke me the next morning by letting steam from a fresh cup of coffee waft under my nose. I sat up and took the mug, hoping that the reasonable Hamlet was the one sitting beside me. His eyes, twinkling and focused, told me that it was. He said he wanted to make up for missing the movie by taking me to the museum of my choice. Funny thing was, the best art around was housed in the old part of the castle, so I suggested we start there. I would be ditching school, but as long as none of the guards ratted me out and I intercepted any messages from the school secretary before my dad came home, he would be none the wiser. Staying in had the added benefit of no security detail and no crowd, we could carry our coffee (which was terribly important, given my uncontrolled coffee addiction), and we could talk about whatever we wanted (which we could never do out, because the public always eavesdropped on his conversations).

We wandered the corridors, and after an hour, we had made our way to the former royal residences. Their brocade canopied beds, imposing doors, and gold leaf moldings made me glad Hamlet's parents had created something new. While impressive to tourists, these rooms didn't suit the times or the personalities of the former king and current queen, which was why they had built and moved into the other building.

At the far end of what had traditionally been the reigning queen's bedroom there hung a tiny photograph, too small for tourists to see. It was of Hamlet as a toddler sitting on his father's shoulders while his mother, standing to the side, beamed at them both. I was never sure why it had not been brought over to the new part of the castle, since the canopy hid it from public view, but I had loved being able to cross the velvet barriers in order to see it. As I neared the photo that Hamlet once cherished, I froze, realizing too late that it might pain him.

Hamlet pressed forward and studied it, sighing. "We were happy once."

"You'll be happy again," I offered, drifting to his side.

"You make me happy," he said, pulling me onto his lap as he sat on the formal chair beneath the frame. "I'm sorry about last night. I just lose myself. I need to figure out what happened, is all."

"If your dad's death was natural, then it's awful, but that's it. And if it was Claudius, and Claudius wants this covered up, there's probably nothing you can do about it. I'd love to have you around all the time, but you have to get on with your life." I wasn't sure if I thought it was possible, but it seemed like the right thing to say.

He pushed his nose into my neck and nodded. "I know you're right, but I have to find out for sure. And I have to avenge my father."

"Avenge? What are you talking about?" Fear slithered through me, and I pulled back to look at his face. When Hamlet didn't answer, I begged, "Don't do anything crazy, okay? If this is about Gertrude and Claudius—"

Hamlet winced.

"We could go somewhere," I suggested. "Leave all this behind. Start a new life."

Hamlet shook his head and looked back at the photograph. "No. My father needs me to do this."

"Your father?" I asked.

His face was suddenly relaxed. He brushed his hair out of his eyes, turned to me, and said, "Forget it, Phee. Nothing serious today, okay?" He lifted me up, tossed me over his shoulder, and lightly spanked my behind. I fleetingly thought that anyone who could change moods so quickly had to be kidding about avenging or revenging or whatever he had been saying, and as he ran us out of the room, I let that idea chase away my concerns. My peace of mind did not last long.

Every night for a couple of weeks, Hamlet came to my room after my father was asleep, only to rise again and leave just before dawn. I asked him where he was going, but he wouldn't tell me. After the first few times, I stopped asking.

During the hours he was with me, he usually sat awake by the window or wrapped his arms around me and stared at the ceiling. I couldn't figure out how to help him. All I knew was the lack of sleep was helping neither his judgment nor his mental state, and it wasn't helping mine, either.

One night, he shook me awake. "I need you to come with me," he said.

"Where?" I asked. Forcing my sandpapery eyelids to stay open, I looked out the window at the still-dark sky.

"Please."

My head ached, and my body wouldn't move as fast as I wanted it to. Hamlet lifted me to my feet, took my hand, and led me to the elevator without saying anything.

My mind was lagging, so it took me a minute to realize he was taking me out. "My shoes," I whispered, not even considering that I was in my pajama bottoms and a T-shirt with no bra. I moved to grab my sneakers.

"Forget them," he said, and the doors opened. I hesitated, but he pulled me in after him and pushed the button for the conservatory. I was tempted to ask him questions, but my mind couldn't form them fast enough. He ran his fingers through his hair roughly, then pushed the already lit button. Then again. And again. All the way up he pushed the button. I squeezed his hand, hoping at least that would make him stop or look at me, but to no avail. I peered up at the security camera in the corner of the elevator and wondered if it recorded sound as well as picture. I decided to wait before asking any questions and bit my nails instead.

We exited the elevator, and Hamlet escorted me inside the conservatory. I shuddered, suddenly wide awake. I hadn't been in there since the king had died, and I doubted many others had, either. The air felt stifling, not tropical and romantic, as it used to feel.

Hamlet let go of my hand and walked quickly along the path. He returned to where I was standing, then continued in the other direction, pausing only to check the dim corner where his father's body had been found.

He waved me over, and I forced myself to go. His eyes darted around and he asked, "Do you believe in ghosts?"

I lifted my eyebrows and replied, "Not really."

He looked over my shoulder and, fearful of what might be behind me, I turned around slowly, but nothing was there.

He frowned. "Neither did I. But my father..." he began. "My father has been talking to me."

"Like in your head?"

"No, like standing in front of me. On the roof. And right here."

The cold was seeping into my feet, and I started to shiver. Or maybe it was the ghost talk that got me. Either way, Hamlet didn't put his arm around me. He didn't even notice.

I stood trembling and wondered what to say. "I know you're upset, but—"

He shook his head quickly. "He was here. On this spot. You don't believe me. I knew it. God! Why did I bother telling—"

He stormed across the garden, peering behind bushes as he went.

"Hamlet, you might have thought—"

"Don't say it didn't happen," he said, running back at me. Stopping short in front of me, he waved his finger in my face. "I talked to him. I talked to my father. He told me things. Things no one else could have known. Now I have to kill Claudius." He ran both hands through his hair before spinning around and exiting through the glass doors. I hustled down the stairs to my apartment as fast as my quaking legs would take me.

I didn't believe in ghosts. Hamlet didn't believe in ghosts. We used to watch those ghost-hunter shows and laugh our butts off at the "experts" and the ridiculous suckers who hired them. And now Hamlet was telling me that not only had he *seen* a ghost, it was telling him to do things. I thought it might be schizophrenia but then remembered that he'd have voices in his head, not ghosts of dead fathers ordering him around. I just didn't get it.

I sat on my bed, trying to catch my breath. Rubbing my leaden eyelids, I hoped that I hadn't actually woken up at all and that when I removed my hands from my eyes, I would find Hamlet sitting by the window. Sadly, the room was occupied by only me. I twisted my pajama bottoms between my fingers, my stomach aching, and hoped he wasn't anywhere murdering anyone. Ghost hunting, I could hope, was the extent of his pre-dawn weirdness.

When the hour seemed decent enough, I texted Horatio.

Me: H says he saw hs fathers gost. Wtf?
Horatio: i saw it 2

134

Me: b.s.

Horatio: my last night in elsinr. aftr u lft. kng ws in unifrm. scry as hell.

Me: i can't believe this

My phone rang. It was Horatio.

"Seriously, Ophelia, I'm not lying. We saw him."

I lay flat on my back, unable to believe the turn the conversation had taken. I considered hanging up, but the stronger part of me had to know more. "What did"—I paused, stunned that I was actually entertaining the thought—"the ghost say?"

"Nothing. Not to me."

I explained, "Hamlet says he has to avenge his father's death. If the ghost didn't speak, then how does Hamlet know?"

"Well...I wasn't with Hamlet the whole time. Apparently the ghost will speak only to Hamlet." I scoffed, but Horatio ignored it. He continued, "The ghost—or Hamlet's dad or whatever—told Hamlet that Claudius poisoned him."

I didn't say anything for a while. It was like having static in my head. Too much nonsense. If Horatio hadn't confirmed the ghost sighting, I would have dismissed it out of hand. I mean, if I got as little sleep as Hamlet had been getting, I would have seen pink elephants crashing through my apartment. But what did Horatio gain from being part of this delusion? I had to call it a delusion. I wasn't ready to believe in ghosts.

"That's insane," I finally said, though Claudius holding that bottle was pretty damning.

"Maybe. But it's true."

I hung up and put on my uniform. I would have been better

off skipping class altogether because I couldn't concentrate on anything that was being said. I ignored school rules and kept my phone on but received no messages.

When I got back to the castle, Marcellus was waiting behind the security booth with a handwritten note. He said, "He told me not to leave it with anyone else."

> O—
>
> I couldn't stick around. I hurt you every time we're together. And I don't think being in Elsinore is good for me right now.
>
> I'm trying to sort this all out, but I'm doing a crap job of it. Maybe I'll have more perspective from far away. It's at the point where I'm not sure what's right or wrong anymore. And if what I believe to be true _is_ true, then I have to do something about it. But I'm afraid to.
>
> I know you don't believe what I've been telling you. That's okay. I wouldn't believe me either.
>
> Better go back to school for now. Sorry about everything. I love you.
>
> H

Francisco: So Hamlet threatened to kill the king and you didn't think to warn anyone?
Ophelia: Like who?
Barnardo: The authorities.

Ophelia: He *was* the authorities.

Francisco: Interesting.

Ophelia: What?

Francisco: So you're saying Hamlet ruled over you?

Ophelia: No. Yes. Everyone. He was the goddamned prince.

Francisco: And Gertrude?

Ophelia: She definitely ruled over me. And so did Claudius, in case you're about to ask.

Francisco: You didn't think to mention his plan to them?

Ophelia: Why would I mention it to them?

Barnardo: Because it was a plot to kill Claudius! *(banging on the table)*

Ophelia: It didn't sound like a plot. It sounded like Hamlet talking, which he did a lot.

Barnardo: And you're saying you saw Claudius in the garden. Why didn't you report it?

Ophelia: It didn't seem like anything at the time.

Francisco: You keep saying that. A rather convenient answer.

Ophelia: There were cameras in the hall outside the conservatory. You must have some video that showed who came and went that day.

Barnardo: The, uh, tape disappeared.

Ophelia: Talk about convenient.

12

"You went to visit Hamlet a couple of weeks after he returned to Wittenberg."

"Yes."

"Why did you go?"

Ophelia pauses and looks at the audience. "He needed me." Ophelia's gaze turns anxiously to the screen behind her on which only Zara's name is floating.

"I'm not going to show any pictures of what went on," she says, "but what would you say to anyone wondering about that night?"

"Well..." Ophelia begins. "It was...a frat party...girls go wild." Her half smile fades. "If I could do it all over again, though, I wouldn't go."

After Hamlet went back to school, I was kicked off the lacrosse team. As far as my coach was concerned (and she *was* concerned), I had already quit. She said if she'd known about my lack of commitment to the swim team earlier in the year, she wouldn't have taken me on this team in the first place. Then she gave me quite a lecture about not changing my life for a boy, even if that boy was a prince. I liked the coach and I liked the game, but I'd only joined to keep myself busy after my mom died. Still, I felt awful knowing I'd let everyone down by skipping so many practices.

I left the field and headed for the art studio, hoping to focus on a drawing I owed. When I got there, the place was mercifully empty, so I grabbed a sheet of white paper and a box of charcoals and perched on my stool. The paper was blank—so full of possibility. And I had no idea what to put on it.

I startled at a noise behind me.

"Ophelia!" said Ms. Hill, who was coming out of the supply closet. "I haven't seen you after school in ages."

I bit my lip and nodded.

She pushed strands of her wild red hair off her forehead. "Are you finally finishing your pieces for the portfolio?"

"What portfolio?"

"For art school."

I frowned, not sure if it was dogged determination or blindness that was preventing her from seeing that I had trashed all my plans and that there was no turning back. I rolled the charcoal in my palm and said, "You know I didn't apply to art school."

"Not this year," she said, her voice breezy. Then she walked over and sat on the stool next to mine. "But I also know Denmark State isn't where you want to be. Or where you'll end up staying. So let's put the portfolio together in case you change your mind."

Not knowing what else to do, I nodded. My life had been looking like a windowless room, but here she was, offering a way out. Satisfied, she leaped up and went back to organizing paints.

The assignment had been to draw something important

to us, and the first thing that came to mind was Hamlet. That just pissed me off. There was more to me than him. Wasn't there? I closed my eyes and thought about what I loved. I considered drawing my art supplies, but I already had a still life, and the portfolio needed variety. A portrait was the way to go, so I considered who else I could do. My brother? My father? Hamlet's father? And then it came to me. My mother.

I reached into my bag and unzipped a hidden compartment, pulling out a crinkled magazine article about her death. There was a picture of the bullet-riddled, crushed limo she'd been riding in when the assassin attacked. I had stared at the image so often that it no longer stung. It was more like the pressure of getting your teeth drilled after a shot of Novocain. Anyway, next to the car photo was a picture of her and my dad from before Laertes and I were born, which I'd always loved because they looked so young and hopeful.

I was sitting and considering whether to do just the portrait or to combine it with the accident — an idea that made my stomach hurt, but I knew would get a reaction from a viewer — when the studio door opened. I snatched the article off the worktable and held it in my lap.

Sebastian walked in and in the split second that I saw him before he saw me, I wished myself invisible.

Sebastian was one of the people I used to hang out with most, but our relationship had always been complicated. And I just didn't want any more complications at that moment.

Sebastian's feelings for me had been obvious for a long time. I would catch him staring at me at lunch or even watching me during study hall. I had deflected his attentions, but I admit I liked them. He was sexy and cute and totally different from Hamlet. He was taller and more solid, his black hair was cut very short, and his dark eyes smoldered—a fact I knew because on one drunken night I didn't look away but let him stare at me and I stared back, locking him with my eyes, sharing in the mutual longing. But the next day, hungover and back to my senses, I remembered that I was taken and acted accordingly. He had continued to follow me around like a puppy, a damn attractive puppy, but to no avail. Until Hamlet and I broke up last spring.

Sebastian and I had gone to see the Poor Yoricks alone because none of our friends liked the band enough to pay scalpers' prices to the sold-out show. Everything started out fine, but then when the equipment was being set up for the main act, the recorded music was really loud, so we had to lean in to hear each other. I was close enough to feel his heat and to smell the gel he used to make his hair perfectly messy. Something shifted, and I wanted so much to lean in and kiss him right behind the ear. Well, he must have felt the same, because at that moment, he inched forward and stroked my bare arm. A chill passed over me and I was about to touch my lips to his skin when over his shoulder, I caught a guy lifting his camera phone and pointing it at us.

I leaped back and ran, weaving through the crowd.

"I'm sorry, Ophelia," I heard Sebastian calling after me.

I waited for him by the door. "It's not you. But— I can't have this in the papers."

"You're not with *him* anymore, so what do you care?"

Sebastian rarely called Hamlet by name, and at that moment, it upset me even more. "I love *him*, okay? We're having problems right now, but we'll get over them. We always do. And that's not why I came out with you." It kind of was, and we both knew it, but at least Sebastian didn't argue the point. "I like you, and I can't risk messing up our friendship. Or having my dad see what I do when he actually lets me go out."

Sebastian rocked back on his heels, his face red. "So, you wanna leave?"

I looked at the stage, where the microphones were being set up. "No. But we can't….Just friends, okay?"

His shoulders had drooped, and he followed me back toward the stage.

In the art studio doorway, Sebastian stopped short when he saw me and asked, "Don't you have practice?"

I shook my head. "Kicked off the team." Saying it aloud, I was even more embarrassed than I had been before.

"You're kidding," he said, pulling his bag off his shoulder and setting it next to his easel. "That sucks."

"Too much missed practice."

He pursed his lips, holding back a comment about Hamlet, I'm sure, and said, "Well, it's nice to have you back in here."

I rubbed my forehead and said, "Thanks."

"Keren and Justine are grabbing coffee. Wanna go after we work for a while?"

"Can't."

"Is *he* waiting for you?"

"*He* is back at school," I snapped. "My dad told me to come straight home today." Sebastian cocked his head, measuring his next move, I'm sure, but I added, "I'll ask if we can all go out tomorrow."

I know he caught the "all" I had carefully added to the phrase. He stooped to grab paint off a low shelf, and we both went back to work.

I spent the next while trying to catch up with my studies and my friends and trying not to worry about Hamlet. I figured if he was out of the castle, it was safer for everyone. I had finally begun to breathe, eat, and sleep normally when Horatio called.

Skipping all pleasantries, he opened with, "Hamlet's bad."

"What is it?"

"You have to visit. He's dying here."

"Well, it wasn't so hot in Elsinore for him, so how much worse can it be?"

"He can't sleep. He won't go to class. He just sits around scribbling weird crap in journals and then burning the pages. He's set off the fire alarm a few times, which is starting to piss off the other guys. He keeps saying he has to go back and finish business. I hope it doesn't mean what I think it means. I keep reminding him how much he hated being around his mom and the Claw, but he won't listen to reason."

"The Claw?"

"It's what we've taken to calling Claudius. It's about the only thing that gets him to lighten up."

I smiled. "I like that."

"Can you come today?"

"Today? No. I have to—"

"He needs you."

"Tomorrow. I think. I have to talk to my father."

"Your father? Seriously, Ophelia, Hamlet's right. You gotta get out from under his thumb."

My cheeks burned. "Screw you, Horatio. I know you asked permission to go places right through the end of high school. I've already put so much on—" My phone clicked. Call-waiting. "I gotta go."

"Ophelia—"

I hung up on him. Then I felt bad because he and I never

ended arguments like that. I'd apologize when called him with my plans.

"Hey," I said to Sebastian, who was on the other line.

"Hey. There's a gallery opening tonight. Wanna go with me?"

I hesitated. It would be good to go out, to be with someone else, but I needed to talk to my dad about Wittenberg. And I didn't think going out with just Sebastian was a good idea. "I, uh…I need to be with Hamlet right now," I said.

"But he's at school."

"Yeaaah. I think I'm going there this weekend."

There was a pause. "Oh. Got it."

He hung up.

A few minutes later, my phone rang again. "What'd you do to Sebastian?" asked Lauren.

"Do? Nothing. I told him I'm going to Wittenberg."

"Wittenberg? Ophelia, come on. You can go a weekend without him."

"You and I went out last weekend. And the weekend before that."

"Two in a row? Wow. You're right. Time to disappear again."

"You don't understand. He's really— I think he might—"

"What?"

"I can't tell you."

Lauren sighed. "Of course not. Fine, Ophelia. We'll be here when you want us. God knows why, but we will."

All I was doing was disappointing people. But I couldn't fix the situation, since I didn't know what was going on. I couldn't share my problems with anyone because, even if I did have any information, which I didn't, I didn't really trust anyone. The whole thing was turning me into a lunatic.

* * *

That night over stir-fry I told my dad I was going to Wittenberg. He put down his chopsticks and began, "There's a Swahili saying: 'When elephants fight, the grass gets hurt.' You, my dear, are bound to be the grass in all this. Perhaps you ought to stay out of Hamlet's fight. Perhaps you ought to stay away from Hamlet altogether. Let his return to school be an opportunity. They say, 'Absence makes the heart grow fonder.' I say it's worth giving absence a try."

"*If* the object was to make him fonder, I might agree. But I can't imagine that's what *you* would want. An even fonder Hamlet?"

He smiled at my small verbal victory.

I sidled up to him and put my arm around his shoulder. "And as for my being grass among elephants, stop worrying. I'll be fine. Hamlet isn't fine and that's what matters right now."

My father tried to circle back to why my being with Hamlet was a mistake.

"Dad, I'm not asking, actually. I'm telling you. I'm going tomorrow and I'll be back Sunday night. I'm taking the train because I can get some work done, but I am going." I shakily lifted my chopsticks and concentrated very hard on picking up the food. The adrenaline rush created a momentary high as I congratulated myself on standing up for myself.

I heard my father say, "I love you, Ophelia. You're my baby. I don't want you getting hurt."

"I love you, too. But Dad, you have to let me grow up." I grabbed the bottle of wine and poured more into his glass. "Maybe you ought to try for a romance of your own."

"My dear, 'An old man in love is like a flower in winter,'" he said, raising his glass to his lips.

"Swahili?"

"Chinese. I'm done with romance. Your mom was my one and only." He toasted the picture of her, which hung on our fridge, and put the glass down again.

"Dad, no one's saying you have to get married. But a little fun never hurt anyone."

"You're not thinking this through, my dear. If I went out, how would I find the time to memorize quotes for our little talks?" He winked, and I kissed him on the cheek.

When I finally reached Hamlet's frat house, I was amazed, as I had been the year before, at how run-down it was. The floors were warped; the carpet was threadbare and stained; the banisters shook if you grabbed them too hard. Food containers were left in all the common areas—and the smell seemed to indicate they'd been there for some time. Not exactly the place one expected to find a prince, but I suppose that had been the point when Hamlet chose it.

I knocked on Hamlet's door and no one answered. I pushed it open and the stale smell sent me back a few steps. "Hamlet?" I called, but still no reply. I crept forward and saw him at his desk, hunched over and scribbling. "Hamlet!" I said loudly, and he swiveled in his seat.

He rubbed his eyes. "Ophelia? Is that you?"

I had a moment of utter confusion. "Yeah. Didn't Horatio tell you I was coming?"

"Oh, was that today?" he asked. "I guess…I'm sure…How are you?" He took out his earbuds and came to hug me.

I hugged him back but asked, "Hamlet, when was the last time you went out…or showered?"

He ran his fingers through his greasy hair and looked like

146

I was waking him up from a peculiar dream. "I don't know. What day is it?"

"Saturday," I said, my stomach tightening. How had he gotten to this point? "Hamlet, what are you on?"

"Me? Nothing. I've just been…I haven't wanted to go out.…I kind of lost track of time, so…" His eyes scanned his room and he suddenly looked embarrassed.

"Listen," I began, setting my bag against the wall and closing the door, "why don't you shower? I'll open the windows, and we'll do some laundry. Then you can tell me what's going on and…yeah, we'll start with that, okay?"

He nodded, looking relieved that someone was taking charge of his well-being. He grabbed his towel and started for the door. I brought him the basket that contained his shampoo and razor, then watched him make his way up the stairs to bathe. I thought of the afternoon the past summer when we walked through the Museo Firenze for the private viewing he'd arranged. Could that solemn, dazed person walking up the stairs be the same Hamlet I had hung out with months earlier?

I picked up my cell and texted Horatio.

wtf?

Hamlet returned after I had already gathered the dirty clothes strewn around the room and changed the sheets. I didn't even change my own sheets, so this was quite a feat. He looked much more mentally present as he entered, and he crossed the room immediately to kiss me. "Hey, baby."

"Hey, yourself. You better?" I asked, touching his wet hair.

"Yeah." He breathed deeply and looked at the fluttering papers on his desk. "That breeze feels good."

"We should go out. Get some air and something to eat. I'm starved, and you look like you haven't eaten in a while." I was trying not to sound like a mother hen, but I was failing miserably.

He shrugged. "I ate…yesterday, I think."

"Think? Come on, sweet prince," I said, taking his hand in mine. "Let's dump the laundry somewhere in town and get—"

"Coffee."

"And food. Man cannot live on coffee alone."

He threw the laundry bag over his shoulder and led me down the stairs. "I could just trash all this and buy new stuff," he joked.

"Where would you get the money?" I teased.

Hamlet's phone *bing*ed. "Horatio," he said to me. "Where should he meet us?"

"Well, how about my favorite place, I Don't Go to School Around Here."

He hip-checked me, typed, "Dolly's," and snapped his phone shut. "I'm surprised your dad let you come."

"I didn't exactly ask," I said.

He looked impressed but added, "Did he have you followed?"

I smiled. "Probably." I put my arm around his waist and soon we found a pay-by-the-pound laundry service. Hamlet usually did his own, but that would have meant staying in the stinky house, and that was something I just didn't want to do.

While Hamlet ordered at the counter, Horatio had a few minutes to fill me in. "I've been basically living at Kim's, so I didn't notice at first that Hamlet was MIA. I mean, his door was closed, so I thought he was out. Actually, he never used to close his door half the time when he did go out, so I should have known...."

"Don't blame yourself. Look, I'm here for the weekend and you know to keep an eye on him from now on—"

"He's messed up."

"He'll be all right," I reassured him. "You worry too much."

"And you have too much faith," he said gravely.

As if on cue, Hamlet returned, followed closely by a slim brunette who seemed rather proud of her very tight shirt. "Hey, Hamlet. Been missing you in class. You going to the party at G's tonight?"

He looked at me and answered, "Uh, maybe. We'll see. This is my, uh..."

"Girlfriend." I glowered, pulling back my arm, which had been around Hamlet's chair.

"Ophelia. Of course. You can come, too," she said in her very pert voice. "Later," she said to him, then bounced back to her friends, who immediately giggled upon her return.

I tried not to look at Horatio, who was looking embarrassed for me. "A party sounds good," I said, swallowing my pride.

"I'm not drinking—" Hamlet started.

I interrupted, "You don't have to. Or you can. One night couldn't hurt, right?"

He nodded. "I could use a drink...and some fun."

"It'll be like before," Horatio said, getting swept up in the plan.

The lights were flashing red, blue, green, yellow, red, blue, green, yellow. The whole place smelled of beer with a vague hint of socks. It smelled like college heaven. "Woo!" I shouted, grabbing Hamlet with one arm and Horatio with the other. We pushed our way past a thick-necked guy who took our tickets toward the crowd on the other side of the entryway. The band was singing something about "being easier to play on than a pipe," which might have been more suggestive if they weren't screaming and pounding on their guitars and drums and one another. Horatio made a cup motion and ran off to the basement to get beer. Hamlet and I waded farther in.

Some girl, not the one from Dolly's, recognized Hamlet and whispered in his ear. I couldn't hear, but he looked at me sidelong, which was worse than her talking to him. I decided not to worry about it too much. Every girl wants to save the brooding guy, but he was mine to save, so I yanked him in the other direction. She screwed up her face and mouthed something at me that I pretended not to see.

We stood listening to the hideous music, if you could even call it that, for another minute. He gestured like he was going to hang himself, which made us laugh, and he pointed toward the basement. I really didn't want to go down, but I followed him, anyway. In the half day I had been with him, he'd seemed to transform back to his old self, or at least to the one who had left Elsinore a couple of weeks prior. Even so, I thought I ought to stay close.

Horatio was in the middle of a very long line. When we reached him, Hamlet leaned in and yelled, "Screw this. I brought my own." He pulled out a fifth of whiskey.

"What the hell did you let me wait all this time for?" Horatio laughed, grabbing the bottle and taking a swig. He passed it to me, and I wrinkled my nose. "It's this or crap beer."

I grabbed it and did a dance of pain as it charred its way

down to my stomach. "Christ, what is with you boys?" I gasped, fanning air into my mouth.

"That is quality stuff. Stolen right from Claudi-ass himself," hissed Hamlet.

"No talking about him tonight. That was the deal," Horatio said, playfully shaking Hamlet by the shoulder.

Hamlet grabbed the fifth and drank deeply, then handed the bottle to me again. I rolled my eyes and held my breath. I hoped I wouldn't need to drink much more before I was drunk. It had been a long time since I'd really cut loose, and I wanted to take my mind off all the crazy stuff that had been happening. I figured if Horatio and Hamlet were going to drink themselves silly, I might as well, too. And it was a perfect time. No slinking into my apartment and avoiding my dad. No worrying about class the next day. Most important, I was with Hamlet, so no guy was gonna try anything if I got wasted. My face was still burning as I passed the bottle to Horatio. The black lights made the iridescent wall paintings glow brightly, and the whiskey made them swirl. I stepped in a puddle of something as we headed back upstairs and was really glad the weather hadn't been warm enough for sandals.

A new band was setting up, so someone had put on a stereo. "How Like an Angel" was blasting, one of my favorite songs to dance to. I started leaping up and down and spotted an empty table pushed in the corner. I climbed up and, to my surprise, Hamlet and Horatio hopped up, too. The table was pretty small, but we all managed to fit. The music was in me and all around, and the lights flashed faster. I did not think about the flashes of white coming from a few feet away.

The next band was either really amazing or I was really drunk. Probably both. They played a long set. Everyone in the room seemed to know who they were because they screamed out the musicians' names between songs and knew all their lyrics. I guess the band went to Wittenberg.

They played a few slow songs, which was a great chance to sit down and lean against the wall. I sat wedged between my two guys, happy that Kim didn't want to come with Horatio, and closed my eyes for a while. Soon, Hamlet leaned close and whispered, "Let's get out of here."

Keeping my eyes closed, I replied, "It's still early, Hamlet."

I looked over at Horatio, who suddenly snored, which seemed outrageously funny. As our laughter died down, Hamlet pulled out the whiskey again and offered it, but I waved it away. With Horatio asleep, I suddenly felt free to climb onto Hamlet's lap. He pulled me into a kiss, and there were more white flashes.

"Get out of here!" Hamlet yelled, waving at someone in the dark. He tried to get up, nearly knocking me off the table. Whoever it was vanished into the crowd while we struggled to keep our balance.

"Who was that?"

"I don't know. The university promised my father that I wouldn't be hassled here. Promises," he spat.

The band started playing a faster song. We looked at each other and knew we were too tired to keep dancing. We patted Horatio awake and steered him back out through the crowd. He stopped in the bushes to puke and then fell to his knees, luckily not landing in the former contents of his stomach. "Why do I let you drag me into these things?" implored Horatio.

"You did this willingly, my friend," replied Hamlet, hoisting Horatio back onto his feet.

As we rounded the corner, we nearly bumped into two

guys, both of whom were wearing absurd beanies. "Rosen-crantz! Guildenstern!" shouted Hamlet too loudly.

"Good party?" asked the tall one, eyeing Horatio.

"Decent music. Foul beer. What the hell are those?" Hamlet asked, gesturing sloppily to his own head.

"Pledge thing."

Hamlet stumbled as he cackled, dragging us away. "Good luck with that," he yelled over his shoulder.

I woke up the next morning in agony. My head pulsated, and my mouth was furry. As I rolled over to get out from under Hamlet, my stomach burned. I moaned and tried to shut out the day with my hands. Why Hamlet was unable to hang a simple curtain or shade was beyond me.

I dug into my overnight bag and grabbed a pair of jeans. That amount of movement was too much, so I put my head back on the pillow. I wanted to shower and get all the grime off from the night before, but I dreaded the comments I knew I would hear if any of the frat brothers were in the hall. They always had off-color remarks for any girl who spent the night.

I stood up and shoved on the jeans, deciding to take my chance with the hall and the guys' bathroom. I grabbed Hamlet's towel, which we had neglected to get laundered, and smelled it. A little mildew but clean enough. When I entered the harshly lit hallway, some guy was sitting on the stained carpet steps that led up to the showers. As he scooted aside to let me pass, he said, "Nice pictures," not bothering to look up from his paper.

"Excuse me?" I scowled at him, wishing I'd brought some toothpaste with me, knowing there would be none I would want to touch upstairs.

"Nice pictures, I said. Front cover. Impressive." He swiveled around and let me see the front page of the paper he was holding. His eyes danced with excitement. There above the fold were two startlingly clear pictures from the party the night before. One was of Hamlet, bottle in mouth, me dancing in a skirt I had not realized looked so indecently short, my hair flying every which way, and Horatio, arms in the air, head back, making him unidentifiable. The other picture was of me sitting astride Hamlet on the table in the corner, his tongue down my throat. The white flashes of light.

"Crap," I whispered, my legs weak. I grabbed the sticky banister to steady myself.

"He's the most famous guy around. Why are you doing anything you don't want the whole world to see?" He smirked and handed the paper to me. I clutched it and sat. The guy bounded down the creaky steps and disappeared into the living room.

As he clicked on the TV, I heard a reporter, glee in his voice, saying, "That kind of picture makes me wish I were back in college."

A female reporter replied with mock concern, "That kind of picture makes me hope my daughters don't want to go at all." They chuckled, then her tone grew serious as she changed topics.

I stood on shaking legs and made my way back to Hamlet's room. I put down the paper and the stinky towel and pulled my hair into a ponytail, trying to catch my breath. I was jealous of Hamlet's sleep and furious that he wasn't awake to share in this horrible moment. I was about to wake him when a ruckus outside caught my attention. I walked to the window and saw a white news van pulling up. Students passing by were stopping to watch, and one pointed to the window where I was standing. I was glad I had put on my pants. Another news van with an outsize satellite dish on top slowed, its brakes squealing.

I scooted to the side of the window and slid down the wall. "Hamlet. We are so dead."

Three hours later, Elsinore's skyline loomed overhead, making me feel as if I were at the bottom of a deep canyon. Horatio had an exam the next day, so he stayed. Hamlet, thinking himself gentlemanly, escorted me home in his limo.

"This was so stupid," I muttered.

"It may have been stupid, but it sure was fun. I haven't felt that happy and free in a while," Hamlet said. He took my hand and I fought the urge to pull it back. Then I squeezed his fingers and tried to relax. What he said was cold comfort, but in a way, I guess I was glad. Despite the consequences, which I knew would be severe, we had accomplished what we had set out to do. We got Hamlet out of his head and we all had a night that wasn't about our parents.

A text message *bing*ed at me. I pulled out my phone.

Laertes: R u stupid? what did I say?

I couldn't face Laertes in any form just then, so I turned off the phone and shoved it back in my bag. I stared out the window at the shops I loved to go to. It occurred to me it might be a while before I was comfortable enough to show my face in public again.

The driver pulled into the underground garage, which was

wise. Not exactly to our surprise, Gertrude, Claudius, and my father were all waiting by the elevator bank. The fluorescent lights made them look sallow and exaggerated their expressions, which ranged from irritation to dismay. I sank deeper in my seat, and Hamlet followed me down. He turned to me and stroked my cheek gently. "Hey," he said, "no regrets, okay? I loved what you two did for me, making me go have fun. They'll forget all about this, but I won't."

I knew he was wrong about anyone forgetting.

The car stopped, and my father didn't even wait for the driver to open the door. He yanked it wide, and I knew I had to go first. I looked back at Hamlet, who winked. Claudius didn't look at me, but Gertrude studied me as if to figure out what kind of fool had been in her presence for the past however many years. I looked away and followed my father.

No sooner had the elevator doors closed than he began shouting. "What kind of lunatic goes out in public dressed like that with the future king? What kind of person puts herself in a position to be so exposed?" We arrived in our apartment and he marched me into his study, where he continued. "You sell yourself short by becoming his plaything, and you made a fool out of me for trusting you!"

My body felt weak and I tingled from head to foot with nerves. "I'm sorry."

"Sorry? You can never be sorry enough. I will be lucky if I maintain my post or am allowed to keep you in the castle at this point. If I were the king and queen, I wouldn't allow it. If I were advising them on anyone *but* you, your removal is precisely what I would suggest."

I opened my mouth to speak, but he would not let me.

"Do you not understand, Ophelia, that Hamlet, as a young

man, and a prince at that, walks with a longer leash than may be given to you? I forbid you to talk to Hamlet until further notice. Are we clear?"

I nodded and kept my tears back until I had turned away and walked out of his office.

When I got to my room, tons of e-mails were waiting for me. Most were from friends, but from the subject lines I knew I couldn't face what they had to say, even the friends who found the whole thing very funny. I spotted one from Hamlet with the subject line: "Never Surrender." I wondered if our parents could read our messages if they so desired. There seemed to be precious little privacy in the castle in general. I wanted to open it but was afraid of where it might lead. Then again, my father had said not to "talk" to Hamlet, which didn't necessarily cover electronic messages, if one were inclined to argue the point. I wasn't sure just then if I was so inclined. I walked away from my computer.

Later that morning, as expected, I was summoned by Gertrude. She was sitting very still at her tea table, delicately painted cups and saucers laid out perfectly. She did not stand in welcome. After some perfunctory utterances of shock, she took a moment to create a meaningful silence between us. She sipped and held the cup to her lips longer than she needed to. "Given my son's inexplicable attachment to you, I had begun to think that you and Hamlet might get married someday." Her lips curled in disgust, and she lowered the cup slowly. "But after this? How could the people honestly accept you as their queen after see-ing you like...that?"

"Gertrude, I—"

"There is nothing you can say."

My anger flared. "The people were shocked by you and Claudius, yet you go on being queen!" I shouted.

Gertrude pursed her lips and crossed her arms, daring me to say another word.

I softened my voice. "The pictures make it look much worse than it really was."

Gertrude looked at the ceiling. "Hamlet tried to say the same thing. I say it does not matter what the reality was. You look like a whore. I've sent him back to school. You are not to go there again. Stay away from my son." She stood abruptly and clacked away, leaving me in her empty salon feeling like she had kicked me in the chest.

Barnardo: You dragged him to that party knowing that bad publicity would come out of it.

Ophelia: No, I didn't.

Francisco: Admit it. You and Horatio arranged the whole episode knowing it would further undermine his credibility and unravel their family stability.

Ophelia: That is not why. We wanted Hamlet to have fun—

Barnardo: Bull. You knew photographers would be there.

Ophelia: In four years, no one had ever taken a picture of him at school unless it was official and prearranged.

Francisco: How convenient. So you knew you could catch him by surprise. Who did you pay to take those pictures?

Ophelia: Why would I do that? I'm the one who got the most grief for that. A guy can do whatever he wants with whomever he wants. But a girl? Forget it. Everyone had something to say about my skirt, how drunk I was, Christ, even how I kiss!

Barnardo: Small price to pay. A little humiliation for—

Ophelia: For what? What do you think I gained from those pictures?

Francisco: Sympathy from Hamlet.

Barnardo: A great cover. It got him back to the castle.

Ophelia: Yeah, that worked out for everyone so well.

Barnardo: My point exactly.

13

Zara narrows her eyes at Ophelia as she leans back on the cream couch. "The queen could not have been happy about that kind of publicity."

Ophelia clears her throat and says, "Happy would be an overstatement. But she was pretty understanding. Don't forget, Gertrude was young once, too."

"And your father?"

"He was...less understanding."

One afternoon a couple of weeks later, I was in my room supposedly reading about the painter John Everett Millais but really staring off into space thinking about the fact that I should be reading. I had just looked at my book again when I heard Hamlet calling, "Ophelia?"

I jumped up, a thrill passing through me at the sound of his voice. But as I ran down the hall, Gertrude's angry face popped into my mind. The image slowed my step, and when I saw Hamlet, as desperate as I was to touch him, I checked myself.

Standing at the end of my hall and forcing myself not to go into the entry area, I called to him, "When did you get back?"

"This morning," he replied, kicking off his shoes next to the elevator.

He was going to stay, and I couldn't allow it. "Get out of here, Hamlet. I'm not supposed to see you right now."

"That's ridiculous," he said, flopping onto the couch. "We've been on the phone and texting since I left. What's the difference?"

"There's a big difference. You have to go!"

"Why? Because your dad said so?"

I crossed my arms, not liking his tone, and added, "Yeah, and your mom."

He rolled his eyes.

"Hamlet, I'm not kidding."

He peered over the back of the couch at me, cocked his head, and smiled. That charm was why the people of Denmark, myself included, loved him so. Except at that moment I didn't want to be charmed. I turned to walk away.

He said, "Ophelia, seriously, what are they gonna do about it if we hang out?"

I spun around, even more annoyed by his stupidity. "Oh, well, your mother could fire my dad, for one. I could get thrown out of here, for the other. They both told me as much."

"I doubt either of those things will happen."

"I can't take that chance. I have to put everything I want aside like always. I have to wear this mask and be who everyone else wants me to be all the time."

"And my girlfriend. Is that part of your act?" he asked.

My heart was racing. How could he even ask that? I wanted to smack him as much as I wanted to kiss him. "No. That's the only time I get to be myself."

"So enough phoniness. I can't take it anymore. Let's go be ourselves and show the world that we're meant to be together."

"No. One time I really cut loose and look what happened."

"So you're embarrassed. So what?"

He always got his way, and this time I wanted to win. I leveled my gaze at him and said slowly, "Get out, Hamlet."

"I can't believe this," he said, standing. "How long am I supposed to stay away?"

"I don't know. Until this all blows over, I guess."

He smirked and said, "I've spent some time studying those pictures, and I can honestly say that if *I* were one of our parents, it'd be a long time till I'd let it blow over." I nodded, and he sauntered toward me suggestively. "I'm afraid that's going to be too long."

Despite myself, I felt my resolve vanishing. "Then go back to school and it won't seem so long."

"I'm too depressed to go back to school. I can't be without you," he answered, creeping even closer.

My heart started pulsing, and invisible hands pushed me to him. "Yeah, you seem real depressed."

Standing right in front of me, he winked, and it was over. I gave no resistance. My dad wasn't there, and there were no cameras in the apartment, so what harm could it do? I stretched up and let my lips brush his. His mouth twitched into a smile and he took a mini step forward; our bodies were close enough to exchange heat, but we didn't touch.

"Should I go?" he asked.

I shook my head, took his hand in mine, and walked him toward my room.

He stopped in the doorway and kissed me, pressing his whole body against mine.

Something in his sweatshirt pocket jabbed into my ribs. I yelped and stepped back.

"Oh," he said, frowning. "Sorry." He stepped away and reached into his pocket. He pulled out a gun and set it on my dresser. Seriously. A gun.

I took a few steps back, my face suddenly numb. "Why do you have that?" I asked, afraid I might know.

"Claudius is trying to have me killed. What am I supposed to do?"

I leaned on the wall, unable to take my eyes off the jet-black handgun, as if watching it closely could keep it from firing on its own. "I'm not a fan of Claudius either, but are you sure you're not just being paranoid?"

"He canceled my security detail, for starters. That's how the photographer was able to get into the party. And I got some information from Marcellus that makes me really suspicious about Claudius's other plans. I'd rather be paranoid than dead."

The word *dead* hung in the air between us. Hearing it felt no more significant or real than talking about characters from a play. Yet this was his life, our life, so I tried to be sensible. "So you're not planning to, like, do anything to him first, are you?"

Hamlet grabbed a hat that was hanging on my closet handle and threw it over the gun, which released me from its hypnotizing effect. When I finally looked back at Hamlet, his face was eerily calm given the subject at hand. His blue eyes were soft and his voice soothing as he said, "You're worrying too much. I knew you were miserable, and I wanted to see you." Stepping forward and tucking strands of hair behind my ears, he added, "But you didn't expect me to come back home unprotected, did you?"

I shook my head slowly, hoping he was telling me the truth.

He took my face in his hands and kissed me gently. It almost made me forget about the gun.

The next day he came back, and the next, and the next. We got pretty comfortable with our routine and our privacy. And complacent. We didn't take into account the possibility that my father might have a budget meeting requiring files that he might have forgotten in his study. I was trying to finish a paper while Hamlet sat on my bed flipping through magazines when we heard the elevator door open. We froze. My father walked directly to his study, so I was nearly ready to consider us safe. I listened to his footsteps come down his hall then stop abruptly in the sitting room. Double-time he pounded through the apartment and filled my doorway holding a pair of sneakers. Hamlet always kicked them off when he walked in. My father looked at Hamlet and then at me with ferocious disappointment, almost more than the morning we came back from Wittenberg. He dropped the sneakers and whipped back around without speaking. I heard the elevator doors open and shut, and then silence.

I put my face in my hands and listened to my breath echo off my palms. The veins in my neck were throbbing, and my ears filled with a panicked whine. Hamlet sank to his knees next to my chair and gently pulled my hands away from my face.

I squeezed his hands in mine and said softly, "You should go."

"Cat's out of the bag now...." he replied.

I didn't even want to think about the cat or the bag or the little mouse the cat was going to murder when it finished with its meeting upstairs. "Go, Hamlet," I insisted.

He looked up earnestly and explained, "But I feel so much better when I'm with you. Don't make me go off by myself. I think too much when I'm alone."

I sat picturing my dad's disappointed face but also knowing that Hamlet *did* think too much when he was alone and that he'd been almost himself since he'd returned from Wittenberg and that I really did want him to stay. Even so, I couldn't. Not that day. I shook my head.

Hamlet's eyes darkened and he sat back on his haunches. "So you'd choose your dad over me?"

"What are you talking about?"

"You are choosing to play the obedient daughter rather than do what you know is right for you...and me? You're not a child anymore."

My temper was starting to rise. "No, I'm not, but he asked me, and I have to respect that."

"And I'm asking you to be with me."

"I can't."

He stood up. "Give me a break, Ophelia. If you really wanted to be with me, you would."

"Don't be so dramatic. This isn't forever."

"Maybe it should be."

"What?"

His eyes were full of accusation and fury. "Choose. Choose now."

"Don't," I begged.

"Choose."

"You don't want me to do that." It was both a plea and a threat.

"Choose," he said slowly, his eyes mere slits.

I stood to match his gaze, fuming. "I have put everything aside to be with you. Everything. My friends. My ambition. Don't make a face. I used to have it. But in the last few months, I let everything else slide. You want to know what I want? Well, so do I! But I can't see past this little world we have when we're together. I can't see a future that doesn't include you."

He took a step forward, as if those last words were encouraging him, but I put my hand up to stop his progress and continued. "Hamlet, as much as it's crushed me when we've broken up, it's almost a relief, because it forces me to think about myself. But then you change your mind. And every time you've wanted to get back together, I've said yes. Every time you've asked for forgiveness, I've given it. Everything that's mine has been yours. For as long as I can remember, it's been this way. It was my choice to give up everything, but this time I need something. I need to obey my father for a while. Let me do this."

"Let you? What kind of relationship do you imagine we have?" He yanked on the hood of his sweatshirt, but didn't go. "Do what you want."

"Like you? You let yourself be manipulated by responsibility and by your mother. You might hem and haw, even break from what's expected once in a while, but you always come back to what you have to do. You always end up agreeing to what your mother wants."

"Not anymore," he said, his fists clenching and unclenching. Then he touched his pocket, where I could only assume he was keeping the gun I'd seen earlier.

I didn't want to think about it, so I refocused on our fight. "Well, she still controls me. And if I'm with you, she always will. She will be the wedge between us forever. How long can we stand up to that? And at what point will your responsibilities come between us?"

"It'll be different when I'm in charge."

"When will that be? Claudius is young enough that he could be in power for twenty years, easy. Are we going to sneak around until then? This is crazy. We should just—" I stopped myself and stood frozen but for the rise and fall of my chest as irregular breaths escaped. I had thought it but couldn't bring myself to say it. Couldn't think about the pain I would cause him. Couldn't think of what it would mean for me. And I loved him. How could I say it if I loved him?

"What?" he asked.

Drawing strength from the core of my being, I forced out, "End it now. Before it gets even harder." Pressure on my lungs ceased my ability to say more. I wanted to take back what I'd just said and hold him. I wanted to push him out the door and start a new life for myself.

He stared at me. Only the traffic outside filled the silence. He pulled his hood lower on his forehead and shoved his hands in his pockets. "Is that what you want?"

"Yes," I said. His face fell, and my stomach contracted. "No," I whispered. I had thought that once I said it, it would be real and done and I would feel better. But it only made me more confused. All strength left my legs and I sank against my desk. "I don't know."

He grabbed the magazines I had left on the floor and threw them across the room before racing out. He forgot his sneakers but didn't bother to come back for them. I sat in misery, watching the empty doorway, hoping he would return and hoping he wouldn't.

That night, my father didn't come speak to me, which was actually worse than if he had yelled. I spent the balance of the afternoon and evening worrying about Hamlet, and feeling both sorry and relieved that we had broken up. I waited for my father to lecture me, to share allegories and sayings meant to defend his point of view, and to have him remind me for the umpteenth time about the public nature of our private lives. I would almost have welcomed being reprimanded over what did happen. I had given up on dinner, which had grown cold and clotted-looking, and sat on the couch watching the television absently when he entered. He looked around to see if I was alone, sighed, and walked to his room, shutting the door behind him.

My insides roiled. If my father wouldn't even give me the chance to tell him that I'd finally done what he'd asked, then what the hell was the point of having broken Hamlet's heart? And my own. But maybe I had actually been looking for an excuse to end things. Hamlet was scaring me. Talk of murder and suicide and ghosts was too much, and I knew if I stayed close to him, I'd get sucked further into his plans. And that thought scared me more than trying to come up with a Hamlet-less identity. Completely wrung out, I went to my room.

Francisco: By cutting off communication with Hamlet, you intentionally drove him deeper into madness.
Ophelia: Is that a question?
Francisco: Yeah, smartmouth, it is.

Ophelia: You're wondering if that was my plan? *(pause)* I felt terrible about it, but my father asked me to.

Francisco: He also asked you not to date Hamlet from the outset.

Ophelia: I tried to be a good daughter.

Barnardo: You failed Hamlet and your father.

Ophelia: That is so—

Barnardo: What?

Ophelia: If I tell you to screw yourself, will you arrest me?

Barnardo: Yes.

Ophelia: Then never mind.

14

Zara shows a picture of Ophelia in her school uniform sitting close to Sebastian. "Who's this?"

Ophelia shifts in her seat, her face stony. "A friend from school."

"Just a friend?" Zara asks, her voice full of untold information.

Ophelia looks at her hard. "Yeah."

"Mm-hm." Zara flips her hair as another photo comes up of two college guys in Wittenberg T-shirts standing in front of Hamlet's fraternity house. "Who are these guys?"

Ophelia shrugs. "Friends of Hamlet's, I guess."

A new picture comes up of Ophelia standing with the same guys while holding a cup of coffee.

"Clearly you talked to them," Zara presses her.

Ophelia shrugs again and looks like she might yawn. "People talk to me a lot. Doesn't mean I know them."

Zara crosses her arms, looks at her producer, and then turns to the audience with a dazzling smile. "Well, ladies, they sure make 'em cute at Wittenberg, huh?"

The audience applauds.

I couldn't sleep at all that night, tossing and turning and regretting what I'd done. How could I live without him? But how could I stay with him? I was damned no matter what I did. I missed him. It had been only half a day and I genuinely missed him.

I watched the hours tick by. There was a part of me that thought Hamlet might sneak into my room as he had for weeks, and that we would embrace and maybe cry and definitely say we were both sorry for being stupid. At least I would. And he should. He should have been sorry for dragging me out of bed to the conservatory only to yell at me. He should have been sorry for bringing a gun to my room and acting like it was no big deal. He should have been sorry for throwing my magazines and telling me that obeying my father was wrong.

My fury swelled, and I tossed angrily in bed until I started thinking about him wandering the castle all night with no one to trust and no one to talk to, surrounded by people who would all profit from his downfall. I even sat up once and started to put on my shoes, ready to go find him. But then I thought again of that gun and slipped back under my sheets, watching the minutes pass and the sky grow light.

After the sun rose, I went to the coffee shop across the street from the castle, intending to order whatever they had that was sweet and strong. *Like I like my men*, I joked to myself, but even thinking that put me in a snit.

"Ophelia," a voice said behind me.

I spun around and saw two guys around my age whose faces I didn't know. I turned back and paid for my coffee, planning to walk away from the counter as quickly as possible.

"Damn, that's rude," said the taller one to his friend, or me, or both of us.

"Do I know you?"

"Billy Rosencrantz."

"Dave Guildenstern."

When I showed no sign of recognition, they went on. "We met at Wittenberg. You probably heard us called by our last names."

"I don't go to Wittenberg," I said, even more irritated, used to confused posers but not in the mood to humor one just then.

Guildenstern sneered. "I know. You were visiting. You were pretty drunk, so…"

All of a sudden I remembered them. "I wasn't that drunk," I said. "I remember now. You had on beanies."

"Yeah," Rosencrantz said, frowning and pulling at his baseball cap.

"So why are you here?" I asked.

"Oh, the queen invited us personally," Guildenstern said, exchanging a smile with Rosencrantz.

"Really," I said. I couldn't think of one occasion when Gertrude had invited anyone to the castle on behalf of Hamlet. Even his birthday parties had been arranged by a social secretary.

Guildenstern said, "Wanted us to cheer him up. Hamlet, that is."

"Hamlet?" I asked, trying not to lose it at the mention of his name. "Why you?"

Rosencrantz leaned casually on the counter holding the sugar and cream canisters and explained, "We're friends with him."

"You are?"

"From school," Guildenstern said slowly, as if I were a stupid child.

The coffee was burning my hands, and as much as I wanted to throw it at them or just get away, I wanted to know what was happening more. "I've never heard him talk about you."

Rosencrantz answered, "Maybe he doesn't tell you everything."

"I'm sure he doesn't," Guildenstern said, looking at Rosencrantz, and they snickered.

I felt really peevish and exposed, and was tempted to ask what they meant, but then thought better of it. Did I even want to know? "How would the queen know to ask for you two?" I prodded, steering the conversation away from my possible humiliation and toward theirs, if I was lucky.

Guildenstern answered, "Our dads have been working for Claudius on a PR project. Claudius wants a profile done of himself. A soft news piece, you know. Make him look good as the new king. While they were meeting, my dad asked Claudius how Hamlet was doing, said that I hadn't seen him in a while and was worried." Guildenstern puffed himself up.

Rosencrantz smiled. "And when he and the queen learned that we had been friends at school, they asked us to come and try to cheer up Hamlet."

"And did you?" I asked.

"Cheer him up? I think so," he answered.

I thought of how angry Hamlet had been the day before and could not imagine what could have turned his mood around so quickly.

Rosencrantz went on to explain. "We had met up with Wittenberg's improv comedy troupe at a rest stop off the highway. They were coming to Elsinore, too, which was totally random. When we got here, we told Hamlet about them, and he was really excited and ran off to work with them on something or other."

It struck me as weird, given how upset we'd both been the night before, that he was excited about anything, let alone a comedy troupe. But I needed to keep my focus on these guys and why they'd come to Elsinore. I asked, "So what's in it for you…being here?"

"Seeing Hamlet," replied Rosencrantz. He glanced at Guildenstern, who looked like he wanted to get away as soon as possible. Their little intrusion on my peace hadn't quite turned out as they had hoped.

"And?"

"That's not enough?" asked Rosencrantz.

I sighed, feigning boredom.

He looked at Guildenstern, who nodded some kind of permission, so he continued, "Claudius said if we could get Hamlet to forget his troubles a bit, we would get internships here next summer."

"What kind of internship?"

Guildenstern shrugged. "Dunno. Politics. Or PR. Or communications. Whatever."

"You'll be perfect at it," I said, before walking with my cup of coffee out the door and back across the street.

The crowd of tourists that were huddled around the front entrance of the castle started pointing and pulling out their cameras. All I had wanted to do was find Hamlet before having to drag myself to school, but instead I was having an impromptu photo shoot. My hair was a rat's nest and my uniform blouse wasn't tucked in. I figured that when she saw the pictures posted on the Internet later that day, my headmistress would be pissed. She was a stickler about proper uniform etiquette and notorious for lecturing students on how we all represented Elsinore Academy both on campus and off. I knew my father wouldn't be pleased either that I was dumb enough to get caught looking like a freak, which just made the morning that much more craptacular.

When I finally made it past the tourists and into the castle lobby, Marcellus was at the security desk chatting. When I approached, he gestured to the other guard to step aside so we could have some privacy.

"Have you seen Hamlet?" I asked.

"He was in the theater last time I checked."

I looked in the direction of the old castle as if I would miraculously sprout X-ray vision and detect him on its upper floors.

He looped his thumbs through his gun belt. "Aren't you late for class?"

I looked at my watch. "Damn," I mumbled. Mr. Norquest, my first-period teacher, was gonna freak out. Again.

"Been happening a lot lately."

I squinted at Marcellus. "You keeping tabs on me?"

"Someone should. Your dad know what's going on with you at school?"

"What do you mean?" I asked, forcing my face into a mask of innocence.

He leaned back against the security desk and crossed his arms extra slowly. "Well, you don't stay for practice anymore, you're late all the time, and I know you've skipped school completely at least three times a month in as many months." He widened his dark eyes, as if daring me to pretend that he was mistaken.

I tapped my fingers on the polished black counter, unable to dispute it but totally stunned that he'd noticed. "I thought you were in charge of Hamlet."

He cocked his head. "You're important to him, so you're important to me."

"Well then, I guess your job with me is done."

"Trouble in paradise?"

"Trouble in hell." I felt a pressure in my eyes and took a sip of coffee to swallow the lump in my throat. "I actually need to talk to him, though. There were these guys at the coffee shop—forget it. I'm just gonna run up to the theater and—"

Marcellus shook his head. "Go to school, Ophelia. He'll still be here when you come back."

I started to argue but changed my mind. Every second that passed would make the reprimands I got from the school secretary and Mr. Norquest last that much longer.

That afternoon, I ran from the parking garage directly to the theater, climbing three flights of stairs while trying not to spill the cappuccino I'd picked up on the way home. When I reached the landing, I saw that Hamlet was standing alone by the large windows in the theater's lobby. His clothes—the same ones he had been wearing the day before—were wrinkled, and I wondered where he had slept after I told him to leave my place. My heart hammered, and I wanted nothing more than to run to him and take back what I had said about breaking up. But then I reminded myself that this was what needed to be.

"Hamlet?"

He spun around to face me. His face was so weary, so pained.

"You okay?" I asked, more sure that my next words should be an apology.

He shook his head but didn't say anything.

I opened my mouth to speak but hesitated. I wanted to put

my arms around him, to ease his pain, but if we were going to be apart, I had to train myself to keep my distance. I'd also have to stop seeking him out. But I was already there, so I kept my voice clipped and my sympathy in check. "I heard you were up here with a group of improv guys."

"Yeah, the Wit Burgers. They're working on an idea I had for a show."

"A show? When have you ever cared about theater, Hamlet?"

Ignoring my question, he said, "It'll be next week." His eyes brightened for a moment, but then a veil of anger dropped over them. "I thought we weren't talking."

"I'm not sure what we're doing. *I* said we shouldn't hang out until—"

He slammed his palm on the window and growled, "I swear to God, Ophelia, if you say anything about your father I'll flippin' lose it."

My fury flashed, and I considered walking away. But I wanted to discuss those college guys more than I wanted to make him stop being a jerk about my father.

My eyes were mere slits as I returned his glare, and I said slowly, "I came to ask about your friends from school."

"Who?" he asked.

"Two guys. Long last names."

He hit the window again, this time with two hands. "Those bastards were wearing wires."

"Wires?"

He put his forehead on the glass and closed his eyes. "To record our conversations. To get information from me."

I stepped closer and asked, "Get information for who?"

"Claudius and my mother."

"Why would they—"

He turned to look me straight in the eyes. "They want to find out why I'm running around the castle at crazy hours and why I'm angry all the time. As if my mother doesn't know. I'm starting to wonder if she was in on killing my…No, I can't even think of that. Claudius must have acted alone. He must have. *Uch*, I don't know!"

"Hamlet, do you really think that—"

He banged the side of his head on the window a couple of times and looked up at the ornately carved ceiling. "I don't know what to think anymore. I got rid of Rosencrantz and Guildenstern for now, but I'll deal with them when I go back to school. They won't get away with this. No one's getting away with any of this."

The night before, my father's happiness had seemed more important than anything. But standing there with Hamlet, watching him deal with being betrayed by his friends and family, the thought of appeasing my dad suddenly didn't matter. So even though there was a voice in my head warning me that this was all too serious and I should stop trying to heroically save Hamlet by myself, I couldn't help it. You can't just turn off loving someone, and he was my best friend, not just some boyfriend. What other choice did I really have?

I walked closer and put my hand on Hamlet's arm. My touch seemed to quiet him. I said, "I can help you through this."

He closed his eyes and whispered, "No, you can't."

"Let me try."

Gently placing his hand on mine, he said, "I think you were right last night. I think you should listen to your father. It's not safe for you to be with me right now. Everyone has a price, and who knows what's coming next?"

"I can take care of myself. You need someone, Hamlet. Put your trust in me."

Then, stroking my face, he added, his voice urgent, "They'll get to you. It's only a matter of time before my mother and Claudius find a way to get to you, I'm sure of it. I don't want you any more wrapped up in my family's mess than you have to be. Walk away, Ophelia. Get out while you can."

I took a step back, and his hand dropped. I'm not gonna lie: Wondering what his mother and uncle would do next scared me, but the thought of facing the danger without Hamlet was even scarier. I said quietly, "I don't want to walk away. I'm here for you. I love you."

Suddenly he was angry again. "Don't. Don't love me." When I didn't move, his voice got loud enough that it echoed off the lobby walls. "And I can't rely on you. You've already proven that. One embarrassing photo spread and you were willing to throw what we have away."

"That is not fair," I protested, my chin trembling.

"Maybe not. But it's true. Walk away, Ophelia."

I couldn't. I wanted to say something, but I couldn't even manage that. He shook his head, turned his back to me, and disappeared into the theater. After the door whispered shut, I stood waiting for him to come out again. Minutes passed, but the only thing that came out of the theater door was the sound of laughter. Eventually, I threw my coffee in the trash and went home to watercolor my worries away.

Francisco: How well did you know Rosencrantz and Guildenstern?

Ophelia: I didn't.

Francisco: Liar.

Ophelia: I met them a couple of times, but we weren't friends.

Barnardo: Here's a photo of you three together just before things got really crazy. Seems like this meeting was a catalyst.

Ophelia: Big word. I'm impressed.

Barnardo: Tell us what you talked about.

Ophelia: The show Hamlet was planning.

Barnardo: And.

Ophelia: And nothing. *(pause)* Fine. They were brought to Elsinore to spy on Hamlet.

Barnardo: For you?

Ophelia: No. For Claudius.

Francisco: Interesting. We found a document in Claudius's files that says you asked the boys to come.

Ophelia: It's not true.

Barnardo: Your word against theirs. Which one of them should we ask?

15

Zara asks sympathetically, "After your visit to Wittenberg, we understand you and Hamlet broke things off."

"For a while."

"What was that like?"

Ophelia breathes out slowly. "Hard."

"So you missed him?" Zara asks as if she has already answered her own question.

"Sure. But my father asked me not to be with him."

"Did you always listen to your father's requests?" Zara probes.

"More than Hamlet wanted, less than my father would have liked." Ophelia smiles sadly.

Zara nods. "Hard to balance the wishes of two such important men."

Ophelia nods and bites her bottom lip.

Later that evening, I was sitting on the couch reading when Hamlet came out of the elevator. I was relieved to see him, actually, and would have said as much if he hadn't had such a wild look in his eyes. I stayed in my seat and braced myself. I thought for sure he was coming to hit me. He had never been violent toward me, so I don't even know why I thought that was his plan. It's just that no one ever races at you with such speed, with such terrifying anger, if they don't plan on hitting you, I guess. He dashed right for me, and then, of all things, sat on the cushion where I was stretched out. He grabbed my hand, and his was absolutely freezing. He clearly had been outside — on the rooftop would be my guess — yet he had no coat, no gloves, no hat. There was snow on the ground outside, but he was wearing his flip-flops. It was then that I noticed his wet hair and that he wasn't even wearing a shirt under his hoodie. No shirt at all. I couldn't fathom why he was such a wreck. For a split second I thought he had just nailed some girl and that was why he was looking so guilty, but the wet hair, the cold hands…I knew that wasn't it. If I had to pick a cliché, I'd say he looked like he'd seen a ghost. And then I realized that was precisely it. I sat really still and waited for him to tell me he'd seen his father again, hoping he wouldn't because I knew he'd be pissed if I reminded him that I didn't believe in ghosts.

Here's the weirdest thing: He never even said a word. He never spoke; he just looked at me, studied me like he was memorizing my face, like he was going to draw it, or, worse, never see it again. The thought made me shiver. He looked choked, and all that escaped from his tightened throat was a pitiful sigh, not one of relief or fatigue but of strangling pain. Then he stood up and started walking away, only he didn't look at the elevator, he looked at me as he walked. He made it all the way to the elevator, steps we had taken together in joy so many times, and pushed the button without watching what he was doing. The doors slipped shut and the last thing I saw was a sliver of his pained face.

I raced to push the button, but it was too late.

What had I expected if I did catch him? Was I planning on stopping him? I knew it wouldn't work. Would I join him in ghost hunting? In people hunting? Not a chance. But where did that leave me? I was being pushed more and more to the outside of Hamlet's life—or had I moved myself there?—and I was both relieved by and hated that fact. Not getting involved with revenge and schemes seemed the safer, saner choice, but it meant that I had to wait for the drama and the information to come to me, and I wasn't one to wait around. And now that it *had* come—whatever it was that had just happened when Hamlet walked through my door—it was finally too scary for me to deal with alone.

By the time the elevator came, I was so undone, so perplexed, I knew the only choice I had was to tell my father what had happened. I hurried to his office, passing his secretary without stopping to answer her questions. My father was clearly in the middle of something, but I didn't give him a chance to tell me to wait.

"Dad," I panted, "something's wrong with Hamlet. I mean, really wrong."

"What's happened?" he asked.

After I told him what I had seen in our apartment, carefully not mentioning the gun or the talk of ghosts and death and revenge, he asked if I thought Hamlet was sick with love. I was shocked. Love? Who on Earth acts that insane over love? I couldn't imagine it. He seemed more suicidal or homicidal than lovesick. I was about to tell my dad as much when I realized that if he thought this was about love, he might allow me to be with Hamlet again, though just then, I wasn't sure I wanted to be. I realized I was staring, and I had to say something. All I could think to answer was, "I don't know, Dad, but it scared me."

"Have you spoken harshly to him lately?" he asked.

My father's tone infuriated me. "You told me not to talk to him and not to see him! I sent him away. I refused to communicate with him and said nothing would change until you said otherwise." I left out the part about our last two arguments.

My father nodded approvingly, then knitted his brow and said, "I was wrong when I said not to speak with him." He put his arm around my shoulder as he escorted me out of his office. "I'm going to talk to Gertrude and Claudius about this."

I stopped walking. "No, Dad. Don't do that. This is between me and Hamlet."

He shook his head. "I think it is larger than the two of you. No man is an island."

Realizing my error in going to my father, I begged, "Dad, please don't."

"Nonsense. I will tell them about Hamlet's visit to you and show them one of your e-mails—"

"How do you have—" I began, but realized I just didn't want to know what kind of access he had to my computer and accounts. Things were getting too weird, and I couldn't take another revelation. I decided on a different question and tried not to sound as horrified as I felt. "Which one?"

He went to his computer and clicked a few times, and the printer whirred. He put on his glasses and read, "'Doubt that the stars are fire / Doubt that the sun moves / Doubt truth to be a liar / But never doubt I love.'" He slid his reading glasses to the tip of his nose and, peering over the frame, added, "He's quite a poet, that prince of yours."

"I *doubt* he made it up," I said, pushing away the memory

of how I had melted reading that same message a few weeks before. "God, how could you? That's an old e-mail, and it's private!"

"No such thing, my sweet. I am doing this to help you. As the Bible says, 'A good name is more desirable than great riches, and loving favor is better than silver and gold.' Claudius and Gertrude are eager to find out the reason for Hamlet's strange behavior, and I am anxious for them to forgive you for the party. Perhaps if you provide the key to unlocking this mystery, they'll come around. I'll bring this e-mail, swear it is love that is the source of the problem, and I will promise they can take my job if I am wrong."

"Dad, no! Don't do that."

He patted my arm. "Nothing ventured, nothing gained. Go back to the apartment and wait for me," he declared, paper in hand.

Back home, I waited in misery. Only the irritating ticking of our one nondigital clock broke the silence. It wasn't going to work, and my father would be fired because of me. I tried to remind myself that it had been his choice and to reassure myself that he could find other work. He was well liked and had had a long career as an adviser. He could parlay that into something. At the very least, he could hit the lecture circuit and let rich people pay for him to offer platitudes and anecdotes instead of making the rest of us suffer them for free. Or maybe it was time for him to retire. My stomach turned. Whether or not it was his decision to offer up his job, it would be a shame if his storied career ended because of a relationship he was against from the outset.

Leaning on the kitchen island, I tried to think back on when my father had begun to mistrust Hamlet so much.

Hamlet's parents were often traveling or at formal occasions, so rather than leaving him at the mercy of the court nannies, my parents invited him to spend evenings with us. They had treated him like a second son, especially my mother. Once we started dating, however, everything changed, especially for my father. They still invited him over, but less frequently, and they were more watchful of us. My door always had to be open, they always seemed to have questions to ask one of us, and they frequently had to get things that could, mysteriously, only be found in my room. It became laughable some nights by the third or fourth pop-in. Hamlet wanted to hang out elsewhere, but my parents wouldn't allow it on weeknights. Weekends, we were on our own, and I knew they were anxious about what we were doing, though they never asked.

I slept with Hamlet for the first time the night of my mother's funeral. The days between her death and the funeral were intense and showed me the best of what Hamlet was—giving, funny, and astute. Those days, he rarely left my apartment, insisting that he skip school to be with me, bringing me food, movies, listening to me cry, making me laugh. My father was a wreck but was busy with plans and trying to hide his grief from us. Laertes stayed in his room much of the time. Hamlet was what they couldn't be. Our importance in each other's lives solidified the day my mother was killed instead of his father.

As soon as my mother's funeral was over, Laertes went back to school, and my father stayed with Hamlet's parents, as well as with his colleagues, until late into the night. Hamlet and I slipped off to my apartment, and I remember the sinking feeling I had when I realized that, without my mom around, no one noticed I was even gone. And that feeling got mixed up with my nervousness at being alone with Hamlet, with suggesting what I was about to suggest. It was a confusing time — a time when my desire to push away my pain got mixed up with my desire to be with Hamlet, to replace pain with pain, or pain with love. I didn't know which. But I knew I loved Hamlet and that he loved me. And so I let the warmth of his hand on mine quiet my fears.

All the lights had been off except the one in my parents' bedroom. I stopped and listened for movement, but no one was there. My dad had just forgotten to turn the light off before heading to the funeral. It was the kind of thing my mother, used to my father's distractibility, would have checked on before leaving.

Trying to hold it together, I walked quickly to my room, Hamlet in tow. I grabbed my pajamas and slipped into the bathroom to change without saying anything. When I came out, Hamlet had taken off his suit jacket and tie and was sitting on my bed, leaning against the wall. He smiled the smallest of smiles while reaching a hand out to me. As I approached, I noticed his eyes were filled with worry. Something in his expression worked its way into my emptiness. I walked over to him, rested one knee on the bed, and asked him to have sex with me.

He was surprised, especially since I had been the one pushing away his advances all along. He sat up straighter. "Do you think today is —"

"Yes. Today. This is the perfect day," I insisted, sitting down and facing him, my hands shaking. "I don't want this day to be the day my mother was buried. I want to remember it as the day we first slept together, the day I lost my virginity."

He frowned and took my hand. "Ophelia, I don't know. I mean, take some time. You're pretty emotional and —"

"I want to do it, and I want to do it with you. I want to

know what all the fuss is about, and I want my first time to be with someone I trust."

He hesitated and scooted a few inches away, dropping my hand. "You know I want to, but Phee, this has been a big day… and what you're asking…it's forever. You can't undo it once it's done."

I was feeling a little frantic; I had to make him understand how important this was to me. I inched forward and clutched his leg. "I won't want to undo anything. This is what I want."

He was almost as nervous as I was, I think. He was shaking and stopped a few times to make sure I still wanted to go through with it. When he finally pushed himself inside me, I started to cry. I had to urge him to go on, and he looked so worried. It was overwhelming to be completely connected to someone and to have it come with such pain. All I could think about was my mother buried mere miles from where her baby was leaving behind the last of her childhood.

He kissed me as tears melted down my cheeks. "I love you," he whispered.

"I love you, too," I whispered back, both to him and to my mom, whom I wanted to know I had found love.

I'm not sure how much time passed between my father going to Gertrude and Claudius with my e-mail and the elevator doors opening. Long or short, it didn't matter. The meeting had not gone well.

My father shouted from within, "Come with me now!"

I popped up, stunned by the change in his mood, and grabbed my shoes. I put them on inside as the doors were closing. When I stood back up, he wouldn't look at me. His hands, which held what I can only assume was my e-mail, twisted and mangled the paper. His knuckles were white, and the rest of his hands were deep red. He muttered under his breath, but I couldn't hear what he said. I noticed that the back of his neck, the part sticking above the collar of his white dress shirt, was the same color as his hands. I tapped my feet anxiously while I tried to figure out what had happened. If given a million guesses, I never would have guessed what was coming.

"I thought…" Gertrude began, once I was standing before her, "No, I was *sure* that those pictures of you at that party would have been the end of the humiliation you would bring upon my family, but it seems I was wrong." She sniffed and crossed her arms, leaning daintily on the edge of her desk.

My mouth was dry and I wanted to sit down, too, but if she didn't sit on a chair, I was expected to stand.

Claudius, who was standing next to Gertrude, his arms also crossed and his face set, continued. "Just this evening we received a disturbing message. A threat really. A video of you and Hamlet…how shall I say?…engaged in…indelicate acts…has been uncovered."

I wrapped my arms around myself and squeezed hard, as if covering my suddenly naked body. I turned to look at my father, who had retreated to the wall and had loosened his tie. "How can that be?" I asked. "Hamlet and I never recorded…" I couldn't continue. I shuddered and wound my arms tighter across my chest.

"Who's to say how these things happen?" Gertrude said in a clipped voice. "The point is," she continued, tapping her fingertips together quickly, "it is in the hands of someone who wants to hurt us, and that someone is demanding money. Now, we are willing to pay to keep you safe from public scorn, but in return, you must do something for us."

"What?" I rasped.

Claudius leaned back on the dark wood desk next to his wife. Sinking down, a whisper of a smile on his face, he explained, "We need you to get information from Hamlet."

"What kind of information?" I asked, swallowing hard.

Gertrude straightened up and touched her French knot. "Ask him why he's been behaving so strangely. Find out his plans. He's been so secretive lately. Your father says that love is the reason, but we're not convinced."

I put up my hands, gesturing for them to stop. None of it made sense. I wanted to ask where the video was taken. And how. Hamlet and I never had sex in a public place. Not once. I wondered momentarily if Hamlet had secretly taped us, but I dismissed the idea. He was a lot of things, but sleazy wasn't one of them. It didn't have to be Hamlet, I realized with dismay. All kinds of people had access to every room and crawl space in the castle. It could have been anyone. Hamlet had warned that someone would try to get to me. I should have believed him.

"I don't understand," I said. "It seems to me that paying would be in your best interest. I mean, Hamlet's in the video, too."

Claudius took a step forward and was suddenly too close. "Let us just say that there's far more of you to be worried about."

My arms, which had slipped down, popped back across my chest and I stepped away from Claudius. "I'm not doing this. You've been using everyone to get to Hamlet, and I'm not going to allow myself to be used by you."

Gertrude sniffed and began walking to sit behind her desk. "Then the video will come out. And you will leave the castle. Indefinitely."

I spun around to face my father. "Dad," I begged.

"Do this, Ophelia. Or leave my home."

I couldn't believe he meant it. And yet, deep inside, I knew he and I had reached the breaking point. He no longer wanted to deal with my crap. He had warned me, as had my mother, that being with Hamlet would come at a price. What never occurred to me was that my family would end up paying, not just me. Protecting me blindly was no longer an option for him, and, even if it was, I couldn't ask him to do it.

I shifted from foot to foot, looking at my three accusers. "I'll make it easy for everyone. I'll leave tomorrow for Paris and live with Laertes for a while."

Claudius snarled, his gaze drifting the length of my body. "If those images come out, there won't be a person in the Western world who won't know your face…etcetera." He squinted at me, and the corners of his mouth turned up slightly again.

I took another step back. If I didn't like the way he was looking at me, how would I feel about the rest of the world doing the same? It was humiliating enough when my clothes had been on and the pictures published just showed a kiss. But more? I shuddered and shut my eyes tight, trying not to imagine what might be on the video.

But then a thought occurred to me. "How do I know you're not making this up? Dad, have you even seen the video?"

"I didn't want to," he said, pulling at his face.

"Well, I do," I announced, not really sure that I did but certain that if I watched, I would make sure my dad was elsewhere.

Gertrude smoothed her skirt. "Security has it locked away. It's for the best."

I gritted my teeth. "Why should I believe you?"

"Do you have a birthmark on your left hip?" Claudius asked, his eyes twinkling.

I hesitated and said yes.

"And you like being kissed by Hamlet on the neck?" he pressed.

My father leaped out of his seat. "Enough!" He turned to me. "Ophelia, you will do this or, so help me, I will never speak to you again."

I couldn't lose my dad. Not over Hamlet. I would do what they wanted, even though I knew I would never forgive myself for it.

Quietly I said, "I'll talk to him tomorrow."

"And one more thing," Claudius said, his smirk clear to see if anyone else had been looking at him. "Hamlet is going to a charity function tomorrow morning, and you will ride with him. During that drive, you'd best get some information. And since we don't trust that you will tell us the truth about what Hamlet might say, your father and I will be in the car with you. Hidden in front, of course."

I sucked in my breath and looked over my shoulder. My dad was sitting with his back to me, his head in his hands. My own head dropped. "Fine," I said, trying not to think of how I was joining the long line of deceivers waiting to bring Hamlet down. Hamlet knew me better than I knew myself, and he had been right not to trust in me. Once again, I regretted confiding in my father. And I regretted that I had ever been brought to live at the castle.

I had planned on going home but hit the button for the basement level instead. I walked out of the elevator following the trail of fluorescent lights to an anonymous, freshly painted white door and knocked. It swung open quickly, revealing three walls of small television screens all showing different parts of the castle. I gasped when I spotted a black-and-white image of my father sitting in his office.

"What the— Ophelia!" exclaimed the short blond security officer who had reached behind his swivel chair to open the door. He leaped up and moved to block my view of the TV screens in the room.

A guard with a dark beard and angry eyes rose from his chair and flicked a switch, turning all of the TVs off. "How did you find this room?"

"I've lived in the castle my whole life. Security has always been here."

"What do you want?" growled the dark-haired one.

"I—"

"Get out," he barked.

"When we were kids, the guards always let us—"

"Well, you're not a child anymore."

"No kidding," said the blond guard, his blue eyes sparkling.

I wanted to twist the smirk off his face but was so shamed by the insinuation in his voice that all I could do was look at my feet. What had he seen? Where the hell were those cameras?

The dark-haired guy stepped closer. "The rules are different now. You are never to come here again."

His tone was definite to the point of being a threat, so I backed away. He slammed the door, and I heard it lock.

"Damn it," I muttered as I headed back down the hall. A camera was pointed right at the elevator, so I turned and headed for the stairwell.

As I reached for the door, Marcellus opened it and we both jumped in surprise.

"Ophelia, what are you doing here?"

"Nothing. I'm leaving." I squeezed past him and started up the stairs, unsure of what those men knew, but wanting to run away from their leers.

"Hey, are you all right?"

I hesitated. Marcellus was nice, but he wasn't a friend. Until recently, we had never exchanged more than a few words. His job was to be invisible to us, a menace to others, and a pair of watchful eyes. I had only seen him laugh twice, both about some comment Hamlet made directly to him. At all other times, Marcellus was professional, impenetrable. He could be trusted with our lives, but I didn't know if he could be trusted with my secrets.

When I offered no reply, he asked, "Can I help?"

I hesitated again. "I came...I wanted to know about the cameras."

"What about them?"

"Where they are. What they see."

This time, it was Marcellus who filled the stairwell with silence. His eyes glanced into the corner and I saw a little red light. Another camera. A small one. So small you wouldn't have seen it if you weren't looking for it. He turned his back to it and lowered his voice. "I can't tell you that." Then he added, even softer, "But I can tell you there are more than you think."

My gaze met his. I chewed on my lips and absently twisted one leg around the other. Gripping the railing, I tried to remember what I had seen in that brief moment in the security room. Elevators, the rooftop, offices. What else? The lobby, the old castle's staircase. It was too quick. Had I seen any of the residences? I couldn't remember.

"What specifically are you asking about?" he asked.

My face flushed. "I was just wondering what they've seen...

of me and, uh…" I wanted to fold into myself rather than finish the sentence. "Hamlet."

Marcellus's eyes widened in understanding, and he looked away. Did it mean he had seen it and was embarrassed to tell me? Or was he embarrassed by my asking? By the time he spoke, his face had settled into professional neutrality.

"I'm not aware of anything that would…cause you special concern. But since Hamlet is my charge, I can ask around."

"They'll know I'm the one who wants to know," I answered.

"Let me handle the others. I've been here longer than most. Though you wouldn't know it, since the king—" He stopped himself. "I'll get back to you."

I nodded and pinched my eyes shut again at the thought of my dad seeing anything that I did with Hamlet.

Marcellus leaned in close and whispered, "Meantime, Ophelia, watch your step 'round here. I can't say I understand anyone's motivations anymore."

If he were a different man, he might have patted my shoulder or cheek. But he stood rod-straight and strode back into the hall toward the security room.

The next morning, when Hamlet saw me sitting in the limo, he started to walk away.

"Please come in," I called after him.

He hesitated.

"Just let me ride with you, okay?" I asked, trying to sound calm. "We need to talk."

His jaw was clenched and his face was flushed, but he got in anyway. Dark purple circles rimmed his bloodshot eyes, and his hair was completely askew. His clothes were even more wrinkled than the day we'd spoken outside the theater, and I had to wonder again where he was living. Somewhere in the castle, I assumed, but not, perhaps, in his room. But why had he stopped taking care of himself completely? Gone was the effortlessly hot guy I'd known forever, replaced by someone who seemed to find living itself a trial.

My heart was pounding. I wanted to reach up and turn off the intercom, to grab Hamlet and kiss him despite all that had happened. But the thought of the video and of being kicked out of my home kept me in my place, literally and figuratively. The limo began to move. I thought of the crowded seat up front and prayed it would be a short, painless, fruitless drive that would be enough to get those intrusive men off my back.

"You getting any sleep?" I asked, barely above a whisper.

He shrugged.

"Are you eating?"

"A little."

I bit my lip. "I'm worr—"

"No you're not. And if you wanted to check up on me, you could have just asked Marcellus," he snapped. "What do you really want, Ophelia?"

I reached deep inside myself for the strength to tell a string of lies. "Hamlet, I wanted to give you back some of your things. Some of the gifts you…" I opened my backpack and pulled out a T-shirt from a band we'd seen play and some CDs he'd burned for me, all of which I was finding especially hard to offer over at that moment. Pretending to not want those treasures, knowing my father and Claudius were on the other side of the partition listening to my every word, my stomach ached.

"I never gave you those," he said, looking with irritation out the window.

This surprised me more than anything else he could have said. Did he know someone was listening? Was he just being contrary? Was he accusing me of cheating? I tried not to show my shock, and replied, "You know you did. They were heartfelt and I loved them when you gave them to me." I thought of his face as he had walked away from me outside the theater and tried to use that image to help me continue with what I was supposed to say. "But now...since we're not together, I don't want them. I can't even look at them anymore." He didn't move to take them, so I tossed the pile onto the seat next to him.

We sat in silence for a few moments. I was determined to say nothing more. I had done what I had promised to do.

Suddenly he asked, "Are you honest?"

I was confused. Was he asking about my reasons for returning the stuff? Was he asking about my faithfulness? Did he know our conversation was being overheard? After a pause that I felt sure would give away my guilt, I clasped my hands, willing them to stop shaking, and asked, "What do you mean?"

"Have you ever been honest with me?"

"I've always been honest," I answered, trying not to sound as guilty as I felt.

He studied me for a moment, his face looking as if he were trying to puzzle out the meaning of one of the abstract paintings he found so laughable. "It's a shame you're so beautiful. It's easy to hide one's true self with beauty, don't you think? No one ever looks past the outside to see the filth that truly lies inside."

I took a moment to compose myself before I spoke, letting his word *filth* hang in the air. He had to know someone was listening. Or if he did not, he truly hated me. Never, in all the times we had broken up, was he anything but jovial and reassuring. He had never insulted me. It was always an attempt "to be practical," which was a thinly veiled excuse to play the field. But this…was new, and it hurt. "I don't know why you're saying this."

"You're suggesting that I loved you once," he said.

I whispered, "You made me believe it."

"You shouldn't have. I never loved you."

I looked for signs of a laugh that would follow this ridiculous statement, a laugh that would be used to placate me. But no laugh came. "Wow. Then I…am a fool," I said.

His face was blank. How could he make such a claim so calmly? He was the one who freaked out when I told him we shouldn't talk for a while. He was the one who reached for me each time I came near. He was the one who whispered words of love and sent the kind of messages only someone with feelings, real feelings, for another person could write. Or was I wrong? All the times I tried to protect myself. All the times I tried to listen to Laertes (if not my father) and keep Hamlet at a distance…Each time Hamlet begged me to be his, to surrender to this love. I did. My brother asked it best: "R u stupid?" burned in my mind. Maybe I was.

I turned to the partition behind me, hoping someone would understand that this was enough. I had been humiliated and the game was over. But there was no movement, so I took a moment to wipe away my tears and see my own anguished expression in the smoky reflection.

He got onto his knees, leaned close to my face, and whispered, "Men are pigs. Don't believe any of us."

Then he kissed me. I was angry and confused, unsure of whether to give in or to push him away. Every moment since he'd opened the door had been so wrong, and kissing Hamlet always felt right. But this was different. If a kiss could be revenge, this was it. Its aggression deepened my fear.

And yet, part of me thought that his final words might be the key. Maybe this was an act, and the kiss was to let me know he knew others were watching. I thought that maybe if I kissed him back, he might know I understood. Or if he was serious, my kiss might make him remember that we loved each other and remind him that I was not the enemy.

Wanting to erase all of the trickery I had committed in luring him into the conversation in the first place, I kissed him back. I let him pull me down onto the seat. But then I remembered we weren't alone, and I turned my head toward the partition. I tried to push away, panic-stricken by the thought of my father witnessing any of what we were doing.

Hamlet pulled back and asked, "Where's your father?"

Involuntarily, my gaze went to the control panel above our heads. He saw me look at it and, seeing the red Speak button lit, reached for the adjacent Open Partition button, but the window separating us from the front seat did not budge. He pushed the button harder, and when the window still didn't move, he stared at me.

"Why is this locked?" He slapped at the thin plate of plastic with his palm, calling, "Lower this right now!" When nothing happened, he turned to me. "Who's up there?"

I opened my mouth but could not admit to my crime.

He reached into his pocket and I thought he might be grabbing for his gun. My hands flew to cover my head, and a strangled cry escaped my throat. But if he was going to shoot, he changed his mind and instead began pounding the black partition wildly, his face reddening.

"Enough!" I yelled, both to Hamlet and to my father, who I hoped could still hear.

There was a *click* and a *whir* as the partition began to lower, revealing a full front seat. Hamlet's look wasn't even angry at first, just blank. Then the scale of my betrayal sank in, and he reached for the door handle. He opened the door and looked as if he were going to jump out while the car was charging down the street. My father yelled, and the driver slammed on the brakes, throwing us all forward. Hamlet fell against my seat. He scrambled up and grabbed at me. Holding me down, he snarled, "You two-faced bitch!" His weight pressed down, pushing the air out of my lungs. His face was twisted with fury, and in his eyes was more pain than I thought could be expressed in a look.

My father, who had been in the middle seat, was trying to grab Hamlet through the now-open partition while Claudius jumped out of the car and opened the door. Hamlet got off me, pushed Claudius out of the way, and managed to close and lock the doors. Hamlet took my father by the shoulders and shoved him so hard that his back hit the dashboard. Then Hamlet raised and locked the partition.

I could hear my father pounding as I whispered to Hamlet, "I'm sorry." Guilt and terror were fighting equally inside me.

He grabbed my shirt collar and pulled himself close to my face again. "If you ever manage to find someone else to be with," he began, spitting venom with every word, "no matter what you do, this will follow you. You will never be able to undo it." His grip tightened, and my shirt cut into the back of my neck. He face was red, and veins were popping at the temples. "And if you ever find someone to marry, make sure he's a fool, because anyone with half a brain knows that women screw up men's lives."

He let go, and I scooted into the corner away from him, but he dove at me again. "Why don't you become a nun? Or a whore? Seems sometimes you are both, no?" The first smile crept across his face, only it wasn't the least bit joyful or kind. He mused on, "Better a nun. Why would you want to bring more sinners into the world?" He patted my stomach, then let his hand drift lower. I tried to push his hand away, but he gripped my jeans, his fingers digging into my flesh. Then he released me and reached for the button to open the sunroof.

I was breathing hard, terrified. As he waited for it to open, I pleaded, "I'm sorry. They made me —"

"I can't take this anymore," he muttered as he climbed onto the roof. "You're making me crazy with these lies!"

I scrambled to unlock the door and bolted out. Hamlet had climbed on the top of the car, attracting the attention of passersby who had not already stopped to watch when our car slammed to a halt and the king emerged unannounced onto the street. Hamlet had his arms up in the air and was addressing the crowd. "I say no one else should marry. Everyone who's married already, except one," he declared, pointing at Claudius, "should go on living as they are, but no one else can marry." He jumped onto the hood of the limo and pointed at me. "Go become a nun, you whore!" he shouted, and ran down the street toward the subway.

"Love?" Claudius yelled at my father. "You still think he's insane with love?" His look was of pure disrespect and distaste for my father, and for me, too. "The kid's just plain insane. And violent. You heard that threat. He means to do all of us harm. I'm sending Hamlet to England. He'll be on a plane by week's end. Maybe that'll do him some good. And if not him, then us." He signaled to the driver, who opened the door for him.

My father came over and tried to put his arms around me. I yanked my body away from him and stumbled down the street.

Ohgod ohgod ohgod, what had I done? How could I have been so stupid? How could I have hurt him like that? I hated myself more than I ever had, more than I ever would. I knew at that moment that I was no better than his mother or Claudius or Rosencrantz or Guildenstern. In fact, I was worse, because I still loved him and, despite what he said, I knew he still loved me, and I chose to hurt him anyway. And if there was a breaking point for him, I had to guess this was it. I wanted to scream or curse or weep or all of the above, but there were people watching, and I didn't want my reaction to become news. As I ran away from my father, I wished I could erase every second of the last ten minutes. No, the last few months.

"What's wrong? Ophelia, why are you crying?" asked Laertes.

I couldn't stop myself long enough to tell him. I leaned against an office building's cinder-block wall, looking through my tears at the end of the deserted alleyway. I hoped no one would come around the corner.

"Is it Dad? Are you hurt? Ophelia, what is it?"

"I…I…" I kept sobbing. I shouldn't have dialed his number. I wanted to confide in him and had calmed down before I hit Send, but as soon as I heard his voice, I fell apart again. "It's nothing," I managed finally.

"It doesn't sound like nothing," he replied, but it was enough of an answer for him to stop asking questions.

"I did a really bad thing to Hamlet."

"Speak of the devil," Laertes replied. "He's on TV. And so

are you. And Dad. What's going on? Why is Hamlet screaming? Has he completely lost his mind?"

I couldn't believe it was out there already. The speed with
which life became news mystified me. It was so fast, I couldn't
even comprehend what had happened—and I was there. I
didn't know how to explain it to Laertes. It was too much, and
I couldn't admit what I did. I was embarrassed for myself. I was
embarrassed for our father. I was embarrassed for Hamlet.

But Hamlet's words stuck in me like a needle. *"You shouldn't
have believed it. I never loved you....No matter what you do, this
will follow you. You will never be able to undo it."*

Aching all over, I moaned, "I hate Hamlet." Yes, I hated
him for how he acted. Even before he realized what was happening in the car, he had hurt me with his indifference and
then his accusations. But, no matter what he had done and
said, I hated myself more for my part in what had followed.

Laertes paused. He had heard me say that I hated Hamlet
so many times over the years. The first few times he had
believed it and had become invested in my upset. Then he
got used to the ups and downs and tried to stay relatively
uninvolved.

"Can you come back?" I asked. "Things are so...I need you."

"You never need me," he answered. Probably realizing that
since I never did need him, it must be bad, he added, "Listen,
it's a really busy semester. I can't just leave. But call me anytime
you need, okay? Anytime. Five times a day if you want."

I slumped against the wall, my stomach aching even more.
"Okay."

I wouldn't call him. I reached out that once, but I would go
back to dealing with things on my own. Straightening out and

ignoring the pain, I checked to make sure my face was dry and set out to find a cup of coffee.

As I walked, I texted Horatio:

i thnk i jst put the finl nail n th coffin. find H.

Barnardo: Glad you weren't my girlfriend.

Ophelia: Thanks.

Barnardo: With friends like his...

Francisco: I know, right?

Barnardo: "I put the final nail in the coffin." How can you explain that away?

Ophelia: It's an expression.

Francisco: Or proof of conspiracy.

Barnardo: We think you asked Claudius and your father to get into that limo with you.

Ophelia: I asked? You don't know anything about anything.

16

"People say Hamlet grew very paranoid. Was there any reason for it?"

"Yes. Absolutely. Everyone he thought he could trust betrayed him."

"Even you?" Zara asks with a twinkle in her eye.

Ophelia sighs, then her chin begins to tremble. "Yeah."

Zara hands her a tissue. "In what way?"

"I didn't believe him when he told me there was gonna be trouble."

That night, against my better judgment, I called Hamlet's cell phone. Each mini-click after the ring sent my heart into my throat. By the time his voice-mail message came on, I was barely able to stand. "Okay. You're not there. Or you can see it's me and you're not picking up. Probably that. I wouldn't pick up if I were you. So, well, here's the thing. You were right. Your mother and Claudius blackmailed me. There's this video. Of us. God, you knew I couldn't deal with being embarrassed, and look what I did. I'm so sorry."

I was standing outside myself, distracted by my own lameness.

"I'm not sure where you are, but when you get this, could you just call? You probably don't want to. I wouldn't blame you if you never wanted to talk to me again, but...Listen, if I don't hear from you in two days, I'll have my answer. Okay? If I don't hear from you within two days, I'll know we're really through and...I'll leave you alone."

Three days later, I still hadn't heard from Hamlet or Horatio. I had kept to myself, staying out of my father's sight, not talking to anyone at school, literally hiding in stairwells and bathrooms until the bell rang. But on the third day, I picked myself up and tried to act normal again. If a walk of a thousand miles begins with just one step, I figured the road to recovering from Hamlet might begin by getting out of his world.

I got to first-period art history early for the first time in a while, and though Mr. Norquest didn't say anything, he did raise his eyebrows as I took my seat next to my friends Lauren and Sebastian.

"Wanna ditch PE and grab coffee after class? You look terrible," Sebastian whispered as the lights dimmed for a slide show.

"Thanks," I whispered back, elbowing his ribs. "Coffee sounds good." The circles under my eyes had grown rather pronounced, and I rubbed my face, hoping to stay awake in the darkened classroom.

Mr. Norquest intoned, "Note the difference between Ingres's *Grande Odalisque* and Manet's *Le déjeuner sur l'herbe*, or *The Lunch on the Grass*. This painting caused quite a stir when it was unveiled. Comments?"

The class pontificated about the sexism in having the woman nude while the men were clothed, admired her direct gaze, and noted the fact that in Manet's painting the woman seemed comfortable among the men. Additionally, students observed that she was clearly of their class, unlike the classic odalisques who were exotic slaves meant to be pitied while lusted after.

When the teacher called on me, I admitted in a rare moment of truth, "Sometimes I feel like her."

"Why is that?" he asked, pulling his glasses off and tucking them into his pocket.

I opened my mouth to speak, but nothing came out. Regretting I had spoken up, I shrugged and slumped a little in my seat.

Sebastian nudged me and whispered, "Go on."

I sat up slightly and fortified myself. "She's so exposed, and everyone is completely casual about the fact."

"But is she bothered by it?" prodded Mr. Norquest, leaning against an empty chair in the first row.

"Not always easy to tell just by an expression," I mused. "Maybe she's used to playing their game, hiding her true self."

Mr. Norquest nodded and looked back at the painting, wondering at this perspective.

"Or maybe she really likes being the center of attention," retorted a snippy girl with purple hair sitting right in front.

"At least she doesn't have to dye her hair crazy colors to get people to look at her," I jabbed.

Mr. Norquest's head whipped around and he shot me a look. Dye Job was one of his favorites, and I was not to mess with her. I slumped down in my seat again as Lauren snickered.

"You're awesome," Sebastian whispered to me when the next picture flashed on-screen. When Lauren rolled her eyes at him, he muttered, "What? She is."

"You don't have to try so hard. She already knows you're in love with her."

It was true. I did. That said, I didn't want to think about love or boys or the trouble both brought, so I slumped further in my seat and let the two of them whisper-fight over my head until Mr. Norquest shushed them.

I sat silently for the rest of class and managed to stay awake. After coffee, I considered going home. If I went, my father might ignore me, or he might be working late. Either way, I would end up eating alone. I could stare at my phone and hope that it would ring. Or I could finish out the day and try to enjoy an evening out.

After school, our friend Justine invited us all to her parents' condo for pizza, and that night we sat around talking and laughing. Well, they laughed. I mostly sat back and watched normal life going on. People who didn't watch everything they said. People who didn't think anyone was out to kill them. People who didn't use anyone to learn secrets or to get ahead. Or if they did use people, the whole world didn't have to know about it.

We were waiting for the start of *Denmark Divas*, which everyone except me seemed to be obsessed with. My friends were all talking about which singer might win this season, and everyone was completely ignoring the entertainment "news" show that preceded it. I had gone into the kitchen to grab a soda when I heard the name Hamlet spoken by the hosts. I hustled out of the kitchen and caught an image I'll never forget: a still photo of a girl wearing boxing gloves, skimpy satin shorts, and a sequined sports bra being carried by Hamlet, who was wearing horns and a painted-on mustache.

"Lord Hamlet is the devil, indeed. Here he is at a party in Amsterdam, and look at that knockout with him."

"When Ophelia sees this, she's gonna call for a rematch."

"Let's hope she doesn't greet him with a sucker punch!" The reporters smirked at each other.

Everyone in the room was silent and staring at me. Dan was merciful and grabbed the remote. The screen snapped to black, and I swallowed hard. Looking around the room, I realized I could have been stark naked and doing the chicken dance, and they would not have been more embarrassed for me.

After a prolonged, awkward silence, Lauren offered, "Hamlet's a jerk."

"Don't know what you saw in him," added Keren.

"Duh. He's the future king and he's loaded." Dan laughed. Keren slapped his leg.

"He'd better at least be great in bed," Greg offered, shoving a handful of potato chips into his mouth.

Justine grabbed the bowl from Greg and said to me, "Men are dogs." Turning back to Greg, she added, "All of you are dogs."

He grabbed the bowl back and kissed her. "And you love us anyway. So who's more ridiculous?" She threw a chip at him, and they started to laugh.

My pain had been quickly forgotten, and so I started backing out of the room. If I was going to be miserable I preferred doing it alone anyway, and I certainly didn't want to hear any more hackneyed quips or assurances.

Standing alone in the kitchen, I tried to gain control of my enraged mind long enough to decide whether to go home or not. I hated the singing show anyway, and I knew everyone was either going to spend the evening asking me how I was doing or pretending to ignore what had happened, neither of which seemed like fun for anyone. I put the soda down and grabbed my keys, which were, fortunately, on a table right next to the front door.

"Where are you going?" Sebastian called across the sitting room.

Caught. I didn't know how I expected to sneak out or why I was too chicken to even say good-bye. Wedged in the doorway, I answered, "Home. Thanks, Justine, I'll, uh…yeah." I sighed and walked out, letting the door slam behind me. *I could kill Hamlet,* I thought as I stormed toward the exit of her building. "Crap, crap, crap," I mumbled, marching to the beat of each expletive.

Halfway down the hall I heard someone coming out of Justine's, following me, I knew. When I looked over my shoulder, I wasn't surprised to see Sebastian. "Go back in," I called to him, but he picked up his pace to a near jog instead. He was going to catch up with me and would want to talk, so I figured I would just wait where I was, rather than chance having the discussion out on the street with the prying eyes and ears of strangers around us.

In three long paces, he caught up with me. "You don't have to run away. No one's judging you."

"They're all judging me. And him. Everyone does." I scowled.

He opened his mouth as if to protest, then clapped it shut when he realized I was right. Unable to contain himself, he proceeded. "Why do you put up with that guy?"

I rolled my eyes, not wanting to explain myself. There was no more putting up with Hamlet, as far as I could tell, but Sebastian didn't need to know that. The fact that our latest breakup had stayed out of the papers was a miracle, and I wanted to keep it to myself as long as possible. "There's a lot to us that you don't know about."

"Because you never tell us anything about your relationship."

"Can't imagine why," I snapped.

"You think we would sell your stories?"

I shrugged. Hamlet and I had each had trusted "friends" find the temptation of money or fifteen minutes of fame too hard to resist. "I just... It's my business."

Little wrinkles of concern sprang up around Sebastian's eyes as he stared at me, thinking. "Here's what I know: He drinks."

"So do I."

"He cheats."

"So have I."

Sebastian flinched. Then I could see his mind working, wondering how true that was, with whom, and if that meant he had a chance with me.

"Look, Sebastian, what Hamlet and I have works. Most of the time."

He slapped at the wall next to me. "Does Hamlet even like art?"

"He tolerates it to please me." When Sebastian made a face, I recanted. "He likes it. Just not the way we do."

Sebastian shook his head. "He has more of it than anyone. What a waste. Seems he doesn't appreciate anything he has as much as he should. As much as others would."

"Sebastian, don't," I warned.

"Sorry," he said. He looked down, but then his eyes flicked back to mine. As he did, I noticed the gold flecks in his brown eyes. Then my gaze wandered to his full eyebrows and strong nose, his square jaw covered in stubble. He wore a braided leather necklace tight around his neck and I had a sudden urge to kiss it and put my tongue in the space between the rope and his throat.

Shoot, I thought. *Hamlet. Keep your mind on Hamlet. You've got to fix what you messed up, not make it worse.* But then I remembered the girl in the boxing gloves and the little shorts. I stared at Sebastian's bare arms, muscular from lacrosse, and then let my gaze be drawn up to his shoulders, and back to his throat. My facial expression must have changed because he asked me what was up.

"Go back in," I instructed him.

"Why?"

"Because if you stay, I'm going to sleep with you for revenge."

"Oh," he said. After a pause, he laughed. "And I don't want that?"

My only response was a shrug and a nervous, flirtatious smile. I made up my mind. Hamlet could go screw himself or boxer girl or whomever he pleased. If we were done, I wasn't waiting around, especially when I had an attractive, attentive guy right in front of me who clearly wanted me.

"Can I kiss you?" he asked.

I nodded and leaned my head against the wall, waiting, hoping it would be a good kiss. And it was. My heart beat faster and I was greedy for more, but I scooted away. He looked concerned that I was changing my mind.

"I can't risk being seen like this," I reassured him, looking up and down the hallway.

"Wanna go to your place?"

"You a big fan of my father's?" I laughed, but even the mention of my father saddened me.

Sebastian blushed and tried, "My apartment? My parents are out of town for the week."

I nodded, and he took my hand, leading me out.

As we walked, I tried my damnedest to stop thinking about anything but Sebastian and how much I wanted him. But it didn't work. By the time we got to his apartment, I was wary of going through with it.

He kissed me, and I pulled back. "I'm not sure," I said.

Sebastian nodded. He tugged on his necklace and looked away.

My chest ached to see his disappointment, so I added, "It's not you. It's just…there's a lot going on in my…" It sounded like a line, one Hamlet had used on me, which made it even worse. There was very little I could tell him about my life, and without any details he wouldn't believe that it wasn't personal.

The one thing that wasn't technically a secret, I was reluctant to admit. But I had to say something. My cheeks burned as I tried to explain my hesitation and spare Sebastian his feelings. "I've actually never slept with anyone but Hamlet."

"How is that possible?" he asked, his mouth hanging open.

If I wasn't so embarrassed, I might have laughed at his expression.

When he regained his composure slightly, he added, "A girl like you?"

Staring at my sneakers, I asked, "What do you mean, a girl like me?"

"Nothing."

"Do I seem slutty?" I asked, my cheeks stinging from the

blood rushing to them. Thinking of the party photos and the secret video, I pulled my arms tight across myself again and wondered how quickly I could make it home before I embarrassed myself further.

"Not slutty," he said, putting his hand on my arm.

I pulled away but let him finish.

He leaned back against his door and looked me over. "Just, like, sexy. And self-confident."

"I don't know what I am or how I ended up just with Hamlet....It just never felt—" I reached into my pocket to check that my keys were there and said, "This was a mistake. I'm gonna go." I was about to walk away, but then I looked into his eyes, his chocolaty, passion-filled, temporarily hangdog eyes, and my resolve melted away.

"Don't. I meant it as a compliment. We don't have to do anything, but don't go. Not yet." He kissed me gently on the forehead, and I let him pull me close. "Let's just take this slowly and see what happens. No pressure."

My body relaxed and sank into his. Sebastian didn't live in the castle. He didn't know what I'd done. He wasn't acting crazy or violent or threatening to kill anyone or to expose me. He just wanted the girl he liked to like him back.

We kissed, and my arms gripped his muscular back. I had nearly lost myself in the moment when an alarming thought crossed my mind. I turned my head, and my eyes scanned the room, lingering in the corners and on the bookshelf.

"What are you looking for?" Sebastian asked, his arms still around my waist.

I looked down again, hoping he'd change the subject, but he didn't say anything else. I didn't want to lie anymore. "Cameras."

Sebastian backed away. "You honestly think— What kind of person would— Did Hamlet—"

"No," I answered quickly. Claudius's leer, Gertrude's scowl, and my father's humiliation all filled my mind.

I considered walking out, but then Sebastian asked the perfect question. "What kind of people do you spend time with?"

I laughed. "You have no idea."

And with that, the thought that had been forming in my mind solidified all at once. I was done. I didn't want any part of Elsinore. I didn't want to be a queen. I didn't want to be in the public eye. Even if the Hamlet of the past—not the Hamlet with the gun, not the Hamlet who saw ghosts, not the Hamlet who attacked me in the limo, but the Hamlet I loved—showed up at that moment, I wouldn't take him back. Because he came with all the trappings of royalty and was constantly in the public eye, and no matter how blasé he was about it, no matter how he might try to create a life for us that could be considered within the realm of normal, it wouldn't be. Sebastian, or a guy like him, could be normal—God, even boring—without trying. Boring sounded amazing. Yet, from the way Sebastian kissed and talked, he could not be considered boring. And I wanted another kiss.

I trusted him. I don't know how or why, after everything that had happened, but I did. For the first time in a long time, my trust wasn't betrayed, and I didn't have to pretend to be anything I was not.

Even if we'd just sat around talking, I think Sebastian would have been okay with it. But we did more than talk, and it was…nice. Hey, don't underestimate the awesomeness of "nice," and don't think I'm giving details. I'm not one to do more than kiss and tell, so just know that it made me happy.

No regrets. It was weird at first, being with someone other than Hamlet. But Sebastian was sweet and funny and so happy to have me with him. And *I* was happy to be there with *him*. Especially 'cause he wasn't crazy or suspicious or on the edge. He was the un-Hamlet. It was my first move toward freedom. And if you gotta move on from a situation, I highly recommend a boy like Sebastian.

The next morning, we didn't want to leave his place, but I had already missed too much class. We showered and dressed and headed for the door. I grabbed my bag and turned on my phone. Five voice messages and three texts were waiting for me. Seeing Hamlet's name snapped me out of my bliss and I shut the phone, looking at Sebastian.

"I'm just…I'm not gonna check the rest now," I started to say, trying to take the quake out of my voice. "I should call my dad, though. I'm sure at least one was from him."

Sebastian nodded and walked across the room, flopping on his bed.

"Dad?" I began. I paused, waiting for him to stop yelling at me. "Dad, you know I wasn't dead in a ditch." I paused as he continued lecturing me. "I know I—" I paused again, and bored holes in the ceiling with my eyes. "But—" My guilt started to overwhelm me. I leaned against the door, avoiding Sebastian's gaze. "Okay. I'll be home before dinner. O…Okay. Bye, Dad. Bye.

"He's pretty pissed," I explained, trying to catch my breath. "We're lucky the DDI didn't come bursting in here looking for me," I added, only half joking. I stretched my hand out to the wary young man in front of me, and it seemed to put him at ease.

At lunch we met up again and went across the street to

grab some coffee. He reached for my hand as we walked, and when I pulled mine back, his face went pale. I said quietly, "Off campus, people have cameras, Sebastian. Not yet, okay?"

He nodded and breathed a little easier. "Maybe leaving campus wasn't such a good idea," he said.

I laughed. "It's five minutes of not touching. You'll live." But while we were waiting for our drinks, I noticed his fingers twitching, like it was a real effort for him to keep his hands to himself. It was really kinda cute.

As soon as we were safe behind the school's tall gates, he threw his arm around my shoulder. There was a part of me that was nervous about what people would say or think about my moving on so quickly, and there was a part of me that wanted to make the breakup definitive and mine. Plus he was hot and I liked him, so for those brief, wonderful moments, his arm around me was what I wanted most.

We headed to the coolest spot on campus, a courtyard with a giant bear sculpture, where the more artistic students would sit and read or play guitar or draw, even on cold days like this one. Dan, Lauren, Greg, and Keren were already there and scooted over, making space for us to sit. Their knowing smiles spoke for them, and they pretended to go on with their conversation, but they were watching our every move.

I stirred my coffee more than I needed to because every time I looked down, Sebastian would lean over and kiss the back of my neck. His expression was relief mixed with pure joy, like a child who gets precisely what he wants for Christmas but still can't believe his luck. We sat close as he whispered stories in my ear as an excuse to sneak a gentle kiss every now and then.

"What the hell?" I heard over my shoulder, and my stomach

clenched. Hamlet. I closed my eyes in a foolish attempt to turn back time. When I opened them, all I saw was the back of his head, and I went chasing after him without so much as an explanation to the boy who had thought he had won, or to our friends, who had looked on in horror. Even at a dead run I was unable to keep up.

"Hamlet!" I tried to shout, but I was out of breath.

People stopped to watch us and started pointing and pulling out camera phones. His driver was driving away by the time I reached the street.

"God, could you just leave us alone?" I screamed at the kids standing behind me.

Some snickered, some complied. Two security guards walked over to reprimand them for breaking school rules but didn't take the phones, so I was screwed again.

I yanked up the hood of my sweater and scuttled off to ground zero. My crowd waited in silent expectation as I grabbed my bag.

"What did he want?" asked Lauren, her voice sharp.

I shrugged as I took out my phone. Still panting, I punched in the code. "You have five messages," declared the gentle robotic voice.

Beep. "Ophelia, Horatio made me leave town with him and I forgot my phone, so I didn't get your message until just now. I guess I should have called either way, but I was pissed. It took me a few days to calm down, but I have, and I need to talk to you. Things are so messed up. I said some things in the car— I don't— I don't know what's going on with me. Or us. I was ready to kill you for— But now...Call me."

Beep. "Phee, you didn't call back. I don't know what you saw on TV, but you can't believe what they're showing. I didn't do anything with that girl. She got hurt and I was helping her. Seriously. Please call."

Beep. "Young lady, it's your father. It's almost midnight, and you're not home. Not like you. Not like you at all. If this is your idea of independence, then we shall have a talk. You tread dangerously, my dear. How çan I trust—? It is a bold mouse that nestles in the cat's ear. Come home this instant! Do you think—" I pressed Delete.

Beep. "Ophelia? Horatio. Hamlet's telling the truth about Amsterdam. So…your dad said you didn't come home last night. You're killing him. Hamlet, I mean. Your dad's pretty ticked, too. Hamlet's on his way to find you. Call him. Or me."

Beep. "Damn it, Phee. Where are you?"

I stood staring at my phone and shaking. What a mess.

I walked away from Sebastian and our friends like a coward, without explanation, without apology, without public tears. I felt guilty and confused, but I couldn't share my pain. Not with anyone. I'm aware that technically I didn't do anything wrong since, really, Hamlet and I had broken up. In my apartment. Again outside the theater. And, quite memorably, for a third time in the limo. Foolishly, I had thought that being with Sebastian would make things easier. Clearer. That it would help me make a break from the past. From Hamlet. From his family. Yet being with Sebastian had only made it worse, and when I realized that fact, sickening disappointment overwhelmed me, and all I could think was that I had to be alone.

I would try to tell Sebastian about it someday, and maybe he would understand. Until then, I would sit separately in art history. I would avoid the courtyard. And I would risk losing my friends and pretend I didn't care. And I prayed that they wouldn't try to make a buck off of our time together.

219

That evening, after listening to my father go on and on about how disappointed he was in me, I retreated to my room. I had messed things up with Sebastian. I had messed things up with Hamlet. Or he had messed things up with me. How do you go back to someone who says such disgusting things and scares the hell out of you? You don't. Or you shouldn't. Sitting alone in my room that night, I realized that neither Hamlet's desire to talk to me nor his disappointment that I'd been with another guy changed my decision. I wanted out of Elsinore. Maybe even Denmark. At the very least, I needed to get away from Hamlet. Even though the old Hamlet, the sane Hamlet, had returned from Amsterdam, I wanted to be done.

I flipped on the TV, catching the end of the news. "With apologies again to our prince and the viewing public, let us say once more that we should not have run a story so irresponsibly. The young lady was hurt, and our prince was a hero for rescuing her from what could have been a dangerous stampede at the club."

I wasn't sure I believed them. It would have been as easy for Gertrude or Claudius to force a retraction for a true story as it would have been for the media to fabricate a false one. It didn't matter. Mistakes and miscommunications. Violent love and violent hate. Betrayals and desire. Our beginning, our middle, and our end.

Francisco: Your father sent out security to look for you the night before Hamlet returned from Amsterdam.
Ophelia: Doesn't surprise me.
Barnardo: Where were you?
Ophelia: None of your business.

Francisco: Everything's our business.

Barnardo: We think your disappearance was meant to further upset Hamlet and trigger some sort of violent act.

Ophelia: Think what you want. This is outrageous.

Barnardo: Okay. Try this one. Would you say Hamlet was crazy?

Ophelia: I don't know. I'm not a psychiatrist.

Francisco: What do you think?

Ophelia: Like "go to a nuthouse" crazy? No. Disturbed, yes.

Barnardo: Is there a difference?

Ophelia: Yeah. He was depressed. He was angry. He was totally obsessed with finding out what happened to his dad.

Francisco: Here's a picture of Hamlet on the roof of a limo. Here's a picture of Hamlet jumping on chairs in the theater. Was his behavior in either of these cases normal?

Ophelia: There was nothing normal about what happened at the castle after the king died.

Barnardo: Even so, there are no pictures of you being destructive.

Ophelia: Well then, someone hasn't done enough research.

17

"We hear there was a dustup at a comedy show. Some of Hamlet's schoolmates were even arrested for what they did onstage. What was that about?"

Ophelia runs her fingers through her hair and takes a deep breath. "Claudius had a hard time looking at the truth. And when you're in power, you can make the truth disappear."

"Interesting," Zara says, drawing out the word. "Care to elaborate?"

"Making things disappear seemed to be Claudius's specialty," Ophelia replies.

The audience laughs, and Zara looks amused. "There was, apparently, a recording of the show, but it has been destroyed."

"I'm not surprised."

I had hoped to get to the theater early enough to enter unnoticed. No such luck. Horatio, whom I'd been avoiding for two days, was scowling as he leaned against the rail of the lobby's balcony. When I redirected my walk away from him, he cleared his throat and beckoned me with his index finger.

I stopped in my tracks. "What?" I asked, the word slicing the air.

"Hamlet told me what you did," he said, his jaw set.

I crossed my arms and glared at him. "I'm sure."

"Why'd you do it?"

"I didn't have a choice."

"You just fell on that guy?"

"Screw you. I was talking about the limo thing." I turned to leave.

"Wait."

"Why? You've already decided I was solely to blame."

Horatio walked toward me. "That's not true. But Ophelia, I dragged Hamlet to Amsterdam. He never—"

Backing up, I said, "Honestly, Horatio, I don't care. I'm not explaining the guy from school, and I'm not sorry. I've had enough of Hamlet and this place."

As I spun away from Horatio, I slammed into a girl of about eleven or twelve. I tried to catch her arm, but she fell to the floor, and the contents of her pink canvas bag spilled everywhere. Horatio and I both rushed to help her up, but when she saw my face, she screamed and we both let her go.

She scrambled to her feet, smoothing out her plaid uniform skirt and squealing, "Ohmygod, ohmygod. You're Ophelia, right? I've seen you at school. Oh my *God!*"

I nodded, shrinking from her enthusiasm.

Before I could say anything, she asked, "Can I have your autograph?"

I tried to force a smile. "I'm kind of in the middle of—"

"I, like, totally love you and even though my mom thinks you're, like, a bad influence because of those pictures, I'm like, 'Whatever.' I just love you and I don't care what she says, and

I've wanted to meet you since, like, forever, but you're always with your friends in the hall and it's, like, too intimidating, which is why I asked to come to this show even though I'm supposed to be at tennis practice. She told me employees and their families could be in the audience so I said I totally had to come. She's on the way down from her office now. Ohmygod, I shouldstoptalkingnow." She was breathless and, I realized, still hanging on to my arm.

"Well, it's really nice to meet you," I said, trying to take my arm back.

She held tightly, panting. "Ohmygod, your hair is *so* pretty. I wanted to dye my hair to match yours, but my mother said not to be ridiculous, that only dumb girls have hair like that, and I should concentrate on my studies instead."

I pursed my lips as she spoke, then said, "Your mom is right about needing to focus on your work. And your hair is naturally pretty, so —"

"Ohmygod!" she squealed again, pinching my arm with her fingers. "You think it's pretty?"

I opened my mouth to speak, but movement over her shoulder caught my attention. A statuesque woman with thick black hair and bronze skin had her hands on her hips and was tapping her foot. "Tara," the woman called out. "Let's go in."

As Tara released her grip on me, she looked like someone had just spit on her birthday cake. "It was nice to meet you," she whispered, before galloping over to her mother.

Horatio was fighting a laugh, so I kicked at him. I started to laugh, too, but my smile faded as Tara's mother took a moment to glare at me before disappearing into the darkness.

"This is the problem," I said, gesturing at the theater door. "Why I have to get out of here."

He looked over his shoulder, but mother and daughter were already gone. "What's the big deal? You and Hamlet are stopped all the time."

"Since the wedding and the party pictures, it's different. And no matter what strangers say to me, I have to be nice because otherwise my rudeness will end up being the new buzz."

"That girl was sweet."

"Yeah, but I don't want to be anyone's role model...or their cautionary tale, for that matter." My stomach sank at the thought of daughters being warned not to be like me. "I just wanted to argue with you in peace."

He half smiled. "It's peaceful now. Argue away."

I looked down and shook my head. "I'm going inside."

"If you hate it so much, why are you here?"

I scanned the lobby. People were starting to trickle into the theater, so I lowered my voice. "My dad told me I had to come see this show. Gertrude and Claudius are coming. Gertrude wants to placate Hamlet by having a big crowd for this show he's put together, and Claudius doesn't want his wife to be anywhere near Hamlet unaccompanied. And Claudius told my dad it's a command performance for everyone. So, according to my dad, even though Hamlet hates me, 'everyone' means I attend, too. And until I'm ready to make a clean break from this place, I'm going to play the dutiful daughter. My father's barely talking to me as it is."

"Help me understand why you did what you did. I can't imagine a reason big enough that you'd hurt Hamlet like that."

"I was embarrassed, Horatio. I'm eighteen, for Christ's sake. What other eighteen-year-old has a sex tape floating out there?" I paused. "Maybe there are some, but I never thought it would happen to me. I didn't want everyone— Everything that's happened helped me see how much I don't want this anymore. I don't want *him* anymore."

He furrowed his brow and studied me. "I don't believe you."

I sighed and felt a lump forming in my throat. "Okay."

I wouldn't have believed me, either. It had been a tumultuous few years, and Horatio had been close enough to know that Hamlet and I always ended up together in the end. For some reason, we couldn't help ourselves. Yet Horatio wasn't in my head. He couldn't know the shift I felt. He couldn't know that I was convinced that this time I meant it. At least, I thought I did.

Strangers and friends were milling around the lobby, some blatantly watching us, some pretending not to. He suggested quietly, "Let's go in. It should be a laugh at least."

"Yeah. Maybe."

We started walking toward the ornately carved double doors that lead into the elegant theater, but Hamlet came up the stairs, so Horatio changed course. Hamlet said hi to Horatio while eyeing me hatefully. Unable to stand his gaze, I went inside and sat alone, hoping to slip away at some point.

The audience buzzed around me, and I pretended to lose myself in studying my surroundings. Carved cherubs danced around the proscenium arch, and in the middle of the painted oval ceiling, flights of angels sang a sleeping baby to rest. Molded crowns jutted out between the boxes, and banners hung floor to ceiling on each side of the stage. So much care had been taken to decorate a room that remained dark for most of its existence.

Horatio and Hamlet entered together and stood under the

box seats talking for a few minutes while Gertrude and Claudius sat up front at Hamlet's instruction.

Claudius called out, "Dear Hamlet—note I did not call you 'son'—how are you?"

"Great, though things seem to change so quickly around here. Who knows how I'll be in a minute? But being with you makes everything better, doesn't it? Just ask my mother. Or my father. Oh, right, you can't because of what you did."

Claudius looked at Gertrude, then back at Hamlet. "I don't know what you're talking about."

Hamlet smiled with angry eyes. "Me neither."

"Dearest," called out Gertrude with her sweet manipulation, "come sit with me."

"No, Mother, here's someone more attractive." He acted as if I were a magnet and, against his will, he was being pulled to me. His comment would have stung Gertrude for a variety of reasons, and he knew it. First, he shunned her loudly enough for all to hear. Second, her insecurity about her appearance, though she had nothing to worry about, was legendary, at least to her inner circle. There was a reason it took her over an hour to get ready each morning and why she had a startlingly large staff of stylists, makeup artists, and hairdressers ready to jump into action at a moment's notice. Third, she hated that he always came to me instead of her.

"Ophelia," he proclaimed, to my great apprehension, "can I lie in your lap?"

I looked around with embarrassment, and as I did so, saw my father's trepidation, Horatio's concern, and the amused glances of nearly everyone else. "No," I replied uncomfortably.

In a stage whisper he said, "I mean, my *head* in your lap."

I whispered back, "Whatever body part you are suggesting, I don't think so." I didn't trust him, and I wanted him to go away.

"Do you think I'm suggesting something dirty? *Moi?*" He leered, then laughed.

"You're in a good mood," I said through a clenched jaw.

"Yeah, because I'm ready to give as good as I get. Speaking of bitches, look at my mother. She's in a pretty good mood, too, and my father's been dead for only two hours."

I had had enough and said sharply, "Months. Nearly four months, Hamlet. Enough of this."

As he rose to tower over me, he asked loud enough for all to hear, "Enough of what? Enough of me or enough of my father's death? Wow, four months have passed and he hasn't been forgotten yet? Then there's hope that a *great* man's memory might last longer than a year."

Thankfully, at that moment a recorded trumpet sounded, indicating the show was starting. To my surprise, Hamlet sat back down next to me. It would seem that my punishment was not yet at its end. The recording came from a little speaker set in the corner of the stage, and the sound was intentionally puny, making the fanfare practically ridiculous.

The troupe marched out, yelling, "All hail King Claudius!"

Claudius nodded but did not smile. All five guys were wearing sailor outfits, and the tallest, thinnest one with a twinkle in his eye stepped forward. "Welcome! Ladies and gentlemen, my name is Mike, and we are the King's Sea Men."

A couple of people guffawed but quieted down once they realized they were the only ones to find the double entendre amusing...or at least the only ones bold enough to laugh at it.

"What's this?" I whispered to Hamlet, remembering that

228

these guys, known as the Wit Burgers, usually wore T-shirts with the troupe's logo plus jeans.

He lifted his eyebrows, not taking his eyes off Claudius. "Mischief," he whispered back.

Mike continued, "If we shadows do offend / Think but this, and all will mend / That you have but slumbered here / While these visions did appear."

"What the hell does that mean?" called out one of his fellow comedians.

Tall Mike grinned and added, "All that follows is meant in good fun. We hope you will take it as such." He winked, and they all ran into new places on the stage, tearing off their sailor costumes as they moved.

Hamlet muttered, "I hope it will be good and fun…but only for some. I'm waiting for the outcome."

"You're not making sense," I whispered.

"Just like a woman," he said, glowering.

I cleared my throat and stared at the stage.

Mike explained that they would begin with an improvised scene, which would need a purpose. "Do I have a suggestion from the audience?" he asked.

Hamlet cleared his throat, and Rosencrantz turned around. When his eyes met Hamlet's, Hamlet nodded and Rosencrantz yelled out, "Murder. Murder most foul."

Gertrude froze, and Claudius glared at Hamlet. Rosencrantz, suddenly realizing he had done something to displease the king, slid down in his seat.

At this point, a guy, clearly meant to be Gertrude (judging by the blond wig done in a French knot), came onto the stage. He swirled, his skirt flowing delicately, then kissed an actor wearing a crown. I cringed.

"No, no," minced the "queen." "Do not kiss me!"

Hamlet stood at this point and asked Gertrude loudly, "Mother, how do you like the act?"

"I think the lady is protesting too much," she said, her voice light but her smile stiff.

"*Son*," Claudius said, "I do not find this particularly funny. In fact, it seems rather offensive."

"No, no, no, they're kidding. *Poisonously* funny, though, huh?" Hamlet spoke quickly, his brimming emotions impossible to read.

My worry was deepening. I didn't know what game he was playing or how far he would take it. As usual, my desire to protect him overtook my good senses. Quietly enough for him alone to hear, I said, "Seems a little pointed to me."

Hamlet roughly ran his fingers through his hair and took in the actors onstage, who made to carry on with the scene after the unintended interruption. "Stop, stop. Do the next one," Hamlet called out, full of excited rage.

The troupe froze and looked at one another, then bowed and regrouped. After a moment, Mike announced, his voice faltering, "W-we call this game the mousetrap."

The game went like this: All of the men were supposedly at a cocktail party. One guy was selected to go beyond earshot while the audience suggested maladies the other comedians would have. The actor who had left would come back in knowing only that he was supposed to play a doctor and that he would have to figure out the sicknesses of the players, then suggest cures.

Two actors stepped forward wearing crowns, the "king" seeming to be stuck to the "queen." To remove the unwanted "king" from her back, the "doctor" suggested poison, at which point all the actors sang a lullaby and the "doctor" pantomimed pouring poison in the ear of the sleeping "king." Once the poisoned "king" had fallen to the ground, the "doctor" took the crown and put it on his own head. Then he asked the "queen" to marry him, at which she squealed in delight, knocked the "doctor" to the ground, and kissed him passionately.

"Enough!" roared Claudius, rising.

The actors froze.

"Turn on the lights! Let's go. And take them away!" he bellowed, pointing at the comedians who looked ready to piss themselves.

"Lights, lights, lights!" shouted my father, and the house lights popped on.

I slipped out the side door in time to hear Claudius shouting at Gertrude, "I told you Hamlet was trouble. I told you to get him out of here, but you insisted on keeping him close. Enough is enough. He goes to England tomorrow!"

Gertrude might have argued against it, but I don't know. The elevator doors opened and they were whisked away.

I stuck my head back in the side door of the theater to see what was happening. There was an intense commotion as the rest of the audience rushed down the aisles, some chatting excitedly, some nervously, about the bizarre situation they'd witnessed. Tara's mother had her daughter by the arm despite Tara's protest that she'd left her pink canvas bag.

Hamlet leaped onto his velvet seat and called out to Horatio, "Did you see that?" He crossed the theater by walking on the armrests. "Did you see Claudius's reaction?"

"I did. He totally freaked out at the poison part," I heard Horatio say.

"No doubt about it. He killed my father. I knew it!" Hamlet

shouted as he leaped onto the stage. He checked his back pocket, and he and Horatio disappeared behind the curtains.

As I exited, I was nearly knocked over by a crowd of royal guardsmen running in. I ran for the elevators, but all were full and moving to other floors. I put my fingers in my ears to drown out the sound of the college comedians being dragged roughly down the back stairs.

After all was quiet, I decided to look for Hamlet. I know. I should have just gone home. But I wasn't making the wisest choices at the time, so this idiot move should come as no surprise. The way I figured it, if Hamlet really was leaving town, I ought to say good-bye. I didn't think he wanted to see me, and I wasn't sure I really wanted to see him, but it seemed like the right thing to do. I couldn't leave things the way they were. Maybe I should have, but how could I turn my back on someone with whom I literally had a lifetime of history? Claudius hadn't said how long Hamlet would be in England. It might be long enough for us to forgive each other. Maybe not. Either way, I spent the better part of an hour searching.

I had been looking everywhere I could think of for Hamlet and finally stopped at a conference room door, convinced I heard his voice. He sounded angry, so I was afraid to go in. Then I heard what sounded like a chair being thrown, and I found myself propelled inside to make sure Hamlet wasn't in danger. When I entered, I saw he was standing alone by the large window. Rolling chairs were all over the room, some pushed away from the table, some overturned, like cockroaches stuck on their backs.

"Hamlet?"

He spun around to face me. "Get out of here. Haven't you done enough damage already?"

I considered walking out, but my guilt kept me rooted. Checking on him was the least I could do. "Where's Horatio?" I asked.

"Why? You gonna screw him, too?"

I crossed my arms forcefully and gritted my teeth. I had gone in there to check on him to be a good friend, and this was how he repaid me? His words were as powerful as a slap, and I wanted to hurt him back. "What do you care what I do or *who* I do, Hamlet?" The shock and deepening anger on his face egged me on. "You've made it pretty damn clear that you hate me. And apparently, you never loved me. So why would I wait around? I'll screw whoever I want whenever I want. You did."

"Liar." He growled.

Hamlet climbed onto the conference table and sat down. He stared at me like a vulture, his chin low, glowering from under his brow. But I stood my ground. Then he reached behind his back, lifted his shirt, and pulled out the gun, the one he'd had in my room weeks before.

I froze, wondering if I was going to get shot for telling the truth. "Jesus, Hamlet," I managed. "Are you still carrying that around?"

He laid it on the table between his feet and stared at it, then rubbed his face hard and shook out his hair. Tapping at the gun with one finger, he said to himself as much as to me, "I had the perfect chance to use it."

I opened my mouth to speak, but a soft gasp was all that came out.

"But I didn't," he said. "I couldn't. Claudius was right there, right in front of me. After the show, in the chapel. No security. No secretaries. On his kneeeees. And I thought, *Well, he's alone. Just get it done.*

"But then I," Hamlet continued, tapping the gun harder, "I couldn't do it. I couldn't shoot someone who was praying. It was too disturbing. As if shooting someone isn't disturbing, right? Maybe I just don't have the balls to kill someone."

Hamlet picked up the gun and pointed it at his own heart. "And I don't know if I have the balls to kill myself. But someone's gotta go."

My heart pounded, and I wasn't sure if I should run for help or keep talking to him. I didn't want to leave him with a gun pointed at his chest. "Hamlet," I said, forcing my dry mouth to speak, "killing Claudius…or yourself…" I couldn't think. "I don't want to lose you."

"Liar," he said, but he lowered the gun and rested it on the table. Then he began spinning it. Every time it slowed down, he'd spin it again.

I couldn't make my body walk closer to his, not with that gun between us. "Hamlet, don't."

He slammed his palm onto the gun. "Maybe you should take this," he said, and slid the gun across the table at me.

I shook my head, unable to speak.

He kicked over another chair as he jumped off the table, then rounded the corner and came toward me. Standing so close I could feel his breath on my face, he whispered, "You should've taken it while you had the chance." He reached across me, his arm grazing mine, grabbed the gun, and shoved it under his shirt. Then he walked out without another word.

He was right. I should have taken it.

Barnardo: You said Hamlet wouldn't speak to you, but, in what's left of the surveillance tape from before the show, he's seen whispering to you. Part of his plot again?

Ophelia: He wanted to humiliate me.

Barnardo: By doing what?

Ophelia: Suggesting I– do lewd things with him in front of everyone.

Barnardo: And did you?

Ophelia: Are you always this rude, or do you just hate women?

Barnardo: Watch it.

Francisco: What did you think of the show?

Ophelia: Funny.

Francisco: It's pretty insulting to the queen and the king.

Ophelia: Yeah.

Barnardo: You don't seem too upset.

Ophelia: They deserved it after what they did, don't you think?

Barnardo: What else did they deserve?

Francisco: *(pause)* Again with the silence. *(pause)* Take her back to her cell.

18

"What happened after the improv show?"

Ophelia looks down. "I'd rather not talk about this."

Zara tilts her head and croons to the camera, "We'll be right back after a word from our sponsors."

Later that evening, I was making dinner when the elevator doors opened. Marcellus and a guard I didn't recognize were standing inside. Marcellus stepped forward while the other man remained. "Ophelia, you need to come with us."

"Why?"

"I'm not at liberty to say. Please come now."

I put down the knife I was using to cut tomatoes and turned off the burner for the pasta. My heart quickened, but I tried to tell myself that it was nothing. Since the king's death, however, nothing seemed like nothing anymore. I followed Marcellus into the elevator, and he pushed the PH button. So we were going to Gertrude. *Ugh,* I thought. *What now?* I looked up and saw my pinched face in the mirrored ceiling. The guards looked straight ahead. I wished they would say something.

When we emerged, the entry was quiet, which I took as a good sign. Marcellus allowed the other guard to open the door to Gertrude's chambers, and he took me by the elbow. He leaned in and whispered, "Signal if you need me," before he pushed me ahead of him.

My eyes were instantly drawn to a small cohort by the window, which had been shattered. One of the curtains had been pulled down and left crumpled in the corner. Gertrude and Claudius were together across the room. He looked pale and sick, and she had mascara tracks down her face like on the day her husband, her first husband, had been buried. Lastly, I saw Hamlet, flanked by two guards. When he saw me, he tried to stand up from the overstuffed burgundy chair, but they forced him back down and he hit his elbows on the carved wooden armrests.

Everyone turned to face me, and the group in the corner whispered furiously. I shoved my hands into my pockets, my muscles tense. VanDerwater, head of security, came forward and said, "There has been an incident."

Hamlet was there, Claudius, Gertrude. What could have happened? I looked at the fallen curtain and noticed shining black shoes sticking out from underneath. Unable to imagine whose they might be, I looked back at VanDerwater for more of an explanation.

He removed his hat slowly, letting it rest across his heart. He cleared his throat and began, "Your father—"

I gasped and clapped one hand over my brow. "No, no, no." My brain hummed with this solitary word. *No, no, no*, I thought. *No, no, no.* Choking on my own breath, my chest heaved. My other hand flew atop the hand covering my eyes. Together, the palms pressed hard, and red and blue lights danced in the darkness. The pain forced thought away and was welcome relief, brief as it was.

"I'm sorry," I heard Hamlet call out. "It was an accident."

My legs began to buckle, and my stomach dropped. Still shielding my eyes from the sight too horrible to comprehend, I turned away from Hamlet's voice and called for Marcellus. "I need—" I pulled in more breath, but it stopped at the top of my throat. I heard his handcuffs and flashlight jangling together as he stepped forward to touch my back. My jaw was chattering, so I could barely whisper, "I'm gonna be sick."

He guided me swiftly across the room and opened the door of Gertrude's bathroom. He flicked on the light and closed me in the room. The confined space was soothing, though I had to keep my eyes closed to shut out the golden poodles she inexplicably had painted everywhere. I leaned over the toilet and waited, but did not vomit, so I lay down on the cool marble floor. Outside I could hear chatter and the clacking and thudding of feet hurrying around, but no single sound, voice, or word came through.

My nausea subsided, but my head continued to throb. Thoughts swirled so fast, they ceased to make sense. What kind of accident had there been? Was it possible that my father was dead? Would he be buried with my mother? Was my mother in heaven? Who would take care of me now? Would I be able to stay in the castle? Did I want to? What had happened? What was Hamlet sorry for?

I focused on the chill of the marble seeping into my skin. I could think of no reason to ever open the door again, and even if I did think of one, I did not believe I had the will to do it.

Sooner than I would have liked, a gentle tapping came at the door. I didn't answer.

"Ophelia?" called Gertrude. "Are you ready to come out yet?"

I didn't answer again.

"Ophelia, they are going to move your father's body. We have some things to discuss."

At the word *body* I felt ill again. He wasn't a body. He was my dad. My dad who liked blueberry pancakes but only if the blueberries were cooked inside. My dad who knew every employee in the castle by name, even the waiters who worked the occasional banquets. But had he ever been more than just a "body" to Gertrude, a person necessary to fill a job? Or was he as disposable to her as a tissue or a paper cup?

I pushed myself to a sitting position, allowed the dizziness to pass, checked to be sure I was not going to puke, and then stood gradually. What I knew after all my years living in the castle was that, no matter how nicely she asked, Gertrude was, in reality, giving an order. I had to hold on to the cream-colored vanity with one hand while I reached for the poodle-shaped doorknob with the other.

Everything got very, very silent in my head. It was the absence of thought and sound that allowed me to step out of the bathroom. Arms rigid at my sides, I did not feel my own steps as I walked into the middle of Gertrude's bedroom. Marcellus drifted next to me, but I did not acknowledge him. I vaguely noted the overturned full-length mirror and stopped next to the burgundy comforter, which lay strewn at the foot of Gertrude's four-poster bed. There had been a struggle and my father had died. Again I wondered how.

No one spoke, so I had time to take in more of the room. The window was not exactly shattered, as I had originally thought. There was a single hole in it from which cracks spiderwebbed outward. Blood had sprayed on the window, on the ceiling, on the still-hanging curtains, and more blood had seeped and pooled around where my father lay. The most distant part of my brain realized that the blood belonged to my father, but it was too awful to register, too awful to feel. On the floor next to the disheveled comforter, I spotted a gun, a handgun that looked just like the one Hamlet had been spinning on the conference table not two hours before.

My eyes flicked to Hamlet, who was still flanked by guards. He was watching me with dread. "You?" I asked in a strangled whisper, hoping I was wrong.

"I didn't mean to," he wailed, trying to rush past the guards, who caught him instantly and held him in place.

I stood with my mouth agape. I blinked several times as everyone watched me. The silence gripped me again. Without my even realizing it, my legs gave out and, if not for Marcellus, I would have fallen.

I wriggled out of his hold and stumbled toward my dad. The sheet covered only his torso and head. His hands rested still and soft, and just next to his violet-shaped cuff link, a single drop of blood stained the pure white shirt. My eyes could not leave that spot of red. That spot, which he would have insisted on treating right away, pushed the truth into my silence. My face crumpled and I fell to my knees.

A gurney rolled up beside me, and the side rails clanged into place. Workers in blue booties surrounded my father and hoisted his body onto the sheeted stretcher. I looked up as they rolled him away but said nothing, as nothing was said to me. The pool of blood left behind was dark and thick, and I would have been unable to look away if someone had not thrown a new blue sheet over it. I turned my head as the stretcher was wheeled out of the room. Part of me knew I should be following the stretcher, but I couldn't force my legs to cooperate.

My head snapped toward a new sound, and my breath grew more irregular. Officers were bagging the gun, and the plastic crinkled noisily. They whispered to one another, then hurried out of the room. I watched Hamlet watch them leave. He yanked at his hair, his face turning red.

He looked at the ceiling and then shut his eyes tightly as he muttered, "Oh God. Oh God." Standing suddenly, he begged, "Please let me talk to her."

The still-alert part of me thought he would be denied. Claudius nodded, and the guards let Hamlet go. I froze as Hamlet knelt beside me.

"It was an accident. Someone was eavesdropping on my mother and me. I didn't know who was hiding behind the curtain. I thought"—he looked over his shoulder and, putting his hand on mine, whispered even more quietly—"I thought it was Claudius."

Fury swept over me, and my mind snapped into clarity. I jerked my hand out from under his. "And that makes it better?"

"Not exactly," he replied. "But it does change things, right?" He put his hand on my knee, and I leaped up.

"You must be joking." My pulse was so fast, I could feel the veins in my neck throbbing. I was light-headed but determined to stay on my feet, and damned if he was going to soothe me into forgiveness.

He stood, too, and his eyes bounced between me and the group huddled across the room watching us. He leaned in to whisper, "I confronted my mother about Claudius, told her I knew about the poisoning. I begged her to see Claudius for what he is and to admit her part in bringing down my father. She cried, Ophelia. She actually cried. And I think she —"

"Hamlet, I don't care."

He stopped. Blood drained from his face, and he wrung his hands. He looked over at the group again, then met my eyes. My body tingled with hate, and my lips curled into a snarl.

He winced and added, "And I saw my father."

It was like having cool water poured over my head. How many times in the past months had we talked of suicide, revenge, fear, and hate? My efforts to stop his plans were halfhearted at best and cowardice-driven denials at worst. I knew I had allowed this catastrophe to happen by not insisting he stop the pursuit of his father's killer…if there even was one. But I never thought it would come to this. Or maybe I did. Maybe I'd just hoped the body being wheeled out would belong to Claudius.

I breathed deeply and paused. With all the calm I could muster, I explained quietly, "Hamlet, I have been trying to understand what has been happening with you lately. I know this has all been a shock, but at what point will it end? Your father is dead. Now my father is, too." I swallowed hard and rubbed my forehead. "Your mother will continue to be married to your uncle no matter how many times you claim to see ghosts, or do skits, or kill. You can't change what's done. Now please, please leave me alone."

I turned and planned to walk away, but he caught me forcefully. Gertrude gasped. Everyone present turned to look at us, and Marcellus stepped forward. Hamlet let go and put his hands up. I stopped Marcellus from continuing toward me, torn between sympathy and hatred.

"Don't go," Hamlet whispered. "I love you."

I stared into his drooping eyes, looking for a sign that he

realized what a ridiculous statement it was. I rubbed my forehead again, trying to understand. A few hours ago, he'd treated me like garbage in front of hundreds of people. Two days ago, he'd caught me with another guy. Six days ago, he'd told me to stay away from him. Either he was crazy or he was faking. I wasn't sure what to believe.

He was seeing ghosts, which seemed crazy, but Horatio backed him up. He was running around at all hours of the night, but if he went to his apartment, he'd be living with his mom and Claudius, making it the last place he'd find rest. And I had kicked him out. Everywhere he turned, someone he loved betrayed him. He was so sure his uncle had murdered his father and he seemed unable to do anything about it. It was enough to make anyone crazy, or seem crazy. But which? I wanted to ask him, but I couldn't.

And then, over my shoulder, I heard an officer whisper my father's name, and what Hamlet *was* suddenly didn't matter.

"You murdered my dad. You. My dad was all I—" A horrifying thought stopped me. Could he have done it on purpose? My dad had wanted us apart, and my dad was winning. Was this Hamlet's psychotic attempt to make sure no one stood between us? He wasn't that cruel. And he wasn't that desperate. No. He was. My dad's blood sinking into the carpet was proof of it.

Suddenly I understood Hamlet's obsession with revenge. I realized that if the gun were within my reach, I would have shot Hamlet.

"Get away from me."

His face twisted with agony. The guards stepped forward, caught his wrists, and pulled them down to his sides.

I turned away but could hear him calling after me as

Marcellus escorted me to the royal couple, who had walked ahead to the reception room.

Claudius was sitting while Gertrude paced. She stopped when I came toward them. "My dear, sweet Ophelia," she said, her arms outstretched.

I stopped where I was, unwilling to accept her embrace.

Self-consciously she put her arms by her side. Gertrude's face had been wiped, though traces of the mascara lingered. She tried to force a smile on her face, but it looked more like a grimace. "We're sending Polonius to the morgue, but it will remain a secret. Only one of our men will work on him." Before I could ask why, she continued. "This must all remain a secret."

"I'm sorry, did you say 'secret'?" I asked.

She nodded, and I asked why.

Smoothing the stray hairs that had escaped her French knot, she explained, "We have had so many tragedies and scandals lately. I simply do not think the public is ready for another."

"The public or you?" I attacked.

She let out a little outraged *harrumph*.

"After thirty years of service to you, are you saying that my father will not have a state funeral?" My voice rose dangerously.

"I'm afraid not, dear. At least not right away," she said, and before I could continue, she clacked toward Claudius. When she was safely at his side, she laced her fingers together and added, "Darling, I am so sorry that your father's death cannot be made public."

The word *cannot* irked me as much as being called "darling." I asked, "What's your plan, then? To say my father is on vacation?"

Gertrude shot a shocked look at Claudius, as if I had guessed their carefully conceived plan. She nodded and sat down primly. "Something along those lines."

Anger flashed through me again. "Are you crazy or just a—"

Marcellus cleared his throat. My head snapped to look at him over my shoulder, but he was staring at the chandelier. I thought he might have shaken his head slightly, but I couldn't say for sure.

I felt dizzy again but certainly didn't want to sit next to Gertrude or Claudius. There was a chair a fair distance from Claudius, so I headed for it slowly. I sat on the edge and looked out the window. The city was covered in a layer of smog, which seemed oddly fitting.

"Is someone at least going to get my brother?" I asked, still studying the skyline.

"I don't think so," replied Claudius.

I whipped my head around. "What?"

Claudius puffed himself up. "When we said secret, we meant secret."

"Where are you going to bury my father? Someone will notice, even if it's just me at the cemetery."

"We're not going to bury him," Claudius explained in a low voice.

I shuddered, unable to imagine what they planned. My mind raced to horrible possibilities, so I was compelled to ask, "What are you going to do?"

Gertrude said to Claudius, "She doesn't need the details." Then she turned her strained sympathy my way. "My dear, it will all happen eventually."

"He has a plot…next to my mother. He's supposed to be buried there."

"In due time," said Claudius.

I wanted to walk over and grab him by his ridiculous, short beard, which I was sure he thought made him look younger, and whack him in the face. "You're sick. I want Laertes."

"I'm afraid that's not possible," Gertrude said.

"Just send a plane for him!"

Claudius stood and folded his arms. "No."

"Damn it. Why?"

Claudius crossed to the window. "The fewer outside contacts the better. The pilots and stewardesses have confidentiality agreements, but you never know. He does not need to come right away."

I had two choices: find something to throw at them or go home. My limbs felt too heavy to grab the vase on the table next to me, so I headed for the elevator. "I'm going to call my brother," I announced.

Marcellus blocked my way. "No, Ophelia," he said gently.

Claudius shouted, "No outside contact!"

"Not until you have recovered from your shock," Gertrude added.

I whipped back around. "You can't keep me here like a prisoner!"

Claudius said, "Actually, we can."

"Sweetheart…" began Gertrude.

"Don't you dare call me that!"

She turned away and walked to the window, tapping the pane rapidly with her red nails.

"Phee," Hamlet called out desperately as the guards crossed him through the reception room toward his bedroom. "You saw Claudius in the garden that day. You know I'm right!"

"Wait!" Gertrude called to the guards, lifting her hand. "What did you say?"

Hamlet looked at me, then his mother, and while staring directly at Claudius replied, "She saw Claudius leaving the conservatory. Right before Dad, your *husband*, was rushed to the hospital. Why would that be?"

I stood in petrified silence, wondering if I was going to be dragged out by security next. Why couldn't he keep his mouth shut?

"What do you have to say about this?" Gertrude asked me.

"Nothing." My eyes darted around the room at the various guards who stood nearby. They were all under orders to keep what they heard and saw in these halls a secret or risk imprisonment or worse. Even so, Gertrude and Claudius knew it wouldn't take more than a whisper or a hint from one of them to begin a cascade of bad publicity and questions. It also occurred to me that the guards were under orders to do exactly what Gertrude and Claudius demanded, even if that included imprisoning or harming me. I couldn't feel my arms, and my tongue felt thick. "I didn't see anything. He's making this up." Hamlet's face fell, and I had to look away.

"Take him." Claudius gestured to the guards as he and Gertrude exchanged impenetrable looks. Anger? Fear? Agreement? Impossible to know.

"Phee!" Hamlet cried.

"Talk to me again and I will kill you!" I screamed.

"Do not threaten the prince," Marcellus warned.

"Why not? Will you put me in jail? Okay," I shouted to the other guards, "I plan to kill Queen Gertrude and King Claudius, too! Take me away now. You have to. Get me out of this asylum!"

"Dear girl," Gertrude said, coming toward me again.

"Don't touch me!" I screamed. "You believe Hamlet that this was an accident? What kind of accident? Who was he actually trying to kill?" I looked at Claudius.

His face remained blank as he commanded to Marcellus, "Take her home."

"You don't get it, do you?" I shouted over my shoulder as Marcellus pulled me by the arm toward the elevator. "How safe are any of you? You crazy—"

"Quiet," Marcellus hissed, shoving me inside.

When we got to my apartment, Marcellus started yelling at me. "What do you think you're doing shouting at the king and queen like that?"

"I don't care who I— He killed my father!" I couldn't stand there and argue. I couldn't control my feelings. I couldn't care what I said anymore. I collapsed on the couch and wept. And wept. Marcellus neither walked over nor tried to console me. Even after I had stopped sobbing—and I have no idea how long that was—I couldn't and wouldn't talk. I sat with my fingers pressed into my face, trying to feel something and nothing at the same time.

Eventually I took my sleeves, dried my face, and asked, "What now?"

"You stay here until we hear otherwise."

I watched him walk to the phone in the kitchen and unplug it, then tuck it under his arm. "What are you doing?" I asked, trepidation breaking through the numbness.

He just looked at me, waiting for my mind to catch up. My lip started to quiver. "All of them?" I asked.

He did not answer but walked to my father's room and returned with a phone cord and my father's laptop. "Why are you doing this?" I asked, though I knew exactly why.

"I have to take your cell phone and your computer, too," he said as he walked to my room.

When he disappeared from view, I ran for my purse and grabbed my cell. Maybe I could get a message off before he returned. Marcellus hurried back into the room as if he knew what I would try. He saw me before I could hide my phone and reached out his hand.

"One message. Please," I begged.

He looked skeptical.

"To Horatio. You can read along."

He looked wary but nodded his assent.

i need u. cm hom

He nodded again, and I pressed Send. We waited, looking at each other. It was my one chance to get someone I trusted into the castle.

Bing. I looked at the reply:

Horatio: Cnt miss mor skl. 2 bhnd.

"Shoot," I muttered. "I can't tell him?" I asked, knowing the answer.

Marcellus shook his head sternly and said, "I shouldn't have let you even do this much." He reached for the phone. I gripped it hard, but he pulled it out of my hand. Surprisingly, he remained next to me, holding it in his palm. I was hoping Horatio would say more. Maybe Marcellus was, too.

We waited through an unbearably long pause during which the only sounds we heard were the ticking of the clock that rested on my father's bookshelf and the murmur of traffic passing below. I hoped Horatio was trying to figure out what I needed and hadn't considered the discussion finished.

The *bing* startled Marcellus and me.

Horatio: wil cm fri. ok?

It wasn't okay. That was five days away. Five days! My breath got really jagged, and my hands started shaking. Marcellus typed "ok" and put my phone in his pocket. "Don't try to leave. You know you can't," he said sympathetically. He squeezed my shoulder.

The elevator opened, and another guard walked into my apartment. He nodded at Marcellus, and Marcellus headed for the elevator with the phones and computers in his arms.

The new guard, a baby-faced guy with a crew cut, stood blocking the elevator as the doors slid shut behind him. He clasped his hands in front of him and stared out the window across the room, ignoring my presence.

Leaning against the kitchen island, I tried to process the last hour. I stared furiously at the shiny black uniform blocking my way out. *They can't make me stay in here,* I thought. Looking ahead as if he didn't exist, I marched toward the elevator and pushed the button.

"What are you doing?" he asked.

My heart raced, but I didn't answer.

"You're not getting in that elevator," he said, more of a challenge than an explanation.

Without replying, I studied my vague reflection in the brushed nickel doors. They slid open and I stepped forward. The guard grabbed me by the arm, swung me around, and threw me to the ground. I smacked my cheek as I landed. He pinned my arms behind me and held me down with one knee, not hard enough to hurt but enough to keep me still. "Send

Marcellus," he called into his shoulder walkie-talkie. "And you're going to have to reprogram the elevator. I told you, it can't stop on this floor." He leaned on me until Marcellus returned.

As I lay there, my chest pressed to the floor, I thought of how sorry I was that I'd ever started dating Hamlet, wished that we'd never kissed on a whim back when we were just friends, wished that I'd listened to my father and truly ended things once they had begun. And if I could turn back time, I would have given up the years of kisses and caring and feeling special and feeling loved to have my father back. To have my freedom back.

Marcellus's boots were highly polished, which I only noticed because they were so close to my nose. Calmly he said, "I'm going to have Officer Cornelius get off you now, but if you try to run, we're both coming for you, and this time it'll hurt."

I felt Cornelius lift himself off my back, and I rolled over. Both men extended a hand, but I got up on my own. My cheek was throbbing, but I refused to touch it and give them the satisfaction of seeing the pain they had inflicted.

"How can you be a part of this?" I asked Marcellus, furiously trying not to cry again.

He didn't answer but nodded at Cornelius and pushed the button. It didn't light up.

"You'll have to take the stairs. I had them reprogram it," Cornelius told him.

"They're going to need to switch that back," Marcellus said, and then, speaking into his walkie-talkie, gave the order to change it. When he was done, he said to Cornelius, "Can't have the rotation taking the stairs all the time."

"Rotation?" I asked.

Cornelius said, "There'll be three guards assigned to you, in eight-hour shifts."

"Wait. Someone's going to be in here all the time?"

"For now." Marcellus frowned. He put his hands in his pockets and his voice grew gentle. "Listen, Ophelia, just stop fighting this. You know you hold no cards here. No one can protect you, and no one can release you except the king and queen. The only thing to do is wait it out, and your happiness is not their priority. So get comfortable."

"What are they going to do with Hamlet?" I asked, my voice catching on his name.

"Not your concern. You take care now. We'll make sure you've got food, and someone'll be in to clean each week."

"Week?" I gasped.

Marcellus nodded, his brow furrowed. "Could be a while." He turned to push the button, and it lit up. Then he disappeared, leaving me with Officer Cornelius, questions, and bottomless grief. I sat, completely desolate.

Francisco: I quote, "I plan to kill Queen Gertrude and King Claudius, too! Take me away now." Sounds pretty clear.

Ophelia: I was upset.

Francisco: Obviously.

Barnardo: So if you weren't plotting all along, then was this when you began planning revenge against the royal family?

Francisco: Answer him.

Barnardo: Ophelia. *(pause)* Ophelia!

Francisco: You will answer his questions and you will answer for this.

19

"You disappeared for a while after your father's death. Were you being held prisoner?"

"Yes, I was."

"Under whose orders?"

"Claudius's."

"You see, ladies? I knew that man was no good." Members of the audience nod angrily. Then Zara raises her eyebrows and asks, "What about Queen Gertrude?"

Ophelia looks backstage. "I don't think she knew anything about it." As the audience twitters, Ophelia takes a sip of water.

Wandering around in a daze, I found that everything I looked at dredged up a painful memory. Of my father. Of Laertes. Of Hamlet. Their presence haunted every corner of the apartment. To escape, I went out on the balcony, but the moment I did, I began to recall the many happy, lazy hours I spent out there alone with Hamlet. My mind filled and pulsed as I lowered myself onto the hammock. There I remained, full of breathless anxiety, until the sun came up and turned the high-rises and the river pink.

I rose, suddenly needing to face the truth. I headed into my father's bathroom, noticing that his toothbrush was discarded on the counter rather than resting in its holder — a toothbrush that would never be used again, one of his socks lying on the tile next to the hamper, a few stray bits of stubble left on the side of the sink after he shaved. He was typically fastidious but had been rushing around so much lately that things had been left undone, unfixed, uncared for. I touched his hand towel, and started to bring it to my face to smell it, knowing the scent of his aftershave would be lingering in the fabric, but I realized if I did, I might crack apart.

I let go of the towel, walked back into his bedroom, and found myself opening his sock drawer. The dress socks were rolled into perfect balls and arranged by hue. His white athletic socks were pushed to the back, for he hadn't taken the time to do anything fun like run or play tennis — once his passions — since Hamlet's father had died. I guess he had too much work to do.

With mounting dread, I kept searching through his stuff. By the time I got to the box of cuff links he kept in that drawer and found my mother's wedding ring tucked inside, I was so undone, so distressed, that I barely made it out of the room on my feet. But I would have crawled to get out of there if I had to. No way could I have stayed in that place of painful memory for another second.

"You okay?" asked the guard.

I didn't even stop to answer his stupid question. I staggered down the hall but stopped. My room was full of Hamlet. I couldn't go in there. My father's room was full of loss. I couldn't go back. Only Laertes's was neutral, so I flung open the door and stumbled in. Curling up on the floor, I closed my eyes and wished I could turn back time and have him be there telling me I was annoying and calling for our father to kick me out.

I woke up on the floor in the late afternoon. My stomach was acid, and my cheek—bruised the day before, then slept on for who knows how long—burned. I made my way back to the kitchen. Officer Cornelius was sitting on a folding chair that had come from somewhere else in the castle. It looked out of place in my home and uncomfortable to sit on for long, but I wasn't offering him anything more welcoming.

"You okay?" he asked.

Without acknowledging him, I got a mug down for tea and put bread in the toaster.

"We checked to make sure you were breathing," he said. "And we took the medications out of all the bathrooms."

"How about the household cleaners?" I asked.

He didn't respond, but I noticed they were gone by the next morning.

For the next two days, I stayed in my room almost all the time, bored, depressed, and sick from not eating properly. I was too out of it to read or draw, and I was unwilling to watch television with one of the guards looking over my shoulder. I didn't want to cook in front of them either, so I grabbed whatever packaged food we had around.

Lying on my bed, I felt removed from my body. I would poke at my face to make sure I was still there. I could feel the sensation on both my finger and my face, but it was distant, like having gloves on or like it was happening to someone else. I didn't always try to bring myself back from the numbness. Sometimes I relished it. Numb felt good. Numb meant not thinking. Not feeling. And being numb and awake was far less terrifying than being asleep.

Every time I drifted off, I had nightmares. My dreams were full of broken glass and flashing cameras and flying bullets. In them, I was trying to stop my mother from getting in a car or telling my dad not to hide in Gertrude's room, but neither of them seemed to know I was talking. I would call out, but my voice was nothing more than a rasping whisper. Off they would go, down a hall or into an elevator, and, standing alone, I would hear screams and see blood oozing or flowing or splattering. And then I would wake.

Deprived of sleep and peace of mind, I began to doubt my own sanity. But when I focused and thought about it, I became sure that if I were allowed out, allowed to call my brother or Horatio, or allowed to go to school, the routine and human contact would do me good.

Thursday afternoon, I showered for the first time in days, dressed myself, and marched up to Officer Cornelius, demanding that I be taken to see Gertrude. He looked at me warily. "I don't think they'll allow that."

"Call them," I insisted, pointing sharply at his shoulder.

He did, and we waited for a few minutes as more calls were placed. I hadn't heard the caravan of limos and security sedans, so I knew she was in the castle. Officer Cornelius looked at me with some concern and even opened his mouth to say something. It must have been an inquiry as to my well-being, because he clapped his mouth back shut and held his lips in a tight line. I smiled at my infinitesimal victory.

The speaker crackled awake, and to both of our surprise, someone on the other end said that we could proceed upstairs.

Gertrude sat at her desk with her blessed tea set spread out just so and gestured for me to join her. I stood behind the chair instead. "You're looking…" she began, but could not say I looked well and so said nothing.

Faced with her, my emotions ran higher, but it was my one chance to make my case and I wanted to appear levelheaded. "Gertrude, I know you're worried about Hamlet and what might happen to him if this gets out, but you don't have to keep me a prisoner. I won't tell anyone anything. I swear. I'll go to my brother, and you'll never have to hear from me again. Just let me leave."

Her face was expressionless. "You know I wish I could," she said.

"Can I at least have permission to get out of my apartment? I'm going crazy down there all alone. You could send guards with me. I…I don't have to go back to school, but let me go outside or talk to my friends or get a cup of coffee somewhere."

She tapped her fingernails on the rim of her teacup. "I don't trust you to keep silent. I don't trust you at all."

"What have I done to make you not trust me?"

"Let's not fool ourselves, dearest. It didn't take much for you to betray my son, so…"

"That was your doing. You said—"

She flicked her hand in the air as if swatting the truth away.

"Don't rewrite history, Gertrude. You blackmailed me. We had a deal, and I kept up my side of the bargain."

She laced her fingers together and sat tall, her gaze burning through me. "You got no helpful information from Hamlet. And now we have a new problem."

I paused, not sure what she meant. And when I realized, my anger exploded. I walked around the chair and slammed my palms on her table. "Problem? How is your son killing my father *my* problem?"

She rose slowly and said with terrifying calm, "It would be better for all of us if you weren't around, but you're here, and we have to figure out what to do with you. Until that time, you will stay put."

Figure out what to do with me? My mind reeled as I thought of the possibilities, and fear left me with only enough breath to whisper, "Please, Gertrude. Please let me out."

She shook her head and then left the room.

I wanted to pick up the tea set and fling it at her. I wanted to take the little tongs from the sugar-cube bowl and stab her with them. Instead, I sank into the chair and rested my forehead on one palm, trying to keep my mind in the room where I was. I hadn't the strength. I felt it float out of my body and to the window and imagined seeing all of Elsinore sparkling in the mid-afternoon sun.

I headed half-dazed for the elevator. As I passed Claudius's office, he opened the door and asked me to come in. I hesitated but had no choice. He closed the door behind me, and I stood near it, hoping I could run if I needed to.

Leaning in, he said, "You told my wife that Hamlet was lying about your seeing me in the garden. I think you are the one who is lying. I need the truth and I need it now." He was speaking slowly and measuredly, but behind his facade I detected a sense of nervousness.

"I…" I began, but was afraid to continue. My eyes flicked to the corners of the office, hoping to see a security camera in any of them like there were in so many of the other offices and meeting rooms. Sadly, there were none. I considered lying but realized that if he had evidence, I would be even more screwed.

"The day…the day the ki…your brother died…I…I went into the garden to read."

Claudius's eyes narrowed almost imperceptibly.

"When I came out of the elevator, I…I saw you headed for…for the stairs."

"And?"

My heart was racing, and blood was rushing in my ears. "And that's it."

"Who have you told?" he asked, his lips curling.

"No one."

"You told Hamlet!" he shouted, and grabbed my arm. I tried to move away, but his grip merely tightened.

"Only him. Not even—" My voice broke at the thought of him. "Not even my father." I was too scared to mention Horatio's name for fear of what Claudius would do to him. And I hoped Horatio hadn't casually mentioned it to anyone, though that would have been out of character.

Claudius bent at the knees so his face was level with mine and he squeezed my arm even tighter. "Let me be clear," he growled. "You saw nothing. But if I find out that you so much as mentioned your being in the conservatory that day, let alone the fact that you saw me, I will kill you and whomever you told." He held me for another moment to be sure his message had time to sink in, then opened the door and pushed me through it.

To my astonishment, when Officer Cornelius and I got back to my apartment, Hamlet was waiting. He was standing behind the kitchen island cutting fruit. Seriously. Cutting. Fruit. I couldn't believe he was free, and I was locked up, and I couldn't believe he was standing in my apartment, a place he'd fled from in anger. I wanted to scream, "Are you insane?" and then I thought that he really might be. Who besides a crazy person kills a girl's dad and then comes to cut fruit in her kitchen? And if he was crazy, I didn't want to be anywhere near him, especially if he was armed with more than just that carving knife.

I remained frozen while Cornelius took a step in front of me and asked, "Sir, what are you doing here?"

"I'm making a smoothie. I know how much Ophelia loves them. I'm headed for England tonight, so I thought I'd do this as a farewell gesture."

"Sir," Cornelius insisted, "you're not allowed anywhere near her. Where's your detail?"

Hamlet began cutting again.

I took a step back, but the elevator doors had already closed. The cool surface chilled my shoulder blades. It was such a familiar sight, seeing Hamlet in my kitchen, but it made me feel like I had jumped out of my body. Everything looked jerky and echoed. My mind raced to other days like this when I would have sat with him on my balcony and enjoyed the day doing nothing. But my father would not come home that afternoon; he was hidden somewhere, cold and dead, waiting for a proper burial. Mr. Smoothie himself had cut my father's life short with ease. How much regret could he have had if he was standing there in my kitchen making me a goddamned fruity drink?

I spun around and tried to push the button, but Cornelius grabbed my wrist.

"Hey, what are you doing?" yelled Hamlet, coming toward us.

"She can't leave, sir," Cornelius replied.

Hamlet kept walking.

"Put down the knife, sir."

I shrank back behind Cornelius, terrified of what Hamlet would do next.

"I'm not going to…Jesus," Hamlet said, putting the knife on the end table. He put his hands up and asked, "What do you mean she can't leave?"

"Orders, sir."

"Has she been kept in here since I killed…"

"Yes," I whispered, still cowering behind Officer Cornelius, who I was suddenly glad was in my apartment. Hamlet squatted down, put his head on his knees, and started to cry. The guard moved swiftly to remove the knife from the table.

I was standing alone and exposed, hoping Hamlet was truly feeling the regret he showed. At that moment I believed he was my only chance of escape. "Tell your mother to let me go," I pleaded quietly.

He wiped his tears and looked at me. He stood suddenly, and I shrank back. Officer Cornelius moved forward, but Hamlet merely came over and pushed the button for the elevator. My heart was racing. His scent, so familiar, so loved, wafted over to me, and I felt myself leave my body again. I closed my eyes, hoping to chase my soul back to its proper place. The elevator *ding*ed and Hamlet vanished behind its sliding doors without another word.

I sank to the floor and leaned against the wall, staring at the pile of fruit Hamlet had left on the counter.

"You—you okay?" asked Officer Cornelius. When I winced, he said, "Sorry to ask, but that was…unexpected."

Barely above a tense whisper, I asked, "Unexpected? All of this is unexpected. I don't even…" Without bothering to finish my sentence, I rose and dragged my feet down the hall to my bedroom.

As I entered, I caught sight of a framed photo of Hamlet and me in Florence—one Hamlet had taken of us on the Ponte Vecchio. He had held the camera at arm's length and we had pressed our faces together to fit in the shot. Even though you can hardly see the old bridge or the river behind us, it had been my favorite photo because Hamlet had wanted to commemorate the spot I loved the most. And the photo wasn't staged for anyone. It wasn't *for* anyone. It was just for us. And we were happy.

I picked up the frame and held it close to my eyes and then far away, thinking that if I looked at it from the right angle, I might be able to understand all that had happened, all that had changed. I turned the frame over and pulled out the photo, held it to the light, and then flipped it over. The faintest image of us shone through, remnants of what we had been.

Struck by an idea, I walked over to my wall, grabbed a pushpin from the corner of my Poor Yoricks poster, and stuck the photo to the wall. Then I pulled the rest of the pins out of that poster and from two art prints hanging nearby as well. The points of the pins poked my palm as I clenched them tightly. The pain focused me.

I dove for a photo album that had been kicked under my desk and opened it. Photo after photo of Hamlet and me. Some with Horatio. Some with our families. I pulled out one photo, then another, then another, and started pinning each to the wall. When I ran out of pins, I used tape. When I ran out of photos, I printed more, cropping out anything that wasn't just the two of us. Then I started cropping closer and closer. I printed just my lips. Just his hands. Just my cheek. Just his chin. Just his eyes. Then my eyes. And Gertrude's eyes. And my father's eyes. And Claudius's eyes. I taped the images one above the other, building a tower of faces and eyes. I stepped back. It was eerie.

I reached for my art case and plucked out the thickest brush. Rolling it between my palms, I stared at the wall and decided what I wanted. I picked up a dinner plate I'd neglected to return to the kitchen and squished black paint onto it. Smushing the brush into the dark puddle and disregarding the drops that fell on the carpet, I pushed the brush against the wall. If my father were home and saw what I was doing, he would have lost it. But he wasn't. He never would be again. I froze for a second and then ran the brush higher on the wall. I dipped into the paint over and over and painted black up and down, side to side, above and between the photos. I stepped back. It was not the grid I had set out to paint. It was the castle.

The tower stood menacing, dark; the faces and bits of people peeking through the windows. A home. A monolith. A prison.

The rest of the wall needed to be filled. Purple brushstrokes—coarse and swift—became the sky. Red rain pelted down. The drops grew longer and sharper, becoming daggers. I would paint daggers because I could use none. My thoughts turned angrier. Unearthly flowers of odd shapes and colors sprouted near the floor, under furniture that I did not bother to move. Some flowers had teeth. Some had eyes. Some had fangs. They grew from the ground and crept up and around the tower. Vines. Fingers. Strangling the tower of happy faces, covering the watchful eyes.

With the wall full and my hands aching, I slumped onto the bed and regarded my work. It was wild. It was disturbing. I was the best painting I'd ever done, and no one would see it.

Ophelia: You know they locked me up?
Barnardo: Yeah.

Ophelia: Was that part of my sinister plan?

Barnardo: They knew you were a danger.

Ophelia: So it was my fault?

Francisco: You threatened them. What else would you have had them do?

Ophelia: You seem pretty big on blaming the victim.

Barnardo: I don't see any victim here. I just see the last girl standing.

20

"How did being locked away make you feel?"

Ophelia's eye twitches. "Trapped." She studies her laced fingers.

"And?" Zara pushes.

Ophelia pauses and looks out at the audience. The camera cuts to their expectant faces before she adds, "I guess…Horrible. Lonely. Terrified. I didn't know what Claudius had planned."

"Just Claudius?"

Ophelia nods.

Zara puts her hand on Ophelia's. "So much for a young woman to go through." She dabs at her eye before saying, "We are sooo glad you are safe and free."

"What the hell is going on?" Horatio shouted as he pushed past Officer Cornelius.

I leaped off the couch and ran to him. His presence snapped me out of my malaise, and I clutched him, allowing relief to wash over me. Once I felt ready to let go, I guided him to where I had been sitting for most of the week. Taking his hands in mine, I forced myself to stay composed. "Hamlet killed my father."

He winced. "I know. I went up to see Hamlet first, and he told me." His leg was bouncing. "Where's Laertes?"

I felt my face twitching as I struggled to push down the emotion. "He hasn't been told."

"How can I know but your brother can't? This is outrageous."

I nodded and started to whimper.

Horatio squeezed my hands. "Ophelia, I can't get you out of here."

I nodded again.

"I tried to talk to Gertrude, but she wouldn't hear of it. She told me I wasn't supposed to know and that if I told my parents, she'd fire them and imprison me as a traitor."

I whispered, "She said that?"

He nodded. "It really took me by surprise. Gertrude has never been anything but civil to me. She's scared, Ophelia. And getting desperate."

My lip trembled again. "I don't know what they're gonna do to me."

"They'll let you go. They have to."

I felt an emptiness in the pit of my stomach. "I'm not so sure."

"They're not going to hurt you," he said. Horatio's powers of forgiveness and optimism were usually endearing, but just then he seemed a fool in my eyes.

"You don't know that." Again I thought of Claudius grabbing me, his face so close to mine.

"What would make you think—"

"What would make me think they'd lock me up and hide my father's body? I'm done with making excuses for them. Done with giving anyone the benefit of the doubt. Done with predicting. Nothing makes sense anymore, Horatio, and trying to reason it out hasn't worked so far. I have cause to be afraid, and you know it. There are a million reasons a high school girl could disappear. They could put out any story, and everyone would believe it."

"I wouldn't."

I felt a chill thinking of Horatio as a whistle-blower for my murder or my kidnapping or my banishment or whatever they might have in store for me. "Then you'd better watch out yourself. You're expendable, too...though at least you have parents who would look for you." My father, blue and on a slab somewhere awaiting a proper burial. My mother, deep beneath the ground rotting or already dust. It was too awful to consider.

I leaned back on the couch and looked at the ceiling, willing myself to be as neutral and empty as that expanse. "Gertrude knows that the public will react badly if this comes out. Could her dear Hamlet become king if he's found guilty of murder?"

"People forget, and if not, they certainly forgive. Especially if that someone is powerful and good-looking enough."

I knew he was right. You could drive off a bridge and kill your girlfriend, but if you had gorgeous teeth and your family had a significant enough title, you could go live a happy life in a ducal palace somewhere.

I conceded. "Maybe. But in the end, the public will need someone to blame, and Gertrude will see to it that the blame will fall on me. I know it." Pinpricks of anxiety spread across my back.

Down below, multiple cars squealed to a stop and van doors clanged opened. I vaguely realized that either the king or queen was arriving, and my body immediately tensed.

I had left the television on, and the sound of my own name

made me look up and listen. "We haven't seen Hamlet or Ophelia in a while. Is anything the matter?" asked Stormy Somerville, wearing an uncharacteristically high-necked sweater.

Standing in front of the castle's gleaming entrance, a dozen and a half floors directly below my balcony, Gertrude explained, "Hamlet and Ophelia have gone on a little getaway together."

"We heard they've been fighting lately."

"Thus the need for a getaway." Gertrude winked and disappeared inside.

Horatio exhaled loudly.

A buzzing in Officer Cornelius's earpiece made me turn around. Once he had taken his finger off his ear, he said, "Ophelia, the queen is on her way up. Sir, you should go."

My face went numb, and I couldn't make myself breathe.

Horatio turned to Officer Cornelius and asked, "Why are you even here?"

"Orders, sir," he mumbled.

"There are cameras and guards everywhere. How's she gonna get out undetected?"

Officer Cornelius shrugged and leaned against the wall.

"This is ridiculous." Horatio looked at Officer Cornelius, then at me. Frowning, he said, "I'm not leaving you alone. I'm hiding in your dad's office."

"No. Go. What if they find you?" I stood up quickly. "You'll come back later, though, right?"

He nodded as he stood. Shoving his hands in his pockets, he walked in large strides to the stairwell.

Moments after he left, Gertrude burst into my apartment, silk scarf flapping in her wake. She looked me over, scowled, and announced, "People are starting to ask questions. You need to be seen. Next week should do the trick."

"What about Hamlet?"

"He's being sent to England tonight. The incident with your father delayed—" She pulled out a handkerchief and dabbed her eyes. "The details are none of your concern. We need people to know you are still around but to see you alone. Eventually, the public will assume you two broke up, or we'll tell them you did, and then we can finally end this charade."

I felt a chill as I wondered what exactly her plan for ending it was.

"In one week, you can go with Horatio for that coffee you wanted so bad," she said, and clicked away.

While Horatio waited at the counter for his coffee, I sat silently. I let the steam from my cup tickle my face. The feeling mesmerized me. I had begun finding pleasure in little sensations during the weeks that had passed. I had spent an entire afternoon musing over what part of my arm was the most sensitive and found it curious that, for all the tickling that happens with the armpit, it is hardly as ticklish as the inside of the forearm. I also found that poking oneself with a pin, if done lightly, actually feels more like a tickle than pain.

In that time, I had also grown so used to silence and solitude that it was odd being suddenly surrounded by strangers. They all seemed so loud. They all moved so fast. They were all so fixed on their destination, so serious in their anonymous self-importance. Would it really matter if they made one bus or the next, skipped work that day, or had an affair with the next person they saw? Who would really care or notice?

I watched them walk in and out, ordering their very expensive coffees just so, taking secret pleasure in their complex orders. It occurred to me that those decisions at the coffee shop about what flavor and how much foam might be the only element over which those people had any control for that entire day. Perhaps that was why everyone loved to come for their latte-macchiato-double-shot-light-whipped whatevers.

"Welcome back to town," a redheaded employee said as she wiped the table next to mine.

I stared at her blankly before realizing what she meant. Perhaps it was my look of shock or the close proximity of a regular citizen that tipped him off, but Officer Cornelius strode up next to me.

"I'm sorry, what?" I asked her.

"You and Prince Hamlet have a good trip?"

Cornelius stepped closer to my side.

I looked at him, and he nodded subtly. "Uh…yeah," I said.

"Too bad you couldn't go somewhere to get a tan."

I nodded slightly.

"Hey, mind if I take a picture with you?" She pulled out a camera, handed it to Officer Cornelius, then put her arm around me. I was too stunned to nod or smile. I did, however, notice other people taking our picture as well.

"Thanks." She smiled pertly before going to wipe a table across the store.

Cornelius raised his eyebrows and backed away while I stared out the window and wondered if Gertrude had planted her or if she just happened to ask.

Horatio sat, but I didn't acknowledge him. "Ophelia?" He waved a hand at my face.

"What? Oh, sorry."

"You're freaking me out. Where'd your mind go?" he asked.

I shrugged, not wanting to discuss the girl quite yet.

"Now I've got two of you on my hands." He sighed.

"What do you mean?" He suddenly looked really uncomfortable, and I realized he was talking about Hamlet again. I felt a pain run across my forehead, and I steadied my breath. "You talked to him? How is he?"

Horatio looked over my shoulder at Officer Cornelius, who was standing by the door. Horatio leaned closer and whispered, "I can't believe you want to know."

"Me, either," I said weakly, not sure why this time I was curious rather than infuriated. Maybe it was habit. Or maybe Gertrude's tears had made me wonder if the trip to England was part of a sinister plan.

He squinted at me as if measuring whether or not I really wanted the information. I nodded my assent, and he looked down at his own cup, picking at the cardboard sleeve wrapped around it. In a low voice, he continued, "Bad. Confused. Unpredictable."

I felt nauseous but also like something in me was reaching out for the Hamlet I knew and loved. Part of me was worried for him just then, wanted to be with him and talk to him as much as another part of me wanted to hurt him and his family.

Horatio looked around and then whispered, "He says Claudius wants him dead, but he has no proof. Things are... this can't end well. I'm really getting nervous, Ophelia." Horatio looked over my shoulder.

Officer Cornelius walked up behind me and cleared his throat. "Sorry, sir, but I have to get her back."

Horatio looked as if he were going to protest, but I stood up immediately. All I needed was to get either of us into trouble and end the possibility of a second outing. Even an outing used to manipulate the public was better than being locked away. I would do what I had to do to get out. And to stay alive.

Francisco: You were seen having coffee with Horatio. That's not what I call imprisonment.
Ophelia: That took weeks to achieve.
Francisco: Even so.
Ophelia: A guard was with me, and you know it.
Barnardo: So is that when you worked on your plan for escape?
Ophelia: That's when I worked on my cappuccino.

21

"So here you are just before your disappearance. It's a little fuzzy, because it was taken on a camera phone, but that is you, right?"

Ophelia, looking a little bewildered, nods. "Wow. Look at that picture! I didn't know one like that existed. That's...that's scary, actually." She starts to laugh, and the audience, feeling this gives them permission, giggles a little, too.

Zara tilts her head slightly and smirks. "So the rumor was that you went crazy."

Slightly amused, Ophelia says, "I do look crazy there, but I was, well, distressed, to say the least."

"This is during the time you were being locked away?"

"Yes, and after Claudius threatened to kill me."

Zara looks out at the audience with feigned shock. As the women and men gasp and mutter, nearly undetectable satisfaction registers on Ophelia's face. Zara allows them their moment and then turns her attention back to Ophelia. "It was just an act?"

"Yes. I needed what came next to be believable."

Right after Horatio and I got back from having coffee, Marcellus walked in and asked to speak with me alone. I took him into my room, where he explained, "I know it's been a while since you asked, but things got crazy around here. I wanted to let you know that I checked into the video you asked about, the one with, uh, you and Hamlet," he began. He tugged at his gun belt, and the handcuffs jangled. "No one knows anything about it."

"Maybe it was sent to Gertrude or Claudius personally."

Marcellus shook his head. "I don't think so. Any threat, even the smallest or most personal, is dealt with by security. Not even VanDerwater knew."

"Maybe he's lying. VanDerwater's your boss, so—"

"No, he'd tell me anything involving Hamlet. Far as I can tell, it never existed."

"Well that's just perfect," I said, and sank onto the bed and rubbed my temples.

"I thought you'd be relieved no tape like that was kicking around."

I blinked back tears. "I would if I hadn't—" I swallowed hard and finished our conversation with, "Thanks for checking into it."

He nodded and left the room.

Horatio came in to find me and flinched as he noticed the painted wall. "What the hell is that?"

"A self-portrait," I mumbled.

He squinted and tilted his head, studying my work of art. "It's…uh…a little twisted." When I started to sniffle, he added, "No, it's not that bad."

I shook my head. "It's not that. It's—*ugh*." I fell back onto my bed, staring at the wall of eyes and at my desk, where my computer, phone, and framed photos of Hamlet once sat. "There was no sex tape. They lied. And my father died thinking I was a total slut, and I screwed over Hamlet for nothing. Oh yeah, and my dad's dead." I rubbed my forehead, as if the motion could erase memory and pain.

"You look like you need a drink."

I nodded and sent him into Dad's office to see if he could find the bottle of vodka my father had hidden behind a volume of tax laws. My father didn't know I knew that he nipped at the bottle before important press conferences, and he didn't know that I snuck some before public appearances that involved large crowds. Its lack of odor was perfect for both of our purposes.

Back in my room, I held out the vodka, but Horatio declined because he planned to drive back to school. Horatio and I sat in my room while I drank, and we talked about everything. For once, Horatio didn't suggest prudence when I reached for the bottle. And reach for the bottle I did. The last thing I remember is telling Horatio how pretty I thought the sun looked as it set over the river.

I don't recall what happened that evening in Gertrude's office, but I was shown the video weeks later when officers from the Denmark Department of Investigations were piecing all of these strange and disparate events together. I'm not sure what purpose Gertrude had in installing cameras in the official offices. Then again, maybe she didn't even know they were there. I wondered: If there were cameras in as many places as I later found out there were, how had secrets been kept at all? Yet the biggest, most important moments of the prior year had been kept out of reach of the lenses. Clearly people familiar with the systems had perpetrated the dirtiest deeds, and the surveillance was not meant for them.

On the video I am seen in loosely hanging flannel pajama pants and a T-shirt, drifting into Gertrude's offices looking at no one in particular.

"Ophelia? Is that you?" asks Gertrude.

I appear not to see her but turn my head, dreamily searching the room. I ask, "Where is the king of Denmark? We were supposed to meet and talk about Hamlet, and then I was going to show him my painting, but I can't find him anywhere. He was a good man, a good king. I miss him." I kneel and look under her desk. "I missed him at the coffee house, and I've looked everywhere."

Gertrude looks thoroughly uncomfortable and sends her secretary out.

Claudius walks purposefully into the room reading some paper or other and stops in his tracks. Once he figures out it's me, his expression changes, and he lets his hand, along with the papers, drop to his side. "Look at her," he says in astonishment. "Is she this upset because of her father?" Gertrude shrugs and drifts to Claudius. They huddle together in conversation and amazement.

My head snaps at the sound of his voice and I wander over to him, chanting one of the limericks I'd been writing with Horatio, an activity begun once I'd finished about a quarter of the bottle of vodka.

> *There once was a girl named Ophelia,*
> *Who asked, "Hey, what's the deal-y–uh?"*
> *She knew Hamlet loved her,*
> *But a split did occur,*
> *And then he killed her dad.*

I take Claudius by the face and slap his cheeks playfully. "I can't seem to make the last part rhyme. The last line should rhyme with the first, but my name is tough. Maybe I need a new opener. What rhymes with 'murderous prick'?" I laugh and then turn away, pulling at my T-shirt as if confused by its very presence.

Claudius turns to Gertrude and asks in a low voice, "She looks drunk. I thought the guards cleared her apartment."

Gertrude replies, face strained, "They did, but Horatio's been visiting her. God knows what those clods you hire to protect us let him bring to her." Gertrude then tries to take me by the hand and lead me out of the room, but I pull back and look at her intently.

I say to her shakily, "Is everything set for the funeral? I can't think of anything but my father in the cold ground. It makes me cry just to think of it." I grab Gertrude and begin sobbing on her shoulder. She stiffens and pats me on the back like a child hater who is given a baby to hold.

A door opens, and Horatio rushes in, stopping short when he sees me. I look up at Horatio and quickly step away from Gertrude as if I have no idea why I'm near her. Swiping under my wet nose and eyeing her suspiciously, I walk over to him and say, "My brother will know of it. My brother…" Then my gaze drifts back to Gertrude and Claudius and I say, "Thank you for your good advice. I will fix the rhyme, but after the ball. My father says it's for charity, and we're expected. He hates when I'm late!" I curtsy and continue. "Good night, ladies. And gentlemen. And kings. Wait—where is the king? Dead, too, I think. We will need to find him." I curtsy again and say, "Good night," as I walk out of the room somewhat grandly, though my steps wobble every so often.

Claudius says to Horatio, "Are you responsible for this?"

Horatio's only answer before he leaves is, "I should make sure she's okay."

Claudius turns to Gertrude. "We can use this. It's time to get Laertes home."

Gertrude appears uncertain as she looks in the direction I disappeared.

He continues as he paces, "The people are beginning to whisper about Polonius's absence, and I'm afraid we can't keep his death a secret much longer. We have to act quickly, and I think this is the best option."

Gertrude wrings her hands. "Yes, we should get Laertes on a conference call."

Claudius says, "Dial," as he buzzes the secretary and asks her to get Horatio and me back. Claudius and Gertrude face the large monitor on their wall, and Laertes, clearly having just returned from the gym, answers.

I couldn't bear to watch him learn of our father's death, and that part was skipped. Agents Francisco and Barnardo either took pity on me, or they felt that that part was not enlightening enough to force me to watch. My guess would be the latter.

When the video started up again, it showed Horatio walking me back in. I see Laertes's face, and I run to the screen and kiss it, then wander away. Then, Lord help me, I offer up another poem. "I've got it!" I declare, and stand very straight as if ready to recite an important work.

> *There once lived a prince in Denmark*
> *Who killed my dad on a lark,*
> *He said, "Didn't mean it,*
> *Now get me some peanuts,"*
> *But then I was locked in a pit.*

278

"Darn," I say, my hand wiping away at an imaginary board. "'Peanuts' sounds silly, and the last line has to rhyme with the first. I have to start over again." I begin writing words in the air with my finger. As my hand passes my face, I take a great interest in my thumb and study it.

Laertes asks, "What's wrong with her? And why did she say she was locked in a pit?"

"She's raving." Gertrude reassures him. "We aren't sure why she's behaving so oddly, but we're bringing in our doctors to have a look at her. We think it's grief. This only started after Hamlet killed your father. Though for some time now, Hamlet has been absolutely horrible, even violent, toward her. You must have heard. We thought perhaps seeing your face might help—"

My brother calls out, "Ophelia!"

I turn and look glassy-eyed at the screen, then pick up a pen from Gertrude's desk. With it, I quickly draw a plant up the length of my inner arm, saying, "There's rosemary. That's for remembrance." I walk over to Horatio and scrawl a similar image on his arm, saying, "Please remember." Then I turn to Gertrude and grab her hand. She tries to pull away, but I hold tight and scribble a flower on her palm. "And that's pansies, that's for thoughts." I kiss her on the cheek and then stumble over to Claudius.

Laertes, pale and frantic, calls out, "Can't you make her stop?"

"There's rue for you," I mutter, trying to draw a flower on Claudius's cheek, but he blocks me. "And here's some for me," I say, turning the pen on myself again and marking my cheek with haphazard petals. I turn to the screen, hold up the pen, and tell my brother, "I would give you some violets, but they withered when my father died." I begin to cry and kneel, holding my stomach.

Laertes asks, "Is she high?"

"No, dear," Gertrude answers smoothly. "As I said, when she found out what Hamlet did to your father, she snapped."

Laertes gestures wildly as he screams, "Hamlet did this to her. I knew it. I knew this would happen. I'll kill him! I'm coming back tonight!"

Claudius commands, "Laertes, please calm down."

"Calm down?"

Gertrude says with false sincerity, "We're taking care of her, and Hamlet is not in the castle at present. Soon you can come home and see your sister…as well as your father's burial. But wait until we call for you, all right?"

"I can't!" he shouts.

"Dearest, you must," Gertrude says soothingly.

Laertes would have known as well as anyone that Gertrude meant he would not be allowed home until they were good and ready to have him back. My brother looks right at Claudius and says, "He'd better be in jail when I get there, and well-protected, or else I'm gonna kill him. I'm not kidding. Hamlet is a murderer and—" His voice breaks, and he rests his forehead on his palms. His shoulders shake.

Weeks later, sitting with the DDI agents, I touched the screen, wishing that we could have grieved together.

On the video, I watched as Gertrude, looking nervous, leans in and whispers something in Claudius's ear. Was she nervous that my brother might be planning to murder her son or nervous that the threat and her complicity were being filmed? I have no idea. What does it matter? Neither scenario makes me like her any more or make what happened any less awful.

Claudius nods and says to Laertes, "We'll make sure you have the chance to *speak* with him when you return."

"When?"

Claudius reaches for the remote and says, "Soon," and ends the video conference call with a creepy smile.

After the screen goes blank, I stand up on wobbling legs and begin to rant, snot and tears streaming down my face. "I hate you," I say, pointing at Claudius. "I hate you all. It's your fault he's dead. It's your fault he did it. He was fine before. But then you had to push him and make me part of your plans." I stumble over to Gertrude. "You did this! You should pay for your crimes. You say you love him, but you did this. And I did it, too. It's my fault he— Oh God!" I shriek, holding my head. Horatio runs over and takes me around the shoulders. "I want my life back the way it was."

"I know," he whispers.

"Get. Her. Home," Claudius growls, and Horatio pulls me out of Gertrude's office.

Here's the weirdest thing: The only memory I have from that night was Hamlet's dad sitting next to my bed. Yes, you read that right. And he wasn't a see-through ghost like you see on TV. It was just him, like he always looked on a casual day: sweater vest, deck shoes, perfectly coiffed hair, and a studying gaze. He sat there like he was watching over me. I wasn't scared, but even in my haze I knew he shouldn't be there. After drifting in and out of sleep a few times, all I could think to say was, "Sorry." He put up his finger to his lips and wandered away.

When I came to in the morning, Horatio was lying on the floor next to my bed, which surprised me. "What's going on?" I asked, my voice croaking. "I thought you were going back to Wittenberg."

He sat up and rubbed his cheeks, creating white and red stripes. "I was supposed to, but I couldn't leave you after what happened. God, Ophelia, what a mess you made."

"What?" I asked, sitting up and looking around the bed, thinking he meant it literally.

"You went to Gertrude's office and…you wouldn't believe it if I told you."

"What did I do?"

"You ranted, recited limericks, and drew flowers on everyone."

"Drew?" I started to laugh. "I did?" I looked down at my arm and, sure enough, there was a spiky plant in black ink.

Horatio held up his matching sketch and tried not to laugh himself. "I thought you'd passed out, but when I went to the bathroom, you ran off. I don't know what the new guard was thinking. He said you told him Gertrude wanted you, and you pushed the button for her floor, so he wasn't too concerned. I caught up with you eventually, but man! I can't believe…" I laughed as he shook his head. "Speaking of the bathroom, I guess we should both clean up."

He went into Laertes's bathroom, and I went into mine. One look in the mirror almost sent me running. My face was streaked with mascara. I figured I had been crying, which saddened me. My hair was pointing in all kinds of wild directions, and my pajama pants and black, holey T-shirt were crumpled and hanging limply.

I felt filthy and in serious need of a shower, and once I got in, I was reluctant to come out. I leaned against the cool tiles, rubbing at the drawing on my arm, trying to let go of all thoughts, until Horatio knocked on the door to see if I was all right. I lied and said yes, and heard him pad down the hall. I wrapped myself in the same towel I had been using since my imprisonment had begun and noticed a distinct smell of mildew. At least doing laundry would give me purpose. Then I thought about that prospect, about how ridiculous it was that doing laundry promised to be the only excitement in my day. Pitiful. Infuriating.

My mother's words from our final conversation popped into my head, words that I had thought of countless times since her death. "Let me assure you that you will sacrifice a lot to be with him. If it's worth it, make the sacrifice. If it stops being worth it, let go." Standing in the bathroom, achy and depressed, her words stung. She never could have known how much my being with Hamlet, or even her husband taking a job at the castle, would cost everyone. It had stopped being worth it some time ago; only I was trapped.

The unbearable nature of my unspecified imprisonment came rushing to the surface. I thought about all that had transpired in the past few weeks, about how my life, once full of fun and freedom, had been reduced to thankfulness at being allowed out for coffee. Bile rose into my throat. Gertrude and her deceit. Claudius and his plotting. Hamlet and his revenge. How did their madness become my nightmare? It couldn't continue. One way or another, I would make a change. Somehow I had to get out.

I stewed about it as I dried off. What could I do? I could obediently stay in my apartment, waiting and hoping that Claudius would stay away and that Gertrude would have a change of heart. I could beg again to be released. I could find a way to contact Hamlet and see if he could convince his mother. I could run. But how? How? I felt dizzy, and my head pounded, so I leaned against the sink. I was in no condition to make a decision.

I put on a pink cheerful Mr. Bubble T-shirt, so different from how I was actually feeling; I thought a change on the outside might make me feel different on the inside. It wouldn't take away my hangover, nor would it bring my father back to life, but it was the best I could do.

I walked down the hall and found Horatio in the sitting room. Since the guard was in his place by the elevator, I waved Horatio back to my room and closed the door behind us. I considered discussing an escape but changed my mind. Horatio looked tired, and I felt awful. I stuck with an easier topic.

"So what happened after I, you know, drew flowers?" I laughed at myself, only half-embarrassed because I didn't remember it and, therefore, couldn't own the humiliation completely.

"Your brother freaked out."

"My brother?"

"They called him."

"Does he know about my father?"

"That he's dead, yes. Not the rest." Horatio grimaced and my stomach turned at the thought of my father's corpse hidden somewhere in the castle.

Horatio added, "And he saw you acting, you know…crazy."

"What did he say?"

"He was horrified. Really worried about you." He lowered his eyes. "Watching him watch you was the worst part of last night."

I felt bad for what I'd put them both through and wished to God I could remember what I'd done.

"He wants to come back."

"He's coming home?" I asked, excitement rushing past my despair. "Then I can tell him what they've been doing to me."

"They're not letting him back yet."

I froze. "You're kidding."

"No," he said. "He begged them to let him return, but they're trying to stall him."

"Oh God. Can you send him a message?"

"And tell him what? They'll be watching me. I can't."

We sat miserably for a moment, and I realized how frustrated Hamlet must have been every time I told him I couldn't do something. When you're not the one receiving the royal decrees and instructions to be secretive, it's a lot easier to judge and feel like the other person has options he or she is too weak to take.

"Laertes wants to kill Hamlet," he said.

"Join the club," I mumbled.

"No, Ophelia, he looked like…like he might be serious."

"My brother? Come on." I shook my head.

"He'd better not find Hamlet. That's all I'm saying."

"Find him?"

"Hamlet texted me that he was back from London sooner than expected and that I had to meet him secretly."

Horatio's next statement only added to my panic. "And Rosencrantz and Guildenstern are dead."

I touched my fingers to my lips. "What happened to them?"

"Claudius sent Rosencrantz and Guildenstern with Hamlet, saying it was for his protection, but Hamlet knew it was a lie. He stole Rosencrantz's phone and found a text Claudius sent describing a rendezvous with some paramilitary guys

285

Claudius knows over there. The guys were to kill one kid in a Wittenberg College sweatshirt—no questions asked. Hamlet forwarded the text as if Claudius were making changes to the plan. It would be two kids—the ones *not* wearing the sweatshirt. When they all met up, the paramilitary guys shot Rosencrantz and Guildenstern on the spot."

Two college guys were dead. My dad was dead. My mom was dead. Hamlet's dad was dead. Claudius wanted Hamlet dead. Laertes wanted Hamlet dead.

Was I next?

I closed my eyes tightly, completely panicked. What I had believed were Hamlet's crazy ramblings had actually come to pass. Claudius was even more dangerous than I had imagined.

Despite my mistrust and dislike for Claudius, I never thought he would do such a thing. And why? To maintain power? To hide his secrets? To keep from being murdered? That Claudius would try to kill his own nephew, his wife's son, terrified me.

Did Gertrude know? To the public, she was the beautiful symbol of the nation. Cool. Cultured. Smiling. Fashionable. Maternal. What if they knew what she was willing to do to protect her son? To protect her husband? How far would she go? She seemed perfectly willing to hide me indefinitely, so would disposing of me prove just as simple? Christ, if Hamlet wasn't safe, neither was I. My body went numb.

Horatio checked his phone. "I just…Ophelia, I don't know how this is all going to play out." He rubbed his eyes and checked his phone again.

I knew that what I was about to ask was one more burden for him, perhaps one burden too many, but I couldn't let that stop me. This was it. I couldn't bear to be in my glass prison for another moment. I couldn't wait for Gertrude and Claudius to turn on me. The action had to be mine.

"Horatio, I have to disappear."

"What are you talking about?" He looked like I had announced an alien abduction.

"Help me go into hiding."

Horatio put up his hands to stop me, then went to the door to make sure no one was listening. Even though no one was there, he lowered his voice. "I don't think we can do it."

"Why not?"

"They'll be watching you more carefully now. I would have to get you permission to leave the castle, which I can't imagine they'd allow after yesterday's display, and then I would have to get some guard who can keep a secret."

"Marcellus!"

"I don't know," he replied, shaking his head. He paced the room as if chasing the answer. "You'd have to tell him why, and if he says no, we're screwed."

"I'm willing to try." I was determined. If I had to do it without Horatio's help, I would. If I had to hit that damned guard by the elevator with my brother's chess-club trophy, I would. I didn't care. I wasn't staying.

Horatio and I talked it out all afternoon and finally came up with a plan we thought might work.

Horatio called for Marcellus. When he arrived, Horatio asked if the guard at the elevator could leave, which he did. Marcellus was studying me from the moment he walked in. "You're looking pretty together there, Ophelia. What was that all about yesterday?" he asked, his head cocked.

"She wasn't feeling well," Horatio said.

Marcellus stared at Horatio, then at me. Folding his arms across his uniform, he asked, "What can I do for you two?"

I told him, and while I spoke he did not move except to breathe. His eye twitched involuntarily every so often, but he kept his breath regular. I was impressed by how unreadable he was, but I was simultaneously afraid that his next move would be to speak into the microphone perched on his shoulder and turn us in. He didn't.

"Ophelia, I gotta tell you I'm surprised it's taken you this long to ask for help." He lowered himself slowly onto the overstuffed chair and said, "I've been watching how they've all been treating you, and it's a damned disgrace." He looked at Horatio, who nodded. "I've been starting to wonder how long you'll be safe."

"What does that mean?" Horatio asked, his voice rising.

"I get the feeling they're making plans to get rid of Ophelia."

Horatio grabbed my leg, and I sat frozen.

"That said," Marcellus continued, jangling keys on his overcrowded ring, "I'm not sure we can get this job done."

Tears sprang into my eyes, and I felt my face crinkling up, so much so that I could no longer see Marcellus or anything in the room.

He reached over and patted my leg. "I didn't say we won't try. I just don't know if it'll work."

I clutched his arm and said, "I want to get out of here."

Barnardo: Marcellus and Horatio helped you disappear.
Ophelia: Yes.
Barnardo: Out of the goodness of their hearts, they put their futures and safety at risk?
Ophelia: Yes.

Barnardo: I don't believe it.

Ophelia: Fine. It won't change what happened.

Francisco: What did you offer Marcellus to help get you out?

Ophelia: Nothing. I just asked.

Barnardo: Oh, come on. You must have given him something.

Ophelia: You're disgusting.

Francisco: Then why would he put himself in jeopardy to help you?

Ophelia: Ask him yourself.

Barnardo: We did.

Francisco: He's under arrest.

Ophelia: What?

Francisco: Aiding a fugitive.

Ophelia: I wasn't a fugitive.

Francisco: Then for helping to create a situation that cost the kingdom an extraordinary amount of time and money. Do you have any idea how many officers were pressed into duty to look for you?

Ophelia: Where was their help when I was locked up?

Barnardo: That's not the point.

Ophelia: It is to me!

22

In her lowest, most commanding voice, Zara asks, "Why did Horatio help you escape?"

"He's my friend."

Zara leans in, her mouth slithering into a coy smile. "You had other friends, but you turned to Horatio. Is that all he is to you?"

Ophelia flushes. "Yes."

Zara takes her time sipping her water. "Why is that? Why nothing more?"

Ophelia shrugs. "Just one of those things. We never felt that way about each other. And if we had, well, it sure would have complicated things."

"Did your relationship with Hamlet ever complicate your friendship with Horatio?"

Ophelia puffs out a mouthful of air. "Well, it got real complicated for him in the end."

The next day, our plan was rolling. Marcellus went to speak to Gertrude and Claudius, and they agreed to let me go out for a while. Gertrude asked if I was still distressed, and when

Marcellus said I was, she told Claudius that it would be good for the public to see me that way, that it would help them "explain things when the time came." I shuddered to think what story they were planning.

Before leaving to secure a car, Marcellus said to me, "Once we're out, you should dye your hair."

My hand jumped to my head. I knew he was right, but I loved my hair. I was never one of those girls who dyed their hair as the mood struck them.

"And you should cut it," he added.

I entwined my fingers protectively around the long strands. I considered all I had given up and all that had been taken from me during the past weeks. The hair seemed like one sacrifice too many. And yet I knew it was the best option. I had seen Hamlet try to avoid notice, and a hat practically screamed "Look at me."

"We'll have to do it once we leave, though. They have to see you go."

An hour later, Horatio and I stood marveling at my reflection in a gas station mirror. "Wow, that's dark," he said.

"And short."

"Not that short," he reassured me.

I pulled at the uneven hair I had begun to chop in the back. It was below my ears but still seemed odd.

"Want me to straighten that out?"

I nodded, and he picked up my fingernail scissors and went to work.

"I look like some loser girl trying to be Goth."

He lifted an eyebrow and kept snipping. "Some guys go for that."

"I'm not interested in attracting guys right now. Just in not being locked up." I bit my lip and tried not to think about what might happen if we were caught. I picked some black eyeliner out of my purse and started applying it thickly. "If I'm going for a new look, I might as well go all the way." I hardly recognized myself.

Marcellus checked to make sure the station attendant was still watching a soccer game on TV and that no cars were gassing up. Then he escorted me to Horatio's car. I ducked down, and the three of us drove to the most private banks of the river on the outskirts of the city. We found a place where no one else was nearby, not even at telephoto-lens distance. The two of them ate the picnic lunch we had told the king and queen we would be having. Too nervous to eat, I did a drawing of the banks as I imagined they would look in late spring, blanketed with flowers rather than just the smattering that were actually there. All the while the two of them planned out what they would say to Claudius and Gertrude, making sure the stories were alike but not suspiciously exact. I listened halfheartedly, the blood rushing in my ears.

Soon it was time. I walked to the river and put my feet in. If rescue dogs were sent into the water, they had to lose my scent at the river's edge. It was difficult to stay steady, with the water moving so swiftly, but within moments, Horatio and Marcellus were lifting me out and carrying me back to the car. We passed the remains of our picnic, intentionally left behind, and all kept looking around to see if anyone was watching. We saw nothing. Even so, I couldn't relax.

Once back in the car, I ducked down and we drove farther upriver. We traveled up and over the hills into a desolate little town with motels and fast food and not much else. Marcellus waited in a burger joint while Horatio found me a motel room with a kitchenette.

The Illyria Inn promised anonymity and few comforts, but the former seemed more pressing. I sat in the car while Horatio checked in, willing myself to be still and to not keep peering at the rearview mirror. He said the girl at the front desk barely looked up as she handed him the key.

When I opened the door to the room, I set down my bag, then checked the garish mattress cover for stains before flopping onto it. No matter how I was feeling, I wanted Horatio to believe I was all right. I knew he wouldn't rest, and might refuse to leave, if he saw me anxious or upset. "Home sweet home," I said, half smiling.

He sat down next to me and frowned. "Someone might find you."

"True," I said with a calm that surprised me, and that calm chased away my fear. "But I couldn't stay there quietly anymore. It was time to at least try. And look, we made it this far." I took in a deep breath, hoping to inhale freedom, but breathed in stale air instead. I cleared my throat to hide a cough.

Horatio stood to go, reminding me, "Leave that new phone on at all times. Don't use it unless it's an emergency. I'll call you every few days. And stay inside as much as you can."

"I know, I know." We had gone over the plan many times. He turned to leave and, to both of our surprise, I added, "Go be his friend now. Much as it pains me to say, Hamlet needs you."

He leaned against the dark wood paneling and nodded.

I asked, "Is all this being needed a good thing or a bad thing?"

"I suppose it depends how it ends," he replied with a weary smile.

After he left, I peeked through a narrow opening in the stiff curtains. No one suspicious was out there...at least not of the photographer or security type. The town was a place devoid of beauty and culture, unless pool halls and strip clubs were your thing. I felt pity for the people who made that place their permanent home. Then I checked myself. They might never have been to museums or on overseas trips, but they also didn't have boyfriends who killed their fathers…or, from the look of things, maybe they did.

I turned my mind to more practical matters and worried a little at the scale of the town. It was certain that everyone appeared to want to be left alone, which would work to my advantage. And yet, with few places to buy food and do laundry, it would be hard to stay invisible for long. If nothing changed at home, I would have to move on. Unfortunately, this never became an issue, since the situation in Elsinore changed faster than any of us expected.

Marcellus and Horatio had returned to Elsinore to tell Gertrude and Claudius that, without Marcellus realizing, I had taken some pills that Horatio had brought and insisted on swimming, but I had been swept away by the river's strong current. Later Marcellus told me that they had sent Horatio out of the room and explained to Marcellus that it was just as well, that it would save them following through with the rest of their plan. "Even so," Gertrude had said, more to Claudius than to Marcellus, "we'd best put on a show of trying to find her."

I watched the television and waited for the news of my drowning to break. Late that afternoon, it did. Helicopters circled where I had supposedly fallen in the water and zoomed in on the picnic Marcellus, Horatio, and I had intentionally left behind. Dozens of police officers swarmed the banks of the river, some with dogs, some with nets. I felt terrible for the divers who were shown bobbing in the frigid water. Even the few moments I had my feet in were enough to numb them. Wet suits or not, it had to be uncomfortable.

Newscasters stood on the bank as the sun set and they remained into the night. I loved how they added more and more designer layers as the night wore on and the temperature dropped. Stormy Somerville's hot pink fur-trimmed hooded parka was a bit over the top, given the actual weather, but since the premise of her story was that I might be alive and merely floating in the freezing water, it greatly added to the sense of peril.

Marcellus and Horatio, it was explained, had refused to be interviewed, too distressed by the accident. My father, they said, was also too grief-stricken to speak, and my brother was en route from Paris, so Reynaldo, my father's second-in-command, held a press conference. Gertrude, with Claudius at her side, gave the details of what had apparently befallen me. She had a piece of paper from which she read, her voice strong and steady.

"There are willows that grow along the banks of our glori-ous river, willows that reflect their silver-gray leaves when the water runs low and still," she began.

I wondered who wrote the unexpectedly flowery speech. It would have been Dad, but…I shook away the thought.

"Ophelia liked to make fantastic garlands of crow-flowers, nettles, daisies, and long purples," she continued.

"Make garlands of flowers?" I asked aloud. "When I was six, maybe. Now I draw them. Christ, Gertrude, did you know me at all?"

"Sweet Ophelia…"

"Not what she has been calling me lately. More like 'whore,' but oh well. To*may*to, to*maht*o."

"Dear sweet Ophelia was climbing for flowers when a branch broke, and down she fell into the rushing water. In recent days, Hamlet and Ophelia stopped seeing each other, and it seems that she was so distressed by this that she lost her senses…or her will to live. She seemed to make no attempt to swim for safety. Her clothes spread out, and mermaidlike they kept her afloat. She recited poetry as if unaware of the danger she was in."

Poetry! That's quite an image, I thought, wondering if Horatio and Marcellus had told her that insanity, or if she was basing the colorful detail on my wild presentation from the incident a couple of days prior.

She finished by explaining, "But soon her clothes, heavy from the water, pulled the poor girl down under the surface. It is assumed that she drowned, though we are holding out hope that somehow she will be found."

At that point, the chief of police stepped to the podium and told viewers that they were still considering it a search-and-rescue mission. Divers and boats, he assured everyone, would hunt the length of the river and out into the harbor.

Oh…I thought with mild dread. *That's a lot of people looking. How are they going to explain it when they don't recover my body? And how long are those poor guys going to have to stay in the water?* I had to turn off the television at that point.

By the next morning, the chief of police announced that the search-and-rescue mission had turned into a recovery mission, as there was no hope that I could have stayed alive in cold water for so long. They were asking that if, by any chance, I had crawled out of the river and was found dead or alive, the authorities should be notified immediately.

I had enough food to last a day or two without going out,

so I remained in the dingy wood-paneled room and watched as much of the spectacle as I could. *From one prison into another*, I thought morosely. I was drawn to the tribute montages of my life and wondered how they got the pictures. Did someone go into my apartment? Did Gertrude hand them over? Were there enough on public record to fill the minute or two? When a few of my childhood friends were interviewed, I realized some of them had provided the images willingly. I sat and stared with bemused shock as reporters dissected my life.

At last it was determined that my body was lost, and a funeral was set and arranged for quickly. An empty coffin would be buried, and the funeral would be, of course, televised. This announcement unleashed a different kind of coverage. Late-night talk-show hosts used my death as a springboard for jokes while child psychologists appeared on daytime talk shows to discuss the perils of fame and promiscuity.

I even caught a religious chat circle discussing what kind of burial I ought to have had if my body had been recovered. A tightly wound woman in a dour polyester suit insisted that it had been suicide, or else how could it be explained that I had not tried to get out of the water.

A bearded gentleman refuted her claim, saying that, while it had been reported that I was very depressed and was acting strangely, this didn't automatically mean suicide.

"Hard to say," declared the tweed-wearing and patched-elbows moderator. He gestured broadly as he said, "Here lies the water. Good. Here stands the girl. If the girl goes to the water and drowns herself, it is suicide. But if the water comes to her and drowns her, she has not drowned herself!"

The dour one insisted, "I can't help but think that if she hadn't been from a rich and powerful family, they would have said that she couldn't be buried on hallowed grounds. Would you and I get the same treatment?"

"Well, Grace, then I suggest you don't go swimming anytime soon," the bearded one said, sneering.

I clicked off the television and went to bed.

I was determined not to watch anything for a few days, until I was sure they would have moved on to another person's scandal or tragedy. I read and drew, ducked into a coin-operated Laundromat, and bought food. It was at the market checkout line that my own name on a magazine cover caught my eye, as did a picture of my brother and Hamlet in what appeared to be a fistfight. I pretended to be looking at all the tabloids and that I just so happened to pick the one I really wanted randomly. I paid for it, tucked it under my armpit as I grabbed the crinkly shopping bags, and headed for the privacy of my room. There, standing in the light of the partially open curtains, I read:

Grave Drama at Ophelia's Funeral

Yesterday morning saw the burial of Ophelia, on-again, off-again, then on-again girlfriend of Prince Hamlet. The proceedings for the recently drowned young woman started off as expected but soon turned strange indeed.

Our beloved queen, wearing a perfectly cut suit and too much concealer under her eyes (one need not hide grief at a funeral, right?), stood by the grave and scattered flowers. King Claudius stood possessively by her side. Ophelia's father was nowhere, much to this reporter's surprise. (Has anyone else started to wonder where Polonius is? One could always count on following the hot air, and yet all has been suspiciously cool and proverb-free of late.) Her brother, Laertes, freshly returned from France (and what, our schools aren't good enough for him?), stood by her grave looking positively sick with grief.

As the gravediggers began to lower the coffin, Laertes actually leaped into the grave. Standing with just his head sticking above the ground, he begged them to bury him along with his sister's empty coffin! At this point, and I kid you not, our Lord Hamlet came over the ridge of the cemetery and, seeing the open grave of his supposed love (though why hadn't they been seen together for many weeks?), leaped into the grave himself! The two men began beating each other roundly…though let it be said that Laertes seemed to be the aggressor. The king ordered his men to pull them out while Hamlet's mother shrieked wildly.

Hamlet came out of the grave shouting to Laertes that his love for Ophelia was greater than that of forty thousand brothers. "What will you do?" shouted the unhinged, yet still dashing, prince. "Will you weep? Fight? Fast? Hurt your-self? Eat a crocodile? I'll do it! Did you come here to whine? To outdo me by leaping into her grave? Be buried with her coffin? So will I."

At this, Queen Gertrude screamed, "This is madness!" and tried to go to her son. Her new husband held her arm and asked Horatio, Hamlet's oldest and dearest friend, to take him away. Horatio did, and quiet, though not peace, reigned at last.

Laertes looked murderous and walked away from King Claudius (who pleaded mysteriously for his patience), leaving violets for the gravediggers to place atop the filled-in grave.

I wonder at the ability of the good people of this kingdom to continue bearing such displays. Our royals were once pinnacles of morality, set examples for their subjects to follow. During these past few months, it has been as if the lunatics were running the asylum.

I reread the article, for I could not believe my eyes. Then I crushed the magazine between my hands and tossed it across the room, as if the distance between me and the printed story might make it less horrible. But it didn't. My mind reeled. What was happening at the castle at that very moment? Why had Hamlet been allowed at the funeral? Why hadn't Horatio told my brother that I was alive? How could he let him suffer like that?

I broke the rules and called Horatio.

"Jesus, what if I wasn't alone?" he asked.

I stared at the crumpled magazine on the floor. "But you are, so can you talk?"

He hesitated. "Yeah. Don't do it again, though."

I made no promises. "I read about my funeral. They both jumped into my grave? That's insane."

"Yeah," Horatio said quietly. "Competitive grieving. Not pretty."

Part of me wanted to laugh, but the larger part of me was completely mystified. And saddened by it.

I guess he felt the same because he added, "It was really hard to watch. They both still love you."

I considered what he said for a moment. Did Hamlet's still loving me make him not a murderer? No. Would it bring my dad back or make what he said in the limo less cruel? No. Hamlet thought I was dead, and that fact caused him pain. Good. He deserved it. But my brother didn't.

"Can you get to my brother and tell him I'm alive?" I asked.

Horatio sighed. "No, Ophelia. We've talked about this. It's not safe yet. And now that he's back in town, it's worse. Your brother's been spending a lot of time with Gertrude and Claudius. If he knows you're okay and starts acting calm or different, they might get suspicious and ask questions. He's even at dinner with them right now. Let's give it a few days and move you farther away from Elsinore first."

I didn't like the idea one bit, but I knew he was right. What was the point of all that Horatio and Marcellus had done for me if I got impatient and blew my cover?

Barnardo: Hamlet and your brother made quite a scene.

Ophelia: That's an understatement.

Barnardo: If you knew Hamlet was so upset about your supposed death, why didn't you go rushing back to him? He didn't seem mad about the whole betrayal thing anymore. You two had gotten past squabbles in the past.

Ophelia: Killing my dad was more than a squabble.

Francisco: Once you knew your brother was in town, why didn't you contact him?

Ophelia: It wasn't safe.

Francisco: You knew he was practically destroyed by the news, and yet you kept quiet. Is that love?

Ophelia: You shut your mouth. You know nothing about—

Francisco: What? Love? If I loved someone, I wouldn't let him think I was dead. You could have called him at any point and stopped him. Stopped everything that came next. Or maybe you wanted it to happen.

Ophelia: I hate you.

23

"Was it hard for you to lie about your whereabouts? To fool the public? To watch everyone mourn your death?"

Ophelia looks very serious and explains, "None of this was done to affect the average person. Things were deteriorating at the castle, and it seemed to be the only way out. . . . Yeah, it was hard to know so many people were being misled."

Zara nods appreciatively. "I understand that not even your brother knew you were alive. When were you going to tell him?"

"I had hoped to send him a message—" Ophelia breaks off.

Zara looks at the audience with tear-filled eyes.

Ophelia whispers, "But everything happened too fast."

A few days after my funeral, I got a call from Horatio. "Ophelia," he said, and his voice was so strained that I dropped the package of Pop-Tarts I had just grabbed off the convenience-store shelf.

"What's wrong?"

"I . . . Hamlet is going to play in a lacrosse game."

I had been expecting so much worse, but my adrenaline

was pumping, so I asked, "A what?" too loudly. When other customers turned to look at me, I pulled my hat down and rushed out of the store.

As I made my way into the alley, Horatio said, "You know, the annual Elsinore Academy fund-raiser."

I did know. Each year, for as long as I could remember, a group of lacrosse alumni and members of the current team played to raise scholarship money for the high school. It brought out huge crowds, huge names, and huge money.

"Yeah," I said, "but I can't believe they're going through with it after all that—" My voice broke off as I pushed away the image of my father lying in a pool of blood.

Horatio said, "I know. I don't think Hamlet should be anywhere near that game. I tried talking him out of it by telling him he's too tired and that it's a bad idea for him to be in the same place as Claudius. But he says he wants to play like he has every year for the past five years."

"Hamlet can't believe that, at this point, his inclusion is business as usual. With everything— You'd think Claudius and Gertrude would want him away from public scrutiny."

"I know. Even Hamlet knows it's weird. He admitted that he's really uneasy about the whole thing. So I told him to trust his instincts and that I could tell them he's not feeling up to it. But Hamlet looked at the e-mail invitation like he saw his destiny. It was eerie, Ophelia. He said to me, 'No. I'm prepared for whatever. *Que será será*, you know?' He sort of laughed, but I didn't. And he looked at me all sad and said, 'Let's just do this thing.' He just went to get dressed, and then we're gonna go to the field."

"So you think it's a trap?" I asked.

"Yeah. Claudius had been trying everything to get rid of

Hamlet. Hamlet has to know that Claudius might use this opportunity to make another move."

"Don't go," I begged.

"Hamlet's determined, and I'm not letting him go alone."

I kicked at the cinder-block wall and worried more than I wanted to about Hamlet.

I heard a voice in the background, and Horatio whispered to me, "Gotta go. I'll call later."

I stood in the alley with the disconnected phone pressed against my ear. I was frustrated to be far away but relieved, too. And I felt so sorry that Horatio had to deal with everything alone. As long as Horatio came out unscathed, that was what mattered most. But what if something *did* happen to Hamlet? I wasn't sure how I was going to react. But what could happen at a lacrosse game? A broken nose. A cracked rib. Nothing devastating. With Horatio and a crowd there, Claudius couldn't have Hamlet kidnapped or shot or anything, so he had to be pretty safe. I hoped. And didn't.

I went back into the convenience store and wandered the aisles in a daze. I was so preoccupied by thoughts of the game that when I reached the checkout, I realized that I'd grabbed spray cheese, a can of beets, and a pack of beef jerky. The mixture was so unappetizing that I left it all on the counter and walked out with a muttered, "Sorry."

Back in my room, I checked my phone to see if Horatio had texted. Nothing. I paced the room a few times and checked my phone again. Nothing. I checked to be sure I hadn't accidentally silenced the ringer. I hadn't. I checked my phone again. And again nothing. An hour passed. Still nothing. And every time I felt a kick of worry in my stomach, I was completely disgusted with myself because I was supposed to hate Hamlet enough that I wanted Claudius to do something to him. But I didn't, and that made me feel even worse. Because I was betraying my father by caring about his killer.

Just when I started to consider going back out again for food, the phone rang. "God, that took long enough!" I yelled.

Not even dealing with my rudeness, Horatio said, "Claudius is planning to poison Hamlet."

I sat on the bed in shocked silence.

"Marcellus met us in the parking lot. Said that if Claudius offers him anything to drink, he has to refuse."

My mouth worked over a million questions, and I settled on, "How does Marcellus know?"

"Some of the guys in security like Hamlet better than Claudius. Things are falling apart at all levels here."

"Wait," I said, "how would Claudius get away with doing it in public?"

Horatio lowered his voice and explained, "They were going to announce that it was a drug overdose, which would explain Hamlet's weird behavior leading up to this game."

"God, that's smart," I whispered, and hugged a pillow to my chest. "So is Gertrude in on it, too?"

"I don't know." He hesitated. "Uh, one more thing."

My heart sank. I wasn't sure I could take one more bit of news.

"Your brother's playing in the game. He and Hamlet are going to be captains of the opposing teams."

I couldn't make words get past the tightness in my throat.

Horatio said, "They're telling everyone that Laertes has been slotted to play for weeks."

"That's impossible," I squeaked.

"Yeah, I know. But either way, he'll be playing, and the

press is making it out to be a big deal that he wanted to come back to help his alma mater, blah, blah. This is so messed up, but I can't get Hamlet to back out. I tried to prey on Hamlet's pride by saying that Laertes's team would beat him. But Hamlet said, 'I don't think so. Since Laertes has been in France, my game has really improved.' Ophelia, I've tried everything I can think of to—"

"You can't keep Hamlet from doing something he wants to do," I reassured him, wishing Horatio could be spared from being in the middle of this. "You know him better than that."

"Game's about to start," Horatio said.

"I wish I could watch," I said quietly, sadness washing over me. "I want to see my brother."

Horatio paused. "I think you can. We've got the same model phone, so we should be able to do video chat. But don't forget: We'll see and hear each other, but so will anyone who looks my way. Be quiet and keep the lights off and your hat on."

"Where will you be?" I asked.

"On the sidelines with the spectators."

A few minutes later, I'd downloaded the right application and we were set up. When he called back, I could see that Horatio was standing dangerously close to the platform on which Gertrude sat. Claudius was at the podium addressing the audience, explaining that today's match would greatly benefit students who wanted to attend the fine institution but lacked the funds to do so, and he thanked everyone present for their generosity. I wanted to punch him in his lying face. He had enough money to send every kid there to school for free but was going to use this as an opportunity to go after his brother's son. He made me sick.

Speaking of sick, Gertrude sat next to him not seeming

quite herself. Gertrude was looking elegant, though slightly dressed down, as she always did when attending one of Hamlet's games, but she was noticeably weary and a little twitchy. The quality of the video on the camera phone was so incredible that it even picked up her eyes darting around the field and at the crowd, and how, when Claudius reached for her hand, she flinched.

Horatio panned, so I could see he was standing among parents and students. They were all oblivious to the fact that the event was being hosted by pure evil.

Horatio then turned the camera to the field. Hamlet was with the squad in white, who was warming up with some practice drills. On the other side of the field was a sea of burgundy and black—the other squad, of which my brother was captain. Laertes came into view, and I was so moved by the sight of him that, for a few seconds, tears filled my eyes and the screen blurred. My brother, my last living relative, the person I wanted to talk to more than anyone right then, was far away and had no idea that I was alive and that I could see him leading a bunch of my classmates in stretches.

It was then that I caught sight of Sebastian. I sucked in my breath. Had Hamlet seen him? Had he pieced together that Sebastian was the guy who'd been kissing my neck when he'd surprised me at school? I hoped not.

To great cheers, Hamlet and Laertes came into the center of the field for a face-off. One thing was suddenly clear to me: the game was about them.

With their helmets on, it was impossible to see Hamlet's or Laertes's expressions, but I noticed that as they walked they both held their bodies differently than they once had. Laertes's arms and shoulders were tense, and Hamlet slouched and kept his head down, a posture of resignation that I hadn't seen since his father's funeral.

Claudius signaled, and the referee took his cue to place the ball. But before he could start the game, Hamlet took out his mouthpiece and pulled off his helmet. Laertes tightened his grip on his stick.

Hamlet began to speak to Laertes, and the ref's microphone picked up what he said, broadcasting it to everyone on and off the field. "I'm so sorry for everything I've done to your family." Laertes looked down, but Hamlet continued with urgency. "The past months have been insane. I've been...not myself."

Laertes said nothing but turned the lacrosse stick over in his hands. I wondered if he was going to whack Hamlet with it.

I couldn't believe Hamlet was saying all of this in public, and I wondered why he was doing it. It was possible that they hadn't had a chance to talk, and that Hamlet really wanted to apologize to Laertes. Otherwise he was playing to the crowd. I chewed on my lip, suspicious.

Even though the ref asked if they were ready to play, Hamlet went on. "You have to know that I would never have done any of these things if I could have helped it. I never meant to hurt you. It's...it's like I shot over my house and accidentally hit my brother."

"Shut up, Hamlet," I heard Horatio whisper.

Laertes grumbled, "Yeah...okay."

"How can you accept an apology?" I asked the screen, forgetting that Horatio could hear me.

"*Shh*," warned Horatio.

"Then let's go," said Hamlet, his spirits buoyed as if he had not recognized the begrudging way Laertes had accepted the apology.

Hamlet put his mouth guard back in. The ref called, "Down." Hamlet and Laertes crouched, their hands on the ground. The ref blew the whistle, and Laertes moved quickly, pinning Hamlet's crosse to the grass, then pulled back and flicked the ball to the side. And with that they were off and running.

The ball was shot back and forth between the players. Hamlet, who was a midfielder, was free to run anywhere he wished on the field, while my brother, an attacker, was constrained to the offensive end. That said, every time Hamlet crossed to Laertes's side, which was often, Laertes was right on top of him.

I saw Laertes pull back his stick and slash Hamlet, hitting him full-force across the stomach. The picture jiggled as Horatio reacted to the hit. It seemed everyone saw the foul except for the ref. Even as Hamlet doubled over, the game was allowed to continue. Hamlet's team was calling "foul" when Sebastian successfully made a goal. The ref ignored protests that it shouldn't count.

"Jesus," Horatio mumbled, and turned, catching Gertrude and Claudius exchanging inscrutable glances.

Horatio panned back to the field. Hamlet and Sebastian were set for their face-off. As they crouched Hamlet looked at his opponent and must have realized who it was because he started to rise. At that moment, the whistle blew and Sebastian did a "laser," quickly clamping and raking the ball to the side, which might have been too fast to block even if Hamlet hadn't been too angry or shocked to try.

When Hamlet finally got moving again and was running toward the action, Laertes spread his hands wide on his stick and slammed Hamlet in the back. Hamlet whirled around and shoved Laertes, and the ref called a foul against Hamlet.

Hamlet shouted, "Are you blind? He cross-checked me. His hands were—"

"Illegal check!" another teammate called out. "The ball wasn't anywhere near—"

"Off the field, Hamlet," the ref insisted.

"What the hell?" Horatio and I said at the same time.

Hamlet's teammates looked at one another with outraged confusion.

When Hamlet was behind the sideline, Claudius held up a plastic cup and said, "The king drinks to your success, Hamlet."

"Here we go," Horatio said quietly.

"Hamlet won't—" But I stopped, afraid that someone might hear my voice on Horatio's end.

Claudius rose grandly and announced to the crowd, though addressing Hamlet, "I offer up a pearl, a pearl more valuable than that which has rested in the crown of four kings. Should you get the next goal, it is yours."

The crowd *ooh*ed at one another, and Claudius offered a smirk. When Hamlet didn't respond or move, Claudius dropped the pearl in the cup with a flourish, put the cup back on the table, and appeared to take interest in the game once again.

After a minute, Hamlet was released by the ref and ran back onto the field. He quickly cleared the ball, sending it to a teammate in the attack area. The player was stick-checked, and the ball rolled out of his pocket. Sebastian scooped it and fed it to another teammate, but as Sebastian ran, he crashed into Hamlet, and they both went flying, nearly knocking into people standing on the sidelines, including Horatio. The image shook as Horatio jumped back. Sebastian's helmet popped off, and Hamlet pulled himself up to his knees. When Hamlet saw who was on the ground, he stopped and hovered a moment. Then he reached down and yanked Sebastian to his feet. Without his helmet on, Sebastian looked more vulnerable, but he was seething himself.

"How long were you waiting for your chance with her, huh?" Hamlet growled, his fingers curled around Sebastian's jersey.

"How long did you treat her like crap?" Sebastian countered, knocking Hamlet's hands away.

I covered my mouth with my free hand. Pinpricks of anxiety ran up the back of my neck.

"Are you kidding? I was good to Ophelia," said Hamlet.

"You cheated on her."

"That's a lie. *I* never cheated. Not once," Hamlet said, pushing Sebastian back with the tips of his heavily gloved fingers.

Sebastian jutted out his chin. "She would have been better off with me, and we both know it. At the very least, she'd still be alive."

Hamlet jerked off his glove and punched Sebastian in the face.

"Christ," said Horatio, "see what you've done?" Anyone around would think Horatio was talking to Hamlet, but I knew the comment was for me. I squeezed the pillow harder against my aching stomach.

Sebastian stumbled back just as Laertes tackled Hamlet, sending Hamlet rolling over and over on the grass.

The whistle blew. Hamlet was sent back off the field, to the great protests of his teammates. No call was made against Laertes.

What was going on? The ref had to be on Claudius's side. I laughed at my own naïveté. Of course he was.

Horatio shoved the phone into his pocket but didn't turn it off, so I could hear the crowd shouting and another, louder sound. A *thump-thump*ing. I guessed Horatio was running toward Hamlet.

"Let's get out of here," Horatio was whispering fiercely. No response. "What Marcellus said is true. Who knows what else—"

"Forget it," Hamlet growled. "No way I'm quitting."

"But they're letting you get beaten up out there."

"I can take it. I deserve—" Hamlet stopped and cleared his throat. "I'm seeing this through. Go back with everyone else."

"Damn it," Horatio said, and the thumping commenced as he moved away from Hamlet.

The picture came up again. Hamlet was released and cut toward the goal. His teammate cradled the ball, then passed back to Hamlet. Hamlet shot and scored.

Time was called, ending the quarter, and someone nearby pronounced it a thrilling game.

Claudius called out, "Hamlet, you've won this pearl. Come have a drink."

Hamlet had walked to the sidelines next to Horatio. I couldn't see him, since Horatio kept the camera pointed at the king, but I heard Hamlet say, "Maybe later."

Claudius smiled at Gertrude and said to her loudly, "Our son will win."

I winced involuntarily at the word *son*, and if Horatio had been filming Hamlet, I imagine it would have shown him cringing as well.

Gertrude blinked rapidly as she stared at her husband, then

at Hamlet. She wrung her kerchief in her hands and called out to Hamlet, "Come, my dear, let me give you a kiss for good luck." I heard Hamlet snap his tongue in response, and Gertrude winced. Then she took hold of the cup Claudius had been offering to Hamlet. "Sweetheart, I drink to your fortune."

Claudius grabbed her arm and snapped, "Gertrude, don't." After a momentary pause, his eyes flicking to the crowd, he added, "You know how you get when you drink."

Gertrude's anger flared even as she took in the students and parents staring at her. "I will," she said, straightening up, and pulled her arm back. "Pardon me."

Claudius's eyes widened and his mouth opened as if to speak. He said nothing, nor did Hamlet, but both kept their eyes fixed on her.

Gertrude drank deeply, put down the cup, and called out again, "Hamlet, let me wipe your face."

"I'm fine," he called out, and she turned, putting her hand to her stomach.

Why would she— I thought as Horatio said quietly, "Oh no."

Laertes walked up to Claudius and said, "My lord, I'll hit him now."

Was he asking permission to check or punch Hamlet? It looked to me like he was going after Hamlet as he pleased. I realized I was holding my breath.

Claudius was cagey, his gaze fixed on Hamlet. "I don't think so." Laertes looked at him and at Hamlet again, his eyes narrowing with fury.

The whistle blew to start the second quarter, and the teams took the field, though neither Hamlet nor Laertes moved.

Hamlet glared at Claudius and then Laertes. He urged, "Come on. Let's finish this."

Laertes tapped his own shoulder with the crosse a few times and nodded. Hamlet looked at his mother, shrugged weakly at Horatio, and said, "I guess…It'll be fine," before running onto the field.

The game began again, and I marveled, as I often did, at its speed. Their footwork was incredibly quick. Players pivoted around one another, their sticks moving as fast as swords, sometimes overhead, sometimes to the side, always amazing. The ball whipped from one pocket to the other so quickly that sometimes I couldn't even follow who had the ball. Nor could Horatio.

A guy I recognized from my math class was scooping up the ball when off to the side of the screen I saw Hamlet crumple to the ground. I heard Horatio gasp. Laertes was sprinting away. Hamlet did not get up but held his side, knees to his chest. From the sound of it, the game was continuing on the other side of the field, but the teammates and opponents closest to Hamlet crept closer. Horatio ran onto the field, and the picture went nuts. Grass. Sky. Grass. Sky. Grass. Sky. As Horatio knelt beside Hamlet, he must have shoved the phone into his pocket, and everything went black.

The sound was really muffled, so I plugged my free ear and was able to make out Horatio asking, "Hamlet, is that blood?" Hamlet groaned, and Horatio added, "It's not that deep. No, don't look at— It'll be all right."

What had happened? How did Hamlet get cut?

"Laertes!" Hamlet yelled. "You coward. Don't you slice me open and then run!"

My brother did it? How?

Horatio said to Hamlet, "There's a blade attached to the end of his stick. We need to get out of here. Now."

My first thought was that my brother was going to end up in jail. His life would be ruined, and all because of that horrible family. Then I realized I didn't hear guards grabbing him. I was relieved, but it made no sense.

The crowd had grown silent.

"You don't ruin my family and get away with it, Hamlet," Laertes snarled from somewhere nearby.

"Don't do it, Laertes," Horatio called out, and I heard screaming and jostling. "Hamlet, stop. Stop!"

The phone went dead.

I screamed, "No!" and hit the phone against my knee. I pushed some buttons, and a video game popped up. "No, no, no," I said again as I hit the video-chat icon, but the screen was still blank.

I paced the room, staring at the still-black screen. Horatio had said Laertes wanted revenge, but I didn't think he'd actually do anything. Why had he asked Claudius a question before stabbing Hamlet? Why had he agreed to play the game? Why wasn't Horatio calling back? I hit the phone again in frustration.

It *bing*ed and I leaped, startled and out of breath. I could hardly open it, I was shaking so badly.

Horatio: o gd. all r dead

Francisco: This text message reads, "Good. All are dead."
Ophelia: That's not what it said.

Francisco: Look, I have it right here. "o gd. all r dead."

Ophelia: No. Not "good." He meant "God" or "Goddamn it."

Barnardo: Sure.

Ophelia: It's what he meant! Ask him. *(pause)* Why would he want Hamlet dead?

Barnardo: Maybe he wanted you for himself.

Ophelia: That's ridiculous. Hamlet was his best friend.

Barnardo: I don't know. Horatio sounds relieved that the plan worked.

Ophelia: There was no plan! Honestly, how do you propose that I made all of those people do those things from over a hundred miles away?

Barnardo: You tell us.

24

Photos flash of the aftermath. Ophelia buries her face in her hands. Zara pats Ophelia's back and looks at the audience with grave concern. Ophelia stands and walks off the stage.

I turned on the TV at some point in the evening, though how much later I could not say. I lay curled on the bed, hoping the ceiling would just fall on me and put me out of my misery already. I heard the worried voices of newscasters but could not will myself to look up. They said words like *tragedy* and *revenge*, *catastrophic* and *panic*. Hollow truth.

I listened for hours, paralyzed by shock. I shook with cold but could not get up to cover myself. My head pounded, and the sound of the news was both muffled and piercing at the same time.

At some point in the middle of the night, there was a knock at the door. I couldn't get up. Whoever it was knocked again. A key jangled in the lock, and the door opened. I felt afraid and then my fear vanished as I realized I didn't care if it was a murderer or the police or someone to help. My future was so meaningless. I wished only for sleep, no matter what dreams might come.

"Ophelia?" asked Horatio.

I lay still, but my resolve to absent myself from the world melted away at the sound of his voice.

"Ophelia?" he asked again, kneeling by my bed.

I looked at him and, as our eyes met, he dissolved into tears. He cried and cried as I held his frigid hands. He looked like a boy kneeling in prayer, and that very boyishness made me pity him all the more. Horatio, who had tried to stand by his friends no matter what, had been unable to stop the terrible events that had consumed them. Powerless he had been, powerless he remained. His best friend was gone. His heart was broken.

Eventually, he crawled his way onto the bed and lay a while in silence. "You wouldn't believe what happened if I told you," he eventually mumbled. A hitch in his voice prevented him from continuing for a while. I waited for him to be ready to go on, knowing there was no rush. Where were we going? Where did we ever have to go again?

"What…" I began, but had to stop and gather myself. "What happened to my…brother?"

Horatio sighed and reached for my hand. "Do you really want to know?"

"Yes," I whispered and braced myself.

"You know he cut Hamlet?" he asked.

I nodded, my face contracting in agony.

"Well, he came after Hamlet again. But just before Laertes reached him, Hamlet scrambled to his feet and blocked Laertes with his own handle, knocking the stick out of Laertes's hands.

Both guys reached for it, but Hamlet bodychecked Laertes and got to the stick first. Laertes was turning to run when Hamlet grabbed the crosse by the head and slashed at your brother."

I flinched. "That's…I think that's when the phone…when it stopped."

Horatio looked guiltily at me and said, "I didn't want you to hear."

I couldn't decide if I was furious or relieved.

He continued, "Everyone started screaming, because Hamlet walked up to Laertes, who was on the ground, and lifted the stick, ready to stab your brother again. I shouted at Hamlet to stop, and he looked at me and then your brother like he was deciding something. Then he squeezed his eyes tight and tossed the stick aside. I thought it was all over, but then Hamlet's legs buckled and he fell right onto Laertes. Claudius shouted, 'Part them!' and the other players rolled Hamlet off Laertes. Both of them were covered in blood."

I sucked in my breath.

Horatio touched my hand. "Are you sure you want to hear?"

Tucking my lips between my teeth to hold back the scream rising up within me, I nodded.

Reluctantly he went on. "Then there was a new sound, and when I turned around, I saw the queen was staggering and then she fell over. Hamlet sat up and asked, 'What's wrong with the queen?'

"Claudius was really anxious. Everyone could see it. He answered, 'She fainted because of the blood.'

"So Gertrude called out, 'No, no. The drink. I've been poisoned.' And then…" Horatio rubbed at his face before finishing. "Then I watched froth pour out of her mouth. She turned blue, and her eyes rolled back. It was sick."

"*Ew,*" I whispered, trying not to picture it.

"Hamlet tried to stand up and pointed at Claudius. 'You did this to her!'"

I found my sympathy for Gertrude growing, something I didn't want. What I *did* want to know was where my brother was during all of this.

When I asked, Horatio said slowly, "After he was slashed by Hamlet, he was bleeding bad."

I cringed at the image of my brother's suffering, which made Horatio stop, so I said, "Go on. I need to know."

"Well…people were shouting that ambulances were coming, but Laertes kept shaking his head. Hamlet was hovering over Laertes, saying how sorry he was. Laertes took him by the sleeve of his jersey and said, 'I'm the villain, and you're a dead man.'"

"Wait. My brother was good. Why would he say that about himself?" I asked, ignoring the fact that I'd seen my brother stab Hamlet after ruthlessly attacking him throughout the game.

"Because, Ophelia, your brother…The blade was poisoned."

"I don't believe you," I said, sitting up quickly.

"Neither did Hamlet. He said to Laertes, 'You just cut my side. I'll be fine.' But Laertes told him that he'd be dead in less than a half hour. They both would."

"No," I said, covering my face at the thought of both of them knowing the end was near.

"You'd be proud of him, though, Ophelia. Laertes was able to tell us what happened. He whispered to us, 'The king—'" Horatio swallowed hard. "'The king is to blame.'"

"Claudius was responsible for the poison on the blade, too?" I asked, lowering my hands.

Horatio nodded. "He put Laertes up to the whole thing. Gave him the poison. Got your brother mad enough to attack Hamlet. Neither of them thought Hamlet would be able to get to your brother, though. Or Claudius."

"Claudius?" I asked.

"Yeah. Hamlet grabbed the poisoned stick, got around the crowd, and sliced Claudius across the forearm."

"He did?" I gasped.

Horatio nodded. "Somebody shouted 'Treason!' and Claudius called for help. But even while he was writhing and holding his bleeding arm, he knew he wouldn't live. Undone by his own trick."

"Where were the guards in all of this?" I asked.

Horatio looked at the watermarked ceiling. "I only figured out at that moment that there had been no security guards at the game. Turns out Claudius had ordered them to stay away until they got a radio signal from the ref to have Hamlet or Laertes arrested. He had said anyone who ignored his command would be fired or jailed. He was too arrogant to think it would go any way but his way."

"Jerk."

Horatio half smiled and then winced. "Hamlet wouldn't let it go at the stabbing. I guess he wanted to be sure his uncle really did die. You could see Hamlet was getting weak from the poison and had sunk to the ground, but he—he managed to pull himself to the poisoned cup his mother had drunk from, then he held Claudius down and poured the rest into Claudius's mouth. Hamlet screamed, 'Here, you incestuous, murderous, damned Dane. Drink this and die like my mother!'"

"No way."

"Yeah. It was crazy. Everyone froze and watched Claudius squirm. I couldn't look, and when I turned away, I saw your brother lying all alone. I took the chance to tell him that your dad's death was an accident. And that you're alive."

"He—" My lip was quivering so I hard that I struggled to finish. "He knew?"

"Yeah."

I threw my arms around Horatio. "Thank you."

"I'm sorry he didn't know sooner."

I nodded and buried my face in his neck.

"So Hamlet crawled back and asked your brother to forgive him, which Laertes did."

"Really?" I asked.

Horatio nodded. "And Hamlet asked—asked me to…" He breathed deeply. "Asked me to let everyone know what happened. To let them know the truth. I sat with him while he shuddered and twitched and—and then he—he—" Horatio couldn't finish.

Eventually Horatio was breathing normally again and said, "I just want to die myself, Ophelia. I don't think I'll ever be able to forget what I saw."

I pulled back and looked at him straight in the eyes. "Don't say that. Don't you say that! I can't lose you, too. I can't be alone." I took his hands in mine again and squeezed. "Do what Hamlet asked. Make sure everyone knows the truth."

"I already tried telling them. I was questioned by Fortinbras for hours."

"The head of the DDI?"

Horatio nodded. "I told Fortinbras and every other damned detective what I knew. Over and over I told them the same story. When they finally let me go, I nearly drove over reporters as I peeled out of the parking lot to get to you."

"Now what?" I asked.

Horatio shrugged. "Hell if I know."

The next day we awoke still in our clothes and on top of the bedspread. Too weary to shower, we put on our shoes and found our way to a Daney's. Hamlet and Horatio had loved these restaurants and used to order the biggest breakfasts they served. The game was to try to finish everything on the plate as fast as possible without puking. I always watched in dismayed mirth and swore it would be the last time we would come to a place that served more food than any human should consume in one sitting.

That morning we just ordered coffee and toast. We kept our heads down, and Horatio left his baseball hat on. No one cared who we were, though. They were fixated by the news coverage and their conversations about the terrible events of the night before.

After the check came, I spoke for the first time. "Why would my brother have agreed to something so stupid? He knew he would go to jail after he stabbed Hamlet."

Horatio stared at his cold coffee and turned the cup in his hands. "Suicide mission. Without a doubt. I don't think he cared anymore. God, if I'd been able to get to him before that game, it could have been different. But I didn't expect it to be him....I mean, it happened so fast. If he'd known you weren't..."

"It's my fault. I should have stayed," I moaned, and turned my face to the window. He shushed me, but it was unnecessary. So many people were grieving that my despair didn't stand out.

As I watched beat-up cars and oversize trucks rush by, I

thought about Hamlet. I wanted to hate him. I did. He had killed my brother and my father. And yet I knew that both murders had pained him because neither had been intentional, certainly not as intentional as what had been done to him. Hamlet had been tangled up in the madness as much as I had been. As much as my father and brother, and even my mother, had been. We were like insects caught on a web of deceit. Had there been an alternative? I wasn't sure. And yet it hadn't been Gertrude or Claudius who had done the killing. It had been Hamlet. He had ruined my life. He had taken all that I had. My chest ached.

Unable to think of it anymore, I wondered what to do next. I could keep running, or I could go back. Going back seemed pointless, except that if I didn't, I couldn't see that my father and brother were buried properly. Longer term, I might never see Horatio or any of my friends again. I would have to keep my identity a secret indefinitely and, given how well-known my face had become, I might have to live somewhere far more obscure than I would have wanted. I could never get my stuff back, which wasn't such a big deal, but without money I'd be hard-pressed to replace it. And I needed money to run.

"I have to go back," I murmured, loathing the thought more for having said it. I knew Horatio was looking at me, but I couldn't face him, so I kept staring out the window. I watched a hitchhiker give up and start to stroll. "I don't see any other way. Maybe I can just live a quiet life now that I'm not with…him."

Horatio snickered, which was not what I had expected. I glared at him. "Sorry," he said. "Inappropriate. Like laughing at a funeral." The word jolted us both, and he went back to playing with his mug. I turned toward the TV behind the counter, where a waitress stood, washrag in hand, unable to pry herself away from yet another retelling of the sordid events on the field. Horatio lowered his voice and said, "I think there's very little chance that anyone's gonna let you fade away."

I wished I could be as anonymous as the hitchhiker and choose my path on a whim. But he was right. I had to be realistic. I would be found. I started shredding my napkin. "It's not just that they're going to follow me and invade my world. People are gonna blame me. They'll find a way to twist this and make it my fault."

Horatio gritted his teeth and nodded. "You could put out your version of the story. Do some interviews."

I tore harder at the napkin. "I'm so sick of spin. I don't want to pretend or lie anymore. And I don't want to explain myself." I shuddered and tried to push away memories of Claudius at the conservatory, of Hamlet offering the gun, of Gertrude taking me shopping, of my brother begging me to leave Hamlet. "But if I can't control the way this plays out, I'll spend the rest of my life running."

Horatio clenched and unclenched his fists. "You can control it to a certain extent."

I balled up the remains of the napkin and rolled the bits between my palms.

He cupped his hands over mine. "Look, the press has used you to manipulate public opinion for years. Use them for once."

I nodded and let my gaze drift back to the television. A gorgeous picture of Hamlet from the trip we took to Italy flashed up, and I pinched my eyes shut.

"Or we could drive the other way," Horatio offered. "I'll take you wherever you want to go."

I frowned as I pulled out of his grasp. "What about your life here?"

"I'll come back as soon as you're settled. I mean, there's my folks, and Kim, and graduating. I can't give that all up. But if you need me for a while—"

I interrupted. "Stop helping. I love you, but take care of yourself."

He lowered his drooping eyes and nodded. "So we go back."

Neither of us was ready to face the scene we knew would be awaiting us in Elsinore, so we paid and went back to my motel room. We lay silently staring up at the pitiful acoustic tiles, drifting in and out of sleep throughout that day and for part of the next, hardly speaking. Hunger eventually motivated us. We packed my things, left my key in the door, and hit the road.

As we drove, we talked about how I was going to announce that I was alive. We called Marcellus and he met us across town from the castle at a salon. His sister was the owner, and she dyed my hair back to blond, matching the color using a photo from the cover of a magazine that had done a memorial tribute to me.

As I waited under the dryer, I flipped through the magazine. I spotted a picture of Hamlet and me at the beach. He was kissing my neck, and I had my head thrown back as I giggled. My jaw dropped when I spotted the birthmark on my hip, which I didn't realize my bikini didn't cover. This might have been how Claudius knew what to say when he convinced me that I had been caught with Hamlet on tape. I threw the magazine and closed my eyes, letting the deafening hum of the hairdryer drown out my thoughts.

Then the three of us traveled as close to the castle as

we could get, given the barricades, and Marcellus brought us through the barriers on foot. There were more than enough reporters around, so he tapped our favorite one on the shoulder. Stormy Somerville was standing in front of her news van and almost fainted when she figured out who we were. Who I was.

The frenzy that followed can only be described as overwhelming. It got so crazy that Marcellus called for backup, and they helped us move inside the castle.

My apartment looked as it had the day I left. It was no longer a prison but also not a home. I would have to move somewhere else, just not that day. Marcellus, along with some of his buddies, blocked the elevator, refusing to let curious eyes or security agents enter. I hugged Horatio good-bye, thanked him for the hundredth time, and watched him disappear behind the elevator doors. I wandered back to my room, but the wall painting freaked me out, and I couldn't bring myself to stay in there, or my brother's room, or my father's. I went to the sitting room and stretched out on the couch and, despite the early hour, fell asleep alone.

Barnardo: So when the smoke cleared, you just waltzed back to town. Worked out pretty well for you.

Ophelia: Yeah. It's been a dream come true.

25

As they settle back onto the couch, Zara smiles falsely. "I am so sorry to have upset you with those photos."

Ophelia stares hard at her. "I'm sure."

"How did you feel about coming back to Elsinore?"

Ophelia hesitates and looks over her shoulder. A man in a suit is caught just behind the curtain giving her a thumbs-up. She grimaces and turns back to Zara. "I was relieved. I never hesitated, because I knew the people needed me back."

I woke with a start and sat on the couch, unable to fall back asleep and unable to get up. I sat paralyzed all afternoon, unwilling to look around the apartment for fear of the memories each corner held. The noises on the street told me the news vans were still swarming, but I didn't turn on the television, knowing I would be greeted by my own face and endless speculation and comments about my own life. The sun set. The sun rose. Still I sat.

When the opal sky had turned to cornflower, Horatio walked in and collapsed on the couch. "You sleep much?" he asked.

I shook my head.

"Me either," he said, clenching and unclenching his hands. "Come down to my folks' for breakfast."

I shook my head again.

"They're worried about you, and they're not going to let you sit here alone."

The thought of their kind faces actually made me cringe. I closed my eyes. "I don't want to talk about anything, and I don't want to be watched."

"Yeah. I know. What are you gonna do, then?" he asked.

I shrugged.

"I wish I could just sit here with you. They keep offering to listen, to listen, to listen. But what is there to say?"

I swallowed the lump in my throat. "Maybe by dinner," I offered, thinking I could put them off until then and cancel at the last minute.

I thought he would get up, but he slumped down and stared out the window. Tears streamed down his face, and he clutched his arms tightly across his chest. "Why didn't I drive him off to safety, too? I knew something bad was going to happen. I knew it." When I reached out for his arm, he pulled away. "All of them. All of them. God! I should have stopped it. I knew something was going to happen. I knew it."

"It wasn't your fault."

"It was, Ophelia. Not entirely, but I played a part."

"So did I. So did my brother. So did Hamlet. We all did."

He shook his head violently. "You know I could have stopped it."

I knew that wasn't true, but I wasn't going to argue with him. What good would it have done either of us?

Suddenly he grabbed a pillow off the couch and threw it,

knocking a picture frame off the shelf next to the stereo. "Shoot," he muttered as he crossed to the frame and picked it up. The shattered glass tinkled to the floor. I didn't need to see it to know it held a photo from the awards ceremony at the end of my junior year. I'm holding up my honor roll certificate and sticking out my tongue, Laertes is squishing my face, and my father is looking on, half-amused, half-uncertain as to why his children would behave in such a fashion. Hamlet had taken the picture. Now I looked away as more glass tumbled, and I tried not to throw up. Horatio put the frame on the coffee table and started for the elevator. "Jesus, Ophelia. I'm sorry. I'm sorry for all of it."

"Still not your fault, Horatio," I called after him.

I could say it to him, and I believed it. As for me, no such forgiveness. I blamed myself. I always would. I blamed myself for not believing the things Hamlet had told me. I blamed myself for deceiving Hamlet. I blamed myself for being so drunk in Gertrude's office that I acted like a wild woman, which my brother misinterpreted, which led him to choose revenge. I blamed myself for inviting my father into my business. I blamed myself for my own cowardice at every turn. No matter what anyone would tell me, I knew I should have done something to stop the killing. I felt certain there was more I could have done.

After Horatio left, I grabbed the broken frame and shoved it in a drawer. I started taking the photos from all around the room and putting them away, but I knew it would do no good. Memories were everywhere. Memories were inescapable.

That afternoon, Horatio's mother came in, appearing as weary as he had. When I told her I was fine and didn't want to talk, she fluttered around, looking for ways to help. She started by checking my refrigerator to be sure I had food to eat, which I did, though I couldn't bring myself to eat much. I listened to the freezer door slam. She moved on to the cabinets and then began picking up the remains of the frame. Her chestnut ponytail flopped from shoulder to shoulder as she searched for stray pieces of glass, and I realized how long it had been since another woman had been in the apartment. I wished my mom could be cleaning up instead.

When at last she was finished, she declared with a gentle smile, "We have a meeting with Reynaldo at four o'clock. Get dressed or shower or whatever you need to do. We'll be by for you in an hour. Unless you want me to stay."

I shook my head more vigorously than I should have. "What meeting?"

She cleared her throat. "Funeral plans."

"Oh," I breathed.

"Don't ask that of me," I begged Horatio.

We were standing in the corner of the intimate conference room. Reynaldo had chosen it because our group was so small; however, my desire to discuss matters with Horatio in private made me wish we had been in the larger one.

"You have to come to Hamlet's service," he whispered.

"Why? Don't you think I've earned the right to skip this one?"

"One funeral will be best for the nation," chirped Reynaldo from across the room.

I spun around to face him. "I am not interested in what is good for the nation, and I am not interested in talking to you!" Everyone looked askance, as I would never have answered in such a fashion if my father had been there. But he wasn't. Reynaldo's face flushed and he started shuffling his papers. I turned back to Horatio, who was running his fingers through his hair. The gesture reminded me of Hamlet in his desperate moments. I had to steady myself against the wall.

"I need you with me, Ophelia. I haven't asked anything of you through all of this, but I'm asking you now. Come with me."

I winced. Helpful Horatio. Patient Horatio. Giving Horatio. He had been counselor and guide to me and to Hamlet; he had delivered me to safety and unwillingly delivered Hamlet to his certain death. How could I deny him? And yet that was precisely what I wanted to do.

He interrupted my internal battle with, "If one funeral will get you there, then make it one funeral. Besides, if they're all together, your father will get his due, as will your brother. You know most people think your brother is the only one to blame for all of this, and if it's separate, none of us can predict what might happen."

"Ignorant sons of—" I began, but stopped myself when I realized Horatio's parents could hear us.

Many citizens, despite evidence to the contrary, were choosing to believe that my brother alone had caused the deaths of the royal family. The thought of my brother's funeral being interrupted by protesters finally convinced me. I nodded reluctantly, agreeing to yet another charade, because the only true friend I had left asked me. Reynaldo ran off to write a statement to be delivered at a press conference that afternoon.

After the meeting with Reynaldo had ended, Horatio's parents insisted that I have dinner with them. His mother tried to keep the mood light. She put on piano music and cooked pasta, chattering constantly as she did. I leaned on Horatio, hypnotized by her uninterrupted motion and speech. Finally his father took the spoon out of her hand and told her to give the sauce and herself a rest. She nudged him playfully as they came to sit with us.

Horatio's father offered to have me live with them, which was sweet, but I declined. I wanted to be alone. The irony wasn't lost on me, given how much I had detested being by myself in prior weeks. Even so, his parents would practically adopt me in the coming weeks, and we would spend many evenings eating and talking. My new makeshift family.

I couldn't live with them, but I also couldn't live in my apartment. The home where I'd had a life with my father. The home where I'd had a life with my mother. The home where I'd had a life with my brother. The home where I'd had a life with Hamlet. Remaining was not an option. Everyone understood.

So the following day, the secretary of relocation came to me with photos of furnished apartments used to house dignitaries and officials needing long-term living quarters. I preferred the small brownstones in a tree-lined neighborhood nearby, but we reconsidered when it became clear how easily photographers could climb the fire escapes and how hard it would be for me to come and go safely and in obscurity. We settled on a sleek one-bedroom condo in a high-rise down the block from the castle. The loft would suit me fine, and the tall windows, covered in filmy curtains, reminded me of a sculpture gallery I had once visited with Hamlet. It was a bittersweet memory that fit my mood perfectly. The secretary explained that I could stay there as long as I chose and that the staff would pack and move my things.

I brought some personal items over myself, and when I was done, I charged through the glass doors and headed for my car.

As I did so, I noticed a figure stop dead in his tracks in front of me. Since my return, more strangers than ever wanted to chat, so I checked to make sure Marcellus was within a few paces, kept walking, and unzipped my bag, pretending to be looking for something.

"Ophelia?" a familiar voice asked. I stopped and looked up reluctantly. It was Sebastian.

I sucked in my breath and stared dumbly at him.

"God, it *is* you," he continued. "What are you doing here?"

Marcellus stepped forward, but I signaled that I was okay. I explained to Sebastian, "I, uh, I'm gonna live here for now."

"I live around the corner."

"Oh, that's right," I squeaked through a clenched throat.

"I, well, wow, look at you. You're here. Alive."

All I could do was nod.

"When we saw the reports—man, all those divers looking for you…We didn't leave the TV. We kept waiting and hoping."

"We?"

"Dan, Lauren, Greg, Keren, Justine…all of us."

I flinched at the mention of their names.

Sebastian continued, "After the reporters said you were gone, we all sat around and"—he blushed a little and looked away as he finished—"had a kind of service for you in the courtyard with the bear sculpture."

He had been genuinely concerned and had grieved for me. God. I looked down and asked, "Really? After what I did to you, I would have thought—" Instinctively, I reached out and touched his arm in apology. He looked at my hand on his arm and then into my eyes. His shame began to be replaced by splinters of hope. His gaze drew me in, but then guilt kicked me in the stomach. I snatched my hand back.

He pulled at his leather necklace as he looked away. When he did, I caught sight of the bruise on his cheekbone. The one Hamlet had put there when he punched Sebastian at the end of the lacrosse game.

"Does that hurt?" I asked, starting to reach for his face but then changing my mind.

"Not anymore. And hey, I got in a shot of my own," he said, pride filling him before he remembered what came right after.

We stood in awkward silence for a moment.

"Sebastian," I finally said, "I'm so sorry for what I did to you." I shoved my hands in my pockets and chewed on my lip. I was so sick of regret, but at least this was one person I could still apologize to. "I told you it wasn't personal, that there was so much I couldn't explain."

He looked back, and as our eyes met, my stomach flipped. From within my pockets, I pinched my own legs to remind myself not to feel anything for him.

He said, "I had no idea it was so bad. I wish I could have helped."

"You did. In your own way." I paused and considered telling him how he had helped me see that there was life beyond Elsinore. But it was too complicated, too personal. I settled on, "I'm so sorry I hurt you."

He hesitated and then, through a twisted half smile, asked, "Sorry enough that you'd go out with me again?"

I marveled at his audacious hope and stopped myself before I could reply the way my fluttering heart wanted me to answer. I looked over my shoulder. Marcellus was studying his shoes, but I knew he heard all of it. I was embarrassed by the conversation as much as I was intrigued by it, and I felt guilty for not dismissing Sebastian out of hand.

"Tacky. Bad timing," he said, shifting from foot to foot. "Sorry."

I shrugged and cleared my throat, looking once again for Marcellus's reaction. Marcellus was trained at seeming not to hear other people's private moments, and, though he never broke confidences, I lowered my voice anyway. "I'm going away in a few weeks."

"Oh," Sebastian said, his shoulders slumping slightly. "You plan on coming back?"

Plan? Did I have a plan? My run-for-the-hills plan wasn't quite a plan. More of a feeling. I couldn't give him details I didn't have myself, so I answered, "Probably. At some point. Not anytime soon."

"Oh. Could I come visit?" His warm eyes met mine, sending a shiver through my body.

I pinched my leg again and curled my toes inside my shoes. He was too good, and this was too soon. And yet...*Damn*, I thought. *Walk away.*

I said, "I don't want you to get hurt."

"I can take care of myself."

Oh, how many times I had said that very phrase. I had no doubt I would hurt or disappoint him, and I would have said as much, but it would have done no good. He was smitten and determined, a deadly combination. God, not deadly. No more dead anyone. Hamlet. My father. My mother. My brother. I was falling into the abyss of memory when Sebastian touched my arm, yanking me back to the real conversation, my present life. I needed to let the past slip behind me. I needed care and contact but not the kind that added to my pain. I wasn't sure what kind of contact this was, just that this was complicated.

He cocked his head and said, "You don't have to answer now, okay?" His tenderness pained me.

"I'm not saying never," I clarified. "Let me get myself settled. And then…"

"And then…" he said, his eyes shining.

"And then we'll see," I said as I grabbed for my keys and headed for my car.

Incredibly, the next day, a camera phone showing the game's terrifying end surfaced. One of the spectators, an Elsinore Academy sophomore, had been too scared to show it to anyone, but his girlfriend finally turned it in. I had never been so relieved by a piece of intrusive technology. The nation was able to forgive my brother, and my father would finally be given a proper burial.

Our plans for Claudius became moot, since almost immediately hearings on his grab for power were ordered, and the public flew into a frenzy. He was buried quietly one night with no ceremony and at a distance from his brother and wife.

I spent the days before the funeral separating out what I wanted to keep of my dad's and Laertes's belongings. There wasn't much besides photos, but I kept Laertes's CD collection and my dad's hats. He loved funny ones from our travels, and I didn't have the heart to get rid of them. I found an old lipstick of my mom's and kept that, too. The last item I tossed into the keep pile was a box of Hamlet's gifts, notes, and the crumpled paper he'd thrown under my bed with the prophetic scribbles "To Be" and "Not to Be." I couldn't bear to look carefully at any of it, but I couldn't throw it away, either.

Horatio came to get me when it was time to go to the service.

I did everything in my power not to think, not to notice the crowds, not to hear the cameras clicking. Guards surrounded us and brought us to the car and then escorted us into the cathedral.

Walking toward the coffins at the end of the long cathedral aisle—the aisle I had begrudgingly hobbled down a few months earlier at Gertrude and Claudius's wedding—my body grew weak. Horatio was holding on to my arm, to steady himself or me I couldn't tell. I was relieved when the minister gestured for everyone to sit. The lacquered boxes seemed to mock us with their shining perfection. Such beauty was about to be put underground; their only purpose was turning to dust. The beauty of those I had loved would be forever locked inside, and all would be left to rot.

My brother, tall and wise, scornful and witty. Hitting me with a pillow if my head was blocking the television. Reading thick tomes that he insisted were interesting. His deep voice calling across the hallway telling me to turn down my music or asking how my day was. Smirking at my father's instructions on how to be a better man. We laughed, yet those lessons made Laertes a wonderful man. A young man. So young he never had the chance to be his own man.

My father was not young. His pace was slowing. His hair was graying. His skin was wrinkling. His face was gentle and loving, despite the concern that often hung across it like a veil. Like a shroud. My father had had an opinion on everything, yet his opinions didn't matter anymore. His advice would be dispensed to no one, and I alone held the memory of his private words. I had ignored too much of his advice, sure he would be around when I needed it, when I wanted it…which I had assumed would be never. "We never know the worth of water till the well goes dry," he liked to say. Prophetic.

339

Looking at Gertrude's silver casket, my father's favorite curse sprang to mind: "May the curse of Mary Malone and her nine blind illegitimate children chase you so far over the hills of Damnation that the Lord himself can't find you with a telescope." Inside I smiled a little. *See, Dad?* I thought. *You did teach me something useful.*

My amusement faded as my gaze drifted to Hamlet's casket, the most elaborate, the one most bedecked with flowers. Hamlet tucked a buttercup behind my ear. Hamlet shoved his sunglasses on top of his head. Hamlet strummed his guitar. Hamlet whispered words of love. Hamlet held me down. Hamlet called me a whore. Hamlet killed my father. Hamlet stabbed my brother. Hamlet. Hamlet. Hamlet. Damn him. Damn his name. Damn his memory. Damn the sweet pain I couldn't shake. I closed my eyes, willing the thoughts away. "Good-bye, sweet prince," I whispered to myself. No. No more of his name. No more of his memory.

"Sweet is the wine, but sour is the payment," my father told me each time I chose pleasure over reason. Too bad my choice cost him so dearly. My lip began to quiver, but I forced my face to remain stony lest some cameraman catch my grief and broadcast it to the world. I wouldn't give them what they wanted. I could hear every sound too loudly and yet understood none of it. Horatio whispered something, but I didn't hear his words. I was sweating and cold, detached and overwrought. I wanted to go, but I couldn't stand.

Horatio's sudden absence left a cavern of cool air around me as he moved to the podium. I tried to focus my thoughts on him and his words about Hamlet, the Hamlet we once knew. Hamlet. Hamlet. My old self heard Horatio's words and agreed: Hamlet had once been wonderful. My new self wanted to reach into the air and tear the kind words apart. Hamlet would be remembered as a charming prince who lost his way under the pressures of grief and conspiracy. I would remember him as the murderer of my very soul. Hamlet. Hamlet. The sharp end of his name curled my lips.

I became aware of silence. I looked up. Horatio was standing at the podium so stricken that he could not continue to speak. He laid his head on his arms, and the wrinkled papers shook in his hands. His father rushed forward and covered the microphone, whispering private comforts to his bereaved son. Taking the papers out of Horatio's hands, his father completed the eulogy. The final story drifted around me while I focused on the father and son and how the father held the son as if bearing up the world. A father and son had led us to this moment. A father's absence. A son's rage. A daughter's grief. Fathers and sons. Fathers and daughters. Lovers and deceivers. There was no escape.

26

"How has your return to—well, life—been?" Zara asks, a laugh in her voice.

"Oh, much better than expected." Looking directly at the audience, Ophelia adds, "And I have the great people of Denmark to thank for it."

The morning the movers were set to come, agents from the Denmark Department of Investigations barged into my apartment. Oddly, it was their suits that scared me more than their guns. Anyone who could do dirty work in a tie had methods of getting information I didn't want to know about.

They grabbed my cell phone and went searching for my computer, but I explained that no one had returned it, or my old phone, after my last imprisonment. When they asked me to go with them, I refused. A man, who introduced himself as Special Agent Barnardo, stepped forward and put his stubbly face close to mine. His receding hairline made his forehead look enormous, and he smelled like mint gum and shaving cream, which struck me as funny given the stubble. "You're coming with us. You can walk out, or we can force you. I would suggest you make it easy on yourself."

I had passed being safe and was sick of following orders. "Screw you," I hissed, and braced myself for what I knew would come. He cuffed me and dragged me out of the apartment.

I was brought to DDI headquarters, a soulless poured-concrete building with harsh fluorescent lighting and lots of locked doors. All of my panic was gone, replaced by irritation and disbelief. They put me in an interrogation room, questioned me for a few days while recording every second of it, and then released me. I left unsure of what they would find, and not sure that I cared. I was wrung out and felt utterly disconnected from everything and everyone around me.

After my release, I moved into my new antiseptic apartment, anonymously beige and thoroughly inoffensive, and became a relative recluse. People tried to make contact, but I screened all calls, and for weeks saw no one except for Horatio's family and my lawyer.

My lawyer looked across his desk and tapped his pen on his legal pad. "Ophelia, everyone's been clamoring to hear what happened. An interview on *Zara* could help you quiet things down."

I shook my head.

Sternly he continued, "And it could help your case. If the DDI decides to put you on trial, you need a sympathetic jury. You have to get your version of the events out there."

"Zara is going to ask all kinds of personal questions. I don't want everyone knowing all the details of my life," I said.

"The people already know the majority of what happened."

I grimaced. "Not the most personal stuff."

"Tell as much as you feel you can. And leave out parts that will make you look bad."

"So lie?"

"Weeeell, tell the truth as much as possible—albeit a *patriotic* version of the truth. Try to pin everything on Claudius. The public wants to believe that Gertrude was an innocent bystander. And Hamlet was deeply loved by his subjects, don't forget." When I winced, he added, "The people need to see you as sympathetic and remorseful. And like a regular teenage girl. Only more glamorous. You have to go on *Zara*. This show is important for your image."

I dropped my head and clutched my stomach. I whispered, "I don't want to be a public figure anymore."

He peered over his glasses and reminded me, "It doesn't matter what you want."

Barnardo: We're gonna let you go. For now. But we'll be watching you. Someone out there knows something, and we're going to find it.
Ophelia: Let me know when you do.
Barnardo: Are you always this mouthy?
Ophelia: No. You just bring out the best in me.
(A door opens and closes.)
Francisco: There's a lawyer out there with Horatio. You can talk in our conference room if you'd like, or you can just leave.
Ophelia: Parting is such sweet sorrow and all, but I think I'll get out of here. Gentlemen, it's been a pleasure.
Francisco: We'll see you around.
Ophelia: Can't wait.

Zara crosses her legs and sits back. "So now what? Are you going on tour? Planning to write a tell-all?"

Ophelia sighs and folds her hands in her lap. "No. I just want to put this all behind me."

"Will you be going to college?"

"Yeah, in Paris, actually. I'm going to stay in my brother's apartment. His university called and offered me a spot in their freshman class. Elsinore Academy gave me a pass on everything, once they found out why my grades had dropped, so I get to start with a clean slate. I'll work hard. Like I used to."

"Political science in your future?" Zara asks with a twinkle in her eye.

"Uh, no. Art history. Maybe I'll move to Italy someday. Spend time studying the masters. Get a job in a gallery. I don't know."

"Will you be looking for romance?"

"Oh God, I don't think so. I think I've had enough for a while."

Zara smirks. "You never know. I hear those Parisian boys can be very romantic. Maybe some Romeo is waiting for you."

Ophelia shrugs and forces a smile. "I'm not looking for romance. I'm not looking for anything but time. I'm asking your viewers to please, please leave me alone for a while so I can get my life together."

"You heard it here, folks," Zara says, holding Ophelia's shoulder while staring sternly at the camera. "I don't want any pictures or stories popping up about my dear friend Ophelia. If someone is fool enough to do it, I'll find you, and there will be consequences."

The audience titters. They might be smiling, but they all know she's serious and powerful enough to make good on such a threat.

"One last question before I let you go," Zara says. "Do you think the DDI has enough evidence to put you on trial?"

Ophelia answers quickly. "They have no evidence, because I didn't do anything wrong." Then she pauses for a second, and her forehead wrinkles. She continues, "You know, my dad had two favorite sayings. One is from the Buddha, I think: 'Three things cannot be long hidden: the sun, the moon, and the truth.'" She smiles sadly at the audience. "Perhaps an even more fitting proverb is: 'Truth fears no trial.' If I am put on trial, all I can do is tell the truth."

Zara shakes Ophelia's hand as she says, "Well, thank you so much for joining us today."

"Thank you for having me," Ophelia replies, taking both of Zara's hands in her own. "It's been a real pleasure."

EPILOGUE

Being led step by step through my darkest times, it occurred to me that not everything important was caught on surveillance tape or in text message. There was so much more to us and to that time than what anyone would ever see, both good and bad. I have years of happy memories that can't easily be erased. And though those rosy memories sear my insides as much as the painful ones, they're all here to stay.

If I were interviewing myself, I'd ask, "I understand you have some gentle feelings about Hamlet. Does that mean you forgive him?"

I would say, "No. I don't think I could ever do that."

"Then what?" I would ask myself. "What have you learned?"

And I wouldn't know. I'd probably be flippant and answer, "Never get involved with royalty," but that wouldn't capture it.

I'd have to think about it, and I wouldn't say anything on the spot, especially not during an interview. I try not to answer so quickly anymore. I try to think before I speak, though that's easier said than done.

If given time, I could create a list of things I've learned, things I wish I'd learned before I allowed myself to disappear into Hamlet's love and his family's villainy. But I didn't, and I'm learning to forgive myself for that.

I've learned that all happiness and all answers can't begin and end with one guy. I need to be by myself for a while, because it's too easy for me to put everyone else's needs and wants ahead of my own.

I've learned that no gift is worth keeping a secret for, and that no photo is so bad it should turn me into a liar.

I've learned that I don't mind lying to people I don't trust.

I've learned to trust very few people.

I've learned that I behave better when I'm sober.

I've learned that good behavior is sometimes overrated.

I've learned that peach bridesmaid dresses suck.

I've learned not to believe everything I see on TV (actually, I knew that before) and that I never want to be in a position to be interviewed about anything ever again.

I'd say I should listen to my parents, but it's too late for that. On that note, I've got to forgive myself a little, because it wasn't all my fault. I'm not sure I'll ever convince myself, but I'll try.

I've learned that I do believe in ghosts.

And I've learned that coffee, when it has just the right amount of milk and sugar in it, is about the best damned thing on the planet.

The rest is silence.

AUTHOR'S NOTE

My inspiration for *Falling for Hamlet* came after seeing a magnificent production of *Hamlet* in Washington, D.C. It was set in modern times, which I loved because the focus was not on fancy costumes but on the story. Hamlet was just a confused, depressed guy walking around in a hoodie, being betrayed not only by his enemies but by everyone he loved and trusted. And it was the first time I felt really bad for Hamlet.

The one element that did not sit well with me, however, was Ophelia. The actress playing her was fine, yet I could not reconcile a modern girl losing her mind the way she did. As I walked out of the theater, I asked myself, "What would make a teenager today go crazy?" By the time I reached the subway, the question had morphed into "What if she didn't die at all?"

Because I planned to make my story modern, the triggers for Ophelia's actions had to change, and I wondered how Shakespeare's questions of rank, family loyalty, and duty transferred to today. Her brother, Laertes, for instance, speaks with Ophelia early on about the consequences of losing her honor. In Shakespeare's day, purity was everything to a young woman's future, but not so these days. That said, shame still exists, and even if what causes it might be different, the desire to avoid humiliation leads many of us to do things we never thought we would do — like betray someone we love.

Much of *Hamlet* is about power, and I knew my version needed a setting with a strong hierarchy. In addition, I felt there had to be an awareness on the part of the characters that the public was watching. Shakespeare brought this theme into *Twelfth Night*, when he wrote, "What great ones do the less will prattle of." In other words, commoners loved gossiping about the rich and famous. We still do. Whether it's about celebrity weddings, breakups, or who's wearing what, we still care. In transferring *Hamlet* to now, I considered setting it in a place like Hollywood or the business world of New York. But I felt strongly that keeping Hamlet a prince was important because hanging over all the family drama is a fight for the crown. And in looking at gossip magazines, most specifically at Princess Diana's tabloid-bait sons, it occurred to me that the royals still make great press. In deciding to do this, I wondered what it would be like to be the nonroyal girlfriend of one of them, and to feel the pressure not only of everyone judging you so publicly, but of the prospect of becoming a queen.

Many of the scenes are direct translations of Shakespeare's words. Making Shakespeare's lines sound modern was no easy task, and my friends, agent, editor, and copy editors all called me out when the words of the characters sounded too old-fashioned. At times, I made a joke of it, like Ophelia saying, "Primrose path of dalliance." She's trying to sound smart while talking to her brother, but then I felt I had to follow it with a colloquial translation so readers knew what I meant. Other times, I had to get a bit creative, like Hamlet scribbling "To be" and "Not to be" on a notebook—a line I'd originally cut because having him say it out loud sounded too clunky.

I considered changing character names. However, I decided to keep them because I wanted you, the reader, to recognize the characters and see how their actions matched the original. Although it's odd to read "Laertes," "Horatio," etc., in a modern context, I hoped that readers would grow accustomed to it. I tried to keep the characters similar, too, like having soldiers' names become the guards and so on. For Ophelia's friends, however, I used contemporary names to make a distinction between these two worlds.

While I took liberties with the story—namely that Ophelia stays alive—I tried to stay true to the general structure of *Hamlet*. The interviews, of course, were not in the original, but the basic plot follows the structure of the play. One challenge was that Ophelia is in just a few scenes of *Hamlet*, so I had to think of ways for her to see, or at least hear about, the action. Technology helped. I also had Hamlet bring her with him to scenes she did not originally witness. *Hamlet* begins after the death of his father and remarriage of his mother, but I wanted readers to see what things were like before their world fell apart. I also added a life for Ophelia outside of the castle—an interest in art, attraction to other boys, and friends not afraid to comment on her behavior and choices. I wanted to give her a depth that Shakespeare did not. But heck, his play isn't called *Ophelia*, so I can't blame the guy.

My purpose in writing *Falling for Hamlet*, besides entertaining myself in asking the many "what if" questions, was the hope that readers would become more interested in *Hamlet*. If you're familiar with the original, I hope this book has provided you with an entertaining twist on a great story. If you don't know *Hamlet*, I encourage you to see it. Note I didn't say "read it." As I say to my students, Shakespeare is meant to be performed, not read. Do as you like, but even I, who do this a lot, am challenged by the original text. My recommendation: If you can't go see a stage production, or even if you can, rent one of the many great movie versions — or a few different ones. *Hamlet* is a story people love to tell in their own way, so whether you see the modern one, an Elizabethan one, the uncut version, or one that's super short, enjoy. Then try another Shakespeare. And another. The man could tell a story.

ACKNOWLEDGMENTS

To Jonathan, who told me "once upon a road trip" to start writing down the stories I had in my head, and who kept me going when I considered giving up.

To my sweet girls, who were sometimes quiet enough for me to write.

Love to my parents, who first introduced me to Shakespeare, and who made me appreciate learning of all kinds.

Thanks to the Rays, the best in-laws a girl could ask for.

To Amy, who made me admit to being a writer, and to Kim, for taking me under her writerly wing.

Thanks to my friends and family for support and encouragement. Special thanks to Shari, who liked it first, and Keren, Amanda, Valerie, Phyllis, and Billy for approving and suggesting. And love to Lauren, my trusty reader who never hesitates to tell me when something sucks.

To my Westlake teachers and Tufts drama professors, who gave me an incredible education in literature and in life.

To the Hudson Valley Shakespeare Festival for inspiring me annually with awesomely creative takes on great works, and to D.C.'s Shakespeare Theatre Company for inspiring a new way to look at *Hamlet*.

Thanks to my agent, Ammi-Joan Paquette, who believed

this would happen, and to my editor, Alvina Ling, for making it so. Thanks, as well, to Pam, Bethany, and Connie at Little, Brown for assistance and for suggestions that helped improve the story.

To my teacher buddies, who spend each day trying to make kids better thinkers, readers, learners, and people.

And to my students for making *me* a better thinker, reader, learner, and person. I wrote this for you as part of my ongoing quest to make you love Shakespeare as much as I do.

Where stories bloom.

poppy

Visit us online at
www.pickapoppy.com